The
BOOKSHOP
of
YESTERDAYS

The BOOKSHOP *of* YESTERDAYS

AMY MEYERSON

PARK
ROW
BOOKS

ISBN-13: 978-0-7783-1984-9
ISBN-13: 978-0-7783-6913-4 (International Trade Paperback Edition)

The Bookshop of Yesterdays

For questions and comments about the quality of this book, please contact us at CustomerService@Harlequin.com.

ParkRowBooks.com
BookClubbish.com

Printed in U.S.A.

The
BOOKSHOP
of
YESTERDAYS

What's past is prologue.

—*The Tempest*

CHAPTER ONE

THE LAST TIME I SAW MY UNCLE, HE BOUGHT ME A DOG. A GOLDEN retriever puppy with sad eyes and a heart-shaped nose. I didn't have her long enough to give her a name. One moment she was running around my living room with the promise of many adventures together and the next she was gone. It was the same way with Uncle Billy. One moment he was waving goodbye as he reversed out of my driveway. Then I never saw him again.

Mom never wanted a dog. I'd begged her, promising to walk the dog every day, to scrub the living room rug after any accidents, but Mom was insistent. It wasn't about the rug, or the countless shoes the dog would ruin. It wasn't about love, either. She had no doubt I would love the dog. Of course, she would love it, too, but a pet, like any relationship, was about accountability, not love. I was on the brink of my teenage years, of boys and friends who mattered more than allowance, more than dogs, more than family. We'd been over it. No dog. I knew this. Uncle Billy knew this, too.

The dog was a birthday present. For my twelfth birthday, my parents had rented out an arcade and batting cages in Culver City. It was the beginning of 1998. We always celebrated in January, since I was born so close to the end of the year.

My friends crowded behind the plate, cheering as I nudged the batting helmet out of my face and timidly stepped into the cage. Dad offered me last-minute advice to keep my feet shoulder-distance apart, my right elbow up. I expected Mom to remind me to be careful, but she was at the concession stand, making a phone call.

All right, Miranda, you can do this, Dad said after a swing and a miss. Mom appeared at his side and whispered something into his ear. I swung at the next pitch once it had already sped past the plate. *You should know by now not to count on him,* Dad said to Mom. *Miranda,* he called to me. *Keep your eyes open.*

He promised he'd be here, I heard Mom whisper.

Let's not get into this now, he whispered back.

He shouldn't make promises if he isn't going to keep them.

Suze, not now.

I tried to focus on my cocked elbow, my loose knees, just as Dad had taught me, but their hushed tones distracted me. There was only one person who made them whisper like that. I hated when they talked about Billy that way, like they were trying to protect me from him, like he was someone I needed to be shielded from. I turned away from the pitching machine, toward my parents. They were leaning against the cage, staring each other down.

The impact sounded before I felt it. An incredibly loud clap and then my shoulder ignited. I screamed, falling to the ground. Two more balls whizzed by my head. Dad shouted for someone to turn off the machine as he and Mom raced into the cage.

Sweetheart, are you okay? Mom pulled the helmet off my head and brushed the sweaty hair off my forehead. The pain had knocked the wind out of me. I panted on the cold cement floor, unable to respond. *Miranda, talk to me,* she said a little too frantically.

I'm okay, I said between exerted breaths. *I think I just need some cake.*

Normally, this would have made them laugh, but they continued to cast concerned and disappointed looks at each other as if the welt rising on my shoulder was somehow Billy's fault, too. Mom huffed at Dad, then stormed off to the concession stand to collect my birthday cake.

Is Mom okay? I asked Dad as we watched her talk to the teenager behind the counter.

Nothing a little cake can't fix, Dad said, ruffling my hair.

After the cake was devoured and the bag of ice Mom made me hold on my shoulder had melted down the front of my T-shirt, I joined my friends in the arcade, ignoring the sharp pains that shot down my arm as I rolled the skee-ball up its narrow lane. Between rolls, I glanced over at my parents. They were cleaning up the remains of my birthday cake, Mom furiously scrubbing the plastic tablecloth until Dad pulled her away and held her in his arms. He stroked her hair as he whispered into her ear. I couldn't understand why she was so upset. Billy often didn't show up when he said he would. In fact, I couldn't even remember the last time he'd been to one of my birthday parties. If an earthquake hit in Japan or Italy, he'd be on the first plane out with the other seismologists, engineers, sociologists. He didn't usually have time to let us know he was leaving. Instead of disappointment, I felt pride. My uncle was important. My uncle saved lives. Mom taught me to see him this way. After a recital or debate, a Sunday barbecue without Billy, she would tell me, *Your uncle wants to be here, but he's making the world a safer place.* He was my superhero. Captain Billy, who saved the world not with superhuman powers but with a superior brain. Even when I was too old to believe in superheroes, I still believed in Billy. I thought Mom believed in him, too, yet there she was, crying over a birthday party.

MY BEST FRIEND, JOANIE, AND I WENT TO BED EARLY THAT night. I was half-asleep and hazy, but the ringing doorbell was real, the tiptoes downstairs, the whispers. I slipped out of bed, into the hall where I saw Mom at the front door below, her satin bathrobe pulled snugly around her small frame. Billy stood outside on the porch.

I started to run toward the stairs, ready to pounce on Billy. I was getting too big to jump on him, yet I thought even when I was an adult I would greet him that way, breaking his back with my love for him. When I got to the top of the stairs, Mom's words startled me.

What the fuck is wrong with you? It's 3:00 a.m. I froze. Mom rarely raised her voice. She never cursed. *You've got some nerve, showing up in the middle of the night and blaming me. Some fucking nerve.*

I stood paralyzed at the top of the banister. Her anger was glorious, unlike anything I'd ever seen before.

You made things this way. She tried to keep her voice down. *You hear me? This was your choice. Don't you dare blame me.*

Billy turned away as Mom continued to yell about the hour, telling him he was an asshole and something called a narcissist and other names I didn't understand. When he spotted me at the top of the stairs, his cheeks were red, his eyes were glassy. Mom followed his gaze to me. Her cheeks were pale and she suddenly seemed very old. I looked between their expressive faces. They weren't fighting about my birthday. Something else had happened.

Honey, go back to bed, Mom called to me. When I stalled, she added, *Please.*

I darted back to my room, disturbed and inexplicably embarrassed by what I'd seen.

Joanie tossed when she heard me crawl into bed beside her.

What time is it?

It's after three.

Why is someone coming over so late?

I don't know.

Joanie rolled over, mumbling incoherently. I couldn't fall back to sleep. Mom's words raced through my brain—*some fucking nerve* and *asshole* and *don't you dare blame me. This was your choice.* Sunlight bled through the curtains as dawn became morning. I'd stayed up all night, and I still couldn't figure out what choice Billy had made, what he'd blamed on Mom, what I had witnessed at our front door.

LATER THAT MORNING, DAD TOOK JOANIE AND ME FOR PAN-cakes.

Where's Mom? I asked Dad as we got into his car.

She's sleeping in. Mom never slept past seven, but Dad's tone discouraged further questions.

When we returned from breakfast Mom was still in her satin robe, her auburn hair tangled around her face as she folded chocolate chips into batter. Normally, singing was an essential ingredient in any recipe. Mom's mellifluous voice would weave its way into a pie or lasagna, making the cherries or the toma-toes sweeter. As she continued to flip the cookie dough, over and over again, the kitchen was painfully silent.

She looked up when she heard me in the doorway. Her eyes were puffy, her cheeks still colorless. *How was breakfast?*

Dad let us get three different kinds of pancakes.

Did he? She returned her attention on the bowl of cookie dough. *That was nice of him.* I wanted her to start singing, to break her own trance. She continued to watch the dough thud against the sides of the mixing bowl, and I wondered if the cookies would taste as good without her secret ingredient.

WE DIDN'T HEAR FROM BILLY FOR A FEW WEEKS, NOT UNTIL HE stopped by to take me out for my birthday. I had no idea where we were going. That was the fun of a day with Billy. Whatever activities I would have proposed—an afternoon at the pier or

Six Flags—wouldn't have been half as exciting as whatever adventure he had in store for us.

The labored breaths of Billy's old BMW echoed through the
house. I waited for the familiar sounds of his car door shutting,
of Mom rushing to meet him at the front door, peppering him
with questions. Where were we going? Would there be other
children? Were there cliff edges or high distances I could fall
from? Seat belts? Life jackets? She never seemed completely sat-
isfied with his answers.

That afternoon, Billy honked his horn and Mom called, *Billy's
here*, from behind her closed bedroom door.

Don't you want you say hi? I shouted to her.

Not today, she shouted back.

I hesitated before I left the house. Mom's bedroom door remained closed. It didn't matter, anyway. Billy didn't ring the
bell, just waited in the car with the engine still running.

There's my favorite girl, Billy said as I hopped into the car.
He always called me that, his favorite girl. It would have embarrassed me if my parents said anything so sappy. With Billy,
it made me feel like the kid I still wanted to be but knew at
twelve was no longer cool. We turned out of the driveway, and
my house retreated into the distance. I wondered if Mom was
watching us leave from her bedroom window.

Boy, do I have a surprise for you. Billy shot me one of his over-
sized smiles. I searched his face for any of the strain I'd seen on
Mom's. Billy looked content, giddy.

A surprise? Although I never would have admitted it to Joanie,
a surprise from Billy was still a greater thrill than stealing lipstick from the drugstore, a better rush than driving too fast
down Highway 1 with Joanie's older sisters.

Hey, reach in there for me. Billy pointed toward the glove com-
partment where a black envelope rested on top of his car regis-
tration. It was the right size to hold tickets to Universal Studios
or a concert at the Hollywood Bowl, but Billy never would have

given me a present so straightforwardly. There'd be no fun in it. I had to earn his gifts through solving his clues.

I tore open the envelope and read the riddle aloud. *My flag is red, white and blue, though I'm not a land you call home. You might think it a lozh'*—I didn't know how to pronounce that word—*but at my closest point, I'm two and a half miles from American soil.*

France? I guessed. Billy looked dubiously at me. *Canada?*

Canada's flag is only red and white. You're getting warmer, or should I say colder, much, much colder.

Russia? I asked uncertainly.

Vernvy! he said in his best Russian accent.

You're taking me to Russia? Was there an earthquake? I pictured Billy and me in shearling hats, trekking through snow to survey the damage to a remote town.

I think your mom would have my head for that, Billy said.

With the mention of Mom, Billy and I quieted. I knew we were both remembering how our eyes had locked while he fought with Mom in the middle of the night.

Is everything okay with you and Mom?

Nothing for you to worry about. He paused, began to say something, then paused again before rolling to a stop outside a building on Venice Boulevard that looked condemned. *Now, let's see about that clue.*

This is where we're going? I asked, counting the storefront's boarded-up windows. Usually, his adventures involved state parks and mountaintops, secluded beaches. *Something in that building has to do with Russia?*

Vernvy! He hopped out of the car and bowed, motioning me toward the metal front door. It was unlocked, and he held it open for me.

Are we allowed to be here? I hesitated, peeking behind him into the dark interior. *It looks closed.*

It's not open today, but the manager owes me a favor. It's always more fun to have a museum to yourself, don't you think? He walked inside and waved me to follow. *Trust me*, he called. Trust me. His mantra. And I always did.

The front room was dimly lit. Glass cases lined the austere walls. Opera played softly from hidden speakers. The case beside the door was filled with taxidermy bats, moles and other small rodents. The next case held shimmering gemstones.

It's modeled off nineteeth-century oddity museums, Billy explained. *Science, art and nature displayed together for the well-rounded mind. A* wunderkammer, *if you will.*

A wunderkammer. I tested the word in my mouth, waiting for its magic to hit me. Billy's eyes drifted toward a case in the far corner of the room. It was filled with miniature figurines—painted elephants, clowns, a ringmaster, acrobats. The case was labeled The Russian Circus.

I peeked inside the glass, searching for something amiss, a figurine that didn't belong, a riddle scribbled across the circus tent. Sure enough, the next clue was taped to the back of the case.

Like the fabric of my name, my title is lowly yet noble. I'm named not for the rough wool I bear but the origin of a river in Northumberland.

Billy laughed when he saw the bewildered look on my face. He rubbed my head and guided me into the next room. It was as overwhelming as the first room was sparse. The walls were cluttered with detailed renderings of dogs in garish frames. There was one portrait of a person, a faded painting of a man with a beard and top hat called Baron Tweedmouth. Beside his portrait, a placard offered a brief history of the lord, a Scottish businessman and member of the House of Commons.

Rumor has it, Billy said, *in 1858 Lord Tweedmouth went to a Russian circus where he saw this fantastic performance by Russian sheepdogs. After the show, he made an offer to buy a pair of dogs, but the ringmaster refused to separate the troupe. So, story goes, Tweedmouth bought the whole lot and bred those sheepdogs to create the retriever.*

Billy gestured toward a filing cabinet beside the portrait. *Open it. It's part of the exhibit.* I tore through reproductions of Baron Tweedmouth's papers, fairly certain where this was headed. I loved that about Billy's adventures. Even though I always figured out where the quest was going before we got there, he refused to let me rush through the lesson. Billy stopped me when I discarded a copy of the baron's breeding records. *Historians found those records in the 1950s and realized the Russian circus was a myth.* Billy pointed to a description of a retriever's keen nose. *See here? Retrievers were already used for tracking before 1858, so Lord Tweedmouth couldn't have bred Russian sheepdogs to create the retriever.* His finger continued down the page, tracing the lineage of Tweedmouth's dogs. *Instead, he bred the retrievers he already owned to produce the perfect hunting companion.*

Does this mean what I think it means? I danced like I had to pee.

Depends on what you think it means.

I flipped over the breeding records and found the next clue written on the back.

> **Don't call me a beauty, a goddess, the prettiest of the lot. You might consider these pet names the same but only one has a certain ring to it.**

I examined each portrait until I located a tweed water spaniel named Belle. Beside her portrait, a plaque explained that Belle was bred with Nous, a yellow retriever, to create the golden retriever.

No way, I shouted. *No freaking way.* I jumped up and down, hugging Billy, screaming unintelligibly.

Not so fast, Billy cautioned. *You have to find her first.*

I searched the crowded room for an envelope that may have contained the next clue. On the far wall, a photograph of a modern golden retriever hung between its ancestors. Its simple black frame pulled away from the wall. I slid my hand into the empty space, removing an index card. It listed an address on Culver Boulevard.

Outside, I didn't wait for my eyes to adjust to the light, just took off down Venice past other storefronts that looked condemned and auto-body shops.

Miranda, slow down, Billy shouted, panting as he raced to catch up with me.

At the light at Culver and Venice, I jogged in place like a runner trying to keep her heart rate up. *A dog, a dog, a dog, a dog*, I said. The light changed and I sprinted across the street.

Billy's laughter trailed me as we raced past the historic hotel, the restaurants that lined Culver Boulevard. The address was a few blocks down, a pet shop that sold parakeets.

The owner also breeds goldens, Billy explained as he caught his breath.

Inside, the store smelled faintly of nuts. A large, balding man stood behind the counter reading the paper. When he saw us, he disappeared below the register, returning with a golden retriever puppy. I carefully lifted the dog from his hands. The puppy's body was warm and emitted a sweet barnyard scent. She was drowsy at first. As I nestled her against my chest and rubbed my cheeks across her silky fur, she roused to life, offering me sticky kisses. I did my best to keep hold of her, but she was too excited for the embrace. The storeowner suggested I let her run around the store. We watched her sniff the dusty corners and pounce at the metal bases of the birdcages. Billy rested his arm on my shoulders, and I was ready to tell him that he was positively, absolutely my favorite person in the world, then I remembered Mom.

You talked to Mom? She's okay with this?

Billy lifted the dog off the floor, laughing as she lunged at his face. *How could your mom say no to this face?*

Seriously, Uncle Billy. She said I can't get a dog.

You want a dog, don't you?

More than anything.

Billy put the dog on the floor and put his arm around me. *Sometimes your mom needs a little help seeing things clearly. Once she sees how much you love this dog, no way she'll say no. Trust me, okay?*

Even as he said it—*Trust me*—I knew I shouldn't. Mom was never going to let me keep the dog. But I wanted to believe in the power of Billy, the magic that everything would turn out fine simply because he promised it would. And I wanted Mom to believe in it, too.

JOANIE'S GOING TO BE SO JEALOUS, I GLOATED ON THE DRIVE home. *A puppy. A freaking puppy. Uncle Billy, this is the best birthday present ever.*

We pulled up outside my house, and Billy held the puppy as I lugged the dog supplies out of the back seat. When I went to collect the dog, he didn't let go. He rubbed behind her ears, suddenly serious. *I'm sorry you had to see that, between me and your mom.*

It's no big deal, I said uncertainly.

It is a big deal, he asserted. The dog squirmed in his hands. *Things with me and your mom, whatever happens, I just want you to know it isn't your fault.* I tried to take the puppy, to run into the house so Billy would stop talking, but his grip was too firm. It hadn't occurred to me that anything was my fault until he said that. *Just keep her out of your mom's shoes, and your mom won't be able to resist her.* Billy handed me the dog. *I'll see you soon*, and I decided to trust those words more than the ominous ones that preceded them. We would see Billy soon. Everything would be fine.

Mom, I screamed as I ran inside. *Mom, come quick, you won't believe what Billy got me.*

Mom tore open her bedroom door and raced into the hallway above the foyer. She was in her robe. Dark circles engulfed her eyes. *Jesus, Miranda.* She put her hand on her chest. *You frightened me. I thought something was wrong.*

Look. I held the dog toward her.

Stillness immobilized her face as she looked between me and the yelping puppy. *You can't keep that.* Mom raced downstairs and lifted the puppy from my hands. *We're taking this back immediately.*

You haven't even met her yet. The dog licked Mom's face. *See, she's sweet?*

You know it's not about that, Mom said. The puppy continued to bark.

I just thought once you saw her you'd change your mind.

Miranda, we've been over this. We're all too busy to take care of a dog.

I'll take care of her by myself. You won't have to do anything.

It's too much responsibility, she said.

I'm not a kid anymore. I don't need you to tell me what's too much responsibility. My tone shocked us both. Mom waited for me to calm down. When it became clear she wouldn't engage, I stomped upstairs, screaming, *You won't let me do anything.* I knew I was being dramatic, prematurely acting the temperamental teenager, but I slammed the door so hard my bedroom floor shook.

Mom threw open the door. *Don't you slam this door.* Her voice was calm, her golden eyes clear and furious. *You broke the rules. You knew you weren't allowed to get a dog. You do not get to throw a tantrum.*

I knew she was right, but I was at that age where it didn't matter if she was right, not if it meant I couldn't do what I wanted.

Where's the dog? I said instead. She was no longer holding it.

Crap. Mom raced downstairs and cooed to the puppy. *Miranda*, she called up to me, *where'd Billy take you to get this dog?*

I'm not telling you, I yelled. When she didn't shout back, I admitted, *A pet shop in Culver City.* I didn't tell her it was a bird store.

Once Mom had left with the puppy, I called Billy to tell him what had happened. He didn't answer his car phone, so I tried him at home. *You won't believe it*, I screamed into his machine. *Mom made me return the dog. She's such a bitch.* After I hung up, I felt like I'd been punched in the stomach. I'd never called Mom a bitch before. I said it again to our empty house. *You're such a bitch.* I kept saying it, hoping it might feel fair. It never did.

All afternoon, I stayed in my room. I heard Mom come home. I heard Dad return from the tennis club. I heard them talking in the kitchen. I knew she was telling him what had happened, that Dad would come upstairs and act the mediator.

At six-thirty, Dad knocked on my door.

I'm not hungry.

Dad opened the door and sat on the bed beside me. *I know you're upset. We've been over this. It isn't the right time to get a dog.*

That's bull— Dad shot me a look. *It's never going to be the right time.*

Maybe so. You have to respect that, Mimi. We're a family. We make decisions together. Why don't you come downstairs. We'll have a nice dinner. I think that will be best for everyone. Dad nodded approvingly at me, a gesture I knew well. I would make the right decision. I wouldn't disappoint him.

At the table, I watched Mom poke her chicken breast without taking a bite, uncertain what I should say to her. I wanted to apologize for calling her a bitch even if she hadn't heard me.

Instead, Mom broke the silence. *I'm sorry we fought. Billy shouldn't have put you in that position. That wasn't fair of him.*

I stabbed a bite of chicken and threw it into my mouth, chewing aggressively. So this was how she wanted to play it. It wasn't my fault. It sure wasn't her fault, either. It was all Billy. He had chosen to buy me the dog, just like he had chosen to do whatever it was she'd blamed on him the night of my birthday party.

So, this was Billy's choice, too? You're saying I shouldn't blame you? I'll never forget the wounded expression on Mom's face as she realized I was referring to the fight I'd overheard, that I was using her words against her.

It doesn't have to be anyone's fault, Dad said. *We can all take responsibility for our actions.*

I'm sorry I slammed the door, I said, but the damage was done. Mom nodded, accepting my apology. Accepting what had shifted over that dinner.

LATER THAT NIGHT, I CALLED BILLY AGAIN.

Me and Mom are done, I shouted into his machine. *I'm going to stay mad at her forever.*

When Billy didn't return my message, I figured he probably didn't want to risk Mom answering if he called me back. I tried him again the next day. He didn't pick up, so I told his machine, *I'm going to call you tomorrow at exactly 4:15. Make sure you're home, so we can talk.* The following afternoon, he still wasn't there. The only other place I knew to reach him was at Prospero Books.

In addition to his work with earthquakes, Billy was the owner of a neighborhood bookstore, not in his neighborhood in Pasadena, but in Silver Lake, Los Angeles. Billy called seismology his real job, Prospero Books his fun job. When I asked him why he didn't make his fun job his real job, he said he had a responsibility to protect people because he knew how to learn from earthquakes what others couldn't.

On afternoons when he hadn't planned a scavenger hunt, he would take me to Prospero Books, and the store was its own kind of adventure. We'd walk through the maze of shelves, and Billy would tell me to pick a book, any book, but to choose wisely for I would only get one. It was there I discovered Anne of Green Gables, Mary Lennox and, more recently, Kristy, Claudia, Stacey and their friends in the baby-sitters club.

A male voice that wasn't my uncle's answered the phone. *Prospero Books, where books are prized above dukedom.*

It was probably the manager, Lee, but I didn't want to get into a whole conversation with him about how he couldn't believe that I still hadn't read *Are You There God? It's Me, Margaret.*

Is Billy there?

I think he's at the lab. He's planning to stop by on Sunday. Can I take a message?

I hung up before Lee realized it was me.

Sunday was still five days away. I couldn't wait that long, so I tried Billy's house again that night, once Mom had gone to bed and Dad was in the living room watching the nightly news. *Billy? It's your favorite girl,* I said pathetically into his machine. *Are you getting my messages? I really need to talk to you.*

After a few more messages, I started to panic.

I tried to keep the dog, I pleaded into his machine. *You have to believe me. I did everything I could. You know Mom. You know how she is. Please don't be mad at me. Just call me back.* He didn't return my calls, and by the weekend, I knew calling him again was pointless. Billy's silence spoke louder than words. He wouldn't be coming over for Sunday barbecues, not any time soon. He wouldn't be picking me up for any more adventures.

I decided I needed to see him in person. He couldn't look me in the eye and banish me from his life. I knew where he was going to be on Sunday. I knew I could find him at Prospero Books.

JOANIE HELPED ME PLOT THE ROUTE ACROSS THE CITY. SILVER Lake may as well have been San Francisco, it took so many freeways to get there. The bus took the residential route, Santa Monica Boulevard all the way until it ended at Sunset Junction. No transfers necessary. If everything went smoothly, it would take an hour and a half.

I told Mom I was staying at Joanie's where the supervision consisted of her teenage sisters sequestered in their rooms. I'd gone there enough times without anything terrible happening that Mom had stopped calling Joanie's mother to make sure she was home.

Before I mounted the bus steps, Joanie smothered me in a hug. *You're sure you'll be okay? Remember, when the bus passes Vermont, you have two more stops.*

Thanks, Mom, I said sarcastically, and she stuck her tongue out at me.

The bus wasn't as crowded as I'd expected. I found an empty row and sat by the window. Traffic was slow along Santa Monica Boulevard as we passed Beverly Hills into West Hollywood and the grimier blocks of Hollywood. At Hyperion, I got off the bus and headed toward the sign at Sunset Junction, pretending I was the daughter of an artist or musician, the type of kid who grew up in Silver Lake. Prospero stood tall on the sign above the bookstore, staff in his right hand, a book in his left, purple cape and white hair windblown behind him. I stopped outside the storefront, looking through the picture window filled with books. Jitters rose in my stomach, same as every time I saw the store's lime-green walls. I had a relationship to this space that no one else had, even if they came here every week, every day. Billy didn't tell anyone else to pick a book, any book, free of charge, as though the books were waiting just for them. I threw open the door, certain I would see Billy and everything would be fine.

Prospero Books wasn't a large store, but with high ceilings and well-spaced shelves, it seemed vast, even spacious. It had a unique smell, different from Billy's home in Pasadena, unlike any other bookstore. The earthiness of freshly cut paper mixed with the white musk perfume of the pretty girls who frequented the store and a trace of coffee that was almost floral.

Miranda? Lee said when he noticed me by the door. *What a nice surprise. Is Billy with you?*

I thought he was here. I didn't see Billy's leather satchel beneath the desk chair or his mug with the San Andreas Fault marking California like a scar on one of the tables in the café.

I could feel Lee watching me. I didn't meet his eye because I already knew what he was going to say.

I'm sure he's on his way, Lee said. *Let me go call him.*

Lee told the woman working in the café to get me whatever I wanted. She winked as she handed me an enormous chocolate chip cookie, like it was some sort of secret between us. I took the cookie to a table in the far corner and watched Lee behind the front desk, talking on the telephone. He glanced up and found me watching him, a conflicted look contorting his face.

Billy can't come in today, he said when he sat down at my table. *He told me to call your mother. She's on her way.*

You called my mom? The lies raced through my brain. I wanted to pick up the latest *Baby-Sitters Club.* Dad said I could come. They were transparent lies that would only make Mom angrier. I'd told her I was at Joanie's, then taken the bus to Silver Lake when I wasn't even allowed to take the bus within our neighborhood. I'd gone to see my uncle even though I knew they were in a fight. I'd totally and completely disobeyed her. I was beyond dead. Grounded for eternity. But that wasn't the worst of it. What truly wrecked me was that Billy didn't want to see me. I fought back tears. I was twelve, which was almost a teenager, which was almost an adult. I was too old to cry.

Hey now, Lee said when he noticed I was crying. *What do you say you and me pick out a book? Would you like that?*

Okay, I said even though I didn't want to pick a book, any book, not with Lee. I followed him to the teen fiction section where the spines were bright, the titles blurred from my tears. Lee showed me a few thrillers—R. L. Stine and Christopher Pike, not the type of books he normally tried to get me to read. I shook my head at every offer. I had thought that by the time I graduated high school I would have read every book in Prospero Books. Now I didn't want to read any of them ever again.

Lee had to ring up a customer, so I returned to my chocolate chip cookie, no book in hand. I broke the cookie into pieces, then I broke the pieces into pieces, too upset to eat.

The tables around me emptied and repopulated. Lee remained behind the front desk. Every once in a while, he stood and checked the café to make sure I was still there. The sky began to darken and I started to worry Mom was so mad she'd decided not to get me.

What felt like hours later, the bell on the door chimed. I looked up to find Mom scanning the crowded tables. Relief washed over her face as she spotted me. When our eyes locked, I forgot I was mad at her and ran into her arms. I took in her warmth, the sweet lilac smell of her skin, feeling like a child and not caring who saw.

I'm so sorry.

She kissed my forehead. *I'm just glad you're okay.*

I understood then that my plan had been doomed from the start. Even if Billy had been at Prospero Books, he'd made his choice not to call me back. Here I was blaming Mom when she was the one to come to my rescue, not Billy.

ALONG THE I-10, I COULD TELL MOM WANTED TO TELL ME ALL the ways I'd been stupid, how Silver Lake was dangerous and something could have gone terribly wrong. Instead, she asked, *What were you hoping would happen if Billy was there?* She didn't sound mad, simply curious.

I don't know, I admitted. *I want you guys to make up.*

It's not always that easy with adults.

Why not?

Mom's hands gripped the steering wheel. *Billy and I have a complicated relationship.*

What are you talking about? What happened when I saw you guys fighting?

Her face softened as she turned her attention away from the road toward me. *It's too difficult to explain.*

Will you try? I held my breath. This was Mom's chance to tell me her side of their fight. I was willing to believe anything she said about Billy, no matter how terrible.

Mom's eyes narrowed as if she was having difficulty seeing the traffic ahead.

You're too young to understand. She said this gently, but it would have been better if her words were harsh, if she'd intended them to bruise rather than to protect me. I didn't want to be protected.

Will you work it out? I asked.

I honestly don't know, she said.

She did know. Whatever had passed between her and Billy, it had been too much for them to forgive. They'd said things they couldn't unsay. They lost each other in that fight. Or maybe they'd been lost to each other for years. I had no idea anymore. One thing I did know, what I felt acutely, was that Billy had lost me. I didn't want to be his favorite girl. I didn't want to hear why he'd sent Mom to Prospero Books, why he hadn't met me himself. Even if he turned up next Sunday, our relationship would never be the same.

Turns out it didn't matter what I wanted because Billy didn't stop by our house the following Sunday or the one after that. He didn't pick me up for an afternoon at Prospero Books. He didn't take me on any more adventures.

For months after he disappeared, I searched for signs of his imminent return. Instead of clues that would lead me to him, I found markers of his absence. The cloisonné plates Billy had bought us in Beijing were no longer displayed in the living room. The photograph of Billy and me at the aquarium was replaced with one of Dad pushing me on a swing. The cupcakes from the Cuban bakery in Glendale that Billy always brought over, no longer dessert at our Sunday barbecues.

By the time I reached high school, I stopped looking for Billy. He became a person of my family's past, someone I virtually forgot. When he finally returned, I hadn't thought about him in at least a decade. And at that point he was already dead.

But Billy's death wasn't the end of our story. It was only the beginning.

CHAPTER TWO

I ALWAYS KNEW BILLY WOULD RETURN TO ME IN THE FORM OF A clue; I just didn't think it would take him sixteen years.

By then I was twenty-seven, living in Philadelphia, a dedicated, if overzealous, eighth-grade history teacher. I had just moved in with my boyfriend, the other eigth-grade history teacher at my school, and was testing the waters of cohabitation for the first time. The school year had just ended. Our students' term papers on the Emancipation Proclamation and the Underground Railroad had been marked and returned. Final grades had been submitted, and unless any parents complained, we were officially on summer break. Jay insisted we celebrate with a party. A housewarming party, even though he'd been in the apartment for half a decade, and the only thing new about the space was the fact that I lived there now, too.

Jay was headed out to buy booze for our big night. There was a state store a few blocks from our apartment, but he insisted on driving a half hour to Delaware where he could buy handles of cheap whiskey and vodka at a tax-free rate.

"You know you'll spend as much on gas as you'll save on tax," I argued, watching him dart around our living room, looking for his keys.

"It's the principle." He dug his hand between the couch cushions. It resurfaced with potato chip crumbs and lint, which he
piled on the coffee table.

"That's disgusting," I said, stating the obvious. Jay blew me
a kiss as he continued to mine the couch, unearthing his keys
and jangling them in victory. "You know there's a hook by
the door precisely for that reason." I pointed to the brass hook
with a bird perched on top, my one contribution to the decor
of our apartment.

"Is that what it's there for?" he teased, pulling me onto the
couch. Jay kissed my neck and cheek, pinning me on his lap.
I pictured him at the liquor store in Delaware, filling a shopping cart with enough plastic bottles to make everyone at the
party sick.

"We could just skip town for the weekend, drive up to a
cabin in Vermont, go off the grid."

Jay released me. I remained on his lap. "I thought you wanted
to have a party," he said.

I shrugged. Jay wanted to have a party. I wanted to want to
have a party, but I rarely went to—much less threw—the type
of binge-drinking-until-dawn rager ours promised to be. "It
was just an idea."

Jay lifted me off him and put his wallet and keys in his back
pocket. "It'll be fun," he promised, offering me a quick peck
before he headed out.

Although I'd been living with Jay for three months, the
apartment felt no more mine than it had before my clothes
were folded in his dresser, before my yogurt and grilled chicken
filled his otherwise empty fridge. The apartment was deco-
rated in the style of Jay's mother, how she thought a single,
twentysomething man should live. A dark couch that hid stains,
leather armchairs that thankfully didn't recline, a television
consuming one wall, the others lined with muted abstract art.

The few objects I owned were in a small storage locker. An antique dresser I hadn't sold with my other bedroom furniture. A stone coffee table my mother had bought in the '70s in New York. A few framed prints from the Museum of Art, which weren't worth the fight to put up on the walls of my new apartment. Jay had no great affinity for the artwork his mother had selected, but it would have offended her if we'd taken down the paintings she'd bought from her artist friends. He said it was easier to leave the apartment be, to choose our battles. I wondered what that was like, living in constant fear of upsetting your mother.

I strolled into the kitchen to clear the countertops for the cases of alcohol Jay would be bringing home. My mail was stacked in a haphazard pile next to the fridge, mostly bills and offers for yoga classes, two thank-you cards from students who professed in sloppy handwriting that I was their favorite teacher and they would always remember our trip to Franklin's Print Shop. In addition to the cards, there was a padded envelope, my name carefully inscribed across the front—*Miranda Brooks*—more elegant than by my own hand. It didn't have a return address, but it had been postmarked in Los Angeles. I squeezed the package. Hard and square, clearly a book. Probably one of Mom's little surprises, even if it wasn't her handwriting on the front of the padded envelope. She was always sending me something, overcompensating for how much it hurt her that her only child had decided to live on the opposite coast. A cookbook with recipes far too involved for me to ever make. A how-to book for decorating on a budget, since she'd reasonably assumed that when Jay's apartment became our apartment the decor would be ours, too.

I unsealed the package and pulled out a paperback book wrapped in satiny emerald paper, a greeting card taped to the front. I ripped the paper off the book. It was a play I knew by heart. *The Tempest.* Mom had named me after Miranda, in her estimation the purest, most beautiful girl in all of literature. On the cover of the paperback, a rogue wave threatened to capsize the vessel that transported the king and his entourage—including Prospero's brother, Antonio—home from the princess's wedding. Mom often sent me copies of my namesake when she found them at estate sales and antiques shops. A rare edition with gold leaf. An illustrated version from the '50s. A miniature replica fashioned into a pendant or pin. This was a generic paperback, printed by the thousands, not Mom's type of gift. Only, if the package wasn't from her, I had no idea who else would have sent it.

I took the greeting card out of its envelope. On the front, a sketch of a blonde lounging on a beach smiled back at me. Her eyes were hidden behind cat-eye sunglasses, her pixie cut caught in a strong breeze. *Malibu, California* was printed across the cloudless sky above her, letters as white and glossy as the woman's teeth.

The message written inside the card offered little clarity.

Understanding prepares us for the future.

And that was it. No "hello from your dear old friend you'd entirely forgotten about." No "here's something that always makes me think of you, love your secret admirer." No reference to the king's doomed vessel drawn on the front of the play, to Prospero and his enchanted island. Just those weighty words in ink so dark it still looked wet.

Understanding prepares us for the future. I'd heard that phrase somewhere before. Possibly Dad? He was the type to forget to sign his name. If the message had been an adage on hard work or a Roosevelt quote, I would have assumed the card was from him. This wasn't his brand of fatherly advice. Besides, Dad was more often the type to add his name to whatever present

Mom had bought me. Perhaps the phrase was a song lyric or a fortune-cookie truism, a catchphrase from one of those New Age books Joanie half-jokingly quoted. Only I heard *future* not in Joanie's raspy voice, but in a soft lullaby. A deep, dreamy voice that should have inspired comfort. Instead, it hit me with acute longing, regret.

Maybe the phrase was one of Prospero's lines, although it lacked Shakespeare's measure. Still, it sounded like something Prospero might have said to the audience in his final goodbye. I flipped through the text. The epilogue wasn't marked, but in the second scene of the play, when Prospero told Miranda how his brother had run them out of Milan, Prospero's words were highlighted.

'Tis time I should inform thee farther. Lend thy hand and pluck my magic garment from me. So lie there, my art.

Sit down; for thou must now know farther.

Thou must now know farther. Understanding prepares us for the future. If not for the similarity in theme, I would have assumed the highlighted section was the random marking of the copy's previous owner, but Prospero's words, the line from the card... they were connected. Only, I wasn't certain how.

I plugged the phrase from the card into my phone's search engine. A few hundred musings on education and religion popped up. No direct quotations of the line itself. It wasn't a reference to *The Tempest*. As far as I could tell, it wasn't a saying at all. Still, I was certain I'd heard it before.

I tucked the play into my dresser and taped the card to the fridge, hoping the beach scene might jog my memory. The woman's happy face followed me as I sprayed down the countertops. Although her eyes were shaded, they monitored my every move. When I looked up, I expected her expression to have changed. Of course it never did and after a few glances at her windblown hair, her blank smile, I started to feel like she knew something I didn't.

BY NIGHTFALL, OUR APARTMENT WAS READY FOR THE FESTIVI-ties to begin. A handful of our colleagues, Jay's soccer buddies and my college friends arrived early with salads, couscous, chicken and cake.

We settled onto the living room floor, wineglasses at our sides, paper plates nestled into our laps. Everyone was talking animatedly. It was the party I would have preferred, just close friends, people you didn't have to ask yourself how they'd ended up at your house. I sat between Jay and the art teacher. Jay coached soccer at the high school and had become the other eighth-grade history teacher earlier that year when Teacher Anne's maternity leave turned permanent. Before he joined my ranks, I'd seen him from a distance, knew how his muscular calves looked beneath his mesh shorts, how his whistle burst in sharp tweets when he wanted to get the boys' attention. He was good-looking in a preppy way I wasn't normally attracted to, but he had this magnetic energy that made female teachers young and old giggle when he said hello to them. A charisma so powerful the school was desperate to keep him. They offered him the position of eighth-grade American history teacher even though he'd been an economics major in college and had never taught before. I was tasked with getting him up to speed, a job that involved more history lessons than I would have expected, evenings and weekend study sessions where I taught him about the Federalists and Jeffersonian Republicans, the contentious election of 1800, the duel between Hamilton and Burr. He grinned apishly as I explained to him how candidates used to run on their own and whoever came in second, regardless of party, was awarded the vice presidency. I'd accused him of not listening, and he'd said, *You're so passionate.*

It's adorable, and then I'd grinned apishly, too, and soon those grins had led to something more.

I'd assumed it would be a tryst, greeting each other in the halls as Teacher Miranda and Teacher Jay, as though we'd never seen each other naked, until the secrecy felt rote. Turned out Jay was more than athletic legs and an inviting smile. He spoke about soccer like it was art, a metaphor for life. He knew everyone in his—now our—neighborhood by name, helping the aging Mrs. Peters carry her groceries to her third-floor apartment, and walking his friend Trevor's mutt when Trevor couldn't get out of work in time to let her out. He was close with his parents, never losing patience with his mom, telling her he liked the collared shirts she bought him, shirts that gathered dust in his closet, and hanging her bland artwork across his—now our—walls. He was close to his sister, who lived a few blocks away and was currently sitting across from us, flirting with my college friend as she snuck sideways glances at Jay and me, still not quite accustomed to our partnership.

"How'd your last day go?" I asked Jay. I didn't want to talk about school, but I was still learning how to be with Jay in a crowd. We spent so much of our time alone that I had to remind myself I couldn't pounce on him when others were around; I couldn't ask him to divulge his feelings in the way that caused him to blush.

Jay proceeded to describe his last day of class, a well-plotted game of Murder that the students probably enjoyed more than my lesson on Abraham Lincoln. That was the difference between me and Jay. He knew how to win them over. I knew how to teach them something they might not value today, but in a few years would resonate, at least so I hoped. So much of being a teacher rests in that blind hope. Jay reached over to play with one of my curls, and I kissed him on the cheek, testing out what it felt like to display affection in front of friends and colleagues. That kiss was the physical equivalent of changing your Facebook relationship status, a pronouncement that, while not quite irreversible, was indelible.

By eleven, the randoms started turning up. Friends of friends of friends—Jay greeted them all. He slapped high five to guys in baseball caps and hugged girls in tight, bright tank tops whom I'd never met before. I could imagine the back and forth he had with those tall, muscular guys, details about Saturday morning soccer league and woes of the Phillies' latest loss. I couldn't imagine the conversations Jay had with those girls. I tried not to be too obvious as I watched them talk. Jay's sister caught me staring, an unmistakable smirk on her face.

As more strangers crowded our apartment, the living room became unbearably hot. Someone turned the stereo so loud you couldn't talk, you couldn't think, you could only dance. I stood against the wall with Jay, watching the gaggle of brightly clad girls move effortlessly to the electronic beat. Couples bumped into each other as they danced, sloshing beer onto our hardwood floors. Desire radiated from Jay's body and I wanted to get lost in him, to turn the corner of our living room into our private lair. Jay tapped his foot against the baseboard and asked if I wanted to dance.

We sidled in beside the group of girls, cognizant of their fluidity. I tried to be fluid, too, but dancing always made me overly aware of the orders my brain issued to my body and my legs' inability to enact them. Jay wasn't a good dancer, either, and we laughed at how terribly we moved, inching closer to each other until the beat became ours, until Jay's desires aligned with mine.

My phone vibrated in my pocket. Normally, I would have ignored it, but the buzzer to our apartment worked intermittently despite my countless calls to the super to fix it, and I didn't want one of my friends to be trapped outside. When I saw it was Mom, I knew instantly that something was wrong. Mom and I had spoken that morning. She'd given me her recipe for fresh-squeezed brown derbies, which I hadn't had the heart to tell her would have been wasted on me and my cheap beer-drinking contemporaries. While we often spoke more than once a day, she wouldn't have called during my party unless something had happened.

I angled the phone toward Jay so he could see that it was Mom, and we spoke in gestures. He shrugged his shoulders, asking if everything was okay. I swatted away the worry I felt, motioning that I was slipping outside. I fought the current of people out of the apartment.

"What's wrong?" I asked as I stepped onto the stoop.

"I'm sorry to interrupt your party."

"Is everything okay?" I sat on the top step.

"I figured you'd want to know. I didn't feel right not telling you right away because I thought—"

"Mom, what happened? You're scaring me."

"I just got a call. It's Billy." All the alcohol in my system hit me with the weight of his name. Billy. Uncle Billy. I was suddenly very dizzy. I couldn't recall the last time Mom had mentioned him. I couldn't recall the last time I'd thought of him. I already knew what she was going to say, but I waited for her to tell me.

"He...he passed. This afternoon," she said distractedly, like she'd taken a sedative, and maybe she had. Her voice was unnaturally calm.

An image flashed into my fuzzy brain: Billy sitting behind the wheel of his car after he'd dropped me home for the last time. He'd smiled as he drove off, only his smile was too wide, uneasy. I tried to recall a happier moment, his pleased expression earlier that day when he'd bought me the dog, his face whenever I solved one of his riddles. Instead, I kept seeing that forced smile as he waved goodbye for the last time, how he'd failed to hide his sadness from me.

"Oh, Mom." I didn't know what to say. I couldn't imagine

how she felt. Even though they hadn't spoken in sixteen years, she must have been devastated.

"I should let you get back to your party."

"No, Mom, it's just a party."

"You go have fun. We'll talk soon, all right?"

"Mom," I said before she hung up. "I'm really sorry."

"I'm sorry, too," she said.

I stayed on the stoop, watching her number blink across the screen until it disappeared. It was a sweltering night. Nine years in Philadelphia, and I still wasn't used to the humidity, how it outlasted the sun. I thought back to the last conversation I remembered having about Billy, how Mom had told me she didn't know if they would work it out, and they never did. I must have asked her about Billy after that, but she made it clear that Billy was a ghost, disappearing him from the stories of their childhood, avoiding Temescal Canyon where the three of us used to hike, the scenic beaches in Malibu that had been Billy's favorite. Eventually, I must have stopped asking after him. Billy was dead now, but he'd been gone from us for years. Still, I felt his loss acutely. And I could tell Mom did, too.

The vibrations of Jay's footsteps thundered as he neared the door. I was relieved that he'd come looking for me but wasn't ready to share the moment with him.

"Hey you," he said, offering me that smile that made me dizzy, only I felt the greater dizziness of Mom's words, of thinking about Billy after such a long time. The smile fell from Jay's face. He leaned against the frame like he was posing in an outdoor catalog. "What's wrong?"

"My uncle died."

"Fuck." Jay sat on the step, hugged me toward him. "Should we get rid of everyone?"

"No, I don't want everyone to know. It's just… I haven't seen him in, like, sixteen years. I can't believe he's dead." Even as I said it, it still didn't feel real.

"I can set off the smoke alarm, light a match under the sprinklers. That will get everyone out."

I forced a laugh. "We don't have sprinklers."

"Okay, then, a fire in the trash can? Nothing dangerous."

My smile grew strained. "Please don't set our apartment on fire. Really, I just want to not think about it for now."

Jay didn't seem convinced, but he lifted me off our stoop and led me upstairs. Before we walked into the apartment, he wrapped his arms around me.

"One word and they're all gone," he promised.

But as soon as we were back inside, one of Jay's friends lured him into a circle with the thick promise of a blunt. The walls had begun to sweat. Our couch and coffee table had been pushed against the wall, enlarging the dance floor. My old roommate spotted me from across the room and dragged me onto the dance floor where bodies coupled, their limbs entwined as they swayed to the music.

I couldn't stop thinking about Billy, the scavenger hunts he'd crafted in my backyard, the adventures we took together across the parks and beaches of Los Angeles, the presents he bought me abroad—beaded jewelry from South America and electronics from Japan. I wondered what had happened to those gifts, if they were still in my parents' house, if Mom had thrown them out long ago.

Jay's arms appeared around my waist, swinging my body almost to the beat. I tried to move with him as one, but I was distracted by Mom's words—*I'm sorry, too*—how quickly she'd rushed off the phone before revealing the depths of her grief.

And as suddenly as Jay was there, he disappeared again, to the far corner where there was a commotion over something that had broken. My limbs grew heavy as they mimicked the movements of those around me. Jay crouched down to pick up whatever had fallen, cradling it as he carried it toward the bedroom. The song ended and the couples surrounding me danced to the rhythm of drunken conversations as they waited for the next song to begin. I shut my eyes and saw Billy, his conflicted smile. What was it he called me as a child? "My special girl?" No, "my favorite girl." *There's my favorite girl*, he would say before whisking me off on one of his adventures.

The music kicked in. I tried to get swept up in the rhythm of the room, but I was lost in thoughts of Billy, his lessons on geology and biology and evolution disguised in adventure. He'd taught me almost everything I knew about the world, how it had shifted and collided and evolved, how our lives were shaped by the movements of the earth. I stopped moving and opened my eyes. Of course. I didn't know how I'd missed it. My legs felt like lead, but I forced them to move, jostling between the gyrating couples until I reached the kitchen. The blonde on the greeting card still smiled from the refrigerator, only I now knew as much as she did. *Understanding prepares us for the future.* Those were Billy's words. It was something he said to me after my first earthquake.

CHAPTER THREE

IN THE MORNING, THE REMAINS OF LAST NIGHT'S PARTY LOOKED staged: cups scattered haphazardly across the living room floor; a fedora resting on the couch's arm; the hum of the stereo speakers left on after the music had stopped. It was already hot, the moist air rank with spilled beer and cigarette butts.

"It smells like a frat house in here." Jay coughed harshly.

"I wouldn't know." Although there were several fraternities at Penn, I was more the type to indulge in jugged wine with the other members of the history review, making drinking games out of the presidents and state capitals. *You're such a nerd*, Jay had declared proudly when I'd described my version of college partying.

"Come on, nerd," he flirted. "I'll buy you brunch."

We walked to what had quickly become our regular spot. The tables lining the sidewalk were overcrowded but the dim, cool dining room was mostly unoccupied.

Jay ordered two Bloody Marys. The sight of that red liquid glittering with pepper sent a sharp punch to my gut. Jay gulped his down in a matter of seconds and didn't fight when I pushed my drink toward him. Despite the news of Billy's death and a pounding headache from a night of too much beer and not enough sleep, I couldn't shake an expectant feeling. It couldn't be a coincidence that Billy sent me something before he died. And where there was one clue from Billy, there were always more. I found the card in my bag and slid it across the table. Jay wiped his hands before carefully removing the card from its envelope.

"I got that yesterday from my uncle," I explained.

"What's it mean?" he asked, reading the inside of the card.

"It's something he said to me after my first earthquake."

That night was one of my first vivid memories. My parents had gone out, and Billy was babysitting. We stayed up late to watch *Return to Oz.* I wasn't allowed to watch the movie, but I didn't tell Billy, not that he'd asked whether shock treatments and a demonic Oz were appropriate for a four-year-old. From the entrance of the menacing score, I knew I was in for a sleepless night. When Billy put me to bed, I didn't tell him to leave a light on, even though the shadows from the floodlights etched the monstrous shapes of the Nome King across my walls. I tossed and turned, and soon the floor began to vibrate. The trophies on my bookshelf rattled. The Nome King had overtaken my room, shifting the walls into stone gargoyles and goblins that wanted to eat me. I screamed. The room didn't stop shaking. I screamed louder. By the time Billy opened the door, the bookshelves had stopped moving but the Nome King's minions remained in the shadows across my walls.

Billy sat on my bed and rubbed my back. *It was only a small earthquake,* he said. He tried to turn on the lights but the power had died. He started to leave the room. I shouted for him to stay. *I'll be right back. I just need to find a flashlight.*

I begged him not to go, and he abandoned the hunt for a flashlight, lying beside me on my narrow twin bed. Each time I drifted to sleep, I felt him slip out of bed, and I pleaded for him to stay. Eventually, he stopped trying to leave and fell asleep beside me.

In the morning, sunlight filled the room and Billy was gone. I searched for evidence of the earthquake. Billy was right. It was a small one. Nothing had been jolted so hard that it had moved or broken.

A sugary scent led me to the kitchen where Billy was pouring batter into a pan while Mom flipped pancakes.

Come on, Billy said to Mom, *that looks exactly like a bird.*

I'm just saying, don't quit your day job, Mom teased.

What, you think you can do better?

This isn't a challenge you want to take.

Bring it, sis.

Mom poured batter into the pan, and Billy laughed when he saw her creation.

What are you guys doing? I asked, and they turned in unison, smiling.

Making our favorite girl breakfast, Billy said as he lifted me into the air and carried me to the table.

My brave girl. Your first earthquake. Mom kissed the top of my head and put a plate of pancakes in front of me, the words *I Win* written in batter.

Later that day, Billy knocked on my bedroom door with a riddle.

I'm a type of lot and also a type of amusement. I'm national and in every neighborhood, he read as he uncoiled a sheet of paper.

What? I asked too quickly.

I bet you know, if you think really hard.

Along the drive I tried to get him to tell me the answer.

Where'd we go for your birthday? Billy finally said, watching me in the rearview mirror.

Disneyland.

And what is Disneyland? An amusement... It begins with a P. No guess? Parrr—

Park, I shouted.

Billy pulled into the lot at the base of Malibu Bluffs Park

where an envelope was fastened to the park's sign. My name marked its face. There was a riddle inside.

What's a fruit and also a color?

What? I asked Billy.
Is it a lemon?
No!
How about a grape?
No!
Well, what is it, then?
An orange, I shouted.

A single orange rested on the closest picnic table. Beneath the orange, I found a paring knife and instructions to cut off the rind in large chunks. Billy held my hand as I gripped the knife and together we cut a puzzle into the outside of the orange.

Pretend each of these is a plate. He held an odd-shaped piece of rind. *Not the type of plate you eat off, but a tectonic plate that makes up the crust of the earth. This is the mantle.* He twirled the peeled orange in his right hand. *The lower mantle. It's made of liquid like this orange. Well, will you look at that—* Billy unfurled a piece of paper from the center of the orange. On it, the next clue.

I'm a female deer and also used to make pie. You might like me best in a form that's playful.

I followed Billy's eyes to the far end of the picnic area where a container of Play-Doh hid beneath a bench. Together, we lifted the lid to find a list of instructions folded on top of a ball of blue putty.

Step one, roll the Play-Doh into a flat circle.

Step two, wrap it around the orange. The orange became a blue orb.

This is the upper mantle, Billy explained.

Step three, wrap the rind around the Play-Doh. The puzzle pieces of rind fit roughly together around the orange.

Billy inched two pieces of rind toward each other. *The plates are in constant motion. They move very, very slowly. We only feel their movement during an earthquake.* The pieces collided and blue Play-Doh oozed between the edges of the rind in a rippled formation. *When the plates converge like this, they form mountains and volcanoes.* He spread the rind apart and the blue beneath stretched. *When plates diverge, they create rifts, which on land make lakes and rivers.* Billy rubbed two pieces of rind against each other until they would no longer move. *The plates' edges are rough, so sometimes they get stuck. These edges are called fault lines. When they lock up like this, they create a tremendous amount of stress.* He kept rubbing them together until one piece slid beneath the other. *With too much stress, they'll slip and that's one way we get an earthquake.*

The fourth and final step instructed us to hike to the highest point we could find. I followed Billy up a steep incline. At the peak, we could see Pepperdine University across the Pacific Coast Highway. I gazed down the barrel of Billy's finger as he outlined the Pepperdine Block, how over time it had moved upward and west of the land where we stood.

Is this where the earthquake happened? I asked.

Along the same fault line.

So an earthquake could happen right here? I braced myself for the shaking to begin. Billy laughed.

You might feel an aftershock in the next few days. If you do, just remember it won't be as violent as the earthquake last night. Billy held my shoulders, looking me in the eye. *We can't stop earthquakes from happening, but you don't have to be afraid. After every earthquake, scientists like me review the damage and we use that to make our buildings and bridges stronger, so there's less damage in the future.*

So we need earthquakes? I asked.

You could think of it that way. We need earthquakes to learn. Under-

standing prepares us for the future. Remember that. It's the only way to make us safer.

"I remember all week I was hoping for an aftershock, but I didn't feel any," I said to Jay. "That's how Billy was. He made everything an adventure."

Jay handed the card back to me. "I don't get it. Why remind you of that now that he's dead?" Jay wiped the corners of his mouth and glanced at my barely touched food. He pointed to my eggs, and I nodded, trading my mostly full plate for his empty one.

"It's another one of his adventures." I reached into my bag and pulled out the copy of *The Tempest*, opening to Act 1, Scene 2, where Prospero told Miranda the story of his past. I ran my index finger beneath the highlighted line. *Sit down; for thou must now know farther.* "This is the only section that's highlighted." I explained Prospero's story to Jay, how his cruel brother, Antonio, had betrayed him, overtaking Prospero's kingdom while Prospero was absorbed in his magical studies. With the help of the king, Antonio had banished Prospero and young Miranda to sea.

"You were named after Shakespeare?" Jay asked.

"You didn't know that?"

"*The Tempest* isn't exactly in my wheelhouse." He flipped through the play like it was a guidebook to me. "So what's your uncle want you to know now?"

"He had a huge fight with my mom when I was twelve. She did something to him, or at least he thought she did. I'm not sure. I think he's using Prospero to tell me what happened."

"Miranda," he said carefully, "it can be really confusing when someone close to you dies."

"What are you saying?" I wished those words hadn't come out so defensive.

"Do you think possibly you're trying to give your uncle's death meaning?" Jay reached over and stroked my cheek. His expression was close-lipped, full of pity.

"I know my uncle," I said assuredly. Did I really, though? I hadn't seen him in sixteen years. I knew nothing of his life after us, whether he'd had a family of his own, if he continued to live in Pasadena. Still, the card he'd sent, *The Tempest*... I knew he was leading me somewhere.

The waitress brought over the check and Jay unearthed enough crumpled bills from his pocket to cover the bill.

Outside, the humidity assaulted us. We stood in the doorway, allowing our eyes to adjust to the blinding afternoon.

"What did your mom and uncle fight about?" Jay asked.

"My uncle missed my birthday party, but it was more than that. I just don't know what."

"Your mom never told you what happened?"

"Billy became something we didn't talk about. It was like he never existed."

"That's sad."

"It's just the way it was." Every family has its unspoken stories. Billy was ours. It didn't matter whether or not it was sad.

"Did you tell your mom about the card?" I didn't like the condescension in Jay's tone.

"It'll just upset her," I said.

"You should tell her," he insisted.

"Please don't tell me how to handle my own mother," I snapped. "You've only met her once."

During my parents' most recent visit to Philadelphia, the four of us had gone to dinner. Over small plates, Jay had talked to Dad about baseball and Mom about the gigs her all-girl rock band had had on South Street in the '70s. After dinner, as we'd strolled down the cobblestone streets of Old City, Mom belted the closest thing her band had had to a hit, a rare performance emboldened by the two neat bourbons she'd ordered to impress Jay. Her voice was phlegmy from the liquor but still silky enough to send chills down my arms. We—and other passersby—stopped to applaud her. Jay had thought this was Mom, an impulsive woman who drank whiskey and sang whenever she felt like it, but this wasn't Mom. This was only a role she played because she knew it would make Jay like her.

Jay kicked at the sidewalk, obviously upset over what I'd said. "I didn't mean that."

He pulled me to him, and I hugged him back, trying to ignore the gnawing disappointment that we wouldn't continue to fight.

I started to follow Jay back to our block, but I wasn't ready to return to our smelly, filthy apartment. I told Jay I was going for a walk, and he pretended not to be hurt that I wanted to be alone.

At Walnut, I turned toward the river. The moist, hot air provoked beads of sweat that ran down my thighs and collected behind my knees. From the steps at the Great Plaza, I watched joggers and rollerbladers race down the path that followed the Delaware River. I found my phone in my purse and searched "Billy Silver, Los Angeles, seismologist, obituary." I couldn't think of anything else to include about him. It was enough for the *Los Feliz Ledger*, which had published a brief obituary for Billy that morning. It described the loss of Billy Silver, LA native, seismologist and earthquake chaser, owner of neighborhood staple Prospero Books. The obituary included a somber quote from the store's manager, who vowed to keep Billy's legacy alive through the bookstore and a listing of the funeral, set for Tuesday afternoon at Forrest Lawn.

Prospero Books. I should have made the connection the second I realized the copy of *The Tempest* was from Billy. Of course any reference to the play was also a reference to Billy's bookstore, where books were prized above dukedom, where he'd taken me countless afternoons as a child and told me to pick a book, any book. Somehow, the copy of *The Tempest* Billy had sent had to do with his bookshop.

I took *The Tempest* out of my bag and reread the story Prospero told Miranda. Prospero needed Miranda to know how his brother had betrayed them in order for her to understand why he'd created the storm that stranded Antonio on the island. It'd been years since Billy sent me one of his riddles, yet I could still read his coded messages. *Thou must now know farther*, Prospero's words. *Understanding prepares us for the future*, Billy's. Like Prospero, Billy wanted to tell me of his betrayal, the event that had exiled him from our family. And also like Prospero, Billy had planned his return, wielding not spells and incantations but the magic of his clues, of the adventures he'd plotted for me in my youth. I wasn't a child anymore. Still, I could feel the rush of Billy, the exhilaration of the first riddle, how it always led to another clue. This time was different, though, the excitement bittersweet. This was the last time Billy would reach out to me. My last chance to discover the story Mom would never tell, the truth of what had driven them apart.

MY SCHEDULE WAS WIDE OPEN FOR THE NEXT TWO AND A HALF months, so I booked a flight for Monday, home in time to make Billy's funeral. I had to go. Not just because I wanted to find the next clue. It was the right thing to do. I'd loved him as a child. I would go to his funeral. I would honor what we once were to each other.

Jay lay across our bed, watching as I packed the bulk of my summer clothes.

"Do you have to bring so much?"

I zipped my suitcase and hopped onto the bed beside him. "If I didn't know better I'd think you were going to miss me."

"Of course I'm going to miss you." He rolled me over and lay on top of me, his face so close to mine I could see stubble erupting along his jawbone.

"It'll just be a couple of days." I hadn't bought a return ticket, but I hadn't spent more than five consecutive days in LA since I'd left for college. If I was right and Billy had left me another clue, it wouldn't take more than a few days to uncover the secrets he wanted to tell me.

"Are you sure you don't want me to come to the funeral with you?"

"You've got camp next week."

"It's only soccer."

"Only soccer? Who are you and what have you done with my boyfriend?" I was still getting used to the way that word felt in my mouth.

He ran his hand through my hair in the way I didn't like, unfurling my curls. "You don't have to go alone."

"It's just a few days," I said, shaking my hair free of his touch.

Jay insisted on driving me to the airport even though he had to get a zip car and it would have been cheaper to call a cab. He pulled up to the terminal and walked around to the trunk to get my bag.

"Call me when you land?" He placed my rolling suitcase on the curb. I expected him to tell me to hurry back, but he said, "Take the time you need. You'll regret it if you rush back and aren't there for your family."

"Who knew you were such a sentimentalist?" Jay turned away, clearly hurt. I was tempted to tease him again for being too sensitive. Instead, I kissed him intently, giving him something else to return to in the days we were apart.

ON THE FLIGHT ACROSS COUNTRY, I TRIED TO DECIDE WHAT I should tell Mom about *The Tempest* and the clue Billy had sent. When I'd told her I was coming home for the funeral, she'd asked, *Why would you want to go to that?* with such disbelief, such utter bafflement, I didn't know how to respond.

You aren't planning to go to Billy's funeral? I asked her.

Why would I be?

Because he's your only brother, I thought. *I'll go alone, then,* I said.

Whatever, she said with the cool indifference of one of my students.

How was I supposed to tell her that Billy had reached out to me when she hadn't even forgiven him enough to honor his death, to memorialize the closeness they once had? And what was worse, whatever he wanted to tell me was something Mom didn't want me to know. I just hoped I'd know what to say to her when I saw her in person.

Dad was waiting at baggage claim with a printed sign that read Teacher Miranda. It was what all the teachers in my Quaker school were called. Teacher Anne. Teacher Tom. Teacher Jay. Jay. I texted to tell him I had landed. He blew me an emoji kiss. While I hated how easy and generic emojis were, I liked that Jay was willing to be corny on my account.

Dad was a reluctant hugger. I knew not to take it personally. Mom was the only person he was comfortable offering physical affection to. I would find them slow dancing in the kitchen as Mom sang an old folk song, or him absentmindedly rubbing her feet as they watched a Nora Ephron movie. To most people, he offered his hand. At least he hugged me, even if there always was that stilted discomfort.

"Where's Mom?" I asked as Dad released me from the sideways embrace. Every time I came home, Dad's hair had grown more salt than pepper, his olive skin more leathered, his blue eyes grayer. It made me want to clutch his hand and beg him to stop getting old.

"She went to bed early. Said she'll see you in the morning." Mom never missed an opportunity to meet me at the airport. She always pushed her way through the crowd of limo drivers and multigenerational families waiting in baggage claim, so her face was the first I saw.

"How's she doing?"

Dad took my bag and wheeled it toward the exit. "You know

your mom. She's putting on a brave face, but this is hard on her, harder than she would have guessed."

Outside the arrivals terminal, the air was thick with exhaust and cigarette smoke. Cars lunged at each other as they tried to weave in and out of rings of unmoving traffic. Only a few palm trees in the distance hinted that we were in Los Angeles, not some neglected airport of the developing world.

Dad pulled out of short-term parking into the outer circle of traffic. "How'd Stanton's words go over this year?"

I ended every school year the same way, on Lincoln's deathbed. Moments after the president died, his friend and secretary of war, Edwin Stanton, commemorated the loss, *Now he belongs to the ages*. Or was it, *Now he belongs to the angels*? I'd pose to my students. While Lincoln's doctor had heard Stanton say "ages," the secretary at the scene had heard "angels." So which quote was right—did Stanton fate Lincoln to history or the afterlife? The students would evaluate each option, debating Stanton's true words. In the end, it was a trick question.

"Stanton's words remain an enigma," I said to Dad. *We have to allow for competing experiences of historical events*, I told my students. *Then we can decide how to interpret the past, what makes sense to us today.* "I think a few of them understood. I hope so, anyway."

"You can only do your best. It's up to them to commit to caring about the past." Dad's car screeched to a halt as the Flyaway bus darted in front of us.

"Do you remember when Billy showed up that time, in the middle of the night?"

"Of course." Dad's attention was focused on the bus, squeezing into an impossibly small space between two cars ahead.

"I'm sure Mom must have told me, but I can't remember what they fought about."

"I don't know." Dad honked at an SUV that crossed in front of us. "Come on!"

"You don't know what happened?"

"All I know is Billy showed up drunk and told your mom he never wanted to talk to her again." He wove around traffic, onto Sepulveda where the road opened up. "Then he bought you that stupid dog."

"Billy wasn't drunk." I thought back to his flushed face, his glassy eyes. "Was he?"

Dad turned onto Ocean Park Boulevard where the air grew cooler and saltier as we neared the ocean. I rolled down the window and inhaled deeply. Every time I returned to LA, the city felt a little more my parents' home, somewhere I'd been an extended visitor, never a resident. I couldn't tell Mom this. She was waiting for the time when, like her, I would move back to Southern California, but it was never going to happen. I didn't want to teach the children of movie stars and musicians. Directors. TV executives. I didn't want to teach American history in a state that hadn't been part of the union until the Compromise of 1850. I wasn't an Angelino, a Californian at heart. The salt in my nostrils was the closest I came to feeling homesick.

"Look," Dad said when we were stopped at a light. "I don't want to ruin your memory of Billy. There were sides of him you were too young to see."

"What do you mean 'sides'?"

"Nothing. I shouldn't have said that."

"Don't do that. What sides?"

Dad turned off Ocean Park into our neighborhood. I took in the familiar scene of our quiet street, knowing the colors of all the houses we passed, even if they all appeared charcoal in the evening's pale light. Los Angeles never got dark, no matter how late at night, not completely.

"I get that Billy's death is bringing up a lot of questions. I just don't feel comfortable speaking on behalf of your mother."

"I'm not asking you to speak for her."

"It's her past," he said.

"It's our past," I corrected. Pebbles crackled under the tires as Dad pulled into the driveway. The house was dark, save the porch light, moths swarming in its glow.

"It's up to your mom what she wants to tell you." He hopped out of the car to fetch my bag from the trunk. I watched him in the rearview mirror until the lid of the trunk turned the mirror black and I couldn't see him anymore. Just before it did, I saw an expression sweep across his face, something I hadn't seen before, something that looked a lot like fear.

CHAPTER FOUR

THE FOLLOWING MORNING, MOM WAS ALREADY IN THE KITCHEN when I wandered downstairs in search of coffee. Blueberry muffins cooled on the island that divided the kitchen from the dining and living rooms. I knew the fridge was also stocked with foods she remembered me liking as a teenager. Cool Whip and strawberries, bologna, chocolate milk—foods, if you could call them that, I hadn't eaten in years.

"Where are the other twenty guests?"

"Miranda." Mom dropped her oven mitts and rushed to me. It was only 7:00 a.m., but she was already dressed in black pants and a coral blouse, her curls set to frame her face, her eyes bright with mascara and brown eye shadow.

"I'm so sorry, Mom." As conflicted of a hugger as Dad was, Mom was the opposite. She always hugged me like if it was up to her she'd never let me go.

"I'm okay," she said, like she wanted it to be true.

"Is there anything I can do?"

She pointed to the table. "Sit."

Mom served me a muffin and a cup of coffee like she was my waitress. She sat across from me, watching as I broke the muffin in two. Steam rose from its center.

"It's good to have you home." She reached across the table to brush a matted curl from my forehead.

"Thought any more about coming to the funeral with me today?" I asked casually as I picked at my muffin. "It might offer you some closure."

"I got closure years ago." She stood and headed to the sink, where she began scrubbing the muffin pan.

I finished eating and brought my empty plate to the sink. I stood beside her in the too-close way she liked. "I worry you might regret it, if you don't go."

She turned off the faucet and put her cold, wet hand on my cheek. "How'd I end up with such a sweet daughter?" She returned her attention to the mixer in the sink, "Really, honey, I'm fine."

FORREST LAWN WAS A HALF HOUR DRIVE FROM MY PARENTS' house, so I gave myself forty-five minutes to get there, just in case. My parents loaned me their car and waved goodbye from the driveway.

I rolled down the window before I left. "You're sure I can't convince you to come?"

"Miranda, go," Dad said, too forcefully.

"We'll see you when you get back," Mom added.

I watched her as I reversed out of the driveway, waiting for a crack in her facade that would reveal the pain she'd covered with foundation and blush. She shooed me on as though I was dressed up for prom rather than her only brother's funeral.

When I arrived at Forrest Lawn, the cemetery's wrought-iron gate looked like it belonged on the east coast, harboring an exclusive country club. Despite leaving early, I was late. Twenty-two minutes late to be exact, late even by LA standards, where everything started ten minutes after it was supposed to on account of the pesky traffic.

"The Silver funeral?" I asked the guard. He pointed up

Cathedral Drive toward a hill in the far corner of the property, away from the famous names that lined the more prominently located gravestones.

A crowd of forty people was gathered around the open grave. They were younger, hipper and more diverse than I would have expected, dressed in black jeans and T-shirts, tight dark jersey dresses. I tugged at the collar of my knee-length black dress, feeling acutely conservative and undeniably east coast.

I stood behind the row of people that lined the grave, searching for someone I recognized. I didn't know whom I expected to be there. My grandparents had died before I was born or old enough to remember them. Mom and Billy didn't have other siblings. Their uncles had died on the beaches of Normandy and in the Pacific. No cousins or extended family to speak of. No lifelong friends that had been stand-ins for family. Still, I scanned those young faces hoping for someone familiar, perhaps an old girlfriend of Billy's that I'd forgotten about or Lee the manager or one of the pretty girls who had worked at the café in Prospero Books, now in her forties. Only a few faces looked older than my own. A plump woman in her sixties with plastic-framed glasses and a wiry man with a white goatee and bifocals. The only other person who stood out was a man in a pinstripe suit who, like me, hadn't gotten the memo on funeral casual.

The crowd shifted as a guy in a hooded sweatshirt and faded black pants walked toward the microphone behind the grave. He swept a mop of hair away from his face, his eyes downcast as he dug into his back pocket to retrieve a sheet of notebook paper.

"This is a Dylan Thomas poem that Billy liked." He cleared his throat before reading "Do Not Go Gentle into That Good Night." As he read about fighting the dying light, I studied Billy's tombstone. The dark granite listed his name, Billy Silver, his birth in 1949, his death three days ago. Thomas Jefferson once wrote that the life and soul of history must remain forever unknown. Only the facts—the eternal facts, he called them—were passed down to subsequent generations. These were the external facts of Billy's life, stripped of any details that made him someone to remember. Why wasn't he buried with my grandparents in the Westside? Why did he choose to be buried here, between the equally anonymous gravestones of Evelyn Weston and Richard Cullen, in what appeared to be the singles' corner of Forrest Lawn, wallflowers even in death?

Billy's friend finished reading the Thomas poem and stared solemnly at the crowd. His gaze circled the rows of people, until it stopped on me. His eyes were clear and so unnaturally blue they caught my breath. They were stunning but cold, making me feel like even more of an interloper than I already did. What was I doing here? I'd told myself I'd come home out of duty and decency and grief. Really, it was because of the card my uncle had sent, the prospect of another one of his scavenger hunts. I didn't belong here. I didn't deserve to be beside these sad, beautiful people, commemorating someone I'd practically forgotten.

"You want one?" The girl beside me held a plastic cup in my direction. She was younger than I was, Latina, her sinewy arms covered in ink drawings and Spanish calligraphy. "There's whiskey or whiskey. I'd recommend the whiskey." I took the cup and watched as she poured liberally into it.

The older man with the goatee walked behind the microphone, holding his red solo cup toward the crowd. He shut his eyes, and began singing, "Oh Danny Boy, the pipes, the pipes are calling."

The plump woman in her sixties arrived at the goateed man's side, and threw a freckled arm around his shoulders, swaying his body with hers as she joined in the old hymn. When they finished singing, the man angled his glass toward the open grave, then the sky, before bringing the cup to his lips.

"'To the nights we'll never remember with friends we'll never forget,' as Billy used to say," the girl said, angling her cup toward mine. "You from the neighborhood?"

"What neighborhood?"

"Silver Lake. I haven't seen you around."

"No, I'm Billy's niece." It sounded like a foreign word—
niece—all accented and blunt. Still, I was Billy's niece. He'd
sent me a sign before he died. He'd been thinking of me. We
remained something to each other. "How did you know my
uncle?" I asked, emboldened by the fact that I was family and
these people weren't.

"I work at Prospero."

"Prospero Books," I said longingly. I couldn't remember the
last time I'd said the name aloud and it still hit me with the
amazement it had when I was a kid, the sorcery of Prospero,
the magic of his books.

The whiskey changed the mood, and everyone started chatting energetically. Laughter carried across the open terrain. The
man in the pinstripe suit announced, "If you'd like to continue
the reverie, we'll be convening at Prospero Books."

"It was nice to meet you." I waited for her to add, *I'll see
you at the store*, but she nodded and made her way toward the
wild-haired man who had read the Dylan Thomas poem. She
whispered to him and they turned to look at me, an inscrutable expression on their faces, or maybe it wasn't inscrutable;
maybe I didn't want to decipher the hard truth of their stare.

I sipped my whiskey even after there was nothing left in the
cup, watching everyone walk toward the mass of cars collected
on the side of the road.

"You wouldn't happen to be Miranda?" The man in the
pinstripe suit approached me, his hand extended. He was older
than he'd appeared at a distance, his sandy hair lightened with
peroxide in place of youth. "I was hoping to see you here. I'm
Elijah Greenberg, Billy's lawyer."

I was about to ask him how he knew I'd be here. Billy must have
told him about me. He must have known about *The Tempest*,
the quest that lay ahead.

"I'm so sorry about Billy." He escorted me toward the two cars left on the side of the road. "Are you coming to the celebration?"

"The celebration?"

"Of Billy's life. Strange way to put it, I know. That's how Billy wanted it. 'I don't want any of this sad business,'" he said in a deep voice that I assumed was supposed to be Billy's. "'That shouldn't be your last memory of me.'"

I wanted to go, but I could still hear the girl's tone as she'd said, "Nice to meet you," like she wouldn't be meeting me again. I could picture her facial expression, and that of the big-haired man as they regarded me from afar, the absentee family arriving too late. I couldn't stand the thought of their continued disapproval, no matter how much I wanted to go to Prospero Books.

"My parents are expecting me home," I said.

"Why don't you come by my office tomorrow?" He handed me his card. "There's the matter of the will to discuss."

"The will?"

"Your inheritance."

"My inheritance?"

Elijah unlocked his car and opened the driver side door. "How's ten tomorrow morning?"

I nodded, speechless. Curiosity spread through me like a fever. Delirium. Euphoria. The feeling of Billy. My instincts were right. First Billy called me home with the card, *The Tempest*. Now, the next clue was waiting for me in Elijah Greenberg's office, in the form of my inheritance.

BY THE TIME I FOUND MY WAY BACK TO THE I-5, IT WAS AFTER seven on the east coast. Jay was either home, resting up for another early morning of soccer camp, or at the bar around the corner from our apartment, drinking off eight hours of cocky teenage boys. I decided to take my chances.

"Hey, babe," he answered on the fourth ring. Jay had never

called me *babe*. Sometimes he called me M or Mimi after he heard Dad's nickname for me. Never *babe* or *hon* or *dear*, endearments manufactured for the masses.

"Hey yourself," I said.

"I just finished cleaning the kitchen. It will still be to your standards when you return." The apartment had taken on new levels of cleanliness when I'd moved in. *OCD clean*, Jay called it, a habit drilled into me by Mom, who believed company-ready should be the natural state of any household.

Jay sighed as he flopped audibly onto the couch. I heard the television turn on, and bit my tongue before starting in on that fight again. Jay did everything with the television set to soccer, or when there wasn't a match, to football, baseball, basketball, even hockey if he was so desperate. The only time he didn't have sports on was when we were having sex.

"This a bad time?" I asked coldly.

If Jay intuited that I was annoyed, he decided to play dumb. The television blared in all its glory. "Trevor was out sick today, so I was on my own. Who gets sick on their second day of work? I want to get him a job as my assistant coach. With this bullshit, no way the school's going to hire him."

I didn't want to talk about Jay's friend Trevor.

"As long as you keep putting out a winning team, they'll do what you want to make you happy." I slowed down again when I reached downtown, about a half mile from the entrance to the 10. I shouldn't have called. Jay was in his I-want-to-chill-at-the-end-of-a-long-day mode, which barely included me when I was home and not at all when I was a phone call away. It was something we were working on, breaking him of his single habits and me of mine, although most of mine were stored in a warehouse somewhere in South Philadelphia.

"Sorry, I'm being a jackass. The funeral was today, right?"

"Just coming from it. I didn't know anyone there."

"Did you expect to?"

"No. It still upset me that I didn't."

"Well, there's no reason why you would have known anyone. That shouldn't make you upset," he said. Soccer fans screamed through the car's Bluetooth.

"Turns out I was right, though. My uncle left me something in his will."

"So I guess this means you won't be coming home tomorrow?"

"Who said I was coming home tomorrow?" I shook the steering wheel as though it might make traffic move, but I was trapped on the freeway, hostage to our conversation.

"I figured after the funeral you'd come home."

"Didn't you tell me not to rush back?"

"Was that me?"

"I believe your exact words were 'take the time you need.'"

"For which you called me a sentimentalist," he retorted.

"Touché," I said, and Jay laughed. "A few more days. Billy's lawyer will give me the next clue. I'll figure out what Billy wants to tell me about him and Mom, and I'll be home before you can even miss me."

"I already miss you."

"Well, then, before you can go back on your word to keep the apartment in tiptop shape. The end of the week at the latest," I promised.

MOM INSISTED ON GOING WITH ME TO MEET ELIJAH.

"I can go alone," I said as she handed me a French omelet. I'd told her that Billy had left me something in his will, not that he'd already given me a clue, nor about the hunt that lay ahead. "If it's going to be difficult for you, I'm happy to go on my own."

"I'm coming with you," she said. "End of discussion."

She took off her apron and disappeared upstairs to get ready. I watched her go, feeling like a teenager about to get caught for going to a party or getting a clandestine tattoo. Jay was right. I should have told Mom about the clue before I came home, before Billy became something I kept from her.

Elijah worked on Larchmont, so Mom and I sat in I-10 traffic, crawling our way east. I watched her eyes shift between the rearview and side mirrors to the congested road ahead. She rubbed her cheek the way she did during suspenseful scenes in movies.

"Miranda, please stop staring at me like that. Really, I'm okay."

I continued to watch her more furtively, sneaking sideways glances that she likely saw. Despite her best efforts, she wasn't okay. I didn't understand why she wanted to hide her feelings. I braved a lingering look at her and thought, not for the first time, that I didn't really understand my mother at all.

Mom exited the highway and headed north on La Brea past furniture stores and lighting warehouses.

"The funeral was pretty weird yesterday," I said, realizing she hadn't asked me about it.

"Billy always was a bit eccentric," she said distractedly.

"I keep remembering things about him." I circled my way toward the conversation I wanted to have with her. I needed to tell her about *The Tempest* before we got to Elijah's office and he did the job for me. "Remember the time he built a simulator in our backyard to teach me about hurricanes? Or when he set up the sprinklers to create a rainbow?"

"He was always good with you," she said almost forlornly, almost like she missed him.

"We were so close, then we just stopped seeing him."

"We were close." Mom paused to collect her thoughts. The massive storefronts narrowed to boutiques, cafés and frozen yogurt shops. When she stopped at a light, she added, "But Billy was unreliable. He was always running off. I wouldn't know if he was alive or dead, if he was coming to dinner, if he'd left the country. I was worried all the time. It got to be too much."

"What does that mean, 'it got to be too much?'"

Mom leaned over me to read the names of the streets that ran perpendicular to Larchmont. "Keep an eye out for Rosewood."

I wanted to tell Mom that she couldn't weasel her way out of the conversation that easily, to remind her of Prospero's words— *You must now know farther*—to let her know that Billy was intent on revealing the past to me, and I wanted to hear it from her first. Mom never responded to anything that smelled remotely of a threat. If she didn't want to talk to me about what had torn them apart, nothing I could say would change her mind, not even if I told her that Billy had planned something for me.

A few blocks later, we found Rosewood and parked outside the law offices of Elijah Greenberg. June Gloom sat heavy in the sky, dreary and somber. Throughout June in Los Angeles, the morning's haze promised an overcast day, but without fail, it burned off, and when the afternoon became sunny, it was all the more spectacular for the bleak morning. Today, however, as I studied the sky, I didn't see a hint of a beautiful day to come.

Elijah guided us into his office where we sat in firm leather chairs as we waited for him to find the right file among a large pile of files on his desk. Mom absentmindedly tapped her foot, shaking her leg so violently I could feel the vibration in the seat beside her. I put my hand on her knee to calm her. She flinched, turning to me with an expression of fright I hadn't expected.

Elijah opened a folder in slow, deliberate motion. "As you know, Billy was the sole proprietor of Prospero Books." This caught my attention. I edged forward, curious to see where this was headed. Elijah cleared his throat and read from Billy's will. "'I, Billy Silver, hereby bequeath my property, 4001 Sunset Boulevard, Los Angeles, California, subject to any mortgages or encumbrances thereon, to Miranda Brooks.'" Elijah handed me a set of keys. "The property includes the bookstore and an apartment on the second floor. I've had it prepared for you."

The keys were cold and smooth, their notches worn from use. I'd expected a map or one of Billy's riddles, but the keys to Prospero Books? I was a middle-school history teacher. I didn't know anything about running a business, let alone a business as specialized and important as a bookstore. But I couldn't focus on those pragmatic concerns. Prospero Books. I could still remember its sweet and musty smell, its feeling of springtime throughout the year. After all these years, I would get to return to that smell, that feeling, again.

I looked over at Mom, sitting erect beside me, alert as prey being stalked. Her eyes darted across the will, reading it upside down. She was so still that if I touched her she might have shattered into a thousand pieces.

"Mom?"

She shook her head. "It's okay. Let's keep going."

Elijah closed the file and opened the desk drawer beneath his computer. "In addition to the store, he also asked me to give you this." He handed me a copy of *Jane Eyre*.

The cover depicted Jane's silhouette, her profile dark against the beige background. I ran my finger along the contour of her face. I'd read the novel in high school, again in college, had logged the love between Jane and Mr. Rochester as one of literature's best, even if Mr. Rochester was by all modern accounts a bit of a creep. If it had been one of the Boxcar Children books, a copy of *The Westing Game*, it would have reminded me of the afternoons I'd spent in Prospero Books drinking hot cocoa from an oversize mug as Billy read over my shoulder, together trying to reason the clues Mr. Westing left for the tenants of Sunset Towers. But *Jane Eyre*? I'd never read it with Billy. I had no idea why he would have left it for me now.

I angled the book toward Mom, and she leaned over to see

the title. Her face remained stoic. I couldn't tell if the title meant anything to her, either.

The novel's spine was split in several places, and the middle bulged awkwardly where an antique key was nestled between the pages. On the page behind the key, a few sentences were highlighted.

> **One does not jump, and spring, and shout hurrah! at hearing one has got a fortune; one begins to consider responsibilities, and to ponder business; on a base of steady satisfaction rise certain grave cares, and we contain ourselves, and brood over our bliss with a solemn brow.**

Did Billy know I would feel bliss, that I would rush into excitement? *Fortune. Responsibilities. Grave cares. A solemn brow.* Was he reminding me that my new fortune arrived because of his death? I skimmed the text around the highlighted section and remembered: Jane did not *jump and spring and shout hurrah!* at hearing she'd inherited a fortune from her uncle, John Eyre. Her uncle! Her father's brother whom Jane didn't know. Instead, Jane expressed her dismay that she couldn't have a fortune without her uncle's death, that she'd dreamed of connecting with him and now never would. But Jane's uncle had searched for her. He'd been unable to locate her before he died. Billy hadn't gone looking for me until he was already dead. If he had, in the modern age of the internet and Facebook, he would have found me easily. If he'd thought of me, why hadn't he come looking? Why did he wait until we no longer had a chance to reconnect?

"Is that it?" Mom asked Elijah with the impatience of a student I'd held after class.

"Well, there are several details about the store to discuss. If you're in a rush, Miranda and I can set up another meeting."

"That would be great." Mom motioned me out.

"I'll call you," I told Elijah. As I stood, the cover of *Jane Eyre* fluttered open. I noticed something written inside the front cover. Cursive writing, nearly faded: *Evelyn Weston*. I could picture that name in all caps, carved into the gravestone beside Billy's. So, Billy hadn't been buried alone, after all. But who was Evelyn Weston?

ON THE I-10 WEST, MOM DROVE IN THE FAR LEFT LANE FIVE miles below the speed limit. Cars passed us on the right, drivers honking their horns and raising their fists as they raced past.

"You want me to drive?" I asked, knowing she wouldn't let me.

"I'm fine." She slammed the gas pedal, and the car lurched forward with nervous energy.

"I can't believe Billy left me his bookstore."

"It's inexcusable," Mom said as she pulled onto the ramp for the Bundy Drive exit. "Putting that kind of burden on you."

"It's not a burden. I loved Prospero Books."

"Loving something and being responsible for it are two very different things." She gripped the wheel so forcefully her knuckles turned white.

"Why do you think he left me a copy of *Jane Eyre*?"

"I have no idea." The gift seemed to anger her regardless of whether she knew what it meant.

"Was it an important book to Billy?"

"I just told you I have no idea." Mom turned on the radio to a top forties station, a type of music I knew she didn't like. We listened to syrupy vocals and catchy rhythms until Mom pulled into the driveway of our Spanish Revival. "I'm sorry, I didn't mean to snap at you," she said as she stopped the car. "I don't think Billy considered how much this would hurt me."

I twisted the antique key I'd found in *Jane Eyre* between my fingers. It was oxidized almost completely black. It had to open an old safe or jewelry box tucked away in the other part of my inheritance, Prospero Books. And it had to have something to do with the name left in cursive font in the front of the novel.

"Do you know who Evelyn Weston is?"

Mom jolted. "Where'd you hear that name?"

"At Forrest Lawn. Billy was buried next to her."

"You saw Evelyn's grave?" Mom appeared nervous, suddenly frantic.

"Was she Billy's wife?" It was the only logical reason he would have been buried beside her.

"She was," Mom whispered as she stared at our familiar white house. The lines around her eyes were more pronounced than they'd been last time I'd seen her. Everyone said I looked like Mom. We had the same curly hair, same narrow builds. Her face was longer and narrower than mine; her speckled brown eyes were more golden than mine had ever been. I'd never be as pretty as Mom.

"Was she someone he met after us?"

Mom turned toward me, confused. "You said you saw her grave?"

"I didn't look at it very closely. I don't remember anyone ever mentioning her."

"He was married to her before you were born. She died a long time ago."

"And Billy never remarried? He never had a family?"

"He only ever wanted Evelyn."

"Why'd he name the bookstore Prospero Books? Did it have anything to do with me?" As a child, I thought Prospero Books was named for me, an homage to my namesake, like Prospero Books lived and breathed with me, like when I wasn't there, it ceased to exist.

"It was open before you were born." Her tone remained even.

"Did you name me after the bookstore?"

"I named you after Shakespeare."

"You and Billy just happened to pick the same play?"

"It was Evelyn's favorite play." She smiled, shrugging off her sadness. "How much of a disaster do you think the kitchen's going to be after your father has had free rein of it all afternoon?" Mom patted my leg and stepped out of the car into the bright afternoon.

I watched her navigate the pathway to the front door, piecing together the details I'd just learned. Billy had a wife before I was born. Her name was Evelyn Weston. She loved *The Tempest*. I was named for Shakespeare's Miranda and for Evelyn's. Evelyn Weston must have also loved *Jane Eyre*. Mom had to know this. Even without seeing Evelyn's name in the novel, Mom had to know why Billy left it to me. I didn't know how it hadn't occurred to me before. Mom was keeping a secret.

"DON'T EXPECT YOUR MOTHER'S COOKING," DAD WARNED AS HE put the eggplant parmesan into the oven. "Will you let her know dinner's almost ready?"

I found Mom outside, holding a pair of shears as she decided which flowers to cut for the table. Behind her, the sky was ignited a rich orange lined in pink. I couldn't see the setting sun, but it left its legacy across the sky.

"Tonight's an amaranth night," Mom said, watching the sky. "Amaranth's not right."

"It's carmine. And cerise," I said. Being raised by Mom, I could name more colors than most people knew existed. That was my skill as the daughter of a decorator, but I didn't want to talk about shades of pink, the glorious hues of Southern California sunsets. "Dad says dinner's close." I snuck a final glance at her, trying to remember when she'd become that way, hesitating before she responded in conversation, when she'd fallen into the habit of covering her mouth as she laughed, when she'd replaced her red nail polish with nude, her crimson lipstick with vitamin E stick. She still listened to Jefferson Airplane and Fleetwood

Mac, still meditated for ten minutes each morning, but at some point, everything she owned had faded to muted shades of pink.

When my parents met, they were both living in New York in lives they'd retired before I was born. Mom was twenty with ironed hair and bright miniskirts. She was the lead singer of the Lady Loves, an all-girl band that had a residency at a club in the East Village where Dad represented the owner. When the owner had introduced them, Mom had looked at Dad's extended hand like it was covered in mud. He'd followed her eyes down his suit and tie to his loafers.

I enjoyed your set, Dad said, putting his hand away.

You like rock? she said with the disdain only a twenty-year-old could muster.

Jesus, Suzy. The guy's trying to give you a compliment. Cut him some slack for fuck's sake, the owner said.

Fuck you, Harry. Mom grabbed one of the amps and stormed offstage.

Don't let her get to you, the owner said to Dad. *Suzy thinks 'cause she's a musician she has to act like an asshole every now and again.*

From the first time Mom spoke to Dad, that was it. He went to see the Lady Loves every Friday night. He liked to watch Mom sing, waiting for the moment when she forgot she was onstage, forgot her tough facade, and her face softened as the sweetness of her voice consumed her. It happened during every performance. In that moment, he saw that she was still young, that she hadn't yet been hardened by life.

There was nothing noteworthy about the night Mom sat at his table. After she finished her set, she pulled up a chair and tied her hair away from her face. Her features were small and girlish. She didn't smile, but Dad could tell she wanted to.

How many ties do you own? she asked Dad.

The question startled him, and he adjusted the knot on his wool tie. He owned so many ties he rarely wore the same tie twice. No one had ever asked Dad about his collection. As far as he could tell, no one had ever noticed.

About two hundred, he admitted.

Why would anyone need two hundred ties?

They wouldn't.

So why do you own so many?

Dad didn't know how to explain it to her. His parents and younger brother had died when he was in college. His uncles had been killed in the war before he was born. His grandparents were long gone. He had childhood friends, law school buddies, others at the firm, a steady stream of girlfriends, but no one he could count on to give him a birthday present each year, to make plans every Thanksgiving. So Dad bought himself ties for Christmases and promotions, a reminder that he could look after himself.

It would be weirder if I owned two hundred pairs of shoes, he said.

Mom giggled and ran off to help her band pack up. From the first time Dad made her laugh, that was it for Mom, too.

WHEN I WENT BACK INSIDE, DAD WAS SITTING AT THE DINING room table, trying to fold linen napkins into Mom's perfect origami.

"Here," I said, taking them from his hands. I showed him how to fold it into three long strips, to tuck one side up and then the other into a perfect envelope.

"You make it look so easy," he said, and disappeared behind the island into the kitchen.

Dad rummaged around the cabinets, banging pans as he put them away. I took out my phone and typed "Evelyn Weston," stopping when I couldn't think of anything else to add to my search. Several Evelyn Westons popped up with LinkedIn, Twitter and current IMDB pages. The Evelyn Weston I was looking for had died long ago, in an era before social media and the twenty-four-hour news cycle. I'd have to find out about her the old-fashioned way, by talking to people instead of devices.

Dad returned with two wooden candleholders. The candles sat crookedly in the bases.

"Turns out I'm not a whittler." When Dad retired, he'd needed a hobby. He'd never been particularly handy. Anything more complicated than changing a light bulb had required the aid of a handyman. Now, suddenly in his mid-sixties, Dad was determined to become a craftsman. Mom had suggested he take a class, but Dad insisted that part of being a craftsman was being self-taught, so he bought books and magazines, watched YouTube videos. He started with a rocking chair, then quickly downgraded to a box. "Did I show you the bookshelf I made? I'm staining it now. If you didn't know, you might actually think someone had paid for it."

"Did you know Billy's wife, Evelyn?" I asked more abruptly than I'd intended.

"Your mom told you about Evelyn?" He sounded surprised without being alarmed. Then again, Dad was good at containing his emotions. He'd had practice for years as a lawyer.

"She said she named me after Evelyn, after her love of *The Tempest*." I fudged it a little. If Dad thought Mom told me more than she had, he might tell me more, too. "Were she and Mom close?"

Dad reached for the candleholder, worrying the wood with the pad of his thumb. "Since they were in kindergarten."

"They grew up together?" Dad nodded, his attention still focused on the unstable candleholder. "How'd she die?"

He peered over at me. "Why are you asking?"

"I didn't know Billy was married. I'd never even heard the name Evelyn before today. Do you know how she died?"

"Evelyn had a massive seizure."

"Was she epileptic?"

"I don't think so." Dad looked through the French doors toward Mom in the garden, inspecting the soil beneath her rosebushes. "Why don't you go see what's taking your mom so long."

"She said she'd be in in a minute. What was wrong with Evelyn?"

The oven timer went off, and Dad sprung at its chime. Of course he wasn't going to tell me about Evelyn. He and Mom were a unit, inextricably close, and sometimes it had made me jealous how coupled they were. Of course, if Mom had a secret, Dad did, too.

CHAPTER FIVE

WHILE THE BRICK FACADE OF PROSPERO BOOKS LOOKED JUST AS I remembered, everything around it had changed. Sunset Junction, once little more than a relic of the old railcar system, had become a destination of its own, complete with cafés, a coffee bar, a cheese shop and boutiques. Every metered spot along Sunset Boulevard was taken. The sidewalks were lined with diners brunching under awnings, with couples pushing strollers.

I stood outside Prospero Books, staring at the store's old sign, repainted but otherwise the same. Prospero towered above the window, staff in right hand, a book in left, purple cape and white hair windblown behind him. The picture window looked the same, too, only it displayed titles by Lionel Shriver, Isabel Allende and Michael Pollan in place of the new releases of years before.

The smell of the store hit me as soon as I entered. Freshly cut paper. White musk. Jasmine. Black pepper. Coffee beans. I'd forgotten the sound of the brass bell on the door, the corkboard in the entryway, now covered in flyers for personal trainers and Pilates classes. The store itself was smaller than I remembered. The ceilings not as high. The shelves more narrowly spaced. They were divided, then subdivided. Fiction into literary, popular, banned, historical, classic, feminist, LGBTQ, science fiction and fantasy, mystery, noir, foreign language and small presses. The lime green of the exposed brick walls still looked fresh. The mosaic tables still glittered blue and gold in the café's bright light. I didn't see Lee. I didn't see any of the poets in trench coats sipping espresso, the pretty girls in overalls stalking the shelves. There were still pretty girls. They were skinnier now, without as much eyeliner. Every table in the café was still occupied, customers intensely typing on laptop keyboards instead of writing in notebooks. Everything buzzed with activity, the store still alive with the possibility of Prospero's magic books.

Against the far wall, the wild-haired, Dylan Thomas–reciting man from Billy's funeral was inspecting a shelf, scratching checkmarks beside a list of titles. His T-shirt read Smile, You're on Camera.

"You were at Billy's funeral?" I asked as I approached him. He glanced up from his clipboard. His crystalline eyes regarded me with little recognition. "You read the Dylan Thomas poem? I'm Miranda."

He surveyed me with those candied eyes, their flit clinical rather than flattering. "The prodigal niece appears."

"That's me." I smiled in the way that usually made strangers think I was cute—never sexy, always cute—but he didn't return the smile. I held out my hand. He shook it perfunctorily.

"Malcolm," he said as if I should have already known his name.

The phone rang, and he released my hand to walk over to the desk.

"Prospero," he said as he picked up. His tone changed as soon as he started to talk about books. "*White Teeth* is out of stock. We can order you a copy." He held the phone in the crook of his neck as he typed something into the ancient computer monitor behind the desk. The desk area wasn't private enough to be the mess that it was. An overflowing bin of advance reader copies, unpacked boxes of books, a calendar with first names and publishers scrawled onto several dates. "It should be here in two days. Have you read *On Beauty*? It's more like *White Teeth* than *NW*, but I think you'll find... We have a copy... Sure, I'll set it aside for you."

I wandered around the literature section, listening to Malcolm answer the caller's questions about Zadie Smith, whom I hadn't read. Book after book across the shelves I also hadn't read, many titles I didn't recognize, subsections of literature I hadn't realized needed to be distinguished from each other. I couldn't recall how they'd been organized when I was a kid. I never paid much attention to the adult books. Malcolm continued to talk about the stylistic differences between Smith's older novels and her most recent one. I walked around the stacks, trying to determine why he would pretend not to recognize me when he'd clearly seen me at the funeral, when my eyes had locked with his. The teen section was now termed Young Adult, twice its former size, consuming the entire length of one of the interior shelves. I used to think that all of those books had been selected just for me, but as I scanned the YA titles, I saw only a handful of books I remembered.

"Do you read?" Malcolm asked, reappearing at my side.

"Mostly nonfiction. I'm a history teacher." I waited for him to ask me what grade I taught or what type of history, questions that typically followed *I'm a history teacher* in polite conversation. "Where books are prized above dukedom," I said when he didn't ask me about myself. He looked confused. "That's how we used to answer the phone when I was a kid. 'Prospero Books, where books are prized above dukedom.'" I don't know why I said we. I'd never answered the phone at Prospero Books before.

"I've never heard anyone answer the phone that way." He bent down to pull a copy of *The Perks of Being a Wallflower* stuffed incorrectly in the *T*'s. The cover was as lime green as the walls of Prospero Books.

"It could have been taken right here." I walked over to the wall and did my best to look like one of the young actors on the front of the novel. Nope, nothing from Malcolm, not even upturned lips. I'd never thought of my students as particularly generous but they always humored me with an eye roll at the least, acknowledging, if not appreciating, my effort.

"I hate movie tie-in covers." He filed the copy under *C* where it belonged.

"I'm not here to close the store down, if that's what you're so worried about." It was the most logical explanation for his coldness.

"Who says I'm worried about anything?" he said indignantly, and I could imagine him as an adolescent, defiant and stubborn, likely too smart for his own good.

"Billy used to bring me here as a kid. I know how important this place is," I told Malcolm. He didn't respond, focusing his attention on the toe of his dirty white sneaker as it pressed into the scuffed wood floor. The floorboards creaked under his weight. "Did Billy tell you he was leaving his store to me?"

"His lawyer did. I didn't know Billy had any living family." He turned his focus toward the shelves, crossing his arms across his chest, gestures anyone who spent time with teenagers could recognize as evasion. The wiry man with bifocals who had sung at Billy's funeral signaled to him from a table in the back. "Excuse me," Malcolm said, and headed toward the café.

"Did you know he had any family that *wasn't* living?" I called to him. He shot me a funny look, like I'd asked him if he slept standing up.

Malcolm kept his back to me as he leaned over the wiry man to review one of the many books open on the café table. I continued to reacquaint myself with the store, counting all the sections I'd never paid attention to before, the books I didn't know, the colorful spines aching to be read. In the noir section, a caricature of Malcolm smiled from the shelf. His cheekbones were more pronounced in the drawing than in life, his unruly hair neater, his eyes kinder, less wary. A speech bubble floated on the drawing above his portrait. It described noir as LA's lifeblood. Chandler, its Homer. Philip Marlowe, its Odysseus. I studied Malcolm's picture, wondering what he wasn't telling me. He was close enough to Billy to have read at his funeral. He'd avoided my eye contact when I'd asked him if he'd heard of me. He knew more than he was letting on about Billy's living family, probably about his deceased family, too.

Along the interior shelves, the history section was separated into World, American and Californian. The books were not only divided by region but organized by subject, alphabetically rather than chronologically. Most bookstores organized history books that way, as though history was a collection of discrete episodes rather than a fluid series of events that evolved over time. It reflected the misguided way we often taught history, the erroneous chaptering of the past. Jay often told me I was a hopeless romantic when it came to history. What else could I be? It was our past, something that shouldn't be alphabetized.

I bent down to browse the titles on the lowest shelf of Californian history, filed under seismology and earthquake history. Books on the 1906 earthquake, the San Andreas Fault, predictions and forecasts. Here, on this modest, ankle-level shelf, was the Billy of my youth. I pulled out a book on the Northridge earthquake. It was one of those nights everyone living in Southern California at the time remembered. Joanie and I were asleep, startled awake as books fell off the shelves. When my bedroom stopped shaking, Mom ran in, checking us for cuts and bruises before the room began to rumble again. The first aftershock ended, and Dad screamed that we had to get out of the house. We followed him downstairs where broken glass littered our hardwood floors. Joanie and I didn't have shoes on, so Dad carried us through the living room. In our backyard, the fence hid the damage beyond our property, brick chimneys torn from our neighbors' homes, electrical wires slithering down the street. Dad turned on the radio, and we listened as the reporters filled gaps of information. Dawn brightened the sky. The death toll rose. Mom made Dad turn off the radio. Joanie clung to me, her body shaking like the earthquake was inside her, but a warmth spread through me, an undeniable thrill. The earth had moved here, beneath my feet, and that meant Billy wouldn't have to travel to some distant land to study the damage. He would stay here with us. That was the best gift Billy gave me as a child. Whenever the earth shook, I became excited once the confusion subsided. At some point, I'd stopped connecting that feeling to Billy, but it never went away. Even as an adult, I felt a guilty pleasure whenever the floor oscillated with the earth.

At the center of the store, an oak table displayed the staff recommendations. Malcolm's were *The Sun Also Rises, Infinite Jest, The Maltese Falcon* and *Ask the Dust.* A Lucia offered Roberto Bolaño, Gabriel García Márquez, Julia Alvarez and Junot Díaz. A Charlie displayed *James and the Giant Peach, Hugo Caberet,* two Lemony Snicket titles and an Edward Gorey picture book. Billy's recommendations were all classics: *Portrait of a Lady, The Grapes of Wrath, Tender Is the Night, The Age of Innocence.* I'd expected Billy's books to be classics, but classics of a different nature—*Robinson Crusoe, The Three Musketeers, Sherlock Holmes.* I imagined the assortment of American history books I would have selected for my recommendations, the blurbs I would have written about the women of the Revolution and Lincoln's steadfast cabinet.

I flipped through the novels on Billy's side of the table, unsure what I was looking for. The antique key Billy had left with Elijah was still in my pocket. It had to lead somewhere in Prospero Books, only I didn't see any safes or antique cabinets it may have opened. Still, something in the store had to guide me to the other side of that keyhole. Billy's recommendations were all untouched, save a series of numbers written in faint pencil inside the back cover of *The Grapes of Wrath*.

I felt Malcolm lean over my shoulder to review the page.

"Billy's secret language with the books he resurrected from hospital thrift shops." He lifted the book from my hands and held it closer to his face. Malcolm explained that the two numbers before the decimal indicated the quality of the book. The four after the decimal the date Billy had bought it, although they didn't translate clearly into a year. The letter noted the month. The next series of numbers commented on the different aspects of the book—the edition, the imprint, the font—and the final letter the season where, if the book hadn't sold, its price would be marked down.

"Does it need to be so complicated?"

Malcolm closed the book and returned it to the table. "It was how Billy liked it."

I ran my finger across Billy's name on the card resting beneath his books. A sketch of his middle-aged face stared back at me. Slender nose, wide smile, hair perfectly coiffed. The smile was ripe with melancholy.

"I'm not the enemy," I said.

"That remains to be seen." For the first time, a smile flashed across his face, vanishing as quickly as it had materialized. He was kind of cute when he wasn't glowering at me. "Come on. I'll get you a coffee."

I waited at one of the mosaic tables while Malcolm journeyed behind the café counter, and started texting Jay. We were having difficulty connecting with the three-hour time difference. He had to wake up early for soccer camp, which meant that he went to bed while I was still having dinner with my parents. Other than our phone call after Billy's funeral, we'd only sent text messages. I'd reported to him about my unexpected inheritance, the next clue, about my memories of Prospero Books. *Sounds like a cool place*, he'd said, then proceeded to talk about camp. He sent me a video of his players shouting they missed me and making kissy faces, as well as other equally gushy texts. While I was aware of the vulnerability it required to get a group of teenage boys to participate in a romantic scheme, I wished he'd asked me about *Jane Eyre*, about whether I was nervous to revisit Prospero Books. I snapped a picture of the bookstore and sent it to Jay, along with the message, Welcome to Prospero Books. He sent back a smiley face. It would have been better if he hadn't responded at all.

Behind the café counter, Malcolm stopped to talk to the Latina girl I'd met at Billy's funeral. Her hair was woven into a bun, coffee grinds were smeared across the white apron tied around her waist. When the girl spotted me watching them, she waved enthusiastically. Malcolm looked over, too, his expression more cautious than the girl's. He filled two cups of coffee and carried them over to my table.

I reached for the mug he held out to me and took a sip. The coffee was black and strong, but I drank it, anyway. Adding milk or sugar seemed like admitting weakness.

"Don't you worry?" I pointed to a key dangling unsupervised from the cashbox as the girl wiped down the espresso machine. The key was modern, nickel or some metal composite. It didn't resemble the antique key Billy had left me.

"Our infantry of regulars. They may only buy a cup of coffee, but they're our eyes and ears."

"Do you keep a safe somewhere?" I didn't see any other locks that might match the key.

"There's no money in it. I went to the bank this morning."

"I wasn't asking for money," I said.

"It's upstairs, in the storage closet." Malcolm pointed to a door at the back of the café. His finger traveled to the girl behind the counter. "That's Lucia. She covers the afternoons.

Charlie's here in the morning. Don't be startled if you hear him downstairs at dawn. He gets here early to open the store." I was about to ask him why he thought I'd be here before the store opened, then I remembered Billy's apartment.

"I'm not staying here—upstairs, I mean. My parents live on the Westside."

"It's up to you," he said.

"When did Billy move upstairs? Last I knew, he lived in Pasadena." Billy's house was large and had columns that reminded me of the White House, only it wasn't populated with a first family or aides, just Billy and too many bedrooms.

"He's lived upstairs as long as I've known him."

"And how long is that?"

Malcolm squinted at me. "Why do I feel like this is a job interview?"

"How do you think you're doing so far?"

"Hard to say." And there was that hint of levity across his face before it vanished again. I'd won over arrogant fourteen-year-old girls who wore push-up bras and more makeup than I did. I'd inspired the class clown to write a six-page paper on how the cotton gin increased the South's dependency on slavery. For fifty-minute intervals, I'd even gotten entire classrooms of eighth graders to put away their phones and be present. I could certainly charm a cagey thirty-something-year-old bookstore manager.

"Malcolm!" The man next to us looked up, suddenly realizing who was seated beside him.

Malcolm introduced me to Ray the screenwriter. "Ray promises not to forget us when he's won an Oscar."

"Well, I don't know about that." Ray beamed as if he could picture it happening. His expression grew severe. "You look like him," he said to me.

I instinctively flattened my hair, its reddish brown the same shade as Mom's, the same shade as Billy's. In my periphery, Malcolm stiffened.

Lucia wiped down a nearby table, then joined us for coffee. Her tight tank top revealed several tattoos along her shoulders and chest. When she caught me reading a line of Spanish on her forearm she said it was from *One Hundred Years of Solitude*.

"She doesn't read fiction," Malcolm said to Lucia.

"Come on, Malcolm. Everyone knows *One Hundred Years of Solitude*." Lucia smiled apologetically at me.

"My boyfriend's mom gave it to me actually." Boyfriend. It still sounded funny off my tongue, and Malcolm must have noticed my discomfort with the term because he glanced over, seemingly curious. "I love Márquez," I overcompensated. Jay's mother had left *One Hundred Years of Solitude* in our living room when she came over unannounced, hoping to kill an hour before she met a friend at a gallery nearby. The novel sat on the coffee table for a week until I filed it on the bookshelf beside the other novels Jay had never read.

A girl with an armful of books lingered by the register, and Malcolm rushed to the front desk to help her. Lucia and I watched Malcolm ring up the girl. He said something that made her laugh, and when he laughed, too, I saw the kind eyes from his portrait in the noir section.

"Don't let him intimidate you," Lucia said. "He's really attached to the store. We all are." Her tone was kinder than Malcolm's, but her words carried the same vague threat, should I aim to do anything that might ruin Prospero Books.

I COULDN'T HELP BUT THINK OF *JANE EYRE* AS I ASCENDED THE narrow staircase toward the eerily silent top floor. While I could remember every dusty corner and piquant scent of the bookshop below, I had no recollection of an upstairs. I'd certainly never been up there. There were two doors, one on each side of the hall. I tried the right one first. A storage room, filled with shelves of books, more in boxes, and cleaning supplies. Behind the stacks of books, I located the safe. It had a combination lock. There weren't any vaults hidden under panels in the floor, any keyholes that might match the antique key Billy had given me. That left only Billy's apartment.

I creaked open the door waiting for someone to tell me I was trespassing, invading my uncle's private life. When no one did, I braved a step inside and shut the door behind me.

Sun dust glittered throughout the spacious living room. It looked like a spread from a design magazine: a brown leather couch with an old chest positioned as a coffee table; an antique vanity beside the door with three mismatching vases spaced across its tabletop. I spotted a keyhole on the chest and tried the antique key. It didn't fit. Besides, it was unlocked. Inside, piles of clothing were folded neatly. Collared linen shirts and waterproof khaki pants, the style of clothes Billy had worn when I knew him. I unfolded an olive green button-down and inhaled it deeply. It smelled of baby powder, pleasant and fresh, but it didn't remind me of Billy.

I scanned the room for another keyhole. The kitchen didn't have a door. It reeked of disinfectant. The tiled countertops and stove had been scrubbed clean. The fridge was empty, the ice tray lonely in the freezer. Elijah said he'd had the apartment prepared for me. Logical enough, yet there was so much I could have discovered if the fridge had been stocked with Billy's food, the trash can cluttered with his waste.

The door to the bedroom didn't have a lock. It was as quaint and characterless as the rest of the apartment, complete with white wicker furniture and a modest bookshelf beside the door, hardbacks faded from years of sun exposure. On the dresser, a bouquet of dried wildflowers rested beside a photograph of a blonde woman. I lifted the frame from the dresser, blowing off the dust that had collected on the glass. She leaned against a boulder on a narrow strip of beach below the cliffs, her thin, white-blond hair pulled over her right shoulder. She had translucent skin and somber green eyes that matched her earrings, or perhaps I only imagined that they were somber because I knew she was dead.

I removed the picture from the frame, checking for an inscription. The Kodak emblem was stamped on the back, nothing handwritten, no dates, no names. This had to be Evelyn. Mom had offered no details on Evelyn Weston's appearance, but she looked exactly as I expected. Young, late twenties, early thirties. Blonde. Beautiful, hauntingly so.

I stared at the photograph, searching for some indication where or when it was taken. The rocky bluffs looked like Malibu, but Malibu had countless pockets of beach and this wasn't one I recognized. Evelyn wore no makeup. Her hair was long and straight. Her emerald earrings were antique. Her white T-shirt could have been manufactured at any point in the second half of the twentieth century.

I put the picture back in its frame and positioned it on the dresser exactly as it had been before. Looking at it, I felt a profound sadness. It was the only photograph Billy had displayed in the apartment. While it must have comforted Billy to return to Evelyn's likeness each day, it seemed to magnify how empty his personal life otherwise was. Goose bumps rose on my arms. The muscles of my back tensed. His lonesomeness scared me. I scanned the bedroom one last time for a keyhole, and when I didn't find one, I hurried out, wanting to get as far away from that picture as I could.

In the living room, there was no old bank on the table by the front door. No jewelry box perched on the drop-front mahogany desk against the wall near the kitchen. The desk looked like the one my parents had in their upstairs hall, an ornamental heirloom that had belonged to my father's grandmother. I ran my hand along the smooth wood, wondering whether Billy had seen the similarity between our desk and his, if he'd sat at this desk and occasionally thought of us. I tried to pull down the front, but it was locked. My fingers traced the ivy carved into the front, a brass keyhole cover that deftly hid the lock. When I slid the antique key into the lock, it fit snugly. I twisted it to the right and the lock clicked open.

The first thing that hit me was the stench of the old wood, its musk. The desk was cluttered with receipts and tattered pieces of cream-colored stationery. I sorted through the crumpled heating bills and yellowed pages of the *Los Angeles Times*, inspecting each article for the next clue before deciding it was little more than an abandoned article. Beneath the forsaken artifacts of Billy's daily life, I found a folder filled with the keepsakes he'd concealed for me.

Billy had photographs, a playbill from my middle-school play, flyers from my debate competitions. I laid the artifacts in chronological order and saw the framework of my childhood unfold before me. The timeline began with a photograph of Billy holding me, swaddled in lavender-colored cotton, his expression somewhere between amazed and terrified. Two years later, a snapshot from a dark restaurant, Billy and me eating the same string of spaghetti like in *Lady and the Tramp*. An action shot from 1991, me running in a sequined bikini. The next January, 1993. My seventh birthday party. The only party I remembered Billy attending. In the photograph, Billy and I posed with a goat. I'd begged Mom to turn our backyard into a petting zoo. *I don't know, Miranda. It sounds unsanitary,* she'd said. I'd enlisted Billy, and together we'd prepared a pitch for Mom, filled with facts about the Nigerian dwarf goat—it bred year-round and had a lifespan of fifteen years. About the zedonk—also known as the zonkey, zebrula, zebrinny, zebronkey, zebonkey or zebadonk—which despite its many names was incredibly rare. We outlined the precautions we'd take to ensure cleanliness—a washing station and lots of hand sanitizer—and scientific studies proving how unlikely it was anyone would catch a disease from the Nigerian dwarf goats of Southern California. In the photograph, Billy held the goat like a trophy.

The next picture was from my sixth-grade play, Billy's arms around Joanie and me dressed in Puritan costumes. Identical bonnets and blue dresses, yet in our postures you could tell who was Abigail Williams and who was a forgettable woman she'd accused of witchery.

In the final photograph, the pet shop looked exactly as I remembered. Speckled linoleum floor, metal cages confining colorful birds. Billy held me close to him as I lifted the puppy toward the camera. We both wore exhilarated smiles. We both seemed happy. How quickly thereafter everything had changed.

I rummaged through the desk, searching for anything else that pertained to me. Amid the credit card advertisements and gas station receipts, I found a folded sheet of lined paper. My handwriting looked pretty much the same, but the words were unfamiliar.

Hi, Uncle Billy!

I bet you're surprised to hear from me. I know it's been forever! I graduated high school yesterday. Can you believe it? At graduation, everyone else had tons of family with them. All I had were my parents. That made me think of you, how at one point you might have been there, too.

Do you ever think about me anymore? Sometimes I think about how much fun we used to have together. Anyway, I just wanted to say hi. If you wanted to write back that would be cool. Don't worry, I won't tell Mom. Ha, ha!

Love,

Miranda

I reread the letter, trying to imagine how Billy must have felt receiving it. He never wrote back. I would have remembered that. I would have written to him again, letters back and forth until they amounted to a correspondence, possibly more. He must have wanted to write back. Why else would he have kept the letter? He must have known, for reasons still unclear to me, that he couldn't.

I slowly refolded the letter. Was this it? Had Billy led me to this desk simply to show me that he'd never forgotten me? What an underwhelming end to our last great hunt together.

As I dropped the letter into the desk, I noticed something written along one of its edges in tiny, precise script: *Down*. I didn't make anything of it until I returned the photographs to the desk and saw the word repeated on their backs: *down, down, down, down, down*. And on the photograph from the pet shop, a phrase: *down went Alice*. The next clue.

I raced around the room, looking for a bookshelf or a stack of hardbacks, any battered old copies of *Alice's Adventures in Wonderland*. There wasn't a single book in the living room.

I took a deep breath before returning to the bedroom. I had no choice; I had to go in there again. The spines of the hardbacks on the bookshelf were so muted their titles dissolved into the faded canvas. *Little Women, Death on the Nile, The Color Purple, Even Cowgirls Get the Blues*—novels I couldn't imagine Billy reading. Between Sylvia Plath and Colette, a thin crimson spine all but disappeared. In peeling gold leaf, *Lewis Carroll*.

The cover was understated. Red with a small portrait of Alice in gold at the center. I ran my hands along Alice's embossed hair, her frilly dress, an approximation of which I wore for three Halloweens until I could no longer zip the polyester costume. Did Billy see me in that blue dress? Did he remember that I wanted a pet rabbit to dress in a waistcoat? I flipped the cover to look inside.

Alice fell down, down, down, upon sticks and leaves, unharmed and curious. She tried several doors. They were all locked. She found a golden key, too big for some locks, too small for others until she peeked behind the curtain. The key fit but the passageway was too small, and Alice couldn't reach the garden. There, Carroll's words were highlighted in crisp yellow.

> [S]o many out-of-the-way things had happened lately, that Alice had begun to think that very few things indeed were really impossible.

So Alice got pragmatic or as pragmatic as one could get after she'd followed a talking rabbit down a long and dark tunnel. She looked for a book of rules; instead, she found a bottle. *DRINK ME*, it said. I flipped through the book and found an envelope tucked into the back. *READ ME*, it said.

Inside the envelope was a thick stack of papers. On the cover page, beneath Cedars-Sinai's emblem, a Dr. Nazario had written to Billy: *This letter is to inform you of your results. Our office will be in contact to schedule a follow-up visit.* Dr. Nazario's name was circled in red. The following pages detailed the tests Billy had undergone, the clinical indication of shortness of breath and tightness in chest, the impression of aortic stenosis. The tests were dated March, two years ago.

I read the highlighted passage again. *Very few things indeed were really impossible.* I could picture the illustrated copy of the novel I had as a child. Alice in a blue dress. Hearts and spades and diamonds and clubs floating around her. I'd like to remember Billy giving it to me, that it was from Prospero Books, but Mom had purchased it at a children's bookstore on the Westside. Billy and I never read the novel on those nights when he tucked me in and made me feel indeed that nothing was impossible. Still, he knew, like Alice, I would follow him down, down, down until there was nowhere left to fall.

CHAPTER SIX

IN ADDITION TO ITS MAIN CAMPUS, CEDARS-SINAI HAD OFFICES across the city. When I looked up Dr. Nazario, he worked in three different locations and didn't have an open appointment for another six weeks. I tried to explain to the receptionist who answered my call that I wasn't trying to schedule a consultation—I merely wanted to talk to the doctor about my uncle—and she started in on a long explanation of HIPAA privacy requirements.

"Is there any way I can get in touch with Dr. Nazario?" I asked.

"You can always email him," she said.

"Does he check his email?"

"I'm not his secretary. You want his email or not?"

I jotted a quick note to Dr. Nazario and sent it into the internet void, hoping somewhat futilely that he might read it, let alone respond.

In morning rush hour, the drive from my parents' house to Prospero Books took over an hour. The 10 to the 110 to the 101, through downtown where somehow the 5 also got involved and the cars piled up in the congestion that made Los Angeles's freeways famous. When I arrived at the store, I wanted to see

Billy's San Andreas Fault mug beside the computer, his beaten-up leather satchel on the floor beside the desk chair. I wanted to see Lee racing to answer the phone, reminding all callers that, in Prospero Books, books were prized above all else. Instead, I saw Malcolm behind the front desk, reading. When he heard the back door open, he looked up expectantly until he saw me, sighing when he realized I was back again.

Morning was quieter than the afternoon. At nine, a handful of committed writers worked in the café. A modest crowd waited for their morning coffee as Charlie, the third member of the Prospero clan, frothed milk and ground beans.

Charlie was in his early twenties and had the Big Friendly Giant tattooed on his left forearm, a Wild Thing on his right deltoid. He sat in the chair beside me and rolled up his pant leg, exposing the freckled skin of his pale calf.

"I'm thinking of getting Willy Wonka here. Or maybe the giving tree, I'm not sure," he said.

"Billy gave me *The Giving Tree* when I started kindergarten," I remembered. The week before school, Billy had to go to Northern California, where a small earthquake had rattled the Santa Cruz Mountains. Billy knew I was nervous. A new school. New kids whom I imagined were already friends. He was sorry he couldn't be there. He'd bought me *The Giving Tree* perhaps to teach me about friendship or to assure me that whatever happened at school, he would be my giving tree.

"Billy used to love reading to kids," Charlie said, unfolding his jean leg.

"Did he ever read them *Alice in Wonderland*?" I asked.

"He had an old copy that he would creak open, and it was like all the kids in the neighborhood had a sixth sense and would come running." I found the copy in my bag and handed it to him. "That's it," he confirmed, the lightness fading from his face as he stared into the hardback's fiery red.

"Have you been working here a long time?" I put the book back in my bag.

"Three years. Never thought I'd stay this long, but that's all our stories."

"What made you stay?"

Charlie shifted in his chair, getting comfortable. "Back then I was reading Ken Kesey, Henry Miller, that sort of thing. One day, Billy took *A Clockwork Orange* out of my hand, put *Charlie and the Chocolate Factory* there instead. I'd seen the movie, but I'd never read the book. I'd forgotten how disturbing it was. It was dark, but it wasn't angry. Billy always knew what book you needed. He had this power, like he was some sort of book doctor—like books were a remedy."

"Or like they were magic," I said, and Charlie winked, getting up to help a teenager waiting at the counter.

I sat at the back table, watching the store's morning routines. Ray the screenwriter worked at the table beside mine. I waved hello.

"Miranda, right?" he said, removing his headphones. I nodded as though remembering my name was some noble task. "Do you live in the neighborhood?"

"Philadelphia actually. I'm only here for a few weeks."

"Guess that's why we've never seen you before."

"Have you been coming here for a long time?"

"Every day for the last four years. I'm sorry about Billy. He was one of the good ones. He introduced me to my manager, Jordan. If it wasn't for Billy, I wouldn't have my career."

I scanned the other tables where customers worked, wondering how Billy had changed their lives, if they remembered the Billy that Charlie and Ray the screenwriter remembered, the Billy who, through small acts of kindness, made their lives a little more complete.

My phone chimed with an alert of a new email. Dr. Nazario indeed read his email and I was in luck. He had a cancellation.

Could I stop by that afternoon? I wrote back a quick Yes! and headed out. It wasn't until I was in standstill traffic on Beverly Boulevard that I realized I hadn't even said hello to Malcolm.

DR. NAZARIO WAS TALL WITH A SQUARE JAW, CHISELED LIKE IT would hurt if you kissed him. He looked like a doctor on television, not one who had actually passed his medical exams, but this was LA. Most people looked like the celebrity versions of themselves. Even Malcolm with his bright eyes and pronounced cheekbones was more attractive than the disheveled bookstore manager I'd expected.

The walls of Dr. Nazario's office were lined in framed diplomas and certificates of accreditations. I sat in one of two chairs across from Dr. Nazario's desk. He reached into a desk drawer and withdrew a letter. "Billy left me permission to share his medical history with you."

The note had been notarized by Elijah a year before Billy died.

Dr. Nazario held a plastic heart and opened it. "Aortic stenosis is an abnormal narrowing of the aortic valve. When the valve narrows to the degree that it blocks the flow of blood from the left ventricle to the arteries, it can cause a variety of heart diseases. There's a range of valve replacement surgeries, but Billy didn't come to see me until he already had severe chest pains. By then, treatment was too risky. We gave him some diuretics to reduce the lung pressure and monitored him closely after that. Given the considerable narrowing, Billy was lucky to live with his condition for two years." I studied the textured peach insides of Dr. Nazario's plastic heart until he closed it. He riffled through Billy's folder and handed me an envelope. "He asked me to give this to you."

He stood, motioning me out.

"Why would a healthy person who wasn't epileptic have seizures?" I asked as I followed him down the hall, Billy's clue still unopened in my hand.

"Have you seized?"

"No, Billy's wife. She died of a massive seizure. I'm curious why a young woman might die of a seizure?"

"Well, there are lots of reasons for nonepileptic seizures. It could be psychogenic, for one. Or a drug overdose, or a brain tumor, vascular malformation of the brain, a head injury. It's difficult to say without seeing her medical records."

"I don't have her medical records. Are any of those causes more likely?"

Dr. Nazario frowned. "I'm afraid I can't comfortably make a diagnosis without having more information."

I thanked him and left. Even if he couldn't tell me the cause of Evelyn's seizure, his explanation confirmed my suspicions that my parents were hiding something. If her death was drug-related, Dad should have said she had a drug problem. If she had a tumor, he should have said tumor. If it was a head injury, an accident. Seizures had other causes, root problems. If Evelyn died of a massive seizure, something else must have been going on with her, something, for whatever reason, Dad didn't want me to know.

Outside Cedars-Sinai's automatic doors, I tore open the envelope Dr. Nazario had given me.

> Science is at the root of all life, especially mine. Made of fibres, muscles and brains, eight-feet tall and strong with lustrous black hair and teeth of pearly white, but you would not find me attractive despite these luxuriances.

It wasn't a passage I recognized. When I typed it into my phone, Google listed a series of articles on nerve and muscle cells, websites for kids on how the body worked. Nothing that directly quoted lustrous hair, pearly whites. It wasn't a book excerpt but a riddle.

Details stood out immediately: *fibres* not *fibers*. Exceptional height. Science. Was he leading me to the memoir or biography of some great scientist? The philosophies of Plato or Aristotle? Something fictional? I was out of practice; I didn't know the answer.

I put the clue in my back pocket and searched the other paper Dr. Nazario had given me, the letter granting him permission to talk to me, looking for a hint, something to help solve the riddle. The only thing that struck me was Elijah's signature, notarizing the document. How well did Elijah know Billy? Well enough to be the executor of his will. To be the custodian of *Jane Eyre*. Well enough to have notarized a letter granting me permission to talk to Billy's doctor. Well enough to know what Billy had planned for me, at least so I hoped.

ELIJAH'S OFFICE WAS A SHORT DRIVE FROM CEDARS-SINAI.

"Miranda." He scratched his head as he led me into his office, ruffling his already tousled hair. He wore another gray pinstripe suit, and I wondered whether it was the same suit, if he had multiple ones that were identical. "Did we schedule a meeting?"

"Is this a bad time?" I asked.

"Of course not." He waved me inside. "I'm all yours."

After I'd situated myself in one of his rigid leather chairs, I handed him the letter he'd notarized, granting Dr. Nazario permission to divulge Billy's medical history.

"He was sick for a while. I don't remember notarizing this." Elijah gave the letter back to me.

I showed him Billy's riddle. "Billy also left this with Dr. Nazario."

He scanned it quickly. "Clever," he said before returning it to me.

"You know the answer?"

"If he left it for you, I imagine he wants you alone to solve it."

I eyed him suspiciously, and he matched my look. "Did Billy tell you he was planning a scavenger hunt for me?"

"No, he never mentioned anything like that."

"Did he tell you why he was leaving me the store?"

"Didn't you get the letter?" he said, surprised.

"What letter?"

"I sent it myself, after Billy passed." He must have meant the package with the copy of *The Tempest*.

"How did you start working for Billy?"

"My dad was his lawyer. I took over about fifteen years ago when he retired." Elijah's assistant shuffled in, offering us each a mug of lukewarm coffee. Elijah took a sip and made a face. "Madeline," he shouted to the secretary, "is this from yesterday? How about a fresh pot?" He reached for my cup. "I can't let you drink that."

"What kind of work did your dad do for Billy?" I asked, relinquishing the mug.

"He helped Billy with a dispute over his wife's trust. After that, whenever Billy needed a lawyer, he'd contact my dad."

"A dispute?"

"With her father, I think. She'd bought Prospero Books with money from a trust he set up. When she died, he tried to regain control of her assets."

"Prospero Books was Evelyn's?" It was so obvious I didn't know how it hadn't occurred to me before. It had always seemed odd that Billy owned a bookstore, but then again everything about Billy had been odd, dazzling and unique.

Elijah nodded. "Billy really didn't have anything to do with the store, so her father didn't think it should go to him. It would have been a nonissue if she had a will, but young people, they don't think they need wills unless they're exceedingly rich. Do you have a will?"

"I'm not exceedingly rich," I said.

"Still, you should set one up, especially now that you own

property." Elijah grabbed both mugs and indicated he'd be right back. I reread Billy's riddle while I waited for him. *Science is at the root of all life but especially mine. Made of fibres, muscles, and brains*— Fibres. The British spelling. Perhaps an English scientist? Huxley? Bacon? Darwin? None of those men seemed right. And if Elijah had solved the riddle so quickly, I was missing something obvious. That was the thing about riddles. They were always simple. Cleverer riddles were just better at hiding their simplicity. I stared at *fibres* until it became an odd formation of letters, absent of meaning. The clue grew more indecipherable with every read, so I tucked it away, willing myself to forget it. That was the only way I'd be able to solve it, with fresh eyes.

Elijah returned with a binder and two new cups of coffee. "It still tastes like jet fuel but at least it's fresh," he said, passing me a mug. He sat in the leather chair beside mine and angled the binder so I could see it. "Now's as good a time as any to show you what you're in for." He'd printed copies of the store's operating costs, sales, payroll and freight records for the last two years. Lucia and Charlie only made thirteen dollars per hour. Malcolm was on salary, but he didn't make any more than I did as a private-school teacher. "The good news is the property is worth a lot more than when they bought it in the '80s, and the mortgage payments will be up in two and a half years. As is, they're pretty nominal. Plus, Billy didn't log the used books into the system, so the numbers aren't quite as dire as they look."

"And the bad news?"

"During the recession, Billy sold his house in Pasadena to cover expenses on the store. I advised him not to. The money from the house lasted a few years, but Billy had to take out a line of credit on the store. I'm afraid there's a lot of outstanding debt, and sales aren't what they once were." He flipped to a spreadsheet of the sales, which spiked in December and early summer, never so much that the profits outweighed the cost. In the slower months, August in particular, sales plummeted.

"Bookstores aren't like other types of retail. You can't raise the cost of a book because you need to make a bigger profit. Rare books can be profitable, but most used books aren't rare. Every time I explained this to Billy, he didn't want to hear it." Elijah's finger skimmed the next column. "The coffee shop, however, is profitable, but one can only make so much off cappuccinos and cupcakes."

"What are you saying?"

"I'm afraid the likelihood of Prospero Books staying in business is rather grim. If you sell the building, you'll still have a little left over after you've paid off Billy's debt."

"But Prospero Books has been in business for—how long has it been in business for?"

"About thirty years. I wish I had better news." I must have looked as despondent as I felt, because he added, "No one will blame you if you decide to sell. You can go on a trip to Hawaii, compliments of your uncle." If Elijah was encouraging me to sell, to jet off to Hawaii where I could sit on the beach, sipping drinks with tiny umbrellas for stirrers, thinking how nice it was to get a free trip, he didn't know Billy as well as he assumed he did. He didn't understand that Billy had left me his store because he knew I wouldn't sell it. He knew I wouldn't let it become a fresh-juice distributor or one of those boutiques Silver Lake had in abundance.

"I'm not selling," I told him. "Not unless I can find someone who will keep it a bookstore."

Elijah handed me the folder. "In that case, you'd better figure out a way to turn a profit. There's enough money in the account to get you through September. After that..." He didn't need to finish his sentence.

As Elijah saw me out, I asked, "What happened with the will dispute?"

"Evelyn's father didn't have a case. Even if she paid for it, it was a community property, so it rightfully went to Billy. Most people who dispute wills don't have a case, though. It's never entirely about the money. That's why it's a good field of law to pursue. That and divorce." He waved goodbye as I stepped onto the street.

I walked to my parents' car, kicking the periwinkle petals that littered the sidewalk. I knew nothing about finances, and even I could see that the debt Billy had acquired was reckless.

When I reached my parents' car, I realized I'd forgotten the cardinal rule of jacaranda trees. Never park beneath them when they're in bloom. The windshield was a sheet of sticky purple flowers. I ran the wipers. They swished back and forth, leaving an opaque residue across the glass. As I sprayed more wiper fluid, I tried to recall precisely what Mom had said when I'd asked her about the name of Prospero Books. She'd mentioned that Evelyn had loved *The Tempest*, not that Evelyn had named the store after *The Tempest*. It wasn't a slip. Mom didn't want me to know that the bookstore belonged to Evelyn any more than Dad had wanted me to know the true nature of her death.

I found my phone and located Prospero Books' website. It included a homepage, no "about us," no search engine, no book recommendations. Only a photograph of the storefront, its hours—9:00 a.m. to 7:00 p.m. daily—a telephone number and the year established: 1984.

Were Prospero Books and Evelyn's death somehow connected? And what did it have to do with the lawsuit Evelyn's father brought against Billy? The riddle that Elijah had solved so easily? I needed a sounding board, someone who, between sporting events, liked to watch detective shows.

"I only have a minute," Jay said as he answered. In the background, adolescent boys shouted to each other as though their words were funnier at louder volumes. "They're finishing up the mile. It's nice to hear your voice."

"You haven't heard my voice yet," I said.

"Well, it's nice to hear it now. What are you up to?"

"I just met with Billy's lawyer. We went over the finances—"

"Tyler," he shouted, "knock it off." His voice became clearer in the phone. "What were you saying?"

"Billy owed a lot of money on the store. It's a total mess."

"Tyler, don't make me embarrass you in front of everyone. I told you to cool it." His voice grew louder on the line. "Sorry, Miranda, Tyler's being a little asshole."

"He's always a little asshole. A smart little asshole." Tyler had been in my history class. He sat in the back and made crude jokes, but he consistently wrote the best papers in class. "I don't know what I'm going to do. It would break my heart if it closed."

"So I guess this means you're not going to be home by the end of the week?"

"Did you hear what I said? I might have to close my uncle's store."

"Maybe it's its time." I heard him snap his fingers three times.

"Don't say that."

"Miranda, I'm in the middle of soccer practice. Can we talk about this later?"

"You understand why this is important to me?"

"Kind of. Let's just talk tonight. I'll call you when I get home."

"No, I want to hear what you have to say now," I insisted.

"It's just...you've never even mentioned the bookstore before." His words hit me physically. A slap across the face. A sucker punch to the gut. "Look, the guys are almost done with the last lap. I'll call you later, okay?" He hung up abruptly.

The windshield wipers were still on, screeching as they fanned the dry glass. It was a horrible sound. Nails across a chalkboard. A body being dragged. I didn't turn them off. I kept listening to their shriek. Jay was right. I'd never mentioned Prospero Books before. I hadn't even thought of it when I got the copy of *The Tempest* in the mail. I'd never asked Mom why she loved the play, never connected my name to Billy's book-store. I'd never even thought enough about Billy to realize he was grieving the entire time I knew him. Mom and Dad were hiding something about Evelyn, about Prospero Books, but what right did I have to know their secret when I'd never really cared before?

While Jay may have been right about me, he was equally wrong about Prospero Books. The answer wasn't to shrug my shoulders and say, *Oh, well, all good things must come to an end.* Jay didn't understand and he wouldn't. Only, it wasn't Jay who could help me save Prospero Books.

CHAPTER SEVEN

THE CAFÉ HAD EMPTIED AND REPOPULATED IN THE TIME I WAS gone. Ray the screenwriter was still there, dutifully clocking his nine-to-five. The other writers' tables were now occupied by teenagers talking loudly as they drank mocha lattes. At $5.50 a pop, I calculated how much the store made off the teenage girls, the customers who took their afternoon fix to go. The café was indeed profitable, but like Elijah said, there was only so much you could make off lattes and blueberry scones.

I sat at one of the empty tables and opened the binder Elijah had given me, filled with spreadsheets of the store's finances. I wasn't sure what I was searching for, some glimmer of hope that might reveal how to turn a profit. All I saw were losses at the end of each page, numbers in red that ranged from two thousand dollars around the holidays to eight thousand dollars in August. Even during the most festive of times, Prospero Books was still depressed.

My phone buzzed. I opened a text from Jay, a photo of a donkey with a quotation bubble that read, What an ass! When I didn't write back fast enough, he followed with, Will you ever find it in your heart to forgive me?

When you went to the trouble of finding that picture, how could I resist? I wasn't sure the tone was right over text or if he knew me well enough to intuit my sarcasm as apology accepted, so I quickly added, Already forgiven.

The older man from Billy's funeral sat at the table beside mine, humming as he cleaned his bifocals with a handkerchief. The tune was buoyant, absent of the forlorn timbre his voice had had when he sang at Billy's funeral. Between his white goatee and wire-framed glasses, the broken capillaries across his cheeks, he was the perfect picture of an aging and eccentric intellectual, of someone who would have been Billy's friend.

I introduced myself as Miranda, Billy's niece. He introduced himself as Dr. Howard.

"I liked your hymn, at the funeral."

"I'm afraid I hardly remember it. When there's whiskey flowing, my glass is never empty." Dr. Howard tapped his head and jotted something into his notebook.

"You were close with my uncle?" I asked.

"He taught me the art of science. I taught him the art of poetry. I'm afraid neither of us entirely understood the other's medium, but we shared an affinity for passion."

I closed the binder of spreadsheets. "Do you remember any specific books Billy liked about science? Something about the muscular system or muscle fibers? Or anatomy?"

"Anatomy was far too pedestrian for our Billy. He gave me a biography of Charles Richter once. I'm afraid I found it dreadfully boring." A biography of Charles Richter. That didn't have anything to do with muscles and fibres and exceptional height. It didn't fit with *The Tempest, Jane Eyre, Alice's Adventures in Wonderland*, either. They were famous works of literature. Classics most readers would know. Not the biography of a seismologist, famous for scaling magnitudes of destruction.

"How long have you been coming here?" I asked Dr. Howard.

He counted on his fingers. "Half a score at least."

"So, you didn't know the original owner?"

"Lee?"

"No, Evelyn. Billy's wife."

"I didn't realize Billy was married." Dr. Howard tugged at his long goatee contemplating this fact. "'For the moon never beams, without bringing me dreams/Of the beautiful Annabel Lee/And the stars never rise, but I feel the bright eyes/Of the beautiful Annabel Lee.'"

"That's lovely," I told him. "Did you write it?"

"Oh, how you flatter me. I fear you've never felt love if you don't know Annabel Lee. Worry not, you're still young." And when he saw my embarrassment, he chuckled. "It's Poe, dear," he explained. "Edgar Allan Poe. How he loved his wife, the beautiful Annabel Lee."

The beautiful Annabel Lee. The beautiful Evelyn Weston. Even if Dr. Howard didn't know about Evelyn, he understood that Billy's essential passion wasn't for science. But there was another person at Prospero Books who had been close enough to Billy to have read at his funeral, someone who knew what poems he liked, someone who might have known about the woman buried beside Billy at Forrest Lawn.

Malcolm was stationed in nearly the same position I'd left him in that morning, reading. My chair skidded on the floor as I stood from Dr. Howard's table. I waved goodbye, and he winked back at me before reaching for one of the hardbacks open on his table. I grabbed the financial binder and headed toward the front desk. It was time to find out what Malcolm was keeping from me.

He jumped when I dropped the binder on the desk, as though I'd snuck up on him.

"If you can get the next ten people who walk through that door to each buy a book, I'll give you a raise." I smiled. Malcolm coughed more than laughed at my attempt to be charming, shooting me an uneasy gaze I was beginning to recognize.

"Are you this suspicious of everyone you meet or is there something special about me?"

"Something about you, I suppose," he said, his tone not entirely unfriendly but not quite friendly, either. He closed the advance reader copy he was reading and put it beneath the counter. He folded his hands and leaned against the desk, bracing himself for whatever was about to ensue.

"Did Billy ever talk to you about Evelyn?" I asked.

"Evelyn who?" His expression remained neutral as he kept his gaze fixed on mine. He had a good poker face.

"Evelyn Weston."

He shrugged, the name seemingly unfamiliar to him. Maybe Malcolm hadn't heard of Evelyn. Dr. Howard was the closest thing the store had to an old-timer, and he didn't know who she was. Still, I could see in Malcolm's fidgety fingers, in the way he startled each time he saw me, that if it wasn't Evelyn, he was certainly hiding something.

"Did Billy ever put on any games in the store? Maybe a scavenger hunt? Or a treasure hunt? Something interactive? Or with puzzles?"

"Not that I can think of. Why?" He continued to regard me with his big, cautious eyes. His irises were like gemstones, their facets catching the light and shimmering. An animal instinct kicked in, and I felt intuitively that I shouldn't tell Malcolm about Billy's quest.

"No reason." I angled the folder with the financial numbers toward him. He thumbed through spreadsheets of Prospero Books' financial data, monthly gross margin, occupancy expenses, operating costs and, a number in red at the bottom, net income—better termed *net loss*.

"Did you know how bad it is?"

Malcolm picked at a piece of loose skin on his thumb. "Billy never let me look at the finances."

"I thought you were the manager?"

"I take care of the day-to-day stuff, ordering books, meeting reps, taking inventory, making sure the café's up to code. Billy always took care of the money." He tugged harder at the loose skin until it tore off, creating a bead of blood.

"Did Billy give you a budget for books?"

"We buy a few copies at a time. If it sells out, we'll order more from a wholesaler." He sucked on his bloody finger, then realized I was watching him and hid his hand beneath the desk where I couldn't see it.

"How could you even afford to buy books?"

"You don't have to pay them back for a month or two, sometimes even three. If they don't sell, we'll send them back."

"But sending them back costs money, too?"

"Yeah, it costs money, too." Malcolm pulled the binder toward him to take a closer look at the spreadsheets. "You got this from the lawyer? That guy's been pressing Billy to close for years. You can't trust anything he says."

"His sole purpose is to offer advice," I argued.

"He's an illiterate hack. He has no appreciation for the written word."

"The law's a profession of the written word. Do you know what most lawyers want to be? Writers."

"Not divorce lawyers. That guy sucks the money out of people's bones."

"So why'd Billy trust him?"

"Because Billy had a hard time giving up on people." Malcolm's expression changed, suddenly apologetic. Even if he didn't know about Evelyn, he knew about the people Billy had given up on. He knew about me. "It was easier to stay with him than find a new lawyer. The devil you know sort of thing," he tried to recover.

"Sure, the devil you know," I said.

Malcolm abandoned our conversation for the computer and

began to sort through the store's emails. I wasn't sure why he was pretending to know less about Billy's past than he did or how exactly that gave him the upper hand. I didn't know why I was gauging his actions like we were in a power struggle. If nothing else, being a teacher taught you to be collaborative, a team player. A bookstore seemed like a prime place for a communal spirit, especially when it was a bookstore that we both loved, a bookstore we both didn't want to see fail.

I left the financial binder with Malcolm, hoping he'd review the numbers when I wasn't around, that in privacy he'd seriously consider the doom they foretold. I didn't know enough about the bookstore to know how to save it. I needed his help, but as I watched Malcolm commune with the oversize computer monitor, refusing to look at the binder I'd left open on the counter, I wasn't certain we'd be able to work together.

TRAFFIC WEST WAS LIGHT, SOMEHOW MAKING MY PARENTS' house feel farther away. When I walked inside, Mom was on the couch, watching a network procedural.

"Miranda," she said like she wasn't expecting me. She paused the show on an attractive lab technician leaning over a microscope and squeezed my arm as she walked past me into the kitchen. "I'll fix you something to eat." There was never the question of whether I was hungry.

I sat on a bar stool at the kitchen island, watching Mom cut peppers and cucumbers.

"Where's Dad?"

"Where do you think?" She motioned toward the garage, now Dad's wood shop. A steady grind churned from behind the closed door.

I watched Mom's calm, pretty face focused on the blade of the knife as it sliced through the cucumber's flesh. A picture of domesticity, elegant and poised, as though this was any other trip home, as though I hadn't just come from her dead friend's bookstore.

"Why didn't you tell me Evelyn opened Prospero Books?"

Mom glanced up at me, perplexed. "We talked about this the other day."

"You told me the store was named after her. You never said that she opened it."

"I didn't mean to confuse you." She arranged the cucumbers on a plate and found a Tupperware dish of yogurt dip in the fridge. "I made it with dill, how you like it." She scooped out the dip and placed the plate before me. I searched her face for the glint of a lie, but she looked like Mom, patient and loving, always prettier than I was. I felt the same ambivalence I'd experienced with Malcolm, the tug-of-war between my instincts telling me something was off and my desire to trust what was plain before me. I'd always trusted Mom; then again, I still hadn't told her about Billy's scavenger hunt. She was avoiding me, but I had started to avoid her, too.

"The store's in trouble. The finances are a complete mess. I don't know what I'm going to do."

She looked surprised. "Aren't you going to sell it?"

"How can I sell it? Billy left it to me."

"Honey, no. That's not fair to you."

"I'm not going to quit my job or anything, but I can't let it go bankrupt."

She capped the yogurt dip. "You can't clean up Billy's messes, trust me," she said to the inside of the fridge.

"What's that supposed to mean?" I asked.

"Nothing." Mom shut the fridge and turned to face me. "It's been a really long day. My assistant double-booked appointments and I've been putting out fires ever since." She found the remote and hit Play on the television. "I need to decompress, okay?"

Only, her next day was equally long, just as draining. Then the day after that, she claimed a headache, followed again by

another stressful day. After four days of returning to my parents' home to find Mom vacantly staring at the television, I
couldn't take it anymore. Not her secrecy. Not mine. Not her
sadness, either.

"ARE YOU SURE YOU WOULDN'T RATHER BE HERE WHERE YOU
have your own room?" Mom said when I told my parents I was
going to stay with Joanie.

"It's too much, driving to the east side every day. It's easier
if I'm over there," I said.

"But doesn't Joanie live with her boyfriend? Isn't that a little
intrusive?"

"Susan," Dad said. "It's what she wants to do."

"I'll be home Sunday, for our barbecue," I promised.

"Do you know how long you're staying?" Mom asked.

"Not yet. Another week or two? I want to be back by the
Fourth." Some couples looked forward to spending their first
Valentine's Day together. Others, New Year's. Or Christmas.
For me, it was the Fourth of July. To hold Jay's hand as we
watched the fireworks from the lawn beneath the Museum of
Art's steps. To walk back to our apartment in the balmy night,
passing revelers drunk on American beer and too many hot
dogs. Even if July 4 was an arbitrary selection for our nation's
birthday, the day Congress had approved but neither signed nor
consecrated the Declaration of Independence, I still loved the
Fourth of July, especially in Philadelphia.

"Well." Mom forced a smile. "We're happy to get you for as
long as we can."

As I repacked my suitcase, Mom stood at the threshold of my
childhood bedroom, watching me fold a sundress.

"You know you can always come back. If sleeping on Joanie's
couch gets to be too much, we always have your room here
for you."

"If it gets to be too much, I'll probably stay at the bookstore,"

I said, gingerly placing the dress on the top of the other clothes I'd already packed. "There's an apartment. Billy lived there."

"Billy lived above the bookstore? And you'd want to stay there?"

"It's convenient." I didn't tell her that the apartment gave me chills every time I stepped inside. Partially, it was that Billy had lived there until he died. Mostly, it was that picture of Evelyn, her ominous beauty, the way it forced me to confront a version of Billy I didn't want to know.

"And you're still thinking about keeping the store?" Mom asked.

"At least until I find someone I can trust."

"Just remember you have a whole life. I would hate for you to jeopardize everything you've built over a failing bookstore." She tapped the doorframe before pushing her body back into the hall. "We'll see you Sunday night?" She smiled as though she didn't recognize the threat her words belied.

JOANIE AND HER BOYFRIEND HAD RECENTLY MOVED INTO A BUN-galow a mile from Prospero Books, up the hill from the reservoir. A small grove of fig trees separated their rental from the landlords' home. Joanie said I could stay with them as long as I needed, and if she still lived alone in her bunker in West Hollywood, I would have planned on staying with her for my entire visit, but their one-bedroom was small for two, let alone three, people. Plus, they were in that honeymoon phase where they kissed each other every time they walked into or out of a room, not yet annoyed by each other's television and dish-washing habits.

I wanted to be in that honeymoon stage, too. Instead, I was on the opposite coast from Jay, communicating in bursts of texts when we could steal a few minutes. When we finally managed to connect again on the phone—Jay half-asleep, me on Joanie and Chris's porch, shivering in the cold night—we talked about picnics on the lawn at Independence Hall and the bocce games we would play at Spruce Street Harbor Park, the lineup for the free concert on the Fourth of July, our first summer as a couple, filled with humid nights and fireflies and memories we would build together. Jay didn't ask about Prospero Books. He didn't ask about Billy. In turn, I didn't ask him what he thought fibres and muscles and brains meant. I didn't tell him about the store's finances, to try to make use of his background in economics. Besides, it had been years since Jay studied microeconomics and, despite his current profession, he'd never been much of a student. Instead, Jay said he wished he could warm me up when my jaw started to rattle. I told him he would get to soon, even though nights in Philadelphia stayed hot and I wouldn't need his body heat to increase my own.

In the morning, Joanie was getting ready to audition for a staging of *The Three Sisters*. She painted a heavy coat of black eyeliner on her upper lids and wore a loose beige dress woven from all-natural fibers.

"Are you sure you don't want a little more color?" I asked as she stepped away from the mirror to evaluate her appearance.

"Sensuality is natural. You don't want to look like you're trying too hard." Joanie gathered her bags—she packed for a vacation every time she left the house—and I followed her outside as she walked to her car. The morning was brisk but the sun bled through the fog, etching dark pools in the hollows of the fig trees. Mornings in Los Angeles smelled mildly floral and peppery. I'd forgotten how wonderful that smell was.

"Maybe tonight I can take you to dinner, a thank-you for letting me stay?" I suggested. I still hadn't gotten to tell her about any of the clues Billy had left for me.

"I have to help Jenny. She sold a painting or something." Joanie's other sister was named Jackie. Joanie, Jenny and Jackie. The similarity had no great significance. Their mom had simply been distracted, too uninspired to come up with three distinct names.

"Tomorrow, then?"

"Chris has the night off, so we're going on a date." She squeezed my hand. "Don't worry, we'll have plenty of time to hang." Joanie played hopscotch with the fig trees' roots as she headed to her car. She stopped abruptly. "I forgot. I mean, I remember figuring out the bus route with you, but I forgot his bookstore was in Silver Lake."

"Have you been to Prospero Books?"

She shook her head slowly. "If I'd remembered that was the name…"

"It's not your fault, Joanie."

She solemnly bowed her head before her slender figure disappeared behind the fig trees. It wasn't her responsibility to remember Prospero Books. It wasn't her responsibility to remember Billy, either.

The cloud cover had dissipated and the day was heating up. I gathered my things and walked toward the store. At the base of the hill, the reservoir glistened aqua. In the dog park beside the reservoir, men with geometric tattoos smoked cigarettes as their mutts wrestled in the open terrain. A concrete divide separated the traffic on Silver Lake Boulevard from the path around the reservoir. I leaned against it, letting the wind knot my hair as the cars raced past.

I took the riddle out of my pocket.

> Science is at the root of all life but especially mine. Made of fibres, muscles and brains, eight-feet tall and strong with lustrous black hair and teeth of pearly white, but you would not find me attractive despite these luxuriances.

I tried to approach these words as if for the first time, emptying my mind of assumptions. *Fibres, muscles and brains.* That line meant something. I Googled famous anatomists and one name stood out: da Vinci. Was he leading me to *The Da Vinci Code*? It was certainly popular enough, but it didn't fit with the other canonical novels.

One of the men in the dog park interrupted my musing, joking loudly as he crushed his cigarette under his canvas sneaker. I was overthinking it. I didn't know how not to overthink it. I tucked the clue back into my wallet and continued the trek to Prospero Books.

AS MY DAYS AT PROSPERO BOOKS UNFOLDED INTO A WEEK, I DIS-covered the patterns of the store, none of which led me to the next title in Billy's hunt. The store's activity followed the sun: slow hours in the morning's June Gloom, afternoons bustling with the day's heat, the crowd dwindling as dusk darkened into the empty hours of night, lasting until the next morning when the cycle began again. It was a steady life, so unlike the one Billy had had when I'd known him.

Malcolm came to accept me like one does a stray cat, a feral but presumably harmless animal that won't go away so eventually you give it some milk, hoping it won't give you rabies. He'd wave hello, otherwise keeping his distance, saying little to me beyond one- to two-word sentences—*See you. Thanks. Back soon*—when I'd started covering the desk during his lunch break or meetings with publishers' sales representatives. During those quiet hours without Malcolm, I perused Booklog, the store's point of sale system, teaching myself how to search the inventory until I could locate memoirs I didn't know, novels I hadn't read. After a few blunders with the credit card machine, I managed to ring up customers all by myself. By the end of the week, I could take money in paper or electronic form, although the money was never enough. Malcolm and I didn't talk about the store's monetary troubles again, and I sensed that Malcolm wanted to remain in denial. But each day we didn't talk about the finances, each day the doors stayed open, the lights remained on, the salaries were paid, we were amassing an even greater debt, one that at some point we wouldn't be able to avoid any longer. The end of September was three and a half months away, which seemed longer than it was. It would sneak up on us, an assassin in waiting.

Each night, I would lie awake on Joanie's soft couch, listening to helicopters in the distance and the occasional car huffing and puffing up Joanie's steep block. I would try to picture those pearly whites, that lustrous hair. Joanie had plans most evenings at clubs with private memberships and bars where you weren't allowed to use cell phones on account of the famous clientele. She always invited me, but I'd been to enough of those networking-slash-socializing-slash-ego-deflators with Joanie to know I would feel out of place. Late at night, I would hear her boyfriend, Chris, tiptoe in after his bar shift, having to eat dinner in the dark kitchen because his living room had become my bedroom. I was overstaying my welcome, but I couldn't return to my parents' home, breathing in their secrecy and skirting the conversations we couldn't have. I couldn't stay in Billy's apartment with the ghosts of a woman I'd never met and the uncle I'd known so distantly I couldn't even solve a riddle he'd written expressly for me.

And I was no closer to solving the riddle when I was in Prospero Books. I'd wander up and down the aisles, my fingers grazing hundreds of titles, without reaching for any of them. When Malcolm tried to convince two teenage girls to buy *Slouching Towards Bethlehem* and *Girl, Interrupted*, I listened as though their conversation might hold the answers I needed. The girls popped their gum and stared at him like he was speaking Ancient Greek.

"Don't you have anything interesting?" one asked.

Malcolm made a valiant case for Joan Didion—did any of her essays discuss *teeth*?—for the manic ways of Susanna Kaysen— were any of the girls on her ward *unattractive despite their luxuri-*

ances? I was grasping for anything—but they continued to look at him like he was some alien species until he handed them *The Hunger Games.*

"OMG I loved the movie," the other smacked.

"You'll like the books even better," he promised.

"Baby steps," I advised Malcolm after they left. "You want them to be people but they're teenagers."

When a deliveryman arrived with several boxes of books, Malcolm called me over to the front desk. "Might as well make yourself useful."

He opened one of the boxes. It was filled with used hardbacks in good condition.

"Billy ordered them before... We don't log used books into the system. We just file them." He put the box behind the counter and waved me toward the art section. "Billy had a knack for knowing what was valuable." Malcolm flipped through a hardback on art deco in Los Angeles. "He bought this for three dollars." The book was on sale for twenty-five. In Malcolm's tale of Billy's business acumen, I saw that maybe he was beginning to trust me, at least with the trivial details of Billy's life.

He grabbed a used copy of *The Naked and the Dead.* "Other used books he'd buy 'cause he liked the title or the person selling it. We'll take books in near-mint condition, but not ones that are obviously new, nothing that seems like it was stolen from another bookstore. There are some stores that will do that. Not Prospero Books," he said proudly.

I flipped through the Norman Mailer novel, searching for an eight-foot-tall character. The sale price of the novel was marked on the top corner of the copyright page.

"Over ten dollars for a used book?" I asked.

"With tax, it comes to $11.10. The day Mailer died, November 10. If the book had something to do with religion, Billy would make the price come to $6.66. Politics, $9.11. If the customer got it, he'd give them the book for free."

We walked back to the front desk, where Malcolm pulled five hardbacks out of the box. He handed the box to me. "Most used stuff goes upstairs. If you're looking for something to do, you can go through them, see if there are any titles we've sold out of new copies and bring them downstairs."

"Doesn't that take forever?" I asked.

"It does." He smiled, and in his invitation for my free labor, I thought that maybe he was willing to work with me. More likely, he was simply trying to keep me busy.

"No more free books," I said as I carried the box upstairs.

I filed the used books in the storage closet with the other duplicate copies, none of which had been moved downstairs during my week at Prospero Books. It was a tough squeeze, filing more unwanted titles into the packed shelves. I didn't spot any books about scientists. Nothing that made me go, *Eureka!*

I should have found the next clue already. I should have understood where science and fibres and eight-feet tall was supposed to lead me. The answer to Billy's riddle had to be somewhere in Prospero Books, but that was the thing about the bookstore. There were too many books that didn't sell, too many titles the next clue may have hid behind.

BY THE END OF THE WEEK, IT WAS TIME TO MOVE OUT OF JOANIE'S bungalow. While Joanie would never have asked me to leave, I sensed the tension between her and Chris, heard the hushed conversations behind their closed bedroom door. I still felt like I was being watched every time I stepped inside Billy's apartment, like something might jump out from the shadows. Or someone. I tried to tell myself that staying there might make me less intimidated by his past. It might even help me solve his riddle. At least, I hoped it would. I'd run out of other options.

Joanie helped me lug my suitcase up the creaky stairs to Billy's apartment. We stood outside the door catching our breath.

"You ready?" Joanie asked.

I opened the door. The humming of the overhead light echoed through the spacious living room.

"This place is incredible." Joanie's eyes danced across the leather couch and mahogany desk. "You made it sound like a crypt or something."

"Will you stay with me tonight? I know that's silly, but I don't think I can do this alone." I bit my lower lip, waiting for her to say yes.

Joanie squeezed my arm. "Wouldn't you know, I just happen to have my overnight bag in the trunk." She darted downstairs, returning moments later with an afghan her grandmother had crocheted, a small duffel bag and a jar of the volcanic mud mask we used to steal from her mom in high school.

I hugged her. "Have I told you you're absolutely, positively my favorite person in the world?"

"Only for as long as I can remember." Joanie spread the afghan over Billy's leather sofa. The blanket's green hues calmed the room. The space didn't look like mine, but it looked less like Billy's.

We sat on the couch in our pajamas, eating Thai food from the container. It felt like old times, before she moved in with Chris, before I moved in with Jay, when we would stay up all night talking about the small injustices of our jobs, the ways our bodies had and would continue to betray us, the people from high school who had become inexplicably successful, all the faraway parts of the world we planned to visit together, and it was almost enough to make me forget the bedroom hidden behind its closed door, the photograph on Billy's dresser. Almost enough.

Joanie hummed as she mined the take-out container for pieces of chicken.

"You aren't at all creeped out?" I asked her.

"Of what, the expensive furniture? It is a little too clean for my comfort but there aren't any spirits here, I can sense it."

"So, you're Joanie the medium now?"

"More like Joanie the ingenue." Joanie allowed the smile she'd been hiding to surface. She was happier than I'd seen her in a long time. "I got it. Irina." Joanie beamed, talking all at once about the well-known actresses who had signed on to play Olga and Masha, the older sisters in *The Three Sisters*, the director who in her estimation was a visionary. "It's going to be big."

"Joanie, that's amazing." My tone was a little less enthusiastic than it should have been, so I tried again. "I'm so excited for you." It still came out flat. It was an involuntary feeling I had every time Joanie shared good news with me—when she got into acting school, when she met Chris, when they moved in together, when she'd started spending more time with her sisters—a feeling it took me a long time to admit was jealousy that her life progressed without me.

Joanie dangled noodles into her mouth, lost in thoughts of the Prozorov sisters and Chekhov, her daydreams threatening to close her off from me completely when I wanted her here, in Billy's apartment, in his quest, in the details of his life that were becoming known to me. I walked over to Billy's closed bedroom door. My hand hovered over the doorknob. I inhaled deeply and twisted it open.

The room had been closed for a week and smelled mustier than I remembered. Muted light from streetlamps on Sunset outlined the furniture. In the almost-dark it looked like a bedroom, nondescript, impersonal, nothing to fear, yet I still felt a chill down my spine. I braved the distance to the dresser, grabbed the photo, and raced out as quickly as I could.

"This is Evelyn." I showed Joanie the photograph and explained what little I knew about Evelyn, that she and Billy were married before I was born, that she'd died, that she was Mom's childhood friend.

"She's gorgeous," Joanie said. "Why didn't you tell me this before?" There was an edge to her voice. It wasn't just me.

Joanie felt that she might be losing me, too. Only it was different. I wasn't cocooned in my own world; at least, I didn't want to be.

I found my wallet and handed Joanie the riddle. She unfolded it like she was unwrapping a present, careful not to tear the paper.

"'Science is at the root of all life but especially mine. Made of fibres, muscles and brains, eight-feet tall and strong with lustrous black hair and teeth of pearly white, but you would not find me attractive despite these luxuriances.'" She looked at me quizzically.

"I got that from Billy's doctor." I expected her to ask again why I hadn't wanted her help sooner, but she was lost in the mystery of the riddle.

Joanie paced the living room, hand on chin as though she was acting out a scene: young woman thinking. "Pearly white has got to mean something. And eight feet." She held her arms straight above her head. "Is this eight feet? It's superhuman." She stumbled around the room with her hands raised, mimicking an impossibly tall person. Her legs were stiff, as though she walked without knees, and watching her plod across the room, it hit me—a person impossibly tall and superhuman, a person made of science, or rather, a creature made of science.

I sprinted downstairs and found the light switch. Joanie was right behind me. The store looked different at night, almost neon green without the natural light. I scanned S in Classics. Nothing there. Nothing in Literary, either.

"Miranda, what is it?" Joanie asked. "What'd you figure out?"

I dashed behind the desk and waited as the sluggish computer churned and sputtered, the screen waking from its slumber. My fingers were clumsy across the keyboard as I typed the title into Booklog's search engine, adding extra letters, requiring me to delete and start again.

"*Frankenstein*. In science fiction," I shouted to Joanie, and she rushed over to the section, pulling down a glossy black book, *Frankenstein; or, The Modern Prometheus* and *Mary Wollstonecraft Shelley* in white across the cover. Joanie leaned over me as I opened the novel to peer inside.

CHAPTER EIGHT

CALTECH WAS A TWENTY-MINUTE DRIVE FROM SILVER LAKE.
Two students sat in the hallway outside Dr. Cook's office, text-
books open in their laps.

"Is Dr. Cook in?" I asked the student nearest to the closed
door.

"There's a line," he said without looking up from his textbook.

I took a seat at the end of the line behind the earnest, clean-
shaven boys and reread Shelley's masterpiece while I waited to
see Dr. Cook. I hadn't read *Frankenstein* since high school and
had forgotten how dissimilar the novel was to Frankenstein in
our popular imagination. We'd come to know the creature as
Frankenstein, and perhaps that was fitting, since Victor Frankenstein was indeed the monster of the novel. But Frankenstein
started as a son. A brother. A broken man, who was grieving
his mother's death, until he heard a lecture on the miracles of
modern chemistry that inspired—nay, destroyed—the young
scientist to experiment with the cycle of life.

I'd found Dr. Cook through a flyer left in chapter five when
Victor Frankenstein first saw the results of his toiling, the beau-

tiful creature of his imagination rendered horrifying in life. Billy had highlighted Victor Frankenstein's words.

> **For this I had deprived myself of rest. I had desired it with an ardour that far exceeded moderation; but now that I had finished, the beauty of the dream vanished, and breathless horror and disgust filled my heart.**

The flyer advertised a lecture Dr. John Cook had given at the Aspen Center for Physics—*Recent Advances in String Theory*—during a convention February 17-20, 1986. Although I'd never heard of Dr. John Cook, Google certainly had. His name produced over sixty-five million hits. He'd been teaching particle physics at Caltech since the late '80s and was class of '71, which meant he'd completed his undergraduate degree the same year as Billy did. Something in Dr. Cook's lecture must have inspired Billy. Something Dr. Cook said must have ruined him, too.

One student disappeared into Dr. Cook's office, then another, until I sat alone in the hall. My body ached from leaning against the cold cement wall. I checked my phone. It was after one. I'd been waiting for over an hour. Jay was probably finished with soccer camp, winding his mother's old Volvo through West Philadelphia in the shortcuts he liked to take home from school that were never any faster than the expressway. When the commute became our shared drive home from campus, I'd accused Jay of being lost. *Just because I don't know where I am doesn't mean I'm lost,* he'd said, backtracking across the street we'd recently turned off. *That sounds like it belongs on a T-shirt,* I'd said, and Jay had asked, *Want to go into business with me?* and I thought, I want to do anything with you, but we'd only been dating a few months. It wasn't time to make that kind of promise to each other. For the rest of the school year, I loved getting lost in the car with Jay, jokingly accusing him of not knowing where he was, him insistent that he did. Even on days when he was forced to admit that he was turned around, he wouldn't turn to his cell phone. He'd keep drifting through the streets until, somehow, we always ended up at home.

"You lost yet?" I asked when Jay picked up.

"What do you mean?"

"You're driving home from school. I was wondering if you'd gotten turned around again."

"Why do you always think I have such a bad sense of direction?"

"I don't. I was trying to be cute, you know, 'cause I always tease you about getting lost." I couldn't believe I had to explain it to him.

"Sure," he said. We sat quiet on the line, and suddenly I didn't know why I'd called him. I'd wanted to tell him that I was at Caltech, but he would have asked me why I was there, and I would have had to explain the flyer, that I thought Dr. Cook could tell me something important about Billy, and Jay would have asked me again if I didn't think it was strange, following clues from a dead uncle I'd never mentioned before. I didn't want to get into all that with Jay, not at the moment.

"How was camp?" I asked.

"Pretty good. There's this new kid starting at school in the fall. He's really good." I waited for him to ask me about the store. "How's your mom?"

"She's fine."

"Are you being nice to her?"

"I'm always nice to her." Jay stifled a laugh.

The door to Dr. Cook's office opened, and the fresh-faced boy who had entered twenty minutes before walked out, a lightness to his step as he sauntered down the hall.

"I gotta go," I whispered to Jay.

"Call me later?" he said without asking me why I had to get off the phone.

"Sure," I said, and hung up.

Dr. Cook leaned into the hall to see if anyone else was waiting outside his office. He was significantly puffier than the photographs online and barely resembled the mousy, bearded man displayed on the flyer.

"Dr. Cook?" I asked when he spotted me.

"You aren't in any of my classes," he said.

I stood from the floor and brushed off the back of my pants. "I'm Billy Silver's niece."

Dr. Cook startled then grew solemn. "I was very sorry to hear about Billy."

"Were you close with my uncle?"

"When we were kids." Dr. Cook waved me into his office. It was lined with books, many of which he'd authored.

"I thought you went to college together?" I asked.

"We did, but we'd been friends since elementary school."

"So, you must know my mother, too?"

"You look just like her." I blushed. Whenever anyone told me I looked like my mother, it sounded a lot like someone telling me I was pretty.

He studied me like he was just seeing me for the first time. "Your name wouldn't happen to be Miranda, would it?"

"How'd you know?"

He walked across the room and opened a filing cabinet, picking up a pile of mail and discarding each envelope back in the drawer. "It's here somewhere. I wouldn't have thrown it away." On the bookshelf, he spotted a smaller pile of envelopes. "Aha." He shuffled over to me with an envelope that read, *For Miranda Brooks, in the event she should visit. —BS.* "My wife calls it clutter. I like to think of it as disordered order. Every great scientist was 'messy.'" He put air quotes around the word. "In fact, it'd tell you something about a scientist if he wasn't a little scattered."

I tried to recall whether Billy was messy. I'd never been to his office. If Prospero Books was clean it probably wasn't Billy's doing. I opened the envelope with Dr. Cook watching.

Whatever happened, I knew I would survive it. I knew, above all, that I'd go on working. Surviving meant being

born over and over. It wasn't easy, and it was always painful. But there wasn't any other choice except death.

"Billy sent this to you?" I asked.

"I got that a few days ago," Dr. Cook said. "I thought at first it was a prank, but it's a little macabre for our sensibilities. Last week, my graduate students repainted the parking lot. I arrived at school to find my spot mysteriously dematerialized. But a letter from a dead man..." Dr. Cook shook his head emphatically. "Back in the day, your uncle was the master prankster."

"Billy?" Of course he was. A prank wasn't so different than a scavenger hunt.

"Campus was covered with orange trees. Billy called them sustainable ammunition. Bitter as hell. He made a potato cannon and used to shoot them at Pasadena Community College every day at noon. More often, I was the target of his antics. Twice, he drywalled over my dorm room door. Another time, he moved all my belongings into one of the racquetball courts, recreated my room to a T. I got him back, though. Don't you worry."

"Sounds like you two were close."

"We were," he said forlornly. "For a long time we were quite close."

I handed Dr. Cook the flyer from his lecture in Aspen. "Billy left me that."

Dr. Cook turned the pamphlet toward me so his youthful face stared into mine. "Hard to believe this ugly mug turned even uglier."

"Did something happen at that conference?" Billy could have left me a picture of them as children or as freshmen in college. He could have left a pamphlet from their graduation or some science competition. Instead, he'd left me a seemingly random flyer from a conference on particle physics, and I knew it wasn't random at all. "Was Billy there?"

Cook snapped his fingers and pointed at me. "He was." His face quieted as he gazed into the distance. "He was." I watched the memory wash over him.

"Dr. Cook?" He turned toward me. "What happened?"

He looked conflicted as he debated what he should tell me. This wasn't going to be a flattering story. "If we're going to talk about Aspen, you'd better call me John."

"What happened, John?" I said, repeating his first name in hopes that it might make him comfortable. "Whatever it is, I want to know." Dr. Cook—John—wasn't entirely convinced. I nodded that I could handle it.

"At first, I thought he'd come to cheer me on." He browsed a bookshelf, stopping when he found a thin red book. He filed through it, and handed it to me, pointing to an article entitled "Anomaly Cancellations," which he'd coauthored. "My adviser and I had recently published that paper." I flipped through it, understanding as much as I would have if it was written in ancient runes. "He couldn't make it to the conference, so I went alone. It was the first time I ever lectured on my own, and boy, was I nervous."

John said the nervousness had manifested physically in shaky hands and an unsteady voice, threatening to undo him and his carefully researched findings.

Hello, everyone, John began as he adjusted the microphone and assessed the modest crowd. *Today I want to share some of the recent advancements we've made on modifying an action functional of a quantum field.* His heart beat rapidly wanting to tear through his flesh. Relax, he'd reminded himself. Relax.

"And that's when I saw Billy."

If he'd stopped to think about it, it made zero sense Billy was there. He studied earthquakes, damage everyone understood enough to fear, while John's lecture was on string theory, an area of particle physics few understood, let alone believed in, but John was too nervous to be thinking rationally. He continued to detail the 496 dimensions of the gauge group, lecturing to Billy alone, as if they were back in John's freshman dorm room, not a disappointingly attended lecture hall. He smiled each time his eyes met Billy's, only Billy didn't smile back. His cheeks sunk in from the bone. In Billy's red eyes, John saw the shimmer of death. He rushed through his speech, explaining how the nontrivial coring line bundles on configuration space became trivializable, panicked that something terrible had happened. Something John assumed had to do with him, given Billy was at his convention.

John shook his head sadly at me. "I should have known. I should have known right away that it had to do with Evelyn."

"With Evelyn?"

"She was always the only thing that really mattered to Billy." He said *always* like he was making a promise.

"What do you mean 'always'?"

"Poor guy. He'd been hopelessly in love with her since grade school."

John said, as kids, Billy had lived within the den of his bedroom. He would invite John over to help him rejigger his train set so the cars would travel faster, to watch Billy's pet snake swallow mice whole. For hours, they would sit in Billy's dark and odorous bedroom watching his snake coil and uncoil, taunting the trapped mouse.

John laughed. "He called his snake Cleopatra. I'll never forget that. I always told him it was the closest he'd ever come to having a girl in his room."

"And Evelyn? Did she meet Cleopatra?"

"Billy didn't know much, but he knew enough not to introduce the girl he was sweet on to his pet cork snake. No, she'd be outside with your mom playing stickball with the other normal kids."

Sometimes, they would hear the crack of a bat, a squeal, evidence of the type of fun that had never felt natural to Billy or to John. Billy would shift open the curtains to watch Evelyn below, her white-blond hair trailing her as she ran the bases.

One day I'm going to marry that girl, he would tell Cook.

But it was like saying, one day I'm going to marry Marilyn Monroe, or one day I'll be the first man to land on the moon. *Good luck with that,* John told him.

"But Billy was resolute. He never gave up on her," John said.

By the time John and Billy were seniors, Evelyn was the most popular girl in their high school. She was lanky in the way teenage boys desired. The only sophomore on the cheerleading squad and homecoming queen, Evelyn was also in honors classes and said hello to John when she passed him in the hall, even when she was surrounded by her friends, other beautiful girls who would never have acknowledged his existence. When Evelyn said, *Hi!* John would stare at her speechless, causing all her pretty friends, including Suzy, to giggle.

"Your mother," John explained as if I might not know who Suzy was. And she *was* someone else back then, young, popular and pretty, someone who didn't belong to me. "Evelyn and your mom made quite the pair. As sweet as Evelyn was, your mom was terrifying."

"My mom? Are you sure you're thinking of the right person?"

John nodded. "She'd mouth off to anyone who looked at her for too long, even the teachers."

John said he and Suzy had been in jazz club together. John hid in the back behind his upright bass. Suzy was front and center, swaying her hips as she sang, making John lose track of where he was in the song. "I would hit the wrong note and she would glare at me like my thoughts were much dirtier than they were. Terrifying." He shivered. A familiar warmth spread through me. I loved those stories of Suzy. They made me nostalgic for a version of Mom I'd never known.

"So how did Billy and Evelyn get together?" I asked.

"He took advantage of the fact that she was always at his

house." John said that Evelyn's father wasn't around much and her mother wasn't in the picture—he couldn't remember why. While Billy's room was still crowded with model airplanes, posters of Einstein and Newton, something important had changed. Billy had grown a foot taller. Muscles had developed along his biceps and back. The girls at school didn't notice. Except when he bumped into them in the halls—Billy nose-deep in a textbook—he didn't cross paths with many girls. But Evelyn was at their house all the time. "And he took advantage of the fact that she was terrible at science."

Evelyn was sitting alone in the dining room, staring down a biology textbook. Suzy must have been in detention or jazz club. Evelyn often spent afternoons in the Silvers' dining room, reading as she waited for Suzy to return home. Billy stood in the doorway, watching her shake her head in frustration.

Can I help? he asked.

She put her hand over her heart. *You startled me.*

I'm sorry. He braved a step into the room. *If you haven't noticed, I know my way around a biology textbook.*

I've noticed, and although she was teasing him, Billy was struck that she'd noticed anything about him at all.

He sat close enough that he could smell the chamomile of her shampoo—*How do you know what chamomile smells like?* John had asked Billy when he'd recounted the details of the afternoon— and his shoulder grazed hers as he leaned forward to read the chapter. She was learning about mitochondria. He lifted her pencil out of her hand and drew an oval on a scrap of paper, marking the inner and outer membrane, the matrix.

From then on, any time she had trouble with biology, she would knock on Billy's door, and he would spend the afternoon explaining photosynthesis and DNA replication, forsaking his own homework. *You're a genius,* she would tell him, and he'd repeat these words to John. *A genius. Can you believe she called me that?* John never had the heart to tell him that she was just buttering him up, the poor schmuck who helped her with her homework.

"I guess the joke was on me," John said. "No one would have ever imagined in a million years that Evelyn would fall for one of us guys in the chemistry club." Even one of the guys in the chemistry club who happened to look like Billy.

It started over dinner. Evelyn looked even lovelier when she was distressed.

He says he'll fail me if I don't complete the assignment, she told Suzy and Billy's parents. *I can't do it*, Evelyn continued. *Do you know the frogs are still alive when they put them on the table? It's completely inhumane.*

Let's start a protest, Suzy suggested.

Now, Susan, her father said. *I don't think you need to insert yourself. You're in trouble often enough as it is.* Billy laughed into his hand, and Suzy threw a dinner roll at him.

You've tried explaining how you feel to your biology teacher? their mother asked.

He's totally unsympathetic. He says that death is part of biology, that scientists have to be comfortable with the cycle of life. But I don't want to be a biologist. I don't want to get used to death. She flung her head into her hands in what Billy insisted was true and profound despair.

"So Billy decides this is his big moment." John talked with his hands, swirling them like he was casting a spell. "He's going to win her over in a way none of the guys on the baseball or football team can."

It took him a sleepless weekend. Quarantined in his room, plastic pieces of model airplanes spread across the floor, a cup of green paint and patterns he'd drawn to scale. He didn't have time to recreate the internal anatomy, so he drew the organs, the entire circulatory system on graph paper, and taped it inside the three-dimensional plastic frog he'd assembled.

On Monday morning, before the first bell rang, he was waiting outside the biology lab, shoulders hunched, swaying foot to foot. He saw Evelyn and her entourage traipsing down the hall. Fortunately, Suzy wasn't with them. He told John he wasn't certain he could go through with it if his sister had been with Evelyn.

The other girls disappeared into their classrooms until Evelyn alone walked toward him. She waved when she saw him.

Come to wish me luck before the execution? Evelyn asked. *I really don't think I can go through with this.*

You don't have to. Billy handed her the frog.

You made this? Evelyn held the frog in her left palm, unhooking the hood Billy had assembled on the underside. *It's got lungs and everything.*

You don't have to get used to death to be a scientist, he said.

"Evelyn still ended up failing the assignment, but it was the best thing that could have happened to Billy."

"I can't imagine one of my students being that thoughtful," I said. I couldn't imagine my boyfriend doing something that romantic, either.

"Your uncle could be quite the gentleman." John shook his head forlornly, and I thought about Billy, the gentleman; Billy, the hopeless romantic; Billy, the widower.

"So Billy came to your convention to tell you Evelyn had died?"

"We hadn't been close in years, but I was around the first time he lost Evelyn. I guess he must have felt like I would understand."

"What do you mean 'the first time he lost Evelyn'?"

"Billy acted like he was the only person in the world to get dumped. At least he'd had a girlfriend. I didn't even go on a date until my senior year of college."

John explained that during Evelyn's last two years of high school, she and Billy had stayed together. Caltech was less than an hour away. Evelyn would visit regularly. Billy would walk her around campus, pointing out the orange trees prematurely robbed of their fruit, the abandoned cans of paint and bricks from the weeks' other pranks. To twenty-year-old John, they were the image of a love that was lasting.

"But young love is like that," John said. "It's too intense. And the fallout is just as bad." Or, in Billy's case, worse.

When Evelyn was accepted to Vassar, she had promised to visit each semester, to spend summers in Los Angeles. What was four years apart when they had a lifetime together ahead of them? At first, they spoke once a week. Then winter break approached, and the other girls on her floor were going on a ski trip to Vermont. Evelyn had never been skiing. Just this once, she'd stay on the east coast. She'd be back in the spring. Then there were protests in New York and Washington, a job at a magazine over the summer, and before long the excuses stopped along with the phone calls. It was no one's fault, Evelyn insisted. They'd simply grown apart.

The summer Evelyn ended things with Billy, John's father had died. He'd returned to school his senior year, depressed and defeated, barely able to focus. John couldn't shake the sounds of his father's final breaths. He was hopeful for the distraction of school, the reminder that life was nothing more than particles dictated by math, equations that produced his feelings of grief. John had always liked the emotionlessness of particle physics, but he was having trouble believing it after his father died.

One look at Billy, and John knew something devastating had happened to him over the summer, too. Billy's frame seemed too big for his body. He walked in a way that suggested every step was a battle. Given John's summer, he assumed Evelyn was dead. But they'd merely broken up.

"Of course the loss of your first love feels like the end of the world. Given the summer I had, I don't think I was as sympathetic as Billy wanted me to be."

Billy spent the bulk of his time in his room with the door

shut. A knock would sometimes result in a response. Other times not.

"I guess I should have been more patient with him, but your uncle, he was always more interested in himself than anyone else. I shouldn't say that." I indicated that it was fine, fighting the urge to defend Billy. "Maybe he didn't know how to ask me about my dad. After a while, I couldn't be his sounding board anymore. It was an easy transition. Billy was in the geology department. I was in physics. Then I went east for graduate school, and Billy stayed out here. We kept in sporadic touch, but we didn't have much occasion to see each other. In fact, I'm not sure I'd seen him since college when he turned up at my lecture."

"So he came to talk to you about Evelyn?" I asked, steering the conversation back to her death.

John nodded and continued his story. He said he didn't remember finishing his speech. He didn't remember shaking the hands of colleagues who congratulated him. His thoughts were focused on Billy and whatever terrible news he had to tell John.

When the crowd dissipated, John approached Billy. *What happened?*

Is there somewhere we can talk? Billy asked.

Billy, you're scaring me.

It's Evelyn. Billy burst into tears, and John knew, this time, Evelyn was dead. John recalled the Christmas cards he'd gotten from them over the years. Billy and Evelyn sitting on the beach. Billy and Evelyn in ski boots at the base of Big Bear Mountain.

I need your help, Billy said.

John and Billy walked to Main Street where they found a pink Victorian that had been converted into a cafe. They sat at a table on the back patio. Billy handed John a sheet of paper with a series of calculations written on it.

I need your expert opinion. Short of forming a black hole, parti-

cles can only have a finite amount of arrangements. Thus the patterns must repeat.

That's true, John said, unclear what his old friend was asking him.

"They were calculations of distances to parallel universes. Theories on multiple universes had already been floating around for a while," John explained to me. "But I wasn't sure why Billy was showing them to me. In fact, I remember being surprised at how unsophisticated his calculations were. Any high school student with a decent physics teacher could have calculated them."

John sipped his coffee, waiting for his old friend to explain his rather mundane observations.

We have to assume that the particle arrangements are randomly distributed between realms. There's no reason that our universe would duplicate more frequently than any other. Billy pointed to the first number on the crumpled page. *Within this distance we can assume there will be a cosmic patch identical to ours, where life unfolds exactly as we know it.* Billy pointed to another number. *And here's where we can expect to find a copy of our cosmic patch, not an exact replica.* His finger kept moving. *And this is where a cosmic patch with a world comparable to ours exists but the particles have rearranged to manifest into different scenarios, different fates.* Billy let his finger linger over the last number.

Sure, Billy, theoretically, John said. *Parallel universes are highly speculative. They're beyond our cosmic horizon. We don't have any observational proof.*

Billy kept his finger firmly indented into the paper. *A world like ours, where different outcomes can occur.*

John watched the tip of Billy's finger, wondering whether he would accidentally poke a hole in his series of calculations.

The math works within an inflationary model, too. Billy's mouth widened into a grin. John wanted to get up and leave, to lash out at Billy for disrupting the biggest day of his burgeoning career with shaky theories that could never be enacted in life.

He reminded himself that Billy was grieving. He reminded himself to be patient.

Billy, slow down a moment. I'm not sure what you're asking me.

Somewhere within our multiverse, she's still alive.

Billy, John said gently, *we can't know what lies beyond the cosmic horizon. You know that. Even if there are other realities similar to ours, realities where the dead are still alive, we'll never know for sure. Our reality is the only one we can know.*

I know, Billy said. John folded the sheet of calculations and carefully placed it in Billy's breast pocket. *It helps, knowing we're still happy somewhere.*

John didn't know what to say. He wanted to ask Billy what had happened to Evelyn, but he knew all that he needed. Evelyn was dead, and Billy was trying to find a way to continue living with her. He wanted John to weigh in on his calculations, to help him account for variations in inflationary models. He had come to John because they were old friends, because they'd always spoken to each other through science, and encrypted in these frantic calculations was a grief Billy couldn't express. John left a few dollars on the table, and put his hand on Billy's shoulder. *Come on,* he said, *I'll buy you a drink.*

"Don't go tête-á-tête with a grieving man," John advised me. "He'll wind up sadder and you'll wind up drunker than you've ever been."

Like Victor Frankenstein, Billy had turned to science to assuage his grief. And where Frankenstein could have used a friend to tell him not to reverse the cycle of life—perhaps Victor's childhood companion Henry Clerval—Billy had John Cook to remind him that he couldn't outpace science. Mathematical calculations wouldn't render Evelyn alive. And even if they could, we all knew the story of the creature and the well-intentioned Victor Frankenstein.

"We kept in touch professionally, but I never saw him again." John gathered a few books and an apple from his desk and placed them in his attaché. "I was very sorry to hear about your uncle." He threw the bag over his shoulder, and I followed him into the hall. We walked downstairs toward the main doors.

"Why did he come to your convention, though? I mean, why'd he decide to seek you out then?"

"There was a feature of me around that time, in the alumni magazine. He must have seen it. He must have seen what I was lecturing on and thought I could help," John speculated. I followed him through the glass doors to the shaded pathway.

"Do you think seeing you helped Billy cope with his grief?"

"Sadness is like a maze. You make some mistakes along the way, but eventually you find your way out."

We arrived at the sidewalk, and I motioned that I was parked to the right. John was going left.

"Thanks for telling me about my uncle," I said, and shook his hand.

"He was one of the good ones. He just could never get out of his own head." John waved goodbye as we walked in opposite directions.

When I got to my parents' car, I reread the next clue.

> Whatever happened, I knew I would survive it. I knew, above all, that I'd go on working. Surviving meant being born over and over. It wasn't easy, and it was always painful. But there wasn't any other choice except death.

I tried to hear those words in Billy's voice. Instead, I heard those words in another voice familiar to me. *I would survive. It wasn't easy. There wasn't any other choice.* They sounded perfect in Mom's mellow, patient inflection. I looked at the flyer again. February 17-20, 1986, a few months after I was born. Evelyn must have died sometime between 1984 when Prospero Books opened and Dr. Cook's convention. When I was an infant, Mom must have been grieving. As I got older, she must have hid that pain from me. Why didn't she ever talk about

Evelyn? Why wasn't Evelyn's picture on the bookshelf in our living room, beside our other dead but not forgotten family—Mom's parents, Dad's, his brother. Why didn't we remember Evelyn that way, too?

CHAPTER NINE

EVERY SUNDAY SINCE I COULD REMEMBER, MY PARENTS MARI-nated a slab of meat, fired up the grill and closed the weekend with another edition of the Brooks Family Cookout. Rain or shine. In sickness or in health. Whether I was home or across the country. Every Sunday, they obeyed their routine.

I waited for Mom in the backyard. Along the perimeter of their property, Mom's roses were in full bloom. Ten different shades of pink, they'd overtaken the lawn. In late June, the avocado tree was beginning to show signs of fruit, green orbs as small as olives.

Mom's curly bob trailed her shoulders as she headed toward me with two glasses of wine. She wore one of Dad's old polo shirts and khaki shorts, her gardening uniform. I tried to see Mom of yesteryears: Suzy, with her sleek ironed hair, the lead singer of the Lady Loves who had charmed Dad with her toughness, who had made young John Cook lose track of the song. Suzy, whose very presence in the hallway outside the biology classroom would have been enough to make Billy slip the frog he'd fabricated for Evelyn into his pocket, walking away, possibly forever. As she walked toward me with two glasses of rosé,

I just saw Mom, her soft curls matted from the hat she'd worn to garden, her cheeks flushed from the unrelenting sun.

"The alohas are coming in strong this year," I said as she handed me a glass of wine. They snaked up the fence behind the other rosebushes, covering the wood planks in papery pink petals.

"I didn't realize you knew which ones the alohas were," she said.

"I think I've been your daughter long enough to know the alohas from the hybrid tea roses."

She winced, the air between us not quite hospitable to sarcasm. I wanted her to brush away the strand of hair that had fallen into my face, but she kept her distance.

The sun remained obstinate, broiling the early hours of evening. I found shelter on the porch and we sat at the patio table.

"How's it at Joanie's?" she asked.

"I'm staying in Billy's apartment now. Joanie's house is too small for guests."

"Is it weird, being there?"

"A little," I confessed.

"You know you can always come home," Mom said.

"I know."

We watched the cloudless sky, drinking our wine and avoiding eye contact. I continued to think about John Cook's story, the way he shivered at the memory of Mom. As teenagers, John Cook and Billy were both afraid of Mom. I remembered the cowed look on Billy's face when Mom had yelled at him on my twelfth birthday. As an adult, Billy was afraid of Mom, too. I'd never been afraid of Mom. I wasn't afraid of her now.

"How come you never talk about Evelyn?"

Mom examined the contents of her glass, glimmering ruby in the sunlight. "There's no reason I would talk about her with you."

"But she was your best friend."

"She was my best friend," Mom repeated.

"And Billy's wife?"

"And Billy's wife," she repeated again.

"You don't think it's strange that I've never heard of her before?"

Mom sipped her wine, contemplating.

"Maybe," she admitted. She glanced at her watch and stood to walk inside. "What do you want me to say? I couldn't talk about it. I needed to move on." She frowned as she slid through the French doors.

I followed her into the kitchen. "What was Billy like after she died? I remember there was always something sad about him."

"You thought he was magical." Mom opened the oven and placed a glass dish of gratin potatoes on the top rack.

"Was it because of Evelyn, was that why he was always a little sad?"

"Everything with Billy was because of Evelyn." The oven door blocked my view of Mom, hiding her reaction. When she shut the oven, her face was red from its heat. She set the timer to forty minutes. "I'm going to take a bath before dinner. Will you tell your father to put the meat on in ten?" Her eyes drifted toward the garage where the belt sander roared.

I followed her to the staircase. "Why won't you talk to me?"

She stared down at me from halfway up. "Honey, I've been in the garden all afternoon. I want to get cleaned up before we eat."

"But it's just us. You can have dirt on your face for all we care. You can wear your gardening clothes. Hell, you can wear nothing. We can become a nudist family." Typically, this would have made her laugh.

"Just give me some space," she said firmly. She skipped up the last few stairs and disappeared behind her bedroom door. The walls whined as water coursed through them, rushing up the pipes to her bathtub. I pictured Mom sticking her big toe into the water to test the temperature. I wondered if she was think-ing about me, if she was thinking about Evelyn. While Mom may have survived Evelyn's death, she clearly hadn't moved on from it.

"Dad," I screamed, knocking on the door to the garage. "Dad!" The grind of the belt sander continued. I opened the door. Dad was against the far wall, working the sander up and down the side of a bookshelf. I waved until he saw me, and he turned the sander off, shoving his safety goggles onto the top of his head. "Mom wants you to cook the meat. She's taking a *bath*." Dad cast me a disappointed look. Even I heard the petu-lance in my tone. "I didn't do anything wrong," I insisted, un-willing to admit fault.

"It's not about doing something wrong." Dad unplugged the sander and rested it on his workbench. I followed him through the kitchen and living room to the back porch. "You're being inconsiderate."

"By wanting her to talk to me? To let me in?"

"Sometimes it's better to let the past go." Dad turned on the igniter for the grill. It clicked until the burners caught fire.

"You don't believe that," I argued. So much of our relation-ship revolved around history. The first book Dad bought me was an illustrated history of the presidents. Each night, as he tucked me into bed, we reviewed the life of a president, begin-ning with Washington—his favorite—and ending with George, Senior, who was president at the time.

"Go grab the meat for me, will you?" He motioned with his chin toward the kitchen.

I retrieved the bowl of flank steak marinating on the kitchen island.

When I handed it to Dad, he said, "You're lucky to have two parents who are both here, still together. Most people don't have that." Dad rarely spoke about his parents, but their deaths were a pain he carried daily. "I don't think Billy was trying to hurt your mom by leaving his store to you." Dad jabbed a giant fork into the meat and lifted it from the bowl. He allowed the marinade to drip before tossing the meat onto the grill. It made a satisfying sizzle. "But Billy was never capable of considering other people's feelings. He always thought about himself."

"And Evelyn."

"That's another way of thinking about himself."

"Why do you and Mom see the worst in him?"

"Because we knew him." Dad closed the grill's lid and sat at the patio table across from me. The air grew sweet with soy sauce burning off the meat. "You were just a kid."

"I know Billy wasn't as infallible as I thought he was. I'm with kids all day. They always see more than you think. There was this weight to Billy. I'm only now realizing it was because of Evelyn." Dad and I stared at each other like two lawyers trying to negotiate a deal. "When I first got back, you said Evelyn died of a seizure?"

Dad coughed, trying to mask his surprise. "Did I say that?"

"Did Mom and Billy's fight have anything to do with her death?" Dad gazed through the glass French doors into the living room, expecting Mom to appear any moment. "Please, Dad. Help me understand why Mom won't talk to me."

"Evelyn was always this tension between your mom and Billy," Dad finally said.

"She and Billy were high school sweethearts?" If Dad had asked how I knew they dated in high school, I would have told him about John Cook, about Billy's last scavenger hunt, the clues I found so far, the story I was piecing together. I would have told him everything.

"I wasn't around back then," he said.

"But Mom told you about that time?"

"She did. She thought it was a terrible idea from the start, not that either of them listened to her."

"It wasn't her place to keep them apart," I said.

I expected, *Come on, Mimi*, in Dad's disappointed tone. Instead, he agreed. "You're right, it wasn't."

"How'd he and Evelyn get back together?" Again, I waited for Dad to ask me how I knew they'd broken up. Again, I was prepared to tell him everything, if only he asked.

"Your mom," he said. He walked over to the grill and opened it to check the meat. It wasn't time to turn it yet, so he closed the lid. "Not intentionally, though. Evelyn and your mom reconnected when we moved to LA."

"When was this?"

"It must have been '75, '76. Evelyn turned up at one of my work cocktail parties. Your mom hated those parties. I did, too, frankly."

Dad said that Mom wanted to leave from the moment they arrived.

Last one and we're out, she had whispered to him while he waited in line for a ginger ale. *I mean it. I want to go home.*

Dad agreed, and Mom disappeared in search of the bathroom. Dad got his soda and puttered around the crowded living room. Most of the partygoers were on their third martinis. The lawyers' voices had grown louder. The wives had started to take off their heels. That's when Jerry Holdsbrook showed up.

"The man fancied himself George Hamilton." Dad sat down, leaning back in his chair and resting his hands behind his head. Dad was a born storyteller, pausing at the right moments, glossing over the dry parts. He loved to reminisce, particularly about Mom, and I was thankful for the fact that he liked to tell stories so much he seemed to have forgotten the one he was telling me wasn't one Mom wanted me to know. I was grateful, too, that Mom was taking her time in the bath, that she hadn't resurfaced downstairs, bringing Dad's story to a grinding halt.

"That artificial tan, those bright white teeth," Dad continued. He said it was just like Jerry Holdsbrook to turn up once the lawyers and wives were on their third round, once the forced conversations had given way to the loose talk of inebriation. And it was just like Jerry Holdsbrook to arrive with an ethereal woman on his arm, a woman much too pretty for him. She was tall and blonde, her white jumpsuit so unlike the wives' dark cocktail dresses.

Dad had watched Evelyn waft from the room like she was floating. He locked eyes with Jerry. Jerry tipped his drink to Dad. Dad tipped his soda to Jerry. That asshole, Dad thought.

Dad searched the patio for Mom. After he didn't find her outside, he checked the dining room and kitchen. He was walking toward the bedroom when he heard the distinct sound of female chatter.

Mom and Evelyn turned in unison.

Darling, this is Evelyn, from high school, Mom said, clutching Evelyn's hand.

"From then on, Evelyn and your mom were thick as thieves again," Dad said.

The weekend after Dad's work party, Evelyn invited them to a reading at the bookstore where she worked in Pasadena. Saturday night was their date night—a predictable evening of dinner and a movie—but Mom had said, *Let's do something cultural for once*, and Dad had relented, even though he'd been looking forward to the opening of *All the President's Men* for weeks.

Tall and blonde, dressed in a plunging red polyester dress, Evelyn was easy to spot. The room flowed around her.

I'm so glad you came, Evelyn said, hugging them both. She looped her arms in theirs and guided them toward the writer.

They stood in a circle around the writer, listening to him lecture on his influences—Thomas Pynchon, James Joyce, Bertolt Brecht and some other theorists Dad didn't know. When the writer finished, the other writers lectured on their influences. They cataloged the novels that had recently been published, listing the ones that hadn't gotten the praise they deserved, disparaging others whose success was hardly earned. Dad drank his ginger ale wondering if he hated all parties, not only those hosted by his colleagues.

The next morning, Mom kissed Dad goodbye as she rushed out to meet Evelyn.

So, this is how it's going to be? I have to share you now? Dad joked. Mom didn't laugh. Dad had stacks of files in his lap. Every Sunday he had stacks of files spread across their living room floor. What was she supposed to do, sit around while he worked? Fetch him coffee? *Tell Evelyn I say hello*, Dad said as he kissed her goodbye.

"You didn't like Evelyn?" I asked.

"It was impossible not to like her. All those literary events she took us to, dinners with writers passing through town. She was the only one who talked about anything other than herself." Dad walked over to the grill again. Pleased with the crust that had formed on the steak, he flipped it to cook the other side. "If I'm being honest, their relationship made me jealous. Your mom seemed to prefer Evelyn's company to mine." Of course that wasn't true, and Dad knew it would be a mistake if he'd asked Mom to give up Evelyn.

"So she and Billy reconnected through Mom?"

"Your mom was under the misperception that she shouldn't tell Billy that Evelyn was back."

When they gathered at my grandparents' house for dinner, Mom would sit across from Billy, talking about *Interview with the Vampire* or *Ordinary People* or *Song of Solomon*, whatever she was reading, always leaving out who had recommended it, who had gotten her a discount at an out-of-the-way bookshop in Pasadena.

Don't you think you should tell him you're friends? Dad asked Mom as they drove home.

You weren't around then. You can't understand, Mom said.

He's going to find out, Dad told her.

I don't want him to get hurt again.

It's best he hears it from you.

"It didn't take a crystal ball to see what would happen," Dad said, resuming his storyteller position, elbows out, torso tilted back.

Mom had a gig at a club near the Sunset Strip. It was her first show in the eighteen months they'd been living in LA. She'd auditioned for countless bands, returning from some auditions optimistic, others deflated. How could Los Angeles be harder than New York? But it wasn't the early '70s anymore. People didn't want her sound, her look, whatever either of those things meant. Looks could change. A good voice was a good voice, yet the bands didn't see it that way. Then, out of nowhere, she got a call. One of the backup girls had gotten food poisoning and the lead singer-slash-band-manager asked if she was free that night.

She'd told her parents and Evelyn not because she expected them to come but because finally something was happening. Of course Evelyn would come. Of course her parents wouldn't. They said they were happy that things were starting to fall into place, a notable hesitation in their voices, a reluctance Mom recognized as their disappointment that now she was married and had a successful husband she hadn't grown out of this phase.

Mom was tucked into the back corner of the small stage, beside the other backup singer who was taller and older than Mom. She'd spent the day with her, learning the choruses to the band's songs, trying to remain optimistic as she realized how uninspired and derivative their music was. But a gig was a gig, and you never knew who would be in the audience, even at a club like this. She hadn't considered that her parents might have told Billy about the show, that he might have been looking for something to do to entertain his girlfriend.

After the show, they were all waiting outside for Mom. Billy was beaming as Evelyn spoke to him. Dad felt sorry for the girlfriend, who was standing beside Billy watching them talk.

Dad glimpsed Mom walk out the door to the club, an alarmed expression on her face when she noticed them on the sidewalk.

Suze, Evelyn called, waving to Mom. She ran up and hugged her. With Evelyn's back turned, Billy slid his arm around the girlfriend, and kissed her cheek. When Evelyn released Mom and turned toward Billy, Dad noticed Billy quickly remove his hand from the girlfriend's waist.

Wasn't she fantastic, Evelyn said to the group.

My mic was too low. You couldn't even hear me, she said.

You sounded great, Billy said. Dad couldn't decipher his tone. *And what a nice surprise, having Evelyn here.*

Mom's face turned ghostly.

Where's Jerry? Mom asked Evelyn. Dad shot her a look. Mom shrugged like it was an innocent question.

I'm not sure, Evelyn said, peering over at Billy. *Working, I think.*

They made pained small talk until the girlfriend announced that she was tired. Billy shook Dad's hand, offered Mom a stilted kiss on the cheek, hugged Evelyn. Their embrace was mismatched. Billy tried to hold as much of Evelyn as he could. Evelyn merely patted his back.

Bill, we've really got to be going, the girlfriend said once he'd been holding Evelyn for too long.

You go by Bill now? Evelyn teased.

We all have to grow up sooner or later, Billy said, causing Evelyn to smile. Dad didn't understand what Evelyn had read into Billy's words, but he saw as plain as the girlfriend did that something charged passed between them.

Your brother looks good, Evelyn said as they watched Billy and the girlfriend walk away. Billy turned once to smile bashfully at Evelyn. *Happy, I mean. He looks happy.*

Let him stay happy, Mom said.

Suze, I'm dating Jerry Holdsbrook. But she wasn't dating Jerry Holdsbrook, not for very long.

"Of course, with Evelyn back, the girlfriend was out of the

picture." Dad lifted the steak off the grill and held it over the glass bowl as he carried it inside.

I followed him into the kitchen. Dad laid the meat on a ceramic plate to cool. I checked the timer on the oven. The potatoes had seven minutes left. My time was running up.

"Where was I?" Dad asked.

"Evelyn and Billy had just reconnected."

"That's right." Dad said Billy turned up alone at the next family dinner. Throughout dinner Mom tried to engage Billy. He wouldn't meet her eye, let alone respond to any of her questions.

Mom asked Billy to help her with dessert, and he reluctantly followed her into the kitchen.

A year? Billy said. *You've been back in touch with Evelyn for an entire year, and you didn't think to mention her. Not once in a year?*

I was trying to protect you, Mom said.

I don't need protecting. You need to stop thinking you know what's best for me. He stormed out of the kitchen.

"Did Mom do that a lot, try to protect him?" I asked.

"Your mother always has the best intentions, but no one wants to be mothered by their sister." Dad handed me three plates and sets of silverware.

"*We* hardly want to be mothered by our mothers," I joked. Dad raised his eyebrows, a warning to not push my luck. "So after that, Billy and Evelyn were back together?"

"A few weeks later, Evelyn turned up with Billy for family dinner."

She had a bouquet of flowers for Billy's mother and a bottle of Scotch for his father. They tried to hide their surprise as they thanked her for the gifts. Mom had seen Evelyn the day before. Evelyn hadn't mentioned that she was coming to dinner.

Mom pulled Evelyn aside while she was fetching Billy a beer. *Why didn't you tell me you were coming?*

It wasn't planned. Evelyn said they'd gone for a drive, and Billy hadn't wanted the drive to end, so he invited her to dinner.

So you're back together?

I don't know.

Mom could see that she did know. *What about your boyfriend?*

Jerry was never my boyfriend, Evelyn said.

"Poor Jerry Holdsbrook," I said, setting out the three plates.

"If you knew him, you wouldn't feel sorry for him." Dad tossed three napkins to me, the superior folder. I set to work on Mom's masterly technique.

"I don't get why Mom had a problem with them getting back together. Was she worried Evelyn would break his heart again?" I laid the napkins beside the plates, the silverware on top of the napkins. Dad sat across from me.

Dad shook his head. "It was more that Billy and Evelyn had this energy between them like no one else in the world mattered. I think your mom felt shut out."

Sure, they saw Billy and Evelyn regularly for dinners, for the author events Evelyn hosted. Where Mom had talked freely about the piano classes she was taking, then guitar, then bass, Billy's stories filled the space.

Evelyn would put her hand on Billy's. *Tell them about Peru.*

They don't want to hear about Peru, Billy teased, as if the entire country, the entire Andes region, was their inside joke.

Sure they do, Evelyn insisted. *You guys want to hear about Peru, don't you?* Evelyn smiled, oblivious to the fact that Billy had already spent the appetizer course talking about his lab, the problems with short-term predictions and other things that Dad had tuned out.

Sure we do, Dad said. He put his arm around Mom, and she smirked at him as if to say, Here we go again.

Billy proceeded to tell a long, convoluted story that lasted throughout the main course and dessert about some American seismologist who had predicted that a massive earthquake was imminent in Peru, provoking unwarranted panic across the globe.

He's completely reckless, Billy said, speaking with his hands and almost knocking over a glass of wine.

Completely, Mom said mockingly. Billy was too busy steadying the wineglass to notice her tone. If Evelyn heard the sarcasm in her best friend's voice, she feigned ignorance.

During those meals, Billy never asked Dad about the studio and his legal team. He never asked Mom about the songwriting classes she was taking or the potential manager she'd met. Still, they saw Billy and Evelyn regularly because, to Mom, the alternative, the possibility that she wouldn't get to spend Saturday nights with her best friend, was far worse.

In Dad's story, I recognized the same quality John Cook had noted, how Billy never completely grasped that other people were as real as he was.

"At some level he was still pissed at your mom for keeping Evelyn a secret," Dad said.

"That's understandable," I said, wanting to defend Billy. "Even if Mom was trying to protect him, he deserved to know." And now Mom was trying to protect me, too. "No one likes being lied to."

"True," Dad said. Above our heads, the floorboards whined. We both looked up. "But Billy let it turn into resentment."

"So is that why they stopped talking?" That didn't sound right. Even if he'd been mad at Mom, even if he'd resented her, he and Evelyn had gotten back together. The timer beeped and I rushed into the kitchen to take the potatoes out of the oven. The top had browned without burning. I didn't need to taste the gratin to know it would be perfect.

Upstairs, the bedroom door shut without slamming, loud enough for us to know Mom was coming downstairs.

"What did Evelyn have to do with their estrangement?" I sat back down across from Dad.

"Nothing directly. Like I said, she was always this tension between them." Dad peered over at the steps, waiting for Mom to appear. "Let's keep this conversation between us?"

"Sure, it will be our secret," I promised, feeling farther from Dad than I had before he told me about the past. He hadn't told me anything that got me closer to understanding Mom and Billy's fight. But with the clues Billy had left for me, I would uncover the stories, with or without my parents' help.

"There she is." Dad turned to marvel at Mom as she descended the stairs. She'd washed the makeup from her face. I didn't realize just how much makeup she wore until I saw the sunspots streaking her cheeks, the pale peach of her lips. She pulled her satin bathrobe tightly around her waist, and walked carefully downstairs.

"I know Billy's death is bringing up a lot of questions for you," Mom said as she sat across from me. "And if I thought I had answers that would be productive, I would give them. But all that lies in the past with Billy is pain. It was incredibly hurtful when he stopped talking to me. I never wanted that. He created this rift, and I refuse to validate it by talking about it."

"So that's it, you're going to pretend like he never existed? Like Evelyn never existed?"

"Who's pretending like they never existed?" Dad asked exasperatedly, justifiably so. He'd spent the last twenty minutes bringing them to life. Yet one pronouncement from Mom, and all conversations of Billy or Evelyn were off-limits again.

"What are you hoping you'll learn?" Mom asked me.

"It's pretty natural to be curious about where you come from," I said.

"You know where you come from," Mom said, and Dad put his hand on hers. They stared at me from across the table, two against one, always an uneven battle.

"What do you say to a little Dodgers tonight?" Dad asked, piercing the silence. It was his way of defusing tense situations, talking about baseball or history. But he wasn't going to talk about history, not now. "I was hoping we could all watch the game tonight?"

"I'd like that," I said even though I'd stopped following baseball when I'd moved east. Fighting with my parents wasn't going to encourage them to let me in, to unite us as a team.

"Me, too," Mom said even though she'd never watched baseball with us when I was a kid, never made the long drive across LA to Dodger Stadium.

We finished eating, leaving our plates on the table—something unheard of in the Brooks household—and piled onto the couch. I sat between my parents. Dad turned on the game. It was a blowout, the Dodgers' pitcher throwing strike after strike. By the bottom of the eighth inning, Dad's head fell back. The rise and fall of his breath grew steadily into snoring. Mom and I both startled at particularly loud snort, then laughed. It felt good, laughing together. I wanted to rest my head on her shoulder. I wanted to tell her I was sorry—I would stop asking questions about Billy, I would stop hurting her. And I wanted her to say that she was sorry, too—she would tell me about Billy, she would stop hurting me. Only, she couldn't. Neither of us could. I still didn't understand why. I wouldn't understand until I knew what Mom was keeping from me.

By the time the game ended in the middle of the ninth, it was almost eleven. Mom stood and held her hand to me, helping me off the couch. "Want to stay here tonight?" she asked hopefully.

"I should be getting back." I didn't mention that "back" meant Billy's apartment, and with that, Billy's name was banished again, any conversation of him whisked off to the land of the unspoken. "Traffic will be a nightmare in the morning."

"Sure." Mom dropped my hand. "I understand."

I followed her toward the foyer. When we reached the door, Mom smothered me in one of her suffocating hugs.

"I don't want to fight," she whispered into my ear.

"I don't want to fight, either," I whispered, holding her tighter. That didn't change the fact that we were fighting. Not in screaming matches, in *you're a terrible mother* or *you're an ungrateful daughter*. We were fighting in everything we weren't saying, in the intensity of our embrace, in the fact that, eventually, we'd have to loosen our grip. We'd have to let each other go.

CHAPTER TEN

THE SMELL OF COFFEE LURED ME DOWNSTAIRS WHERE CHARLIE was slicing tomatoes and washing lettuce for the day. He hummed along to a Bob Dylan song as he rinsed out a plastic bin for the onions.

"I love this song," he said. "Whenever it comes on, it makes the onions sweeter."

Charlie sang as he filled the display case with muffins. The scene reminded me of Mom, how her song commenced with the opening of the cookbook and continued until the meal was plated. If I asked her what she was humming, she'd quiet, surprised that the sound existed outside her head. I'd stopped pointing out the melodies of her meals. It was the only time I got to hear her sing.

Charlie broke down an empty box from the bakery that delivered pastries each morning. He handed me a muffin. "It's fig with goat cheese. Sounded nasty to me at first, but they're awesome."

I pinched off a bite of the sugared top and popped it in my mouth. It was indeed awesome. Charlie threw the pastry box into the trash and wiped his hands across the front of his fitted jeans.

"They were Billy's favorite. 'Only two things I need in life,' Billy used to say. 'A good book and one of Tiffany's fig muffins.'" Charlie wiped down the countertops and set out thermoses of coffee.

"Who's Tiffany?" I asked.

"The baker in Atwater. Billy used to tell her she knew the way to a man's heart." Charlie laughed. "'Too bad I like women,' she'd always say."

"Did Billy have any girlfriends?" I continued to nibble at the muffin, savoring it.

"None that I knew of. Billy was all about books. Books and earthquakes. The earthquake stuff only came out when there was a big one in the news, though."

"And fig muffins? Books, earthquakes and fig muffins?" I said, and Charlie winked as he skirted past me to take down the chairs. "Did Billy ever talk about his wife?"

Charlie dropped a chair clumsily. "Billy was married?"

"To Evelyn Weston. She was the original owner of Prospero Books."

"Are you sure?" When I nodded, Charlie said, "Huh, never knew that." He seemed unperturbed by the revelation about Billy and Prospero Books.

At nine, we opened the doors for three women waiting to get first dibs on the fig muffins.

"Where's Malcolm?" I asked. Normally, he'd staked out his domain behind the front desk by now.

"He texted. He's having breakfast with a sales rep. Said to tell you he'd be late." Charlie doled out a muffin to each woman.

"I can handle the front on my own," I said defensively. I wouldn't have expected Malcolm to have texted me—he didn't even have my telephone number—but it still stung that I was an afterthought, extraneous to the daily running of Prospero Books.

"Never doubted it," Charlie said.

The morning rush came and went. Charlie had an easier time managing the café when I wasn't in his way, so I busied myself with the latest clue.

> **Whatever happened, I knew I would survive it. I knew, above all, that I'd go on working. Surviving meant being born over and over. It was easy, and it was always painful. But there wasn't any other choice except death.**

It was from *Fear of Flying*, by Erica Jong. I hadn't heard of the novel, but it had sold over twenty million copies worldwide. We had one copy in literature, another in feminist fiction. I skimmed each one. Neither had a clue burrowed between its pages. According to the inventory system, there weren't any additional copies stocked in the storage closet. Still, something in the novel had to lead me to the next person Billy wanted me to talk to. I occupied Malcolm's position behind the desk and began reading.

At first, I was shocked by Isadora Wing's frank voice. In 1973, she spoke candidly about her sexual desires in ways that, reading it forty years later, made me blush. The novel was chock-full of literary references. Isadora viewed her life through the novels she'd read, the characters she'd come to know. Since Billy hadn't left anything in the novel, hadn't highlighted any passages, the clue must have been somewhere in the books Isadora mentioned. Only there were too many references, too many titles, that may have harbored the next clue.

I needed a distraction, but the near-empty store wasn't offering it. The arrangement of the history books had bothered me every time I walked by their paltry, alphabetized shelves. I pulled the books down and piled them into centuries, restocking them from our forefathers—Native American history was housed on the other side of the store, a subsection of underrepresented voices—to the present. Prohibition into the

Teapot Dome Scandal into the *Spirit of St. Louis* and the stock market crash. Of course, it wasn't that simple. I couldn't decide whether to put the books on FDR together before World War II or to litter them throughout. Or perhaps the historical biographies should have gone with the other biographies. I organized them as best I could. Messy as it was, it was certainly better than storing them alphabetically.

The bell rang and it took me a moment to recognize Elijah without his pinstripe suit. He wore a T-shirt and board shorts to match his surfer hair. When he spotted me kneeling in the history section, he walked over.

"I was in the neighborhood," he claimed. We made our way through awkward small talk about how I was settling in, how his summer was going.

"Can I get you a coffee?" I asked.

"No, I'm late to meet a friend at the observatory for a hike." He leaned against the history shelves I'd just reorganized as he bent down to tug his sock up his calf. "You haven't been returning my calls."

"You called?" I aligned a few books that sat too far forward on the shelf. They definitely looked better chronologically.

"At least half a dozen times. I talked to Malcolm. There was a restaurant looking for a space around here. They found somewhere else, though."

"Why would they think Prospero Books was available?"

"It's a friend of a friend."

"And you told them we wanted to sell?" I couldn't decide who I was angrier with, Elijah for working behind my back or Malcolm for making decisions for me. "I'm still not planning to sell, not until I find someone who will keep Prospero Books Prospero Books."

Elijah frowned. "We should really get ahead of this. We'll get considerably less if the bank forecloses." We, as if we were a team. As if we were aligned.

"I appreciate your effort here." I put my hand on his back, trying to guide him to the door. He was taller than I was, firmly footed, not going anywhere. "But please, no more friends of friends. When the time comes, we'll find a buyer who wants to keep the store going."

"No buyer is going to want that. No sensible buyer, anyway."

"I'll take a nonsensible buyer." A nostalgic buyer. A biblio-phile. A philanthropist. "As long as it's someone who's willing to keep the store a bookstore, that's all that matters to me. This is Billy's legacy."

"Miranda." He said my name like we were playing hide-and-seek and he was trying to lure me out of my hiding spot. "I really don't think you understand the situation here. You're responsible if the store goes bankrupt."

The bell on the door rang, and without turning, I knew it was Malcolm, that he was watching us, his clear eyes stunned and livid. What had he called Elijah? An illiterate hack? What was I, then, for seemingly inviting him to the store the one morning Malcolm was out? And what was Malcolm for not telling me that the illiterate hack had called?

"Elijah," he said, and Elijah saluted him. Malcolm nodded coldly to me. I matched his stare. He disappeared behind the desk where he could hear our conversation while remaining safely out of view.

"This isn't going to go away," Elijah said as he headed to the door. "I'll call you soon. This time, answer my call." His sneakers squeaked on the wood floors as he left.

I walked over to the desk area where Malcolm was reviewing a digital book catalog on the computer.

"Any messages you forgot to tell me about? Maybe a few from a lawyer who just left?"

"They're in the book," Malcolm said, clicking the mouse.

"What book?"

Malcolm handed me a spiral notebook of pink slips. I filed

through eight messages over the last ten days, where Malcolm had written my name at the top, above a message that simply said *The Vulture*. "You're serious?" I flapped the book in his direction.

Malcolm laughed. "It's an apt description."

"Malcolm! This is funny to you?"

"A little." Malcolm shrugged and kept typing notes to himself as he browsed the catalog.

"It won't be funny when you have to return all those books you're ordering because we've gone bankrupt." I didn't realize how loud my voice was until Malcolm was no longer smiling. His shoulders clenched. He was clearly rattled.

Malcolm scanned the store to see if anyone had heard me. The aisles were predictably empty at this time of morning, the writers in the café were fully absorbed in their imagined worlds and Charlie, fortunately, was busy running bagels.

"Upstairs," he said like I was a child.

I followed him to the dark hallway outside Billy's apartment.

"I don't appreciate being reprimanded," I said.

"I'm not going to fight with you in front of the customers," he shot back.

"Why, because they don't realize how broke we are? It's not exactly a shocking secret that our sleepy bookstore is failing."

"It's not sleepy." The hallway was too dark to discern his expression.

"How many books did you sell yesterday? Ten?"

"Seventeen actually," he said as defiant as ever.

"That's how many we should be selling in an hour."

"Miranda, it's the middle of summer." I didn't like the way he said my name any more than I'd liked the way Elijah did.

"No, it's the peak of summer. Things shouldn't slow down until the end of July."

"You're suddenly the expert?" he huffed.

"I've studied the sales reports, which is more than I can say for you."

"They're inaccurate. They don't even include the used sales." The floorboard squeaked beneath his feet as he rocked back and forth, collecting his anger.

"So now you're going to tell me we make the bulk of our money from used books?" My frustration was on the verge of unleashing, too.

"It's not nothing."

I steadied my breath, trying to remain calm. "Look, Malcolm. I get it. I know I seem like a stranger coming off the street, but I spent a lot of time here as a kid. Prospero Books is special to me. I don't want it to close, either." My eyes had adjusted to the dim light and I could make out more of Malcolm, arms crossed against his chest, head turned away from me. Even when it was too dark to see each other, he still couldn't face me. "We can't keep pretending that everything is fine. Things have to change if we're going to find someone who wants to keep Prospero open."

"I thought you weren't selling." The surprise in his voice almost sounded like disappointment.

"I said I wasn't going to close down, and I don't want to, but I'm a schoolteacher. I have about eight hundred dollars in my checking account. I can't keep this place afloat." When he didn't respond, I added, "You know I wouldn't have taken Elijah up on his offer, right?"

"Yeah, I know." His voice was clear, no wariness to it, and at least that was something. As least he believed I wouldn't sell the store behind his back. Malcolm turned to look at me. I still only saw the shape of him, a blurry mass in the otherwise dark hall. As we regarded each other in the low light, I still wasn't sure we'd be able to work together. We wanted the same thing, but we weren't allies. We couldn't be, so long as we kept things from each other.

"HE'S COMPLETELY IMPOSSIBLE," I SAID WHEN JAY PICKED UP. I paced the hall outside Billy's apartment. Anger coursed through me like adrenaline, a fix that made me feel alive, and so I clung to it, even if I wasn't sure why I was so mad.

"Who is?" Jay said, his voice heavy with sleep.

"Are you asleep?"

"Hmm. No. Just a catnap. I'm meeting the fellas later." I hated when Jay called his friends "the fellas." It reminded me that he was a dude, a bro, the kind of guy that played soccer and wore cargo shorts. He yawned, emitting his heavy breath into the phone. "Who's impossible?"

"What?"

"You were complaining about someone." He said *complaining* like it was something I did often.

"The manager," I said dismissively. I suddenly didn't feel like talking about Malcolm anymore.

"Malcolm?" I stopped pacing. Had I told Jay Malcolm's name? I may have mentioned him once in passing, not enough that Jay should remember.

"I don't know how Billy could stand him."

"Why, what'd he do?"

"He…he…" What had Malcolm done? "He's just a dick, is all."

"You think any guy who doesn't have a thing for you is a dick."

"Most guys don't have a thing for me."

"A, that's not true. And B, you think most guys are dicks." Bro or not, Jay could make me laugh.

I slid down to the dusty wood floor and leaned against Billy's apartment door.

"I miss you." His assessment of me was wrong. I was never the girl who got noticed at a bar—that was usually Joanie—and I prided myself on trying to find something good about everyone, a necessary skill if I was going to continue to be a teacher.

The moment you grew cynical about America's future was the beginning of the end.

"We'll see each other soon, right? Do you know when you get in?"

Into what? I almost asked, then I remembered: Fourth of July. I'd said I'd be home. I'd wanted to be home. "I haven't gotten my ticket."

"For next week?"

"If you haven't noticed, I've been a little busy."

Jay paused, waiting for me to apologize for being short. When I didn't, he said, "I gotta shower before meeting the fellas. I'll call you later."

I stayed on the floor after we hung up. If the roles were reversed, I would have been furious that he hadn't bought his ticket. I would have accused him of taking me for granted. Still, I couldn't quite motivate myself to feel sorry. With everything going on, it had merely slipped my mind. Jay should have understood.

FOR THE REST OF THE AFTERNOON, MALCOLM KEPT HIS DIS-tance behind the front desk, setting aside his reading when a customer solicited his help or a deliveryman needed him to sign for a box of books. At one, Lucia replaced Charlie behind the bar. I sat in the back, rereading *Fear of Flying* and watching the quiet habits of the store, habits that were too quiet, habits that needed to change if we had any chance of keeping Prospero Books open.

One by one, the writers left until only a couple clearly on a first date and Dr. Howard sat in the café. Malcolm told Lucia she could take off early, and she hastily wiped down the empty tables, dashing out before he could change his mind. I continued to read about Isadora Wing's sexual exploits. What struck me more were the passages about her relationship with her mother. Isadora both adored and blamed her mother. She said she had two mothers: the one who loved her and made her feel safe and the one who would have been an artist if not for Isadora and her sisters. Maybe all mothers were a bit like Isadora's. My mother certainly was. She was two people, the one I'd always known and the one I never could.

"The zipless fuck?" Dr. Howard said. I quickly shut the book, covering its title with my hands. "Oh, dear, I've embarrassed you."

"I guess I shouldn't be reading it in public," I confessed.

"Don't be silly. That novel transformed generations of women. It encouraged them to masturbate, to claim ownership over their desire, to have zipless fucks. It's a right of passage for the emancipated mind. You should read it so many times the spine cracks in half, bursting Isadora Wing wide open."

Although in earshot, the first-date couple was too busy trying to decode each other to have heard Dr. Howard's monologue. Still, I wanted to crawl under the table.

"Men have been writing about women's desires for centuries. It's only right that a woman should account so candidly for her own. It's only right that you celebrate it." Dr. Howard stood and rose his fist into the air. "'Throughout all of history, books were written with sperm, not menstrual blood,'" he shouted as if Jong's words were a mantra.

The couple stifled laughs, locking eyes with each other as they shared their first real moment together. Malcolm chuckled as he dusted the shelves. I tugged Dr. Howard back to his seat. Sex always embarrassed me, particularly when it was a man my father's age talking about ejaculation and a woman's time of month. I closed *Fear of Flying*, reminding myself not to read it in the presence of Dr. Howard again, lest I wanted a cheerleader for my sexual awakening. Besides, reading it again and again wasn't getting me anywhere. There should have been a riddle or a keepsake in the book, something that led me to the next clue. I tried to ignore the growing fear that Billy may have had too much faith in me.

The couple finished their coffee and left. Dr. Howard began to organize his books into neat piles, the sign he was leaving. All of his books had been read so many times that their spines were cracked in half, and that's when it clicked. Cracked spines. There were hundreds of used books in Prospero Books, editions that Elijah had said weren't logged into the computer system, copies that Malcolm insisted made a sizable dent in our mounting debt. There had to be another copy of *Fear of Flying*, a used copy I'd overlooked.

"My dear friends and humble companions, I bid you adieu." Dr. Howard bowed and sauntered out, leaving Malcolm and me alone.

"Never a dull day when Dr. Howard is around," Malcolm said.

"Have you read it?" I flashed the cover in Malcolm's direction.

Malcolm shuddered. "It was my mom's favorite book. Imagine my horror as a teenager when I realized what it was about."

"Your mom must have been a liberated woman."

Malcolm shuddered again. "Please don't use the words *liberated* and *my mom* in the same sentence again."

Malcolm put down the duster and gestured he'd be right back as he disappeared into the kitchen. I took advantage of my time alone and searched the literary and feminist fiction sections. There weren't any used copies of the novel there.

"Looking for something?" Malcolm asked, returning with two mugs.

"Just browsing," I said. He handed me a mug. It was filled with a few fingers of amber liquid.

"I need a drink if we're going to talk about my mother." He sat down at one of the empty tables in the café. "Billy always kept a bottle of Scotch in the kitchen for slow afternoons."

I held my mug up to him. "'Hugo, I don't much care for

your law, but, by golly, this bourbon is good.'" Malcolm stared blankly at me. "It's a Truman quote, something he said to Hugo Black." He continued to appear as dumbfounded as one of my students, like history was as abstract as calculus, as dull as grammar, as irrelevant as Latin. "The Supreme Court Justice? Of the United States?" I buried my face in my hands, dismayed.

"You're a little strange, aren't you?" Malcolm teased.

"Have to be to teach middle school."

"To be a bookseller, too." Malcolm put down his mug and laid his hands flat on the table. "I think we've gotten off on the wrong foot here. That's my fault. It's just...when you showed up at the store, it all became real. Realer, anyway." He sounded sincere, like he really believed that the first time he saw me was when I arrived at the store, like he really didn't remember locking eyes with me at Billy's funeral. But his mouth twitched nervously; his shoulders tensed as he retreated inside himself. There was still this wall around him. And if it wasn't secrecy, I didn't know what else it could be.

My phone buzzed, and Malcolm and I watched Jay's name flash across the screen. I quickly silenced it. The Scotch was strong, and I stifled a cough. Malcolm held the Scotch in his mouth before swallowing. "I bet your boyfriend's eager to have you back?"

"He's happy for a little time to himself." I wasn't sure why I said that, why I didn't want Malcolm to know how serious Jay and I were. "How'd you get out of talking about your mother?"

"I'd hoped you forgot."

"I don't forget anything," I said, not quite sure what I meant. Malcolm turned away, understanding nonetheless. "Your mom's in LA?"

"No, the Bay Area, where I grew up. My dad works at Berkeley. They split up when I was little, but we stayed nearby. She wanted me to have a relationship with him. She tried, anyway." There was a longer story there, one Malcolm wasn't about to tell. Still, it was more than he'd said to me before. Maybe what I saw as secrecy was merely the fact that we didn't know each other.

"How'd you end up down here? I thought everyone from Northern California hated LA," I said.

"I like the east side. I could take or leave the rest of LA."

"And Prospero Books?"

"Started in college. Going on ten years, next month." Malcolm drank steadily from his mug. "It's surreal to think we could close, but it's happened with a lot of neighborhood staples." Malcolm listed the old hamburger stand that was now a brick oven pizzeria, the donut shop famous for its chess matches now a derelict storefront, the gay bar once the site of protests now a fine foods and mixology bar. "But you can't fight change."

"Sure we can," I said, and Malcolm glanced over at me, his incandescent eyes somewhere between dubious and hopeful. "I meant what I said. Even if I can't keep the store, I don't want it to close. We don't owe anything until the end of September. That gives us a little time." I'd already be a month into school by then, but with the help of Malcolm and Elijah, I could finalize a sale from the other side of the country.

"If we can get the sales up, there're a few people I can approach. A few people Billy may have been okay with…" His voice trailed off. He bit his lower lip, focusing all of his attention on his now-empty glass. "He was my best friend. Pretty pathetic, I know." He steadied his breath. I wondered what his eyes would look like with tears in them, if they would become vast pools of blue, warm lakes you could swim in. "I knew he was sick. He never talked about it, but when you spend every day with someone, you know when something's wrong."

When you spend every day with someone, you know when they're carrying the past with them, too.

"Billy really never mentioned me?" I grew completely still in anticipation of what he might say.

He shook his head subtly and my stomach sank. We'd spoken about his mother, his parents' separation. Still, Malcolm wasn't ready to open up to me about Billy. Then again, I'd lied about Jay. I hadn't told Malcolm about the scavenger hunt, either. Maybe I didn't tell Malcolm because he would have seen it as an ulterior motive, one that made my desire to save the store less sincere. Or maybe he would have wanted to help me solve the clues, to take some part of the quest away from me. Or maybe it was that he had a whole relationship with Billy, filled with details of Billy's life I could never know. Maybe I wanted to know Billy in a way he never could, too.

I reached out and poured Malcolm another mug of whiskey.

"Prospero Books won't close," I promised him. "We won't let it." We sat like that, drinking and making vows to each other that we couldn't keep, hiding the truths we should have told each other.

IT WAS DARK OUTSIDE BY THE TIME MALCOLM LEFT, MAKING the bright interior of Prospero Books almost Technicolor. At night, when the store was no longer a place of business, no longer failing, it became what it had been to me as a child. A library. A collection of stories, with endless possibilities that belonged exclusively to me.

There weren't any used copies of *Fear of Flying* in feminist fiction or literary, so I checked poetry, in case someone assumed that since Isadora Wing and Erica Jong were both poets, the novel belonged with other writers who labored over the rhythm of a line. No Jong there; I searched banned fiction instead. Despite the controversy the novel had stirred, it wasn't stacked with *Tropic of Cancer* and *Lolita*. I checked nonfiction, in case someone had forgotten that, as human as Isadora Wing was, she wasn't real. The only two copies of the novel were the ones I'd already found—one in literature, one in feminist fiction—but the shelves weren't the only place we stored books.

The windowless storage room smelled intensely musty, an intoxicating smell I would associate with Prospero Books long after I left. Feminist fiction was located in the back of the closet. Sure enough, there was one used copy of *Fear of Flying* sandwiched between *The Second Sex* and *The Golden Notebook*.

The novel's cover captured a slice of a woman's naked body, the bottom of her voluminous breast, suggestive without being explicit. I peeked down at my own chest deflated beneath my T-shirt. I'd never be sexy in that lush feminine way.

Tucked inside the back cover, an envelope harbored page after page of faded blue ink.

June 6, 1986

Billy,

I drove to your house yesterday to apologize. You were home. Through the kitchen window, I could see you at the stove, leaning over a frying pan as you cooked eggs. You always worried you would burn them. If anything, your eggs were always undercooked. I suppose that's symbolic of our time together, but I'll resist my writerly urge to make your cooking failures poetic. I watched you for twenty-two minutes. I timed it on my clock. Each time the minutes rolled over I said to myself, When it rolls over again, you will go, you will knock on the door, you will apologize. I never made it out of the car.

I suppose I should apologize for everything. What we did was wrong. I knew that from the first time we fucked on your living room floor, perhaps even earlier when I felt the first trace of lust for you. The lust was real, but it was just that. Desire. Desire for you, desire for Daniel, desire for us to share our pain. Our grief is separate. It will never unite us.

Although we were wrong, there was something fundamentally right about what we did. You helped me take the necessary steps not only in my memoir but in coming to terms with Daniel's death. Did I tell you Daniel committed suicide? We came together because of our beloveds' deaths, yet we never told each other what happened to them, why we blamed ourselves. I was the one to find Daniel. I didn't know he owned a gun. We'd lived together for ten years, and somewhere, beneath the bed, in a box in the closet, in his desk, somewhere the bullets had lived with us. His death wasn't my fault. I understand this now. I believe it. Evelyn's death wasn't your fault, either. You have to believe this, if you ever want to move on.

Knowing you has been a great kindness in my life. You will survive this. We both will. And once we have, I'm certain we will see each other again.

Your friend,

Sheila

Or more precisely, your friend you used to fuck, Sheila. It shouldn't have surprised me that there were women after Evelyn. Billy was still young when Evelyn died, good-looking and strong. Of course there were other women. He was grieving but still alive. Despite the other women, despite Sheila and their affair, his grief persisted and morphed into guilt. *Evelyn's death wasn't your fault.* Even if it was common to blame yourself after your partner died, Sheila's words struck me as extreme. *You have to believe this,* as if Billy couldn't see a way around his culpability, as if he was certain he was responsible for Evelyn's death.

The letter said "writerly," so I dashed downstairs, hoping to find Sheila amid the other writers of Prospero Books. My phone rang as I barreled down the stairs, hitting me with a wave of guilt when I saw who it was.

"I'm right in the middle of something," I said, picking up.

"Well, hello to you, too," Jay slurred.

"Isn't it, like, two in the morning there?" I skipped across the store to the desk area and clicked the mouse, waking the computer from its coma.

"What, you're suddenly my mother?" It was a tone I hadn't heard him use before. It was a tone I didn't want to hear him use again.

"Let's talk tomorrow. I'll call you when I get up." I opened Booklog and typed "Sheila" into the author slot, waiting as the system searched for the right name.

"I want to talk now. Not everything gets to be on your terms," Jay spat.

"Jay, you're drunk." The computer made a soft grunting noise, as if it was annoyed with me for putting it to work.

"So?"

"So let's talk tomorrow when you're not drunk." I clicked the mouse multiple times to get it to go faster.

"Did you buy your ticket home yet?"

"In the seven hours since we last spoke?" Fortunately, Sheila wasn't a common name, at least not for writers. Booklog listed a handful of writers named Sheila. I started to scroll through them.

"Why don't you want to come home?"

"Why are being so intense about me coming back? It's not like you aren't going out with *the fellas* every night." I scrolled through the list of names.

"I have to stay home in order for you to know I miss you?"

"Jay, I'm right in the middle of—"

"Are you fucking him?"

I turned away from the screen. "What? Who?"

"Malcolm." Jay was too drunk to remember Malcolm's name,

yet there it was, the clearest thing he'd said during our short, muddled conversation.

"Don't be a child."

"There must be some reason you aren't rushing home."

"What's wrong with you? I'm not rushing home because of my uncle. What don't you get about that?" I hung up before he could respond. Part of me wanted him to call back, so we could fight about Billy, about Malcolm, but Jay was probably already passed out across the bed, jeans bunched around his ankles. Maybe all guys were like that when they were drunk and spurned, but I couldn't imagine Malcolm with his jeans around his ankles. At least not because he was passed out drunk.

Outside, night had settled into the evening hours where the otherwise sleepy store filled with random chatter of merrymakers walking between bars on Sunset. I kept hearing the way Jay said *Malcolm*, enunciating each syllable like he'd practiced the name many times, and it made me want to scream, drowning out the voices that had drifted into the quiet store. I willed myself to stop thinking about Jay, about Malcolm, refocusing my energy on the task at hand. I swiftly cross-checked the list of nine Sheilas, checking ages and biographies, isolating two Sheilas who were the right age to have had an affair with Billy in 1986. The letter was written a few months after John Cook's convention, so Evelyn had been dead at least three months, possibly over two years. How long had Billy been mourning at that point? There were two Sheilas who might have known. Only one had a memoir titled *Daniel*.

Sheila Crowley had books in literature and in memoir. *Daniel* was about her husband, his bipolar depression. Her writing was evocative, hypnotic. I didn't want to witness Sheila's optimism when Daniel started taking medication, nor the inevitable day when he abandoned the pills. But I couldn't stop reading. I read until the sidewalks emptied and the darkness dissipated, softening to dawn. The diners and coffee shops hadn't opened yet. Outside, everything was still.

Sheila found Daniel on their bathroom floor, gun in hand.

The gates rolled up across the street at Sunset Junction. Baristas wiped down the tables lining the sidewalk.

Sheila stood at Daniel's graveside, withdrawn from a crowd of friends who otherwise hadn't made it into her memoir. She imagined that her isolation felt similar to the loneliness Daniel always experienced, even with her.

On the back of the memoir, Sheila's long hair framed her narrow face in a black-and-white photograph. She stared unapologetically at the camera, her frankness saying, *This is me. I'm not going to try to make you like me.* It made me like her. It made her seem familiar somehow.

I carried the memoir to the desk and found Sheila's website. It listed seven novels she had written, three memoirs including one that had just been published. Her headshot had been updated. Sheila was plumper now and older, better preserved in the portrait than in life, but I recognized her from the funeral with her arm around Dr. Howard, swaying as they belted an Irish hymn.

I reread the passage John Cook had given me, the words that had led me to Sheila. *Whatever happened, I knew I would survive it.* At some point, Billy had learned to survive his grief, his guilt. And Sheila must have known how. She must have known what happened to Evelyn, too.

CHAPTER ELEVEN

"DO YOU KNOW SHEILA CROWLEY?" I ASKED MALCOLM THE NEXT morning while he was filing books from a shipment that had recently been delivered.

"Sure." He wiped his hands together, casting off the dust that had collected from the cardboard box. When he looked up at me, I self-consciously brushed my hair, embarrassed as though he knew Jay and I had been fighting about him, as though he knew I'd imagined him with his pants around his ankles.

"Do you know how I could get in touch with her?"

"She's in New York." Malcolm reached into his back pocket for an X-Acto knife, flipped over the box and cut the tape that held the bottom together. "Or San Francisco, I'm not sure. She's on a book tour. She'll be back by the fourteenth. We're hosting a book launch party for her."

"The fourteenth of July?" That was two and a half weeks away. "She won't be back until then?"

"It's the middle of the summer. People are in and out."

And they were. Ray the screenwriter hadn't been in in over a week. Even Dr. Howard hadn't turned up that morning. His books still covered his table, but he wasn't around for me to quiz him on Sheila Crowley.

"Why do you need to talk to her so badly?" Malcolm asked.

I fidgeted with the seam of my shirt. "No reason."

Malcolm continued to break down the box, unfazed by my evasiveness. It was an uneven matchup, my desire to know his secrets versus his disinterest in mine. My phone buzzed, and I snuck outside to answer it.

I said hello like I was answering a telemarketer's call. The morning was still cool, the sidewalks littered with parents and infants, too early for anyone childless to be out.

"It must have been pretty bad if you're answering like that," Jay said.

"Is that an apology?" I was angrier than I'd realized.

"Come on, I wasn't that bad."

"I thought you didn't remember." I skirted out of the way of two women powerwalking with their strollers.

"Of course I remember. You hung up on me."

"Because you were being an asshole." One of the women turned toward me, rebuking me with her eyes as though her child could hear me. I glared back. I'm sure the child had heard worse.

"I was being an asshole, wasn't I?" Jay had his cute voice on. I wasn't falling victim to it.

"You accused me of sleeping with the manager." I wasn't sure how Malcolm's name would sound if I said it aloud, what Jay would interpret in my tone.

"Isn't it sweet that I'm jealous?" And there was that cute voice again.

"It'd be sweeter if you were nice to me." I kicked at the sidewalk.

"I looked up tickets for next week. They're pretty expensive. I have some miles you can use."

"Jay..." It sounded like I was about to break up with him. "There's so much going on here. I need a few more weeks."

"What if I came there?"

"What?" My voice had more surprise in it than it should have. The excuses swirled through my brain. It was too expensive. He would hate LA. He had camp. His mom would be disappointed if he didn't stop by his parents' barbecue, and we both knew how much he hated to let down his mom. There was no good reason for him not to visit me other than the simple, unfortunate truth that I didn't want him to come. And worse, I didn't even know why.

"It was just a thought," he said when I didn't respond. "I should probably go."

"Jay," I said before he hung up. "I really do want to see you." I wished I hadn't said *really*, as though it was something I needed to prove.

After we hung up, I leaned against Prospero's window, watching a couple at the light on the corner. There was probably an appropriate emoji for neglectful girlfriend atones. A cat or monkey shedding a tear, an explosion of hearts that would rain across his phone, even a selfie of me making a puppy dog face.

But Jay still hadn't asked me about Billy. He hadn't asked me about Prospero Books, either. Why should I want him to visit when he wasn't interested in anything going on here? Anything besides Malcolm, whom Jay accused me of fucking—almost as if he wished I were.

TIME SEEMED TO EXPAND WHILE I WAITED FOR SHEILA. EACH hour, each day, loitered like a customer that wouldn't leave but had no intention of buying anything. Even if I didn't have the next clue, I wasn't about to sit around idly twiddling my thumbs as I waited for her to return. So far as I could tell, Sheila's letter had offered me a key new detail: Billy blamed himself for Evelyn's death. Was he driving on a dark road after one too many drinks? Had he convinced her the headache she complained about was nothing, when really it was the first sign of an aneurism?

I added what little information I'd gathered on Evelyn to my original Google search: Evelyn Weston, Los Angeles, Death, Prospero Books, 1980s. This still wasn't enough for the internet. The Central Library downtown cataloged the *LA Times* and *LA Weekly* since their inception. If her death was a tragedy, it wasn't lurid or unusual enough to have made the papers. I skimmed 1984 for an article on Los Angeles's newest bookstore, Prospero Books, or an advertisement Evelyn may have taken out in the paper. The sole mention of Prospero was in an *LA Weekly* theater review of *The Tempest* at the Ahmanson Theatre. The *Los Feliz Ledger* wasn't in publication until the early 2000s, so no chance of anything being written about her there.

With the library a dead end, I searched the bowels of Billy's apartment. Evelyn wasn't in the top shelf of Billy's closet. She wasn't crammed into the coffee table chest, in the silverware drawer with the disposable chopsticks. She wasn't lingering in Prospero Books, either, not in a folder among the paperwork detailing years of decline, not in a file on the desktop.

"Looking for something?" Malcolm asked when he spotted me on the floor behind the front desk, every paper from the filing cabinet cascading around me.

"Why isn't there any paperwork from before the early 2000s?" I held up a book order from 2002, the earliest document I could find.

"We have a limited amount of space." Malcolm took the paper from my hands and inspected it. "Not even sure why we have this." He balled up the book order and threw it into the trash.

"Hey!" I grabbed it out of the trash and smoothed it as best I could. "That could be important."

"For what? Audits only go back six years."

"It's the store's history," I told him, resisting saying more.

"The store's history?" He took the order from my hands.

"What exactly does the fact that we ordered twenty copies of *The Lovely Bones* tell you about the bookstore?"

That, like the novel, the store was burdened with tragedy. While Susie Salmon might not be narrating from above, death still hovered over the store.

Instead, I said, "In posterity, seemingly unimportant documents reveal the most about daily life, the tastes of the times, details that official documents overlook. It's documents like that—" I pointed to the crumpled paper he was still holding in his hand "—that tell us the most about our past."

"You want a soapbox to go along with that lecture?"

"You want a fist to go along with that attitude?" I curled my hand in protest. Malcolm rolled his eyes and tossed the order into the trash like he was shooting a basketball.

Since our conversation about the store, something had undeniably shifted between me and Malcolm. In the mornings when I arrived downstairs, he'd fetch me a cup of coffee. He maintained his position behind the counter, but he called me over when a customer wanted to place a special order, leaning over me as I typed the request into Booklog, close enough that I could smell the cinnamon of his deodorant mixed with a faint musk of his sweat. When three galleys for books on JFK's assassination arrived, he asked me to choose one to order in honor of the upcoming anniversary.

Before his lunches with reps, we would sit behind the desk, poring over the publisher's catalog. Malcolm would show me how to type questions I had about specific titles, where to mark how many copies I thought we should buy. Together, we printed out the last quarterly report to see what hadn't sold. Together, we pulled down books and paid our respects before packing them up to return to the publishers.

At the end of the day, once Lucia was gone and we flipped the sign on the door to Closed, he would hand me a glass of Scotch. I tried to enjoy the burn of that strong liquor as we plotted ways to save the store. From various bookstores' websites, I'd learned that our competitors were constantly inventing ways to broaden their customer base. Readings. Open mics. Book clubs. Writing workshops. Loyalty rewards.

"No open mics," Malcolm protested. "I'll tear my ears off if I have to hear anyone's slam poetry."

"Too bad we don't sell alcohol. We could make a fortune off people's bad art," I said.

"I'm okay with loyalty rewards," Malcolm added, "so long as you don't get points for *Twilight*."

"You're such a snob."

"Thank you." He smiled. But buy ten books, get one free and flash sales on the Russians, Roald Dahl and our bestsellers wasn't going to be enough to keep the store afloat.

"What if we put frequent buyer cards in the coffee bar across the street?" I suggested.

"You really want to be associated with a place that has tasting notes for its coffee?"

Malcolm was better at rejecting my ideas than offering his own. He didn't want to hold any events beyond the occasional reading and a few monthly book clubs. He refused to sell literary themed matchbooks or tote bags, anything that reduced the classics to kitsch. He wouldn't budge on the locally roasted coffee beans that cost twice as much as nationally distributed beans, on the health insurance plan for our modest staff, not that I wanted to take dental and vision benefits away from Lucia and Charlie. While his oppositions were always on intellectual grounds, they were merely excuses. I called him elitist and pretentious, qualities he embraced, and we both sidestepped an obvious truth. Letting go of parts of the store meant letting parts of Billy go, too. So we created a giant path around Billy, circumventing the Billy that Malcolm had spent each day with, the Billy who had crafted wild adventures for me as a child, the Billy who still plotted journeys for me as an adult. He could have been our point of connection. Instead, we had another common interest, one that was easier to talk about, not so secretive. We had Prospero Books.

ONE THING MALCOLM AND I COULD AGREE UPON WAS SOLICITing help. That meant bringing in Lucia and Charlie. I hoped they could talk some sense into Malcolm, to make him see that changing the store wasn't forgetting Billy but making it possible for us to continue to honor him.

The Fourth of July was the only day that summer the store closed and thus the only day everyone was free to meet. That morning, I woke to an exploding firework emoji Jay had sent. It was the first time he'd initiated contact with me all week. While he'd answered when I'd called him, which I did daily, he'd stopped talking about the picnics, the bocce ball, the beach trips we'd take that summer. I understood why he was hurt, but Jay was close with his family. He dropped everything—dinner plans with me, a movie we'd bought tickets for, a walk along the Schuylkill, everything except soccer—if his sister needed him to help her put together a dresser or if his mother wanted him to go to a brunch or gallery opening. He should have understood that this was my version of those society events, those dressers and bookshelves. When the fireworks dissolved from my phone's screen, I threw the phone across Billy's bed and tried to go back to bed.

No sooner had I drifted to sleep than the phone beeped again. Dad's texts always appeared as orders, no punctuation, no caps— call me, check email, tell me about school, get better. It should have been no surprise when I opened the latest message, confronted simply with, what time tonight. While it was his age revealing itself, his ignorance to the nuances of modern forms of communication, I still read his words stripped of emotion, devoid of excitement at the prospect of seeing me.

Every year, Mom and Dad invited the Conrads, their neighbors and oldest friends, over for a barbecue before walking to the beach to watch the fireworks. I didn't remember Mom inviting me to join them. She must have assumed since I was home, I'd spend the holiday with them. We hadn't spoken in eleven days, not since we watched the Dodgers as Dad snored on the couch. On Sunday, I hadn't called to tell her I wasn't coming to their cookout. In turn, she hadn't called to see why I hadn't shown up.

I can't make it tonight...plans at the store, I wrote.

Okay, he wrote back. He didn't say they'd see me soon or ask if I was planning to come over that Sunday. Just, *okay*. It felt like the seeds of a breakup only worse because family is supposed to be unconditional. But Sunday barbecues and baseball games couldn't make us what we always were to each other. Only talking could, the one thing we were unable to do. So I resigned myself to this continued state of limbo with my parents, with Jay, and decided to focus on Prospero Books and our meeting scheduled for that afternoon.

Lucia and Charlie reluctantly agreed to meet for lunch, making us promise to be done by three. In preparation for the meeting, I printed reports off Booklog, not just the end-of-day sales on our store but averages aggregated from other independent bookshops that were more successful than ours. I made spreadsheets, cataloging our operating costs and break-even point. If we sold only hardback books, we'd have to sell sixty-five each day to make ends meet. A paperback every three and a half minutes. I didn't want to think how many cups of coffee that was.

I bought sandwiches at the cheese shop at Sunset Junction and a six-pack of IPA from Northern California that I knew Malcolm liked. Malcolm arrived before the others, planting himself behind the computer to prepare for our meeting. I opened a beer and brought it to him.

"My favorite." He stared intently at the label. "You think there's any chance this will work?"

"We have to try," I said.

The bell on the front door chimed and Lucia stormed in. "I'm going to need food before I have anything nice to say."

"The things she gets away with by claiming low blood sugar," Charlie said, following closely behind. Lucia saw the sandwiches on the table, unwrapped one and devoured it before she even sat down. "There's something wrong with you," Charlie said as Lucia swallowed the final bite.

Lucia wiped her mouth. "Let's get this over with. Charlie and I have a bonfire to get to."

"It doesn't start for another four hours."

"I can think of a thousand and one things I'd rather be doing than this. No offense," she said to me. I shrugged, pretending not to be hurt.

"I'll make it as quick as I can," I said, knowing that once I told her she might soon be out of a job, she wouldn't be in such a rush to get to a fire on the beach.

"Is something going on?" Charlie asked. "You two have been awfully chummy lately." I snuck a peek at Malcolm and saw the distinctive reddening of his cheeks. I was pretty sure I was ruby, too. "You didn't sign us up for a reality show or something?"

"Charlie," Malcolm said, his voice coated in disgust, "I've turned down literally every location scout who's tried to shoot here. You really think I'd deign to put Prospero Books on a reality show?"

"I would hope not," Charlie said.

"Scouts have wanted to shoot here?" I asked Malcolm.

"It's never been right."

"But think about how much money we could make."

"We'd have to close shop, and it's never worth it. Besides, I wouldn't do that to our customers."

"I'm sure they can find somewhere else to go for a day or two."

"It's not happening, Miranda." Charlie and Lucia shifted

their attention from me to Malcolm, two children caught in the middle, not sure which side to pick.

"Well, we have to do something if we don't want the store to go belly-up," I shouted, exasperated, and Lucia gasped. We all fell silent. "I didn't mean to tell you like that," I said to Lucia and Charlie. "But we're in a bit of a situation."

I walked Charlie and Lucia through the spreadsheets and started the speech I'd prepared, how we had a loyal customer base, which was key. Now we had to double, triple, its size. We needed to attract those who viewed Prospero Books as little more than scenery as they waited at the coffee bar for overpriced lattes. Lucia nodded eagerly. I reiterated the ideas I'd posed to Malcolm. Readings. Open mics. Book clubs. Writing workshops. Loyalty rewards. I was as persuasive as a lawyer in a movie during opening statements. We could sell ebooks. Night-lights. Organizers. If we were going to keep Prospero Books a bookstore, we needed to make each day count, until the fated date of October 1.

After I finished my speech, I gave everyone a few minutes to process the news. Charlie scratched the grout between two tiles until Lucia made him stop. Malcolm finished his beer and opened two more, handing one to Lucia. They drained their beers, and I realized a six-pack wasn't enough.

"Could we really close?" Charlie finally asked. I didn't have the heart to answer him. Neither apparently did Malcolm, who picked at his scabbed-over thumb.

"Well," Lucia said like she'd suddenly been hit with an idea. "We're not going down without a fight."

"You make it sound like we've already lost," Malcolm said.

"It's going to be a challenge," I admitted. I highlighted the amount of minutes we had to sell each children's book.

"You can't isolate one inventory stream," Malcolm protested.

"It's just an example." I showed our sales compared to the average sales of similarly sized indie bookstores across the country.

"This isn't as neat a comparison as you're making it," Malcolm said.

"Why are you fighting me on this?"

"Because you're positing the store unfairly."

"Why aren't we selling as many books as these stores?" Lucia said. "We have a prime location, loyal customers, a great collection. What are we doing wrong?"

Charlie filed through the spreadsheets. "Billy knew about this?" He sounded like a wounded lover.

"Come on now," Malcolm said. "This isn't Billy's fault."

It was Billy's fault, but it didn't do any good pointing that out. "There's enough money in the account to cover our expenses until the end of September. We've got to make some serious changes if we want to stay open through the fall," I said.

"Does that mean you're thinking of staying?" Charlie asked me.

"I have to be back in Philly at the end of August." As soon as I said it, I realized I'd already decided to stay through the summer. I tried to shrug off the guilt, the conversation I'd have to have with Jay, the continued strain it would add to our relationship.

"But you don't have to sell. If we can get the store profitable, then it can stay in the family." Charlie's voice quaked, and I wanted to hug him because he thought of me as part of the clan, a better option than some random outsider, even a charitable outsider who might keep Prospero a bookstore.

"I can't run a business from across the country," I said.

"But Malcolm can run the store. He's been doing it for years."

"Charlie," Malcolm chided. "We'll find the right buyer."

"If we have time to be choosy, it will end up in the right hands," I said. "I'm sorry those aren't mine."

For a moment no one spoke. Lucia motioned she'd be right back and reappeared a few minutes later with a case of beer, a bottle of tequila and four shot glasses. I must have made a face when she handed me a shot because she said, "We're in this together."

We clinked our glasses and drained our tequila.

Across Sunset, the cheese shop, coffee bar and diner all closed for the day. Lucia looked at her watch but said nothing about the hour. Together, we listed the ways people found Prospero Books: foot traffic, the occasional reading and book release party, word of mouth, Yelp. Lucia poured another round of shots. The bottle was half-empty. We listed the ways they could find Prospero Books: ads in local papers, weekly events, book clubs, writers' workshops, magazine launches, monthly specials, a blog.

"We're going to need a real website," I said. "Not just a homepage. And a Facebook account. Instagram, too."

I expected Malcolm to fight me on this. Instead, he confessed, "I've always wanted to write a noir blog."

"I've always wanted to write a crocheting blog," Lucia said hopefully.

"Let's not get carried away," Malcolm told her. She stuck her tongue out at him.

"Why don't we do some stuff for kids, too? I can do a Dr. Seuss day," Charlie said, and I felt that familiar desire to hug him.

We compiled a list of events to advertise on our new website, beginning with Sheila's book launch party, celebrations around the birthdays of Raymond Chandler, Hemingway and other staff favorites.

"We can't do more than one birthday a month," Malcolm argued. "It won't work if we oversaturate the calendar."

"But you're the one who wanted both Chandler and Hemingway," I argued. Their birthdays were two days apart.

"It's called brainstorming," Malcolm said.

"It's called brainstorming," Lucia mimicked, her voice loose with alcohol.

Malcolm hopped up but Lucia was spry. He chased her until he had her cornered in the literature section. When he lunged at her, she sidestepped his hands. They breathed heavily and, just when Lucia turned to smile at me, Malcolm made a quick dive for her legs and tossed her over his shoulder. She kicked, her twig legs flittering in the air, as floppy as a dying fish.

"Malcolm put me down! I'm serious." He held her inches over the trash can as she squealed. After a few moments, he placed her on the floor. She punched his arm with little effort. "You're such a child."

Still breathing heavily, Malcolm sat back down. "August is always slow." He pointed to the names on the birthday list—James Baldwin, Charles Bukowski, Dorothy Parker, the nights blocked off for readings. "We shouldn't plan too much. Maybe one reading. And Bukowski."

"But we have to get sales up in August. No way this is going to work if we have a slow month," I said.

"You can't get people to come in if they're all out of town," he said.

"The whole city is out of town? Everyone in LA?"

"Pretty much."

"I'm still running my crochet circle in August," Lucia said defiantly.

We set the calendar through the end of September, with a lightened schedule for August. In September we'd pick back up, a Roald Dahl day, complete with a chocolate fountain that Charlie promised to pay for if it didn't pay for itself, a Ken Kesey night, regular book clubs and writers-group meetings until the fated day of October 1 when the mortgage payment and line of credit were due. On September 30, we'd throw a blowout party. A gala. A celebration whether we succeeded or failed. Either way, it would be my final goodbye.

When our growling stomachs dominated the conversation, Charlie made turkey sandwiches in Prospero's bare-bones kitchen. Over dinner, Lucia, Charlie and Malcolm swapped their favorite memories of Prospero Books. Lucia said she hated reading until she discovered *How the Garcia Girls Lost Their Accents*. Her memory was photographic. She could recall the eyebrow and lip piercings of each customer she'd sold the novel to, the silver rings and ankle boots they'd worn when they returned weeks later, asking for more recommendations. Charlie described his first day at the store, how he'd forgotten a bagel in the toaster and the whole café had filled with smoke. He'd thought for sure he would get fired, but Billy showed him how to use the timer, how to prevent accidents like that from happening again.

Malcolm remembered the regular who had proposed near the table where we sat. The screenwriter, who could now afford his own office and rarely came into the café. When that writer had sold his first script, Billy had treated everyone to champagne. When another writer had learned his father had died, Billy had closed the café so the man could grieve alone. Once, a young man stampeded the literature section, tearing down one book then another, ripping out the pages of his beloved's favorite romances. Malcolm had tried to intervene, but Billy stopped him. The boy shredded ten books before he calmed. He paid for the books without further outburst. After the boy left, Billy put the pages in a box, and tucked it away in the storage room for safekeeping. As far as Malcolm knew, the box was still there.

In turn, I told them how Billy had brought me here as a kid, how he'd said to pick a book, any book, and those novels contained more magic than if I'd bought them in another bookstore. I told them how Lee and Billy used to answer the phone, *Where books are prized above dukedom*, and Lucia repeated this as though it was a fight song, swinging her fist as she recited it again and again, books and dukedom, sloshing beer onto the table until Malcolm told her to settle down.

I described Silver Lake in the '90s, how there weren't cafes and cheese shops. Instead, cars regularly were broken into, sometimes you even heard the echo of a gunshot.

Malcolm lamented gentrification and displacement until Lucia yawned exaggeratedly and threw her napkin at him. "You live in Echo Park," she said. "Don't act so valiant."

We swapped memories of the store until the sky darkened, and the popping of illegal fireworks echoed outside. We followed the sounds to the roof, where we had a clear view of Echo Park and downtown. The succession of sparklers sounded like a war zone.

Lucia and I dangled our feet off the roof. "I wonder how many fireworks we'll be able to see from here." She pointed east. "Definitely the ones at Dodger Stadium." She drifted her finger west. Her words were slurred. "Maybe even in Century City and Santa Monica. It's pretty clear tonight." Malcolm and Charlie were at the other end of the roof, speaking intensely about something. "Secrets, secrets are no fun, unless I am a part of one," Lucia yelled to them.

"If you want to know what we're talking about, come over here," Charlie shouted.

"I can't move. Literally, I can't feel my legs." She punched her thighs. "Nothing." The sky darkened around us. I could move, but I didn't want to. "Is this what you thought you'd be doing for the Fourth?" she asked me as she took a swig from the tequila bottle.

"You mean did I think I'd be trying to save a store owned by my uncle who I hadn't seen in sixteen years? No, I didn't think I'd be doing that." The alcohol had made me lose control of the volume of my voice. Lucia covered her ears with her hands.

"I'm right next to you. You don't have to shout." We both laughed until Lucia's face stilled. "You haven't seen Billy in sixteen years?"

"I wouldn't make that up."

"That's so sad." She rested her head on my shoulder.

"It is sad," I said, resting my head on hers. "It's really sad."

Charlie shuffled over to our side of the roof and sat down clumsily next to Lucia. He threw his arms around her, grabbing the bottle out of her hand.

"You only want me for my booze," she said.

Malcolm lingered on the other side of the roof. I walked over to him and we watched the firecrackers sparkling in the distance. Despite our teamwork, our promise to work together, I still wasn't quite sure what to say to him when we weren't talking about Prospero Books.

"Sorry if I was being difficult in there," Malcolm said.

"You? Difficult?"

"I was always after Billy to change things. It's just now that he's gone..." He watched the fireworks pop and fade in the faraway sky.

"It's okay. I get it," I said.

"But I stand my ground on open mics. Not everyone should be encouraged to find their inner artist."

I nudged him with my elbow. "Billy was lucky to have you."

Malcolm stared at me like he was seeing me for the first time. "You know, you're different than I thought you were."

"Different how?" My voice was more hopeful than I would have liked.

"You're—" A firework exploded behind us, saving Malcolm from finishing his thought. Lucia jumped to her feet and ran toward us. We turned as the sky ignited in pink and blue. Lucia put her arms around us and howled.

"How am I different?" I shouted over Lucia's shoulder. Malcolm winked at me, then returned his attention to the sky. I wanted to reach for his hand. I wondered what would happen if I pulled him downstairs and pushed him against the literature section, if I would kiss him, if he would kiss me back. He was objectively less attractive than Jay. Soft around the middle.

His hunched shoulders always making him seem slightly un-comfortable. There was something about him I couldn't shake, though, something I couldn't deny, either. Who was I kidding? I would never reach for his hand. I would never make him my zipless fuck, my zipless kiss even. Not simply because I was with Jay. It required an abandon I'd never had. Still, I couldn't help but fantasize what it would be like to be the type of girl who only considered the consequences later.

"Over here!" Charlie pointed west where three separate sets of fireworks flared in the distance. They burst erratically, releas-ing concentric circles of color. They must have looked as bril-liant across the city as the fireworks at Dodger Stadium looked from Prospero's roof. I pictured Mom at the beach, sitting on the blanket beside Dad, their hands entwined as they watched the white filaments fall into the ocean. Was she thinking about me as she watched the fireworks? Was she thinking about Evelyn and Billy, about the stories she could never tell me?

Another firework erupted and Lucia raised her beer. "Here we go," she shouted. Yellow filaments fell like rain as their cen-ters exploded in patriotic blue. Before the blue dissipated, an-other firework went off, followed by the gunshots of a dozen more. We stood shoulder-to-shoulder, watching too many fire-works to count. For ninety seconds, it seemed the sky might never quiet. As the last firework faded to dust, Lucia shouted again. "Here we fucking go."

Several people cheered from the backyards that surrounded us. We joined them, uniting our cries with theirs, draining our vocal cords, but we didn't care. We screamed until we were hoarse and our throats ached.

RENEGADE FIREWORKS BLAZED FOR HOURS. AT SOME POINT, we'd stumbled downstairs where our shouts were too loud for the slumbering store. Drinks materialized. I didn't know what they were. I didn't know how many I had. I didn't know when or how I'd made it upstairs. In the morning, I was on Billy's bed, alone, yesterday's jeans glued to my thighs. I had hazy memories of calling Jay, the slur of sleep in his voice as he reported our bed empty without me. Fuzzy recollections of me offering to do things that would make him feel less alone, trying not to say Malcolm's name by accident, avoiding the fact that I'd decided to remain apart from him for the rest of the summer. Jay laughed at my attempts to talk dirty, telling me he missed me, and we reached a truce because, despite the disappointment, despite the fighting, we still had that thing between us.

Billy's bedroom grew light. I stayed in bed, thinking about Jay. When I finally returned home at the end of the summer, he would meet me at the airport with flowers, and when I saw the flowers, when I saw Jay, I would remember how much I liked him. I would be thankful that I hadn't acted on my desire for Malcolm. School would begin, and we would lesson-plan together. We would take shortcuts home through West Philadelphia that never saved us any time. We would act like colleagues in the halls, we would become lovers again at home, and it would all feel complete.

But as I summoned those images, as I tried to recall how happy I was in my life in Philadelphia, I was distracted by the more immediate image of Prospero Books, of Malcolm's inscrutable stares, of Charlie's dimples, of Lucia's chaos, of Billy's clues. Could I really leave if I hadn't solved Billy's quest? If I hadn't discovered what happened to Evelyn? Why Billy and Mom fought? Could I really take off for the east coast if Mom and I still weren't speaking? If our relationship wasn't repaired? And how could I leave if we saved the store? Was there any chance we would save it? Would any of it help? The book clubs, the parties, the readings? Maybe there was no fighting change, and Prospero Books was just another relic of yesterday's Silver Lake, an obsolete store that couldn't adapt. I tried to convince myself it was the hangover talking, the drop in dopamine that followed the rush of tequila, but in the gray morning after, the whole thing seemed impossible.

Very few things indeed were really impossible. Had I forgotten Alice's words so quickly? Billy believed in these words. He wanted me to believe in them, too. I had to try. I had to do everything I could to save Prospero Books.

CHAPTER TWELVE

WITHIN A WEEK, WE HAD FLYERS AND POSTCARDS TACKED TO every corkboard in every coffee shop and public library in Los Feliz, Silver Lake and Echo Park, complete with famous literary quotes and Prospero Books' insignia.

To learn to read is to light a fire. —Victor Hugo

Good friends, good books and a sleepy conscience: this is the ideal life. —Mark Twain

We read to know that we are not alone. —C. S. Lewis

I have always imagined that Paradise will be a kind of library. —Jorge Luis Borges

Once you learn to read, you will be forever free. —Frederick Douglass

I cannot live without books. —Thomas Jefferson

I contributed the last two.

On our front door, Malcolm tacked a poster for our newly

formed book clubs, four in total. One for small presses and debut authors we hoped to lure to the store. One on literary LA, at Malcolm's insistence. One on world literature, at Lucia's. One on the classics, old and new, which at a store named after Shakespeare seemed to go without saying.

We had finalized the details for our gala: Saturday, September 28. Literary costume. Twenty dollars a ticket. Two hundred tickets in total. Tickets alone wouldn't cover the average monthly loss, but it was a start. We'd have a silent auction to account for the rest. Malcolm put calls into a local furniture store, a few salons and bike shops to solicit sponsors. I drafted a press release, which we would send to local newspapers and blogs. Lucia and Charlie commissioned their friends, bartenders and waiters across the east side, urging their bosses to donate free platters and cocktails for the gala, to auction off prix fixe meals. We needed these donations; more so, we needed the support of the neighborhood, the insistence that everyone from the local florist to the clerk at the hardware store couldn't bear to see us close.

Malcolm had a friend who worked at KCRW and managed to get us at fifteen-second spot on the morning music show to advertise Sheila's reading, so long as we agreed to be part of the station's benefits program. While Malcolm scoffed at the words *ten percent off*, the entire arrangement was a win for us. It would introduce a new cast of public radio-listening Angelenos to Prospero Books.

Of course Sheila's reading had to be on Sunday, at 7:00 p.m., smack in the middle of the Brooks Family Cookout. A few days before Sheila's reading, Dad texted one of his orders, and I knew this one was meant as a command: come sunday. When I wrote back, I'll try, he added, make your mother happy. I wanted to write back that she should make me happy, too. Instead, I told him that I'd do my best to make it. I didn't want to imagine what type of command Dad would issue if I texted to tell him

I couldn't come, after all. Besides, the person I really wanted to talk to was Mom.

It had been three weeks since I talked to her. Once, when I'd joined the art teacher as a chaperone on a tenth-grade trip to Italy, Mom and I hadn't talked for a week. She made me promise to email every day, so she wouldn't have to call the American Embassy to make sure I hadn't been abducted, and I reported to her regularly on the students who had snuck wine, others who smelled of cigarettes, the coupling and uncoupling that occurred almost daily resulting in tears and, once, a fist-fight. When I was stateside, she would become nervous after thirty-six hours of not speaking. At forty-eight hours, the nerves bordered on hysteria. I never minded. It was one of the many ways I felt tethered to her. Even when we lived far apart we were integral to each other's lives. Now that I was close, that hold was loosening. It was up to me to do something if I wanted that grip to tighten again.

Mom picked up on the first ring. "Miranda, I'm at the market. They have rhubarb. I'm going to make a pie for Sunday. Do you want it with or without strawberries?"

I paced Billy's living room, searching for the right words. "I'm sorry to do this, but I can't make it on Sunday." I heard her cart squeak to a halt. "It's our first event at the store. It's not really something I can miss."

"Sure, I understand." The cart rolled again.

"Why don't you come? Sheila Crowley is reading." Momentarily, it seemed like the perfect solution. My parents would come to Sheila's reading. Mom would remember Evelyn's version of Prospero Books. She'd point out what had changed, what had remained the same. I would tell her how we planned to reinvigorate and save the store.

"Sheila Crowley?" she said like it was a name she hadn't heard in a long time.

"She has a new memoir out. She had a big bestseller in the '90s."

"I know who she is." She sounded slightly offended, like I'd accused her of being poorly read.

"So you'll come?" I sat on the edge of Billy's couch, eager for her to say yes.

"I already bought fish for dinner."

"So have it Monday."

"We're going to the Conrads on Monday."

"So have it Tuesday." The cartwheels echoed through the speaker.

"It will be bad by Tuesday."

"So freeze it."

"You can't freeze thawed fish. It will ruin the consistency," she said, appalled by the suggestion.

"So throw it out, then. Please, I want you to come." I scrunched my shorts in my fists, waiting for her to stop coming up with excuses, to just say yes.

"I don't want to see that woman again." The words erupted involuntarily. She'd lost her composure, something that rarely happened.

"You know her?"

"We've met," she said, regaining her cool.

"When she and Billy were dating?"

"They weren't..." I waited for her to ask me how I knew they were dating. "That woman was a horrible influence on Billy." She sniffed, jolting herself out of whatever memory she'd drifted into. "Let's plan for next Sunday, all right?"

"Sure, next Sunday," I said, a sinking suspicion that something would come up the following week, too. "Mom?" I asked before she hung up.

"Yes?"

"I miss you."

"I miss you, too." Her voice quavered. "We'll see you next Sunday."

I hung up and sat back on Billy's couch. I wasn't sure how we'd gotten here. Mom knew every doctor's appointment I had, every movie I saw, whenever I finished a book. She was my stream of consciousness. I never filtered anything. I told her everything. When Sam, the class bully who seemed to think *teacher* was another name for potential victim, left a tampon on my desk, slathered in red paint. When I discovered two girls vomiting in the bathroom during lunch, when I caught my favorite student plagiarizing, when I had a strange bump on my arm and I thought I might be dying. It turned out to be a benign cyst, but Mom still flew to Philadelphia for the outpatient surgery. I told her how my teeth smashed Jay's during our first ineloquent kiss, how I wasn't sure I could date someone so off-type. Mom was the first person I confided in. She was my confidante, my adviser, my cheerleader. In turn, I knew when she had a meeting with a new client, when she was trying a new restaurant, when she and Dorothy Conrad were driving to Arizona to go antiquing. I knew the price and quality of each chandelier, each armoire, each vase she bought, but those stories, they weren't benign cysts. They weren't awkward first kisses. They weren't feelings of fraudulence that I wasn't really a good teacher, after all. She told me anecdotes. I told her insecurities. Maybe we couldn't return to what we always were to each other because we'd never been as close as I'd assumed we were. My mother knew everything about me. I hardly knew anything about her at all.

ON THE AFTERNOON OF SHEILA'S READING, JOANIE CAME OVER to get ready before the event. It was the first time I'd seen her since she'd started rehearsals for *The Three Sisters*. She leaned against the dresser in Billy's bedroom, tousling her hair before the mirror and prattling on about a lunch she'd had with the famous actresses who played Masha and Olga, what it was like to dine with a roomful of people covertly watching you.

"My director says it's good I'm getting a taste of it now. A lot of people think they want fame until they have it." Joanie said *director* with a practiced gusto. *My director. My play. My career. My fame.* I hoped this play would be as important as she assumed it was.

She pulled a tube of lipstick out of her bag and waved me toward her. I sat on the edge of the bed as she angled my face toward the light.

"This reading is a good idea. It should definitely bring in a crowd," Joanie said.

"It was all Malcolm. He had it set up before I even got back."

"Sounds like you two are getting along better?" Joanie pressed the waxy lipstick into my lips.

"I seem to have passed some test. Turns out he's not a total asshole, after all." Joanie stepped back to appraise her master-piece, studying me like she understood my thoughts better than I did. "What?"

She used her forefinger to dab more lipstick onto my bottom lip. "Men always think about kissing when they see scarlet lips."

"You're totally off base." She kept smiling in that Joanie way, where neither logic nor facts could dissuade her. "Joanie, I have a boyfriend."

"And how is the good offensive man? Striker? I guess I should learn my soccer positions if this one's sticking around." She capped the lipstick and tossed it into her overflowing purse.

"He plays defense. I don't know what he's going to say when I tell him I won't be back for another six weeks."

"He misses you, is all." Joanie held her phone out, evaluating her appearance in the camera before snapping a selfie. "There's a reason most long-distance relationships don't work out."

"We're not long distance," I said.

Joanie looked like she was about to argue, then decided

against it. I wanted to press her, but I also didn't want to hear why she thought Jay and I wouldn't work out.

"So Sheila's got the next clue?" Joanie asked instead.

"Let's hope so." I opened the top drawer of Billy's dresser and located Sheila's letter.

She paced the bedroom as she read. "'From the first time we fucked on your living room floor'? Oh, my." Joanie wiped her brow as though she was Scarlett O'Hara.

"Keep reading. The key part's at the end."

"'Knowing you has been a great kindness in my life. You will survive this. We both will. And once we have, I'm certain we will see each other again'?" She squinted, trying to parse out its significance.

"Not that part." I grabbed the letter. "'Evelyn's death wasn't your fault, either. You have to believe this, if you ever want to move on.'" Joanie shrugged, not understanding. "Billy thought he was responsible for Evelyn's death."

"It sounds like survivor's guilt to me." Joanie flopped down on the bed, apparently bored with the conversation. "Besides, what does that have to do with his fight with your mom?"

"I'm not sure. My mom shuts down any time I mention Evelyn or Billy."

"What'd she say when you told her about the scavenger hunt?"

"I haven't told her yet." Joanie perked up. "Things are really awkward between us. We're hardly speaking."

"You think that's a good idea?"

"No, but you know my mom. If she doesn't want to talk, you can't make her."

"So you should stop asking her questions she won't answer." I shot her an indignant look, which she matched, mockingly. "You have a good relationship with your mom. I don't see why you'd want to jeopardize that over an uncle you'd pretty much forgotten."

"You're serious?" Joanie had known me through all of Billy's quests, even participating in a few. She'd been there when he'd disappeared. She'd helped me plot my route across LA to find him again. How could she remember all that and think that just because I was stuck, just because Mom and I weren't speaking, that I would give up on the last quest Billy would ever leave for me? "Since when have you advocated for bowing down to anyone?"

"Don't get all bent out of shape. I'm just saying, you're lucky to have a mom who's invested in your life." Growing up, Joanie had spent countless weekends at our house when her mother was off in Hawaii or Santa Barbara with her latest boyfriend. She ate regular dinners with my family when her sisters forgot to pick her up after school. After each leading role in high school, Joanie would find me waiting in the parking lot with flowers. Me and Mom. "Don't throw away your relationship with your mom over this. It's not worth it."

"Well, don't act like you're the expert on the importance of mother-daughter relationships just because you have a shitty one with your mother." Joanie winced, betrayed. "I didn't mean that." I sat on the bed beside her. She turned away from me. "All of a sudden everything between me and my mom feels fake. I want things to be okay, but she's keeping secrets from me."

"They're her secrets," she said coldly. "You don't deserve to know them simply because you're curious."

"They're my family's secrets."

"Why is this so important to you?" Her voice had calmed, but she was still angled away from me.

"After Billy, it was just me and my parents. I never had siblings or grandparents or cousins. I always felt like I was missing out on something. I want to understand why I never had any extended family."

"And you think you'll feel complete if you know why Billy disappeared? Life doesn't work like that, Miranda."

"At least I'll understand my mom better." Joanie nodded and shifted her knees slightly toward me. I shifted my knees toward her until they touched. "I'm really sorry about what I said. How about we trade mothers? I'll take yours, and you can have my mom in the front row at every single performance of *The Three Sisters*?"

"Those tickets are reserved for famous people," she said, still pouting.

"I'm sure she'd settle for the back row." I batted my eyes and did my best to look repentant. "Can you find it in your heart to forgive me?"

Joanie sighed. "You're lucky you're cute."

AT FIVE, WE CLOSED THE CAFÉ EARLY TO GET READY FOR THE reading. Charlie, Joanie and Lucia wiped down tables while Malcolm and I set up a makeshift bar. We were offering wine and beer for a mandatory donation, since we didn't have a liquor license and couldn't risk the cost of a fine. We put out a row of reds and whites, beer bottles, moving to the beat of the music, gliding in and out of each other's periphery. At seven dollars a drink, it wasn't a bad boost for the store. Like all of our endeavors, it was minimal compared to our accumulating debt.

Fans filed in a half hour before Sheila's reading. The bell on the door rang with the arrival of each patron, and every time I heard its chime, I turned, optimistic that Mom had changed her mind, but it was just another young woman clutching one of Sheila's books against her chest. I chided myself for hoping, yet every time I heard the bell, I turned again.

By the time Malcolm was ready to get started, every seat in the café was occupied. Patrons lined the stacks, angling to see the podium in the back of the café. Heads turned as Sheila entered the room. She wore dark sunglasses and a bright shawl, waving hello to a few people as she made her way through the dense crowd. Before I was able to introduce myself, my phone rang. I motioned to Malcolm that I was going upstairs, and he tapped his wrist.

I ducked into the stairs to answer Jay's call. "Hey, I can't talk right now. I'll call you later?"

"I'm going out later," he said coolly.

"Well, what's up? I have a minute or two." I leaned against the banister. It shifted with my weight.

"My mom's getting tickets for the mummy exhibit at the Franklin Institute. It's closing in August, so she wants to buy them now before it sells out."

While a mummy exhibit was right up my alley, I would have tried to get out of it if I were home. Jay's mother was never cold to me; she simply ignored me lest it appear rude. I didn't believe there was anything particular about me she disliked. I was simply an obstacle between her and her son. Now that I had the perfect excuse, I wished I didn't have to use it.

"There's something I've been meaning to talk to you about. I don't think I can get back to Philly until orientation." I bit my lower lip to prevent myself from apologizing.

Jay didn't say anything for too long. "I think I've been pretty patient." I let out an involuntary cough. "Most guys wouldn't let their girlfriends go away all summer."

"I didn't realize I needed your permission to come home," I snapped.

"I know you've never been in a serious relationship before." He had his teacher voice on, his tone intimating that it was all simple if you approached it in the right way. "But when you're committed to someone—"

"Don't you lecture me on being committed. How many Saturday mornings have I froze my ass off to watch you play soccer? How many times have we canceled plans because your mom has a dinner party or an art show or just calls your name and we go running? Do you realize you haven't asked me a single question about Billy or Prospero Books? Don't you dare talk to me about being committed."

"I didn't realize being part of my life was an obligation to you," he said in a different teacher voice, one reserved for disobedient students.

"Oh, fuck you, Jay."

Malcolm popped his head into the staircase. He must have realized I was in the middle of something because his expression quickly shifted from annoyed to apologetic. "It's time," he whispered.

"Jay, I have to go."

"You're unbelievable, you know that? Sure, go. Stay all summer. Stay forever. Do whatever you want, Miranda. It doesn't matter to me anymore."

"Nice. That's real mature of you, Jay. Real fucking mature." I hung up and turned off my phone before Jay had a chance to say anything else.

MALCOLM WAS A MAGNIFICENT ORATOR. HE ANALOGIZED SHEILA'S prose to ballet and quoted Rilke without sounding pretentious. He fit Sheila into a legacy of female writers, including Joan Didion and Susan Sontag. I tried to focus on Malcolm's eloquent introduction, on making eye contact with Sheila so she would recognize me later, but I had too much adrenaline. Did Jay really think this was what I wanted, to be apart all summer, to reconnect with my uncle only after his death, to have fractured my relationship with my mother, to be tasked with the responsibility of saving Prospero Books?

"Her words captivate, inspire and ignite. So, without further ado, the inimitable Sheila Crowley," Malcolm said, concluding his introduction.

Everyone cheered. Malcolm solemnly thanked the crowd, his eyes poring over everyone until they landed on me. He watched me while Sheila kissed his cheek. I smiled at him. I didn't want to be fighting with Jay. I didn't want to be fighting with Mom, either. But I did want this. I wanted to make eye contact with Malcolm; I wanted to listen to Sheila read, to calculate the precise moment to approach her. There was nowhere else I wanted to be.

For twenty minutes, Sheila read about the summer before her mother went to rehab. Sheila was twelve and they lived in a ranch house in Altadena where her mother bred sheepdogs. One of the females was pregnant. Sheila's mother was passed out on the porch, and Sheila had to supervise the birthing. She had a voice like a jazz singer. I could have listened to her for hours. Mom had a voice like a folk singer. I could have listened to her for hours, too, if only she would talk to me.

Sheila finished the chapter, took off her glasses and bowed her head at the applause of her fans. As she began to field questions, the bell on the door chimed. Instead of my parents, Elijah waved to me from the entryway. I waved back, then searched the room for Malcolm, hoping he didn't think I was colluding with *The Vulture*. Malcolm was busy organizing the signing table and fortunately hadn't noticed Elijah's arrival.

"Last question," Malcolm announced, pointing to a tall brunette leaning against the YA section. She looked like a model and, in Los Angeles, she may have been. A rush of jealousy surprised me as I watched Malcolm nod to the prettiest girl in the room. She proceeded to ask Sheila a question about her writing process. Sheila answered curtly, telling the girl there was no magic formula, that every writer has to figure out her own routine. The girl cowered at Sheila's response, and I felt guilty for the pleasure her dejection aroused in me. I glanced over at Malcolm. He'd already moved on from the pretty girl, back to aligning books on the signing table. As Sheila began to gather her things from beneath the podium, I sidled through the tables to intercept her.

"Ms. Crowley?" I asked.

"Malcolm's having everyone line up against the wall," she said without looking up at me.

"I'm Miranda Brooks. Billy's niece."

Sheila smiled widely at me, revealing a sizable gap between her front teeth. "Miranda! I didn't realize you were here." Her face sobered. "I'm so sorry about Billy. When I got here today, I expected to see him, then it hit me all over again."

"I know what you mean."

"You know, I met you once when you were a baby." She closed the copy of her memoir she'd read from. The page was covered in pencil markings, edits to the draft that had already been published.

"Was that when you and Billy were dating?" I tried to sound casual, but my voice betrayed me.

"I'd hardly call what we did dating. Sorry, you probably don't want to hear that."

"I do. I want to hear everything. I haven't seen Billy in years." Sheila indicated to Malcolm that she'd be a second.

"And I want to tell you everything." She patted my hand. "But right now what I really want is a glass of red. I'm going to need it if anyone else asks me about my *process*." When I told her I'd get her a glass, she said, "Maybe bring the whole bottle with you?"

I carried a plastic glass and a mostly full bottle of Malbec to the table where Sheila had situated herself behind a pile of her books and several black Sharpie pens. The line of fans snaked the length of the fiction section, winding its way around History and the recommendations table in the center of the store.

"I think we're going to get along quite well," she said when I poured her a glass.

"I'd really like to talk to you about Billy," I told her.

"Sheila, you ready?" Malcolm said, carrying another pile of her memoirs over to the table.

"Let's meet here for coffee tomorrow?" she suggested, and we arranged a time for the following morning.

"Ms. Crowley?" a young man asked as he approached the table, holding out her memoir. His hair was cut into a mullet and he wore tortoiseshell glasses that made him seem earnest, although I doubted that was the look he was going for. He was one of a few men at the reading. "I was hoping you could sign this for my mom."

Sheila turned to me. "We may need a second bottle."

I watched Sheila sign the boy's book, signaling to the next eager fan that it was her turn. She was efficient without being cold. Fastidious.

Elijah appeared at my side. "You got a good turnout."

"First of many, I hope. It's nice of you to come."

"Of course I came," he said, surprised that I might think he wouldn't. That made it more obvious the other people who should have been there and weren't. "I can't say I agree with your decision to keep the store open, but you are your uncle's niece. Billy would have done the same thing." We stood shoulder-to-shoulder watching the line crawl toward Sheila, "What else have you got planned?"

Elijah nodded along as I explained the book clubs, the other readings, an advertisement we'd put out in *LA Weekly*. I expected him to tell me it was an expense we couldn't afford.

"I know an editor there. I bet we can get a piece about the store." He made a note to ask his secretary to look into it before shaking my hand goodbye. "Good luck to you," he said as though I needed it.

After Elijah disappeared onto Sunset, Malcolm found me against the history section, marveling at the line of women still waiting to meet Sheila. "What did The Vulture want?"

"Actually, he offered to help."

"You've made an ally of our foe," he said, impressed.

"I seem to have that effect on people."

Malcolm winked at me before dashing back to Sheila and the steady line of readers hoping for personalized inscriptions.

It was nearly midnight by the time we had the chairs stacked on the tables, the floor swept clean. Sheila waved goodbye as Malcolm escorted her onto Sunset. I'd hoped she might have a renewed energy after the last customer lingered out with her signed hardback, but Sheila had turned to Malcolm, her lips lined in red wine, and pronounced she'd never been so tired in her entire life. As if to prove her point, she collapsed against Malcolm as he helped her outside.

Once I was alone, I turned my phone back on, certain I'd have heard from Jay. He would apologize in an emoji I'd never seen before or leave a rambling voice mail where he'd call me all sorts of cruel names, and in his madness I'd see how much he desired me. I had one text from Joanie. Sorry I had to run out. Sheila's totes amazing. Let me know what she says about Billy!

I walked alone upstairs to Billy's apartment, hugging my sweater against my chest, warding off the cold that had collected in the stairway from the back door, propped open all night. I loved how nights in LA had a bite to them no matter how hot the days were. It reminded me that despite the lawns and urban blocks, the free-flowing water from the tap, Los Angeles was a desert, arid and stubborn. I almost called Joanie to tell her about my fight with Jay, but I didn't want her to reaffirm her theory about long distance, to confirm my suspicion that something had transpired we couldn't undo. I didn't want her to try to convince me that I was overreacting, either. I considered calling Mom. She would have grown quiet in that concerned way where she thought I'd made a mistake yet refused to say so. I wanted Mom powerfully in that moment. But whoever I would get, it wasn't the Mom I wanted. So, I kept climbing the stairs, to my dead uncle's apartment, protecting myself from the cold, and for the moment that had to be enough.

CHAPTER THIRTEEN

SHEILA WAS AN HOUR LATE FOR OUR COFFEE DATE. I'D WOKEN at dawn, too animated for sleep. Jay still hadn't called, but I wasn't thinking about him. As I lay awake in Billy's bed, waiting for the familiar sounds of Charlie cranking up the gate, of the grinder hammering beans, I could only think of the story Sheila was going to tell me. She had to know what happened to Evelyn, if her death was somehow Billy's fault.

At ten minutes after we were supposed to meet, I bussed tables to distract myself from the fear that she'd forgotten. At twenty after the hour, I persuaded a girl to buy a memoir I'd never heard of, its metaphorical title revealing little about the book's subject. When the clock finally hit thirty minutes late, I admitted to myself that Sheila wasn't coming, that the wine had been abundant and she was probably still in bed. Thirty minutes later, she burst into the store.

"I had an emergency this morning. It's no excuse, but that's why I'm late."

"It's fine," I assured her, relieved that she'd turned up at all. I found her a cup of tea, and we settled into the table along the back wall, the most private, which oddly made it the least desirable to our customers.

She grabbed my hand. "It's not okay. My mom was always late. She showed up to my high school graduation after I got my diploma." Sheila dropped my hand. "You'll have to forgive me. I've been so embedded in the past I'm having trouble extricating myself."

Mom had never been late to any event in my entire life, but someone was missing from my graduation. I hadn't seen Billy in over six years at that point, and still I'd wanted him to see me walk across the stage. Did Mom want him there, too? Had she noticed his absence not only at my graduation, but at every big event that had passed without him: her fiftieth birthday, the anniversary of their mother's death, of Evelyn's?

"Miranda? Did I lose you?" Sheila asked.

"Sorry, you got me thinking about my mom."

"How is Susan?"

"She's good." My automatic response. "Actually, I don't know. I haven't talked to her in a while." I waited for Sheila to offer me some sage advice about mothers, despite the fact that I hardly knew her. When she didn't, I asked her, "You and Billy were friends for a long time?"

"We met in the mid-'80s. In grief counseling. We both left rather quickly for our own reasons." Sheila said that everything about group had exhausted her. Even its name, Grief United, as though losses could be shared. "Fragments of pain aren't like pieces of a puzzle." She blew into her mug, creating waves across the jasmine surface. "They can't fit together to form something grander. Knowing that others, that strangers, suffered, too, it didn't make me feel less alone."

Sheila said no one made her feel less alone, not her sister, her friends, her therapist, not even her aging Labrador, who trudged around the house, searching for Daniel. If Daniel's own dog couldn't make Sheila feel less alone, she didn't see how a group of depressed middle-aged widows could help her resolve her grief. She saw her sadness that way, as something that could be reduced but never vanquished.

"Refill?" Lucia asked, extending a carafe of coffee toward me. I held my cup to her without looking up. Lucia watched us, wary of our intensity. She tiptoed to another table.

"So why'd you go, if you didn't think it would help?" I asked.

"Same reason as Billy. I promised my sister."

For the first week, Sheila had listened without speaking. The group leader, Pamela, had given them an assignment to visit somewhere important to their loved ones. As the group discussed their beloveds' favorite places, Sheila imagined that she had gone to Muscle Beach. Daniel liked to watch the men bench press. It calmed him. It reminded him that he didn't need to grow his muscles to feel safe. Sheila wondered if something else had given him strength, whether he'd still be alive. Sheila had expected group to be more like the AA meetings she'd attended with her mother, counting the days since their loved ones had died to gauge their progress. This group kept their beloveds alive. They didn't suppress them like addictive desires.

"Malcolm," Sheila shouted suddenly. "The table's clean." I swung around to find Malcolm wiping the pristine table beside us, covertly listening to our conversation. "We're trying to have a conversation here." She and Malcolm held each other's gaze until he relented and cleaned a table that was actually dirty. "He's so nosy," Sheila said to me.

From my experience, Malcolm generally left people alone. If he was listening to our conversation, my interest in Sheila or her interest in me must have unnerved him. Maybe he was even afraid Sheila would tell me something he hadn't.

"Come on." Sheila stood. "Too many spying eyes. Besides, I'm in need of a walk."

I followed her out of Prospero Books. We stood on the corner outside the store, waiting for the walk sign to light up. I turned back. Malcolm was standing at the picture window, watching us leave.

The light changed, and I followed Sheila across the street. I wondered if Malcolm was still watching us. I liked to think he was, his eyes trailing me until we were out of sight.

"I'm thinking of getting one of those walking desks," Sheila said as she unlocked a Prius parked outside the coffee bar. "Hemingway used to stand when he wrote, not that I think I'm Hemingway."

She opened the driver-side door.

"I thought you said we were walking."

"Don't you know in LA you have to drive in order to walk anywhere?" Sheila smiled deviously.

I got in the passenger side and Sheila pulled into traffic on Sunset. We passed a diner that had been renovated to look like the old lunch counter it had replaced, an old church that had survived the changing neighborhood, the desolate stretch of Sunset between Silver Lake and Echo Park.

"I'll give it to Pamela," Sheila said, tugging the wheel like she was driving in a video game. "Her assignments were really thoughtful."

For the next assignment, Pamela had asked them to do something their beloveds had always wanted, but had never gotten to do. Then they visited their beloveds' favorite museums, listened to their favorite music, read their favorite books. While the pain didn't go away, Sheila looked forward to the meetings, to the ways she could share Daniel.

Sheila turned onto Park Avenue and parked by the lake. At the center of Echo Lake, fountains shot water toward the sky, bisecting downtown's skyline. Yellow paddleboats puttered in the blue waters, careful to avoid the beds of lotuses.

"The lake didn't used to be this blue." I followed Sheila through the grass where couples and homeless men lounged. "It wouldn't have been able to hide the bodies."

We followed the sandy path around the north side of the lake. Sheila said she'd remained the group's newest member for two months, which she'd liked. It had prioritized her voice. But before long, a new mourner had arrived.

Billy anxiously walked into the airless hall where group met, wearing a dirty white undershirt and faded jeans. Sheila might have mistaken him for a homeless man, had it not been for his watch. Matte black dial. Steel. Rolex.

I've been staying with my sister and her husband since it happened, Billy explained to the group, fiddling with the face of his expensive watch. The group had enough experience with *it* that they didn't ask who had died, how *it* had happened. *I'm starting to scare them. And the baby.*

"You, dear," she explained. The baby didn't feel like me. It was a time before I had my own memories, a time when I had to rely on my mother's. Now, I could trust Sheila's version of the past instead.

Why do you think you're scaring them? Pamela asked.

They stop talking each time I enter the room. The baby cries every time I go near her.

Those who love us often don't know how to help us, Pamela said. *We have to help ourselves first.*

I'm not sure I can, Billy said.

You have to try, Pamela said.

For the next several weeks, Billy remained silent, hands folded in his lap, erratically tapping his foot as the others shared their beloveds' favorite words, their most embarrassing possessions, as they gave away the clothes they'd always hated. Part of Pamela's strategy was to awaken forgotten moments, to abandon distractions. *Less is more,* she advised, reminding Sheila of writing teachers. During these sessions, Billy never spoke, never brought any mementos of his beloved. Sheila didn't even know who had died.

"It might sound odd," Sheila said. "But Pamela's whole thing was to focus on the memories. We knew the intimate details of the dead, the way their feet smelled and how they snorted when they laughed, but we never told each other how they died. I was glad for that. It might have turned into a morbid competition if I thought someone else's husband had a more painful death than my Daniel did."

No one in the group mentioned the cancer that ravaged their beloveds' bodies, the fatal car crashes, the heart attacks. Still, they talked. Only Billy sat there, mute. Distant.

I don't think it's right, Sheila had overheard one woman whispering to the others as they waited for Pamela to unlock the door. *Each week we pour our hearts out and he just sits there.*

He makes me uncomfortable, a potbellied man agreed. *I don't like talking in front of him.*

During the session, Sheila watched Billy, trying to determine what about him unnerved the group. When the potbellied man held up an olive-green scarf, unraveling at its center, Billy didn't look up. The man explained it was the first and only thing his wife had ever knit. Billy didn't chuckle at the story. He continued to study the face of his watch, counting the minutes until he could leave. Sheila realized that was what scared the group. Pamela's tactics weren't reaching Billy. They might never reach him.

Each week, Sheila watched Billy, wondering why he kept coming. Sheila saw the sleek car that pulled up to the stucco building at the end of each session, how Billy hopped in the passenger seat like a child being picked up from school. Of course. The power of sisters. The fear of their disappointment.

Sheila continued to watch Billy, feeling a pull toward him that it took her weeks to identify as sexual attraction. It was unlike the desire she'd felt for the stranger she'd taken home from a bar or the fellow writer whom she'd allowed to seduce her at a conference. Billy existed for two hours a week. She could linger over his lovely eyes, she could admire the softness of his lips, emboldened by the fact that she would never act on her desire.

Then Billy came in too distressed not to talk.

He's actually suing me, he told the group. *He doesn't need the money. Why is he doing this to me?*

"Evelyn's father?" I remembered Elijah saying that Evelyn's father had sued Billy over her estate.

Sheila nodded and continued her story.

People grieve in different ways, Pamela said, watching Billy pace. The group fidgeted. They were supposed to be sharing their beloveds' favorite foods. Instead, Billy had been talking breathlessly for half the meeting about his wife's father, how he was suing Billy for their home, for Prospero Books.

He doesn't even read, Billy screamed. *What's he going to do with a bookstore?*

A bald man stood. *If he's going to keep going on like this, I'm leaving.*

Billy stared at him, confused. *I listen to you talk about your wife's needlepoint. Her calligraphy. Her homemade jam. I think you can do me the same respect and let me say my piece.*

Those were assignments. Where is your favorite food? Did you bring anything?

There's an order to this, a woman dressed in earth tones said.

And how is that working for you? Billy asked. *Does all this make you feel better?*

Okay, let's take a step back, Pamela intervened. *Billy, why don't we let someone else share?*

After my husband passed, his mom tried to take our dog away. Sheila didn't realize she was talking until everyone turned to look at her. *She didn't even like dogs, but she wanted to shift some of her suffering onto me. You have to feel sorry for him, that he's too afraid to face his grief head-on.*

Billy watched her. The air between them electrified. The room dissolved. Time stopped. Through their gaze, they relayed everything they wanted to do to each other.

Would anyone like some cake? a woman in cashmere said, breaking the silence. She shifted the birthday cake she was holding in her lap.

That's a great idea, Pamela said.

"It was incredible how Billy unhinged everyone." We passed the boathouse café where couples shared sandwiches and glass bottles of soda.

Thank you, Billy said to Sheila as they walked out of the meeting. *You seem to be the only person in there capable of thinking for herself.*

I don't think that's fair, Sheila said.

I don't very much feel like being fair, Billy said.

"I'll never forget the next meeting. They hadn't wanted him there, but they were irate when he quit. They were jealous, really. He had the conviction to follow himself."

He has the audacity not to show? the bald man had said. *He berates me, then doesn't even turn up.*

We can't control those around us, Pamela advised, *only ourselves.* The group nodded. Sheila heard a familiar dogma, similar to religion, similar to AA.

After that meeting, Sheila couldn't go back to Grief United. She wasn't sure whether Billy had ruined group for her or if he had made her realize what she already knew—Pamela's tactics were helpful to a point but redundant in the end. She was ready to move on to the next stage of grief.

"I didn't expect to hear from him again," Sheila said as we rounded the corner of the lake nearest the highway. We could hear the cars idling in traffic above, smell the sourness of their exhaust. "But a few weeks later, he left a message on my machine."

They met at a café on Main Street in Santa Monica where Sheila often wrote. Billy was wearing a collared shirt, tucked into khakis. Sheila wore a black tunic over equally dark pants. Her hair was wild and frizzy. Since Daniel died, she'd stopped dyeing it. When she spotted Billy, she wished she'd put on tinted moisturizer, lined her eyes with a little color. Instead, she looked tired and old. Billy looked young and composed.

There was a deposition this morning, Billy said. *It's such bullshit, but my lawyer says I have to take it seriously. The more disagreeable I am, the longer this will go on.* Billy explained that Evelyn's father was a conservative man who had tried to shape Evelyn into someone she wasn't, who still aimed to control her, even in death. *He can have the house and the cabin, I don't care about that. The bookstore, he's never even been there. I don't know what I'd do if I lost that piece of her.*

You won't. Sheila put her hand on his. She did this without thinking. When she was about to pull back, Billy rested his other hand on top of hers. *I know it's difficult, but you can't give in. If you let him have any of the life that belonged to you and your wife, it validates his anger.*

But her death was my fault, Billy insisted. *He's right to blame me.*

"How was Evelyn's death Billy's fault?" I interrupted.

"It wasn't. That was his grief talking."

"You're sure?"

"Trust me. We all blame ourselves."

"Did he tell you what happened to her?" My pulse raced.

"He never offered, I never asked. That's what enabled us to connect. We didn't need to know what happened."

Sheila continued to describe their first date, if you could call it that. They finished their tea, and wandered down to the beach. It was a clear day, and they could see up the coast to Malibu. Cold waves crashed against their bare calves. When they reached the pier, Billy took hold of Sheila's hand.

Evelyn liked walking on the beach, Billy told Sheila.

Daniel hated the beach. Relaxation made him anxious, Sheila said.

After their walk, they drove across town to Billy's house in Pasadena. The house was white and colonial, large enough for a family of six, but Billy lived there alone. He led Sheila upstairs to a guest room.

"Honey, are you sure you want to hear this part?" Sheila asked. She found an empty patch of grass beneath the thick trunk of a palm tree.

"I have the powers of disassociation." I lay on the grass, staring up at the fronds rustling in the wind. At ground level, the air was calm.

After that night, Sheila and Billy met at her house and his. They went to hotels, parking lots, bathrooms. Sheila didn't mention the affair to her therapist. She assumed Billy didn't, either, if he still visited his doctor. She wasn't sure. As they came to know each other's bodies, they spoke less about their lives.

Sheila was surprised when Billy invited her to his sister's for dinner.

Are you sure that's a good idea?

Why wouldn't it be?

Sheila could account for a dozen reasons why it would be a bad idea, yet she told Billy she would go. She put on a white dress that hugged her waist and hid her stomach. But white was the color of brides, of youth, so she selected a black dress instead. This was the color of mourning. She decided on chartreuse, hoping it would be the perfect compromise.

It wasn't. The dress clashed with the many shades of pink that overwhelmed our house.

"Even you were wearing pink," Sheila said.

Susan hugged Sheila and pretended she'd heard so much about her, though Sheila knew Billy had mentioned little.

David should be home any minute. He needed to run to the office. Susan threw her hands in the air to suggest nonchalance, but Sheila could envision the argument that would commence once the guests were gone and the baby—"You," she emphasized— was in her crib. *I don't know if Billy told you, I'm a huge fan.*

Susan made wine spritzers. Billy drank his too quickly.

Take it easy, Billy. No one's going to take it away from you, Susan said.

It's a spritzer. Billy finished the glass. *How about a real drink?*

Sheila and Susan waited for Billy to apologize. Instead, he took a flask out of his blazer and filled the wineglass with clear liquid.

The sound of gravel under the tires broke the women's spell. David walked through the door in an expensive suit. He kissed Susan, then greeted Sheila.

Ms. Crowley, I'm sorry I'm late. Sheila remembered that he had a firm grip.

Throughout dinner, Susan spoke too much. She gave a synopsis of each of Sheila's novels. Her experiences in New York had been similar to the protagonist's in *Downtown Eleanor*. When the baby fussed— "I mean you," Sheila said. "When you fussed. Sorry, dear. I'm having trouble connecting the sophisticated woman before me to that tiny little creature bawling her eyes out. I've never been particularly fond of children."

"It's fine," I assured her. No one had ever called me sophisticated before. Kooky, certainly. Overzealous, for sure. But sophisticated? Not on my life. "It's not like I remember being a baby, anyway."

When the baby fussed, Susan interrupted herself to rock the cradle. Otherwise, she continued to detail the club from Sheila's first novel, where Eleanor first sang, how it looked a lot like the club where Susan had performed with the Lady Loves. Billy sat at the far end of the table, almost as if he weren't there.

After dinner, David and Billy retired to David's home office.

David's helping Billy with the lawsuit, Susan told Sheila as they cleared the table. The baby started to cry. Susan put down the stack of plates and indicated to Sheila she'd be right back.

So that's still going on? Sheila asked, gathering the napkins. Susan sat down and started to unhook her nursing bra.

Do you mind? she asked Sheila, who stated that she did not. Susan positioned the baby's head, trying to get her to latch. Sheila knew she should turn away, but the baby's constant squirming, how she was hungry yet refused nourishment, fascinated her.

"I was difficult even then," I joked.

"There are worse things than being difficult," Sheila said.

Susan switched breasts, cooing until the baby surrendered. *Evelyn's father is relentless. He always disapproved of Billy, even in high school. Can you imagine, your wife dies in a terrible accident and you have to keep living it over and over again in depositions. It's hard not to feel like it's vindictive.*

I sat up too quickly. Red dots floated in my periphery. "Evelyn's death was an accident?"

"I remember your mom calling it that, 'a terrible accident.'"

I imagined Billy and Evelyn driving down a slippery road, the dark night, the car or tree they couldn't see. "My parents told me she died of a seizure. I can't believe they lied."

"For years, until my memoir was published, I told people that Daniel died at home. We all craft euphemisms to hide behind," she said, defending them. "I remember your mom was really upset. She started pacing with you in her arms, rocking you so aggressively I was worried she might drop you."

I wish this would end, Susan said. *David says it could go on for another few years. I don't know how Billy can move on with this lawsuit still pending.*

Sheila wiped the food scraps onto one plate and stacked the others beneath it.

How's he seem? Susan asked, returning the baby to the crib. She followed Sheila into the kitchen. *I try to talk to him, but he never says anything.*

Sheila hesitated. *Maybe you aren't asking the right questions.*

Everything I say is wrong. I feel like I'm in training for when Miranda's a teenager.

You want him to get over it. It's not that easy. Some people take longer than others.

Susan balled a towel and began wringing it absentmindedly. *I don't know what else to do. I want Evelyn back, too.* Susan wiped the same square of countertop repeatedly and Sheila understood what Billy couldn't.

"She was grieving," Sheila said.

I pictured Mom in the kitchen when I first returned to LA, scrubbing the counter, the muffin pan, anything within her reach. "My mom can be difficult to read."

"No, Billy didn't want to see it. He wanted to feel like he was the only one who deserved to mourn Evelyn."

Sheila watched Susan wipe the same square of countertop until Billy stormed into the kitchen.

I'm not feeling well, he said to Sheila.

David raced in behind him. *Bill, don't walk out on me. I'm trying to help.*

Billy grabbed Sheila's hand and pulled her to the door. Sheila tried to thank my parents for a lovely time, but Billy was tugging her too forcefully.

Neither of them said anything on the drive to her house. Billy stopped the car in the driveway. He didn't unbuckle his seat belt.

So you're going to shut me out, too, now?

I need to be alone.

Billy, they want to be there for you. You need to try.

You sound like her. Billy snorted.

You need to let people in. Eventually, they'll stop trying to find you.

Sheila had several friends who'd called her for months after Daniel died. She'd ignored the phone, erased their messages. The calls dwindled until they stopped completely. She was too embarrassed now to reach out to them.

"We kept seeing each other." Sheila dug her heel into the soft sod. "But it was never the same. I don't even remember when it stopped."

In my back pocket, I found the letter and handed it to her.

Sheila read the letter. "I can't believe he kept this." She tried to hand it back to me.

"Keep it."

Sheila held the letter for a moment before putting it in her purse. "That means a lot to me. Thank you." She peeked at her watch. "I've completely lost track of the time." She gathered her things.

"So Billy never told you what happened to Evelyn? Not even when you reconnected?"

"I know it sounds weird. The less someone talks about a tragedy, the worse you know it is. When we reconnected, I think he needed me not to ask him."

"How did you and Billy get back in touch?"

"Prospero Books." Sheila grabbed my hand. "I'm so glad you're here."

I followed Sheila back to her car.

"You go," I said. "I'm going to walk back."

"But it's over two miles." Sheila shook her head at herself. "I don't know when I became so LA."

"Did Billy give you anything for me?" I asked as she stepped into the car.

"Like what?"

"I'm not sure exactly. You'd know if it was for me, though."

Sheila frowned and shook her head. She waved goodbye as her Prius merged into traffic around the lake. I walked toward Sunset, turning onto the main thoroughfare of Echo Park. There was only one reason you would hide a terrible accident— if it was someone's fault. What had Billy done? Was he drunk? In some other way negligent? And why would Mom keep that from me now? I walked past the old theater that had become a vegan-friendly restaurant. Sheila should have had something to give me. Billy wouldn't have broken the pattern he'd created. He must have assumed she'd tell me about the accident, something that would lead me toward the next clue. I followed Sunset through the stretch where there were no storefronts, no other pedestrians, only steep sandy cliffs harboring the road. I thought about what Sheila said, how we create euphemisms for tragedy to shield ourselves from the pain. Maybe Mom wasn't trying to keep Billy's actions a secret. Maybe she really couldn't return to the scene of Evelyn's death, to pick at the scab time had hardened. Sheila had said that Billy had refused to acknowledge Mom's loss. Was I doing the same thing? Was Mom closing herself off to me because I wasn't willing to listen, really listen?

"Sweetheart." Mom answered the phone as though this was our regular daily call, like there was never a doubt I'd be calling her today. "We're just headed to the movies. Can I call you later?"

"I'm sorry. I wanted to tell you—I'm really sorry I haven't been more considerate of your feelings. I can't imagine how hard this has been for you," I said.

"Miranda, we're running late. Let me call you later, all right?" She hung up before I could respond.

I held the phone in my hand as I continued down Sunset, certain she would call back. I walked past the old burger place that was now a brick oven pizzeria and the empty chess tables behind the derelict donut shop, which Malcolm had said were once an institution of the east side. My phone would ring any moment. She would apologize for rushing off the phone, then I would say, "No, I'm the one who's sorry," and she would say, "No, I am," and we would laugh, and in our laughter we would begin to heal. I clutched my phone all the way back to Prospero Books. It grew wet from my clammy hand, but Mom didn't call back.

CHAPTER FOURTEEN

SHEILA AND I BEGAN TO SEE EACH OTHER REGULARLY. WE WOULD meet for an early morning hike in Griffith Park before the day grew too hot. Although her English cottage sat at the base of the park, we'd hop in her Prius and drive up to Ferndale or Crystal Springs, supporting her theory that, at least in Sheila's LA, you had to drive in order to walk anywhere.

During our meet-ups, I pressed her on Evelyn's death. Sheila had given me a vital detail—Evelyn's death was a terrible accident—but little else to go on.

"You're sure Billy didn't leave you something to give to me?" I asked as we marched across the lawn beside the old, abandoned zoo. "That's the way this works. *Alice in Wonderland* led me to Billy's doctor, who led me to *Frankenstein*, which led me to his physicist friend, who led me to *Fear of Flying* and you."

Sheila smiled as she caught her breath. "Billy always knew I fancied myself a disciple of Erica Jong." She motioned me to keep walking.

"You didn't get any strange packages in the mail? Something you may have accidentally thrown out? Nothing from Billy's lawyer?"

"I'm sure if Billy had sent me the next clue, he would have

made if obvious enough that I wouldn't have thrown it away."
We wound our way around tan hills, Sheila setting a steady
pace despite her labored breath.

"And there haven't been any rumors around Prospero Books
about Evelyn? How she died?"

"There's been at least a generation of patrons since Evelyn
died. I don't think any of the regulars even know there was an
Evelyn."

"Except you," I said.

"Except me."

"And Malcolm?"

"I don't know what Malcolm knows." Her voice had no
hesitation to it, no cageyness. Whatever Malcolm was keeping
from me, Sheila wasn't in on it.

We continued our climb toward Amir's Garden, finding a
bench that overlooked the square buildings of Glendale. Cacti
grew in wild formations around us, stretching and twisting
toward the sky, not quite tall enough to block the man-made
masses in our periphery.

"Quite the view." Sheila wiped sweat from her forehead.

We sat on the bench, trying to cool down. Every time I
started to get up, she said, "Let me sit here one more minute,"
so I settled onto the bench, taking in the little bit of shade the
cacti offered, and confessed Prospero's money problems. I told
her how each month Billy had flushed his own savings into the
store, the financial equivalent of scooping a bucket of water
out of a sinking ship. I detailed the calendar we'd put together
with first-time authors and other writers we'd lured away from
readings at other bookstores around LA, about our new rewards
program, the small bump in sales from the KCRW piece adver-
tising her reading. I explained our plans for the gala, the donations we'd lined up, the tickets we hadn't sold. I tried to sound
upbeat as I listed our programming for the upcoming months,

but my tone revealed my skepticism, my fear that Prospero Books really could go bankrupt.

"Prospero Books can't close. I've got lots of rich friends. Let's gouge them at your gala." Sheila agreed to send them personalized invitations with promises of a reading from her current project—unfinished, something she always advised other writers not to do—and an auction of a one-on-one meal with her, even though they were her friends and could dine with her whenever they desired.

I told Sheila I had to go back to Philadelphia in late August, whether Prospero was likely to stay open or not. I wasn't even certain I would be able to come back for the gala.

"I just hope I have an apartment to go home to," I said. Jay and I hadn't spoken since our fight. Not on the phone. Not over text, either.

Sheila put her sweaty hand on mine. "Honey, don't you know men become children when their egos are bruised? You have to fawn over him a little, let him think he's in control. It's really very simple."

"Aren't you supposed to be giving me some empowered, don't-take-any-shit type of message?"

"There's a time and a place. If you want to be with him, you need to let him be right. That's important, learning how to let someone else be right even when they're wrong. God, when did I become someone who gives life lessons?" She made a sour face, disappointed in herself. It may have been good advice, but I was right. I didn't want to pretend that he was. I didn't want my relationship to depend on me bowing down to him.

"Well." Sheila stood. "This hike isn't going to finish itself."

As we sidestepped down the stairs carved into the side of the hill, I continued to talk, turning the conversation to Mom. I told Sheila that I was ready to let Mom be right, but just because I was ready to listen didn't mean she was ready to talk.

"We've never been this way before," I said. It was going on a month since I'd seen her.

"I remember that time when your mom stops being a parent and becomes a person," she said as we crossed the road toward the parking lot. "It's difficult seeing parents for who they are rather than who we want them to be."

"I don't know who my mom is. I'm not sure I ever really have."

"Then you should try to get to know her," Sheila offered.

As close as we were, there was always a part of Mom I could never know. I identified it as her former life, her faded promise of stardom. I never understood why she gave all that up. I never understood how she'd wanted it in the first place. I assumed she always regretted that she didn't end up with the career she'd envisioned, but maybe the shadow that followed her wasn't her aborted dreams. Maybe that shadow was Billy. Evelyn.

BY LATE JULY, THE STORE WAS STILL IN PEAK SALES BEFORE THEY promised to bottom out in August. Even with that extra income, after the daily operating costs, the payroll and taxes, the utilities, the mortgage, the line of credit, Prospero Books was still firmly in the red.

Charlie held our first book club meeting, *Where'd You Go, Bernadette*, which had recently come out in paperback. He sat with a handful of women in their early twenties, discussing the unique structure of the novel, the role of technology and email in contemporary literature. I counted at least three girls I'd never seen before. Their eyes darted to and from Charlie as they tried not to be too obvious about why they'd joined the book club. Whether it was for Charlie or Maria Semple, that was three books we otherwise wouldn't have sold, three new customers who would come to the next book club meeting, if only to spend more time with its leader.

That Sheila didn't have the next clue ready and waiting, gift-wrapped and addressed to me, didn't mean I was going to squander what time I had left. I had a month until I had to be back for orientation. Every year, we went to a motel in the Poconos that my principal's in-laws owned. We'd sit around a campfire, sharing stories from break. I could recite from memory the locations of the beachfront properties my colleagues rented every summer along the Jersey Shore. The sunburns, the Dippin' Dots. Humid nights on the boardwalk. What would I tell them in turn about my summer in Los Angeles? How peaceful late afternoons were in Prospero Books? The ins and outs of the daily bookkeeping and inventory checks required to run a bookstore? Would I tell them about Dr. Howard and his savant ability to recite Erica Jong and Edgar Allan Poe? About befriending the legendary Sheila Crowley, the hikes we took each morning? I didn't want the English teacher to ask me for book recommendations, the math teacher to say, *That's so interesting*, the way he purported to find everything interesting, even his students' wrong answers. I told myself I would feel differently once I returned, once Jay's arm was around me as we sat by the campfire, once the life I had chosen was mine again, but as I thought about that motel in the mountains, Prospero Books didn't sound like a summer job.

Since Sheila couldn't tell me what happened to Evelyn, I tried the patrons of Prospero Books.

"Evelyn?" Ray the screenwriter asked. "Evelyn Ward?"

"No, Billy's wife, Evelyn Weston."

"Billy was married?" He shoved his glasses up the bridge of his nose, eager for a bit of gossip.

"A long time ago," I said. "She opened Prospero Books. You've never heard anything about her?"

"I always thought Lee was the original owner."

The other regulars weren't any more helpful. The teenagers who savored their mochas each afternoon stared at me with the same skepticism I received from my students when I asked them if they remembered who Andrew Johnson was. "You mean the old guy who died?" the teenagers deigned to respond when I asked them about Prospero Books' owner. The young mothers were too busy cleaning up milk their toddlers had knocked over to have noticed anything amiss in Prospero Books. The writers wore oversize headphones, blocking them off from the world outside. Even Lucia looked at me like I spent too much time with my nose in novels.

"An accident?" she said as she bussed a table. "Here, in Prospero Books?"

"I don't know where. I just know she died in a terrible accident," I explained.

Lucia shook her head emphatically. "If something like that happened, I'd know about it." She grabbed a bus tub and brought it into the kitchen. I thought tragedy lived in a place like old smells, never fully faded, but no one in Prospero Books seemed to know anything about Evelyn. No one except Sheila, who had respected Billy's privacy too much to ask him what had happened, and Malcolm, who knew more than he intimated.

I turned toward Malcolm. He was sitting with a circle of men, an open bottle of whiskey between them as they swapped tales of hunting and brushes with death, copies of Hemingway's *Green Hills of Africa* resting in their laps. I counted two plaid-shirted, brass-belt-buckled men I didn't recognize. Charlie brought in the giggling girls. Malcolm brought in the brooding men. He pantomimed his hunting stance as he described his communion with a buck, how their eyes had locked before he pulled the trigger. His story was grandiose, flourished with details that couldn't possibly be true, the buck's snarl, his grinding teeth, a bead of sweat dripping from Malcolm's brow onto the rifle below. He was a charlatan. A sweet talker. And he was good at it. He could bring these stoic men to the edge of their chairs. He could cajole me, too, feeding me tales of Billy's uncanny ability to know what art books to buy, distracting me with whiskey and biographies of JFK.

"Have you ever really shot a deer?" I asked Malcolm after the lumberjacks left.

"Of course not," he said, capping the bottle of whiskey on the table.

"So you lied to those men?" The humor fell from his face. It wasn't the most persuasive way of getting him to talk to me, but I was frustrated with Sheila for not having the next clue, with Jay for not calling or texting, with the regulars for not exploring the history of the place they supposedly loved, with Prospero Books for hiding secrets, with Malcolm for being so good at keeping those secrets, too. Billy was his best friend, and everything about Billy was because of Evelyn. Malcolm had to know about her. He simply had to.

"We were just bullshitting," he said matter-of-factly. He returned the chairs, collected in a circle, to their respective tables. "What's up with you? You're acting weird. Weirder than usual."

"You said you spent every day with Billy?" His lovely eyes widened as he waited for me to get to the point. "And there's nothing he ever said to you that you want to share with me?"

He sighed. "What do you want me to say? I'm sorry if it's hard for you to hear, but Billy never talked about you. I didn't know you existed until you showed up here."

"Until I showed up at the funeral." I straightened one of the chairs he'd haphazardly pushed into the table. "You saw me at the funeral."

"I don't really remember much about the funeral." He held on to the back of a chair, rocking it gently.

"Too much whiskey?" It came out crueler than I'd meant.

"No. Jesus, Miranda. I'd just lost my friend." Malcolm threw the chair into the table. "Some things aren't about you." He grabbed the whiskey bottle and stormed behind the front desk. I watched him from across the room. His eyes glazed over as he retreated into himself. I felt like an asshole. Callous and selfish. Each day, Malcolm arrived at the store to me instead of Billy.

Each day, he had to face anew that Billy was gone, that Prospero Books might soon be gone, too. I don't know why it took me so long to understand. Malcolm wasn't keeping secrets from me. He was mourning.

MY FAILURES IN BILLY'S QUEST SEEMED IN DIRECT PROPORTION to the gains we were making with the gala. I'd interviewed every regular, scanned every local newspaper, torn apart every drawer upstairs and down, without finding any evidence of Evelyn, but we'd secured three additional readings for the big event. Malcolm contacted the publicist of a debut novel he'd loved. The writer lived in San Francisco and agreed to drive down to Prospero Books for the night. One of Lucia's friends, a DJ of some renown, had offered to do short sets between the readings. Malcolm and I agreed that the EDM should be saved for after hours, once Sheila's friends, the likes of Dr. Howard and whoever else had enough money to bid on the silent auction, had called it a night. It was just about the only thing we were agreeing upon. Malcolm's sentences had quickly resumed their brevity, talking to me only when necessary. I missed our communion more than I'd expected, but Malcolm held on to his injury like it appreciated in value the longer he retained it. He was being petty with his one-word answers, his pretending not to hear me when I spoke to him. It didn't encourage me to apologize to him, even if I knew I was wrong to doubt his grief, to make it about me.

With our Scotch sessions coming to an abrupt halt and the division of labor split neatly in half, Malcolm and I inhabited independent roles in the store. He stayed behind the front desk, ringing up customers and ordering books. I kept to the shelves and the café, filing books that came in, taking down others that didn't sell. As I was packing up a box to return to the distributor, Sheila barreled into the store, emphatically waving an envelope in her right hand. I rested the book I was holding on the shelf and ran over to her.

"Look what turned up in the mail this morning!" She handed me a standard number-ten envelope, PB written in place of a return address. It had been postmarked and processed the day before, in the 90005 zip code of Los Angeles. Hancock Park, my phone told me, where Elijah worked. I wondered why he'd waited so long after her reading to send it to Sheila.

I tore open the envelope, and Sheila leaned over my shoulder as we read the riddle typed on the computer paper inside.

> **A master of charades, the names she gives are never just that. Although he's no Fitzwilliam, when he's gone away, his value is still intact.**

Sheila frowned. "It's grammatically incorrect." She pointed to the comma before *the names*. "*She* is a master of charades, not *the names*. Billy knew better."

"Who?" I asked Sheila.

"Jane Austen. She was known for her charades. In *Emma* particularly. But this isn't referring to *Emma*." She pointed to *Fitzwilliam*. "You know who that is?"

"Should I?"

Sheila frowned. "You're going to have to forfeit your Jane Austen card if you don't."

"I don't think I have a Jane Austen card."

Sheila rolled her eyes. "No one is too good for Jane Austen." Her finger pressed into *Fitzwilliam* on the paper. "And no one is too proud for Mr. Darcy, either, Mr. Fitzwilliam Darcy."

Sheila and I studied the clue.

"You see the end here?" I ran my finger beneath the last line. "'When he's gone away, his value is still intact.' That's the name we're looking for."

We leaned closer to the paper, as if distance was what kept us from solving the rest of the riddle.

"His value." I typed "value" into the thesaurus and read to Sheila. "Amount. Cost. Expense. Worth. Profit."

Sheila snapped her fingers. "Worth," she said authoritatively. "And what's another way of saying gone away, perhaps in the simple past tense?"

"What are you, the grammar Nazi?"

"I never joke about grammar. So, what's the correct answer?" She would have made a good teacher.

Go. Gone. "Went," I marveled, like I'd solved one of the great mysteries of the world.

Sheila nodded approvingly. "Captain Frederick Wentworth." I shot her a puzzled look. "You're hopeless."

Sheila guided me to the classics, where she scanned the *A*'s until she located a Penguin Classics edition of *Persuasion*. The paperback bulged awkwardly where an empty matchbook marked an early page in the novel. Austen's descriptions of the Elliot patriarch were highlighted.

> **Vanity was the beginning and end of Sir Walter Elliot's character: vanity of person and of situation.**

And a sentence later:

> **Few women could think more of their personal appearance than he did, nor could the valet of any new-made lord be more delighted with the place he held in society.**

The matchbook was from a steakhouse in Orange County. Yelp reported that it had been sold and renamed in 2002, trading hands a half dozen times before it finally closed in 2011. The reviews from the most recent iteration pined for the original restaurant. Burt Weston may have been a greedy a-hole, one reviewer wrote. At least he knew how to hire a line staff that could cook an f-ing steak. I angled my phone toward Sheila. She shrugged, not seeing the key detail in that review, and now it was my turn to play the expert.

"Weston," I told Sheila. "As in Evelyn Weston. Burt Weston must have been her father." And he must have been vain and self-important. I already knew that Billy didn't like him.

The information online about Burt Weston was overwhelming. Sole proprietor of Weston Family Farms, the largest fruit distributors in the San Joaquin Valley. He'd been on the cover of several magazines, including *Forbes*. In the '70s and '80s, periodicals praised his rags-to-riches story. By the '90s, exposés detailed harsh work environments, political bribery and massive layoffs. He'd been sued by former employees and unions, by ex-wives. By the late '90s, when he was in his midsixties, he'd sold his farm to a conglomerate and retired. I wondered how much money each of the wives had gotten. I wondered which wife was Evelyn's mother.

People as rich and controversial as Burt Weston didn't publicly list their addresses. But through Sir Walter, Billy had announced Burt Weston's key characteristic: his vanity. He must have wanted people to be able to locate him. Even after he'd sold his business and retired, even as he insisted he was no longer giving interviews, he must have wanted to be found. His address was listed in a gated community in Orange County, about an hour outside Los Angeles.

ORANGE COUNTY WAS A STRAIGHT LINE DOWN THE 5, BUT MY car made a detour, driving itself west before I realized where I was going. I found Mom in the garden, mulching her roses. She wore a wide-brimmed hat to block the sun. I couldn't make out her expression, cast in all that shadow.

"Miranda." Mom stood and called to me from across the yard. "What are you doing here?"

I wanted to run to her like I was a child again, to wrap my arms around her waist in that too-tight way, but I kept my distance. I missed the carefree way I used to embrace Mom. I hadn't thought I could lose that with her.

"Well, hello to you, too," I said.

She took off her hat, and I saw her face clearly, layered in makeup even though she was gardening. "Honey, is everything okay?"

"Of course everything's not okay. How could it be?"

"I don't know." She took off her gloves, wedging them under her arm. "I'm glad you came home, though."

"I'm not home," I said curtly. "I'm just letting you know that I'm on my way to see Burt."

"Burt?" she asked innocently enough.

"Burt Weston."

Mom dropped her hat to the ground. The gloves dislodged from under her arm, trailing her as she raced toward me. She grabbed my arm. "You can't do that."

"You aren't even going to ask how I know who he is?" I tried to shake her hand off me.

"Miranda, please. You can't talk to Burt." She gripped my forearm, pulling me gently, then harder when I wouldn't budge. I was stronger than Mom was. Younger. More stubborn. "We'll go inside. We'll talk."

"We'll talk? You're serious? I've been here almost two months. At any point in the last two months, you could have talked to me. I don't want to talk to you anymore. I don't need to." Mom let go of my arm and hugged herself. Her body trembled as she tried to contain her emotions.

"Burt Weston is a cruel and selfish man." She looked so small hugging herself, staring over at me. I clenched my hands into fists so they didn't reach out to comfort her.

"At least he'll tell me the truth."

"No," she said calmly. "He won't. He only ever saw the worst in your uncle."

"As opposed to you? Since you've been so generous with Billy?"

Mom's face hardened. She unfurled her arms and rested her hands on her hips. "I always saw the best in him. It was him— it was Billy who always blamed me."

"Maybe you deserved it." Mom recoiled like I'd slapped her. Tears welled in her eyes. I'd wanted to hurt Mom, and I'd succeeded. It didn't make me feel any better.

"Please don't see Burt," she said so quietly I almost didn't hear her.

"You do realize that the more you tell me not to see him, the more obvious it is he'll tell me something you don't want me to know." I started pacing back and forth. "And the funny part is I can't even figure out why you won't talk to me. I thought we told each other everything, but maybe we've never been as close as I thought we were."

"Please, honey, you can't go see him." She stepped closer to me, reaching for my shoulder. She smelled of sweat and manure. A pungent, acrid scent that made me nauseous.

"You aren't even listening to me. I'm telling you there's something wrong with us, and all you can talk about is Burt."

She shook her head frantically and rubbed at her face, lost from me and our conversation, from any chance of connecting. I stormed toward the car. "Miranda, please come back," she called, but I was already gone.

CHAPTER FIFTEEN

THE I-5 WAS CLEAR, AND I DROVE FASTER THAN NORMAL, WATCHing the speedometer inch toward eighty, eighty-five, ninety. Hot air gushed in through the open windows, sending my hair into a tornado that partially obscured my view of the road ahead. My phone buzzed in the console. When I saw it was Mom, I hit Ignore. I tuned the radio to something loud and angry. I wanted to be reckless. I wanted to be angsty. I wanted to be someone else, but when I hit ninety-five, something seized in my chest and I let up on the gas. The car slowed down until it leveled off at seventy. I turned down the radio and rolled up the windows. I wasn't someone else, I was me, Miranda Brooks. Even if I didn't answer Mom's calls, I still listened to her voice mails.

"Miranda, it's your mother," she said, as if I otherwise wouldn't have known who it was. "Please call me back. I shouldn't have let you walk away. Please come home."

Her next two voice mails grew more urgent.

"Please, honey. I'm sorry if I haven't been more open with you. This is all tremendously difficult for me. Please call me," and, "Sweetheart, this has all gotten out of hand. We're family. We can't lose each other. I can't lose you. Please, let's just talk about this."

I had to press Delete as soon as I listened to them, so I wouldn't replay them and feel guilty enough to call her back. By her fourth message, the plea was gone. "This is the last time I'll call. I'm not saying I'm perfect or I've done everything right, but I'm trying to protect you. You have to trust me." How was I supposed to trust her now?

I pressed on toward Orange County.

The Orchard Estate, belonging to one Burt Weston, was housed in a community where each home had a name. The guard eyed my parents' Japanese sedan, its black paint speckled gray from weeks of street parking.

"Name?" he asked dubiously.

"I'm Miranda, Miranda Brooks. I don't think my name's on..." I tried to explain as he disappeared into his hut to review the visitors' list.

The guard opened the gate. He pointed toward the road to the right. "Follow it around to the top."

I was about to ask him how my name had been on the list. Instead, I confirmed, "That way, to Burt Weston's?"

"Like I said, the top of the hill. You can't miss it."

I followed the windy road up to the Orchard Estate, impressed that Billy had thought of everything.

I parked outside the stucco, tile-roofed mansion, feeling my pulse in my temples. This was what I'd been waiting for. Finally, some answers. Sweat gathered above my upper lip as I watched Burt's Mediterranean house. Billy, via Jane Austen and Sir Walter, had nothing nice to say about Burt. If Billy was sending me to a man he despised, Burt must have had something to tell me that no one else could. If Mom was so desperate for me not to talk to him, it must have been huge. I unbuckled my seat belt and stepped into the breathless afternoon.

A Filipino nurse answered the door. Behind her the house was dark. The air-conditioning wafted out, like a silk scarf grazing my arms.

"I'm not sure if Mr. Weston is expecting me. I'm Miranda Brooks. My uncle, Billy Silver, sent me to talk to him?" I told her.

"Miranda! Come in, come in." She opened the door wider, and I followed her into a formal living room, shocked that this was all so easy. "It's one of his good days, but be gentle with him. He gets agitated when he can't remember."

Burt sat in a wheelchair, watching a telenovela on the television above the marble mantel. An antique armoire reflected the profile of his long nose, his deadpan face.

"He doesn't understand Spanish, so he watches it on mute. Makes up storylines for what he sees on the TV." The nurse turned on the light. "Burt, you're going to go blind, watching in the dark."

He turned his wheelchair to face us. "Why would I go blind?"

"I was joking, Burt," she explained.

"Oh." He laughed. He looked at me like he wanted to know who I was. "Hello."

"Burt, this is Miranda. Remember I told you she might stop by? She's Billy Silver's niece."

"No, she's not," he said angrily.

The nurse turned to me. "He's been good all day." The nurse put her hand on his shoulder and leaned close to him. "This is Miranda. She's come a long way to see you. Isn't it nice to have a visitor?"

"It is nice." His voice quaked, and whatever vanity he'd had when Billy had known him had been stripped of him in old age. Deep lines carved his cheeks. He was frail. Immobile. Maybe I should have left him be, but as he continued to stare at me his frightened gaze dissolved into something that resembled friendliness.

"I'll be in the other room," the nurse said as she left. "If he starts to act up, just call me."

Once Burt and I were alone, he pressed a button and wheeled his chair to turn off the light.

"I hate sleeping with the windows open." He laughed. "I don't know why I said that."

I sat on the couch and watched him peer into the distance. I'd never spent any time with elderly people, healthy or sick. My grandfather—Mom and Billy's father—was the sole grandparent still living when I was born. He was in his early seventies, a lifelong smoker, already in an assisted-living home. My parents had a picture of me with him in hospice, a visit I didn't remember. Mom said I was terrified of him, which upset both Mom and her father, so she didn't take me to see him very often. He died when I was two. Even though he'd been sick for a long time, his mind was sound. I couldn't imagine how much worse it would have been for Mom if her father was like this. I brushed off thoughts of Mom. I didn't want to be thinking about her. I didn't want to be feeling sorry for her, either.

"Loretta?" Burt asked when he realized I was still in the room. He wheeled over, stopping so close I could smell onions on his breath, see dandruff in his thinning hair.

"Miranda, I'm Miranda," I said, shifting away to create some space between us.

"Right. Of course."

"I was hoping we could talk about your daughter, Evelyn."

"She used to eat pancakes every Sunday. I've never seen a kid who could eat so many pancakes." He paused. "What was I saying?"

"You were telling me about your daughter, Evelyn."

"Loretta?" He wheeled closer to me again.

I rested my hand on his. It was icy, lifeless. "My name is Miranda. Miranda," I shouted as if saying my name at louder volumes might help him to understand who I was. "I'm not Loretta. I'm Miranda."

Burt's eyes watered. I should have called the nurse. Even if he had been as vain as Sir Walter Elliot, even if he was once worthy of Billy's scorn, no one deserved this.

Burt grabbed my forearm with surprising strength. "Why did you leave, Loretta?"

"I'm Miranda. I'm right here." The conversation was making me light-headed.

"Did you think of Evelyn? Did you think of what you were doing to your daughter?" he pled.

"What did Loretta do? Was she Evelyn's mother?" I wasn't going to pretend to be Loretta, but I would talk to him. He wanted to tell me about Loretta. I wanted to listen. "What did Loretta do to Evelyn, Burt?"

"She died, you know," Burt said soberly.

"Evelyn did die. She died thirty years ago." He looked as if he was trying to calculate whether thirty years was a lifetime or barely anytime at all. "Do you remember how Evelyn died?"

"Of course I remember." He was angry again. "You think I would forget how my own daughter died?"

"How did she die, Burt?" I squeezed his cold hand.

"You were supposed to get her." His voice was weak. The tortured expression on his face sent a chill down my arms.

"Burt, what happened to Evelyn?"

"Did you forget?" He clutched my forearm. "How could you forget?"

"Forget what, Burt? What did I forget?" His eyes were focused on mine, but I couldn't tell where he was, whether we were talking about Evelyn's death or something else entirely.

"She waited at the school for you. You never showed." A tear rolled down his right cheek.

"Burt, I don't know what you're talking about. Who was waiting? Did Evelyn die in a car accident?"

"She waited all alone on the school steps. You were supposed to pick her up, Loretta. Why didn't you take her with you? Why did you leave Evelyn with me?"

"Did Loretta leave you, Burt?" Burt nodded. "Did she leave Evelyn?"

"Yes." He drifted in and out. A moment with me. A moment disappeared. The past seemed to be right there, as though he could slip all the way into it.

"What happened to Evelyn, Burt?" I leaned toward him like the nurse had done, trying to create an intimacy that might return him to the present.

"You look so much like Evelyn. And Loretta. Evelyn looked like Loretta when she was pregnant. I always wanted to tell her that, but I didn't know how."

"What do you mean?" It was impossible to tell what was fabricated from the past, what was embellished from his telenovelas, what may have been real. "Was Evelyn pregnant? Did she have a child?"

"Before we left the orchard. She didn't want to raise our child there. If we had, maybe you wouldn't have left."

"You're talking about Loretta," I decided for him. "Loretta was pregnant at the orchard. Not Evelyn."

"That's what I said."

"Do you remember Billy?"

"Billy?" he said like he wasn't sure that was a real name.

"Evelyn's husband, Billy Silver."

"Murderer!" he shouted. "Murderer!"

"Shh." I turned toward the doorway, expecting the nurse to come rushing in. The television blasted from the other room, and if she did hear the commotion, she decided not to investigate. "Shh, Burt. Calm down."

"He killed her. He killed my Evelyn. I tried but I couldn't prove it. He didn't deserve her. He didn't deserve either of them." Burt was shaking his head like the past could be dislodged with a little effort.

"Either of whom?" I was completely turned around. I couldn't find my way through Burt's story.

"Evelyn and the child," he explained.

"What child?" What child?

"Evelyn."

"Evelyn is your child, Burt. Evelyn was your child."

"Evelyn was my child," he said.

"So Evelyn didn't have a child?"

"Evelyn didn't have a child."

I was dizzy, slightly intoxicated. If this was a good day, I didn't want to know what a bad day looked like.

Burt turned away from me toward the television above the fireplace where a tall woman with dyed blond hair and artificially blue eyes paced frantically across the screen. She ranted on mute, waving her arms like she was speaking in tongues.

"She's my favorite. Esmeralda. She gets so enraged. It's beautiful."

I still had so many questions to ask him, but whatever Billy had expected him to tell me, he wasn't capable of it. And yet among all the seemingly irrational things he'd said, one word persisted. *Murderer! Murderer!* Billy wasn't a murderer. That was beyond the realm of possibilities. He'd devoted his career to making the world a safer place, to decreasing death and destruction. No way he murdered his wife, yet Burt's lucidity as he shouted, *Murderer! Murderer!*—it was the only thing he'd said that didn't get wrapped around itself, woven into a spiral of fragmented memories and regret. *Murderer! Murderer!* Burt was so certain Billy had killed her, even if he couldn't prove it. And I already knew that Billy blamed himself. What if Sheila was wrong, if it wasn't grief talking when Billy had said Burt was right to condemn him. What if Evelyn's death really was Billy's fault?

Burt and I watched the telenovela until the nurse returned. He was calm again, not entirely cognizant of me.

"Well, Burt," the nurse said, turning the light back on. "What do you say to a nap? Let's say goodbye to Miranda."

He cast me the same expression of almost recognition he'd had when I first walked in.

I sat alone in the living room, waiting for the nurse. She came back in and sat beside me. "How are you doing?"

"I'm all right. He was confusing me with Loretta."

"He confuses me with her, too. I know it's hard, but you should visit more often. It helps him. Even if he can't express it, it helps to remember."

"Does he ever talk about his daughter, Evelyn? She was my aunt." Was Evelyn my aunt? Did she belong to me?

The nurse nodded.

"I was hoping Burt would tell me about her. I never got to know her."

The nurse walked over to the armoire and dug through a pile of photo albums until she found a faded gold canvas book. She handed me a yearbook, 1969 embossed on the bottom right corner. The year Mom graduated high school. The year Evelyn must have, too.

I opened the cover and saw several handwritten inscriptions to Evelyn. *Good luck at Vassar!* And *I'll miss sitting next to you in drama class! I still think you should act instead of doing set design!* And *I'll never forget when you set the counter on fire in chemistry class* and *Keep fighting the good fight!*

"Burt kept this?" I asked.

"It's amazing what makes the move," the nurse said. "And what doesn't. Even when he can't remember, he likes looking at the old pictures."

"Can I have this?"

She frowned. "I've got to get Burt's dinner ready. Take your time." She left me alone in the cold living room.

I skimmed through the early pages of the yearbook, filled with headshots of the administration and teachers, stopping when I saw a photograph on the newspaper's page, Evelyn in a crocheted vest leaning over a table, a strand of hair bisecting her face. She looked serious and pensive and older than eighteen. Evelyn was one of two girls on the debate team. A member of the Students of Concern Committee, the Key Club, National Honors Society. I scanned the clubs for Mom. She was a member of the Jazz Club, a photograph of her dancing suggestively behind a microphone. She looked disobedient and energetic and young. I flipped through the rest of the yearbook, searching for Evelyn and Mom, for some evidence of how they'd been best friends. In the class portraits, they looked like everyone else, only haircuts to differentiate them. Evelyn's hair was long and straight. Mom's was cut into a pageboy, bangs hiding her eyebrows and ears, shorter than I'd ever seen her wear her hair.

On the second to last page of the yearbook, in the candids, I saw them together. Evelyn and Mom sitting on the floor, leaning against a row of lockers. Evelyn wore jeans and a striped sleeveless shirt, Mom was dressed in black tights and a short A-line skirt. Evelyn's head rested on Mom's shoulder, her face scrunched in laughter. Mom stuck her tongue out and crossed her eyes. Beside the photograph, Mom had written, *Love you forever—Suzy*. I thought about Mom's desperate tone in the voice mails she'd left me, the voice mails I'd erased, how terrified she was of losing me. She'd already lost someone she'd expected to love forever. I snapped a picture of the two of them, and left the closed yearbook on the coffee table.

The sounds of a blender led me to the kitchen where the nurse was making soup. When I started to say goodbye, she signaled for me to hold on as she wiped her hands on a towel. She opened and closed a few drawers before she handed me an envelope.

"Came for you about two months ago." We walked toward the front door. When she opened the heavy door, light poured into the cool, dark house. "Stop by again. Even if he can't express it, he likes the company."

On the porch, I tore open the envelope. Inside was a rebus. A drawing of a tree plus a set of keys. Tree keys? Tree ring?

Spruce ring? Spruce keys? It wasn't a spruce. It was a broad tree with a massive crown of branches and leaves. A maple? A birch? An oak? Oak keys? Okies! There was only one quintessential novel that documented the Okies struggle, one quintessential novel that happened to be displayed on Billy's side of the staff recommendations table between *The Portrait of a Lady, Tender Is the Night, The Age of Innocence,* classics that hadn't seemed like Billy's favorites.

WHEN I GOT BACK TO THE STORE, THE CLOSED SIGN DANGLED on the door even though it was only six o'clock and we should have been open. I unlocked the door and went inside. The stacks were empty, the tables of the café unoccupied.

"Malcolm," I called.

"In the bathroom," he shouted.

Malcolm was mopping the tiled floor, his shirt soaked, his hair frizzed.

"You picked a great day to not show up." His words had a mean edge. Still, it was a sentence that consisted of nine words, which was more than he'd said to me in weeks.

"What happened?"

"I'll give you one guess." He must have realized he was being unnecessarily prickly, because he added, "Some asshole clogged the toilet, then a pipe burst. It's been a fucking day." He squeezed the mop into the bucket.

"Can I help?"

"Now that it's all cleaned up?" He wheeled the bucket into the kitchen.

"Did you fix it yourself?"

"I'm a man of many talents, but cleaning up other people's shit isn't one of them. Plumber left about a half hour ago."

"So, it's fixed?"

"Yeah, it's fixed. A thousand dollars, but we'll be open tomorrow." Malcolm hauled the bucket to the sink and poured the gray water down the drain.

"You spent a thousand dollars on a plumber?"

"It was a rush job." The dirty water ricocheted off the sides of the basin, splashing his face. He wiped it off aggressively.

"You didn't shop around, see if you could find anyone cheaper?"

He dropped the bucket on the ground. "You know what, if you were here, you could do it your way."

He swept past me and stormed out. I wanted to chase him down Sunset to apologize for not being here, for doubting him, for assuming he was lying to me when he was mourning. I wanted to ask him if we could go back to the way we were before. I wanted to scream at him, *What the hell were you thinking, spending a thousand dollars?* and poke my finger into his chest, telling him if Prospero Books closed, it would be his fault. I wanted to use Malcolm as my punching bag, to blame him for my fight with Mom, for Burt's words—*Murderer! Murderer!*—but I couldn't do that to him. I hadn't been there. I hadn't lost my best friend.

I walked over to the recommendations table and spotted the drawing of Billy.

"Why weren't you more careful?" I asked his forlorn face. Billy was methodical as a seismologist. He was precise in each of our scavenger hunts. "How could you have been so reckless with Prospero Books?"

I scanned his recommended titles. *The Portrait of a Lady, Tender Is the Night, The Age of Innocence.* No *Grapes of Wrath.* I raced around the table, tossing books aside. It wasn't under books one and two from *A Series of Unfortunate Events*, between copies of *In the Time of the Butterflies.* I raced behind the desk where Booklog confirmed that we'd sold a copy of *The Grapes of Wrath*, paid for in cash, the ticket stub or dinner receipt or whatever keepsake Billy had left in the book carried onto Sunset, thrown away by an anonymous customer, the destroyer of Billy's hunt forever unknown.

I sat behind the desk, staring at the screen. Could this really be it? Billy's quest undone by one purchase? That would have been a major oversight, and Billy was nothing if not meticulous. Even if he'd been willfully ignorant when it came to the finances of Prospero Books, he wouldn't have left anything in this journey to chance. He wouldn't have allowed the quest to unravel that easily.

We had three copies of *The Grapes of Wrath* in Classics, so I started there. No notes in the used copy. No love letters. Not even an old lunch receipt. Nothing in the mass-market copy, either. The centennial edition—published on what would have been Steinbeck's one hundredth birthday—fell naturally to chapter twenty-nine.

The chapter began with the clouds, how they rolled in from the ocean, trailed by the wind, which brought the trees to life and carried the clouds farther onto the lands. Then the rain came, erratic at first until it found its rhythm, cutting in on the sun and claiming the afternoon. Steinbeck continued to describe the rains that grew heavier and heavier, soaking the earth until it had had its fill. Then the water flooded the orchards, the highways, the car engines, carrying sickness and hunger to the migrants who waited out the deluge. Two pages into the chapter, a single word was circled. When the coroners arrived to take away the bodies of those who had not survived the storm: *dead*. And a page later, circled again: *died*.

And then the rain stopped. The fields were flooded. There would be no jobs for three months, and everyone was scared. Soon the men's fear morphed into anger, and the women trusted that anger because as long as the men could still grow angry, they weren't beaten. Then, a couple of days later, everything began to turn green again.

I remembered the drought in *The Grapes of Wrath*, not the

flood, not the hopeful undercurrents at the end of the novel. Yet, Billy hadn't highlighted those hopeful passages. He hadn't highlighted anything. Only those two words were circled: *dead* and *died*. So sober. So unadorned.

I flipped through the rest of the novel. Nothing was marked, no notecards or envelopes tucked in its pages, nothing to guide me to the next person in the journey. Still, those circled words weren't random. They were Billy's markings, guiding me toward Evelyn, toward her death.

I reread the chapter, possessed by its simple beauty, frightened by its death. I searched the other copies of the novel to see if I'd missed something. They were untouched. As I shut the mass-market copy, I noticed pencil markings on the inside cover, so light I almost overlooked them again. Two numbers followed by a decimal point, four more numbers. The letter *N*, followed by two more numbers, a decimal, four digits, the series ending with a *W*. I checked the used copy, and the same sequence of numbers and letters was written there, too. It had to be the code I'd seen in Billy's recommended copy, a secret language that Malcolm had said was Billy's with the novels he'd salvaged from thrift shops. It was Billy's secret language, all right, just not with the books.

I looked the numbers up in Booklog. It wasn't an ISBN. A Dewey Decimal classification. It wasn't anything that our inventory system recognized. I typed the numbers and letters into Google instead. When nothing matched my search, Google asked if I meant the same numbers and letters with degree signs and periods. In that configuration, *N* stood not for *new* but for *north*. *W* not for *worn* but for *west*. The coordinates aligned in an area called Fawnskin, just north of Big Bear Lake.

CHAPTER SIXTEEN

BIG BEAR WAS A TWO-HOUR DRIVE, INLAND AND EAST FROM LA. On Google Earth, I'd located a house in Fawnskin that sat at the coordinates from *The Grapes of Wrath*, a dark wood cabin surrounded by brown grass thirsty for rain. I couldn't imagine what Billy wanted me to find in that house, what it had to do with wild rains, what it had to do with death, either.

Unable to sleep, I left at dawn, hoping to beat rush hour. Even at 6:00 a.m. cars crawled along the 210. Pasadena slowly retreated in the rearview window, then traffic thinned around Pomona, slowing down again in San Bernadino. At seven, Charlie would have arrived at the store with three boxes of muffins. By the time he had the chairs down, the coffee roasted, Malcolm would have strolled in. He would have checked the voice mail and email, before heading upstairs to the storage closet to unlock the safe and count out enough change for the day. Would he have glanced at my closed door, realizing I'd normally emerged by then? By the time he switched the sign on the front door to Open, would he have asked Charlie if he'd seen me? Would he be thinking how soon all the days at Prospero Books would be free of me? And would that prospect bring him relief or regret?

"Prospero," Malcolm said as he answered the phone.

"It's Miranda."

"Why are you calling from upstairs?"

I wanted to joke, You really think I'm that lazy? "I'm out," I explained. "I won't be back today."

"Are you asking my permission?"

"No."

"Well, we'll see you when you're back, then." His tone was so even, so devoid of emotion, that I wondered if I'd merely imagined we were in some tense, unspoken fight.

The ski mountain stood behind Big Bear Lake, strips of fir and pine trees delineating its snowless trails. The woods continued beyond the ski resort, across the mountain range and onto the flatlands that skirted the lake. Motorboats tugged inner tubes across the still water. Kayaks lined the beach beside North Shore Drive where tourists steadied themselves on bright paddleboards as they rowed away from the shore. The summer season would last until mid-October when the weather cooled and the leaves began to change. Big Bear was one of the few places in Southern California where the leaves turned, cloaking the mountains in crimson and sienna. Fall in Philadelphia was equally magnificent. Brilliant colors against the Schuylkill River. Vibrant leaves littering the stone walkways across campus. By the time the leaves fell, I'd be two months into the first trimester of the school year. By the time the leaves fell, Prospero Books would belong to someone else, if it belonged to anyone at all. By the time the trees were barren, everything would have changed. Everything except my life, back to Jay and our apartment—assuming it was still ours—back to my classroom with Susan B. Anthony and Harriet Tubman on the walls, the same as it had been before.

I turned into Fawnskin, toward the house that matched the coordinates, thinking about the fall, the packs of students eating lunch on the slate benches outside the cafeteria, the lessons I'd taught so many times I could recite them from memory. Teaching was a little like saying your favorite word over and over again. *Fuchsia* or *effervescent* or *luminous*. At first, it felt like butter on your tongue, soft and silky, then as you kept repeating it, it began to sound strange. Fuchsia was bleached of its brightness. Effervescent fell flat. Luminous became dull. I'd explain to my students Patrick Henry's famous speech to the Virginia House of Burgess, and suddenly I could no longer understand what was so important about it, if he'd actually been able to persuade his peers to revolt with a few measly words that no one had even bothered to transcribe, the speech living on only in memory. I never thought history could become bleached or flat. I never imagined it could dull. Teaching did that. The students who were needy. Others I had to chase after. Those who only cared about their grades and those who didn't care at all. I thought about Prospero Books, how much money we still needed to earn, the tickets for the gala we still had to sell, the donations that had been promised but had yet to materialize—somehow, the idea of that work didn't weigh me down the way my life did.

I parked at the coordinates. The house looked worse in person than it did on the internet. Posts were missing from the porch railing. The front yard was mostly dirt, brown grass sprouting like uneven patches of hair. A woman in an apron answered the door. Behind her, children's shouts echoed through the house. Her hair was frizzy, her apron speckled with flour.

"Yes?" The shouts turned shrill and she looked back into the dark house. "Jonathan, don't you dare touch that oven." Several children giggled. She returned to me, expectant.

"I'm not sure if I'm at the right place. My name is Miranda Brooks. I think my uncle, Billy Silver, sent me here to talk to you."

"Who?" She turned again. "Jonathan, what did I just say?" The children squealed again.

"Should I come back?"

"Whatever you're selling, I'm not interested." She started to shut the door.

"Please, I'm wondering if you knew my uncle, Billy Silver?"

Something banged behind her. "Sorry, I can't help you."

She shut the door, blocking the sound, all the life inside. I leaned against the banister, retracing my steps. I must have read the code wrong. It must not have been coordinates. Or I'd plugged the numbers in incorrectly. I entered them into my phone again, and they still led here. My finger caught a splinter on the banister. I winced in pain as a drop of blood formed on my fingertip. I pinched it with my thumb to stop the bleeding. The entire banister was splintered, the paint chipped, revealing the rotten wood below. The column that held up the roof appeared on the verge of collapse. Most of its paint was long stripped away, but white had collected in a carving of a heart, etched into the soft wood. Inside the heart were two unmistakable initials: *B & E.*

The woman's impatience bordered on anger when she found me at her door, knocking again.

"Sorry to bother you." I pointed to the initials on the column. "Do you know who carved this?"

"What?" She didn't even bother to look at the carving.

"I'm looking for the past owners. Did you know them?"

"My parents have owned this house for the last twenty-five years." She began to shut the door.

"Please," I said. "I really need to know who they bought it from."

Half her face peeked out from the edge of the door. "It was on the market for a while. Past owners died during the storm."

"The storm?" Steinbeck's words came to me in images. I saw the wind swirling the rain. The flooding. The death. "Did they both die during a storm?"

"The wife, maybe. My mom never told me the whole story.

I didn't want to know, frankly." Inside, something crashed. Children gasped, then erupted in laughter. "I have to get back."

"Is there anyone who might know what happened to them?"

"Try Dotty at the library," she said as she shut the door. "If there's anyone who'd know what happened, it's Dotty."

THE BIG BEAR LAKE LIBRARY WAS SURROUNDED BY STARVING grass and dying brush. Inside, people worked at carrels. A man with a ponytail filed books. The large, single room carried the mildew of all libraries, so different than the smell of Prospero Books.

A librarian was reading behind the reference desk. She had curled white hair. I figured she'd been here long enough to remember a tragedy almost thirty years past.

I explained to her that I was looking for information on an accident that had happened in the mid-'80s. I still didn't know exactly when Evelyn died, sometime between 1984 and 1986.

"I don't remember anyone dying on the mountain," the librarian said. "There were accidents, sure. Nothing serious. Did you try the hospital? They probably won't release records to you, though, even if the person is dead."

"It wasn't on the mountain. It was at a house. A woman died in a storm?"

Her face grew still. "I remember." She used both arms to lift herself out of the chair and led me to an old microfiche scanner. I waited as she sorted through several archival boxes. "We don't keep copies of the paper that far back." She handed me a binder of negatives. "I don't remember when it happened. It was during a snowstorm. A bad one. So, you can rule out May through October." She started to walk away. "Actually, you might want to check October, just to be safe. Winter was longer back then. May, too."

There was a reason microfiche had gone out of fashion. No easy way to search unless you knew precisely what you were looking for. I had to go through each day's paper, one at a time. Fortunately, the paper was short, a handful of local stories added to the ones from the Associated Press. I started with January 1984. While there were lots of snowstorms, none had a death toll. Nothing in February or March. I breezed through the rest of the year into the next ski season, the start of 1985. There was steady snow that winter, nothing monumental. No recording-breaking storms. Nothing that mirrored the power of Steinbeck's downpour. In April, someone had died in a car accident in the hail, an older gentleman who had driven into a tree. I skipped June, July, August, September. When I didn't find anything in October, I got nervous and looked back over those dry, hot months. The chapter in *The Grapes of Wrath* was about rain, not snow. The librarian may have been mistaken when she said it was during a snowstorm. But there was no rain that summer. The drought lasted through the fall, one of the worst in years. In November, when the snow should have started, it was still dry, threatening the chances of a good ski season. In December, it finally began to snow. Every accumulated inch was allotted a few hundred hopeful words that this was the beginning of the snow they desperately needed. The storms remained small. Fleeting. At the end of the month when the snow really arrived, it was too much at once. The ski mountain had to close. The road was blocked off. Flakes the size of dimes quickly amassed into a whiteout in the early hours of December 30, 1985, the day of my birth.

The paper wasn't printed on the thirtieth on account of the storm. The edition from the thirty-first was longer than usual, filled with photographs. Stills of the restaurants along Big Bear Boulevard with closed signs on their doors, roofs and walkways buried in snow. A pixilated print of a family pushing a car out of a snowbank. A man walking along the sidewalk, his legs buried past his knees, his face masked by a scarf, dark against the white terrain. The caption for the picture read "Man walking down Big Bear Boulevard."

Articles detailed the fire department's efforts to clear the roads. The front page listed the injuries and fatalities from the storm. Six people had died; several others were being treated for hypothermia and frostbite.

The article included one short paragraph per death. Some were listed by age, others by gender or occupation. A forty-three-year-old man had been killed when a tree fell on his mobile home. A retired teacher suffered cardiac arrest while shoveling snow. A marathon runner was hit by a car while training. Honeymooners from Bakersfield were killed when their car skidded off the road. A pregnant woman died of suspected carbon monoxide poisoning. Her husband and newborn were in critical condition.

The article continued to list the car accidents that hadn't killed their passengers. A police officer had broken his leg when his car collided with a truck. A local girl on a sled, hit by an elderly couple trying to make it home. My eyes drifted back to the paragraph about the pregnant woman. It was two sentences long.

Thirty-four-year-old woman dies of suspected carbon monoxide poisoning. Husband, an earthquake scientist, and newborn girl in critical condition.

I had little evidence that the thirty-four-year-old pregnant woman was Evelyn, yet I was certain it was. I had little reason to believe the husband was Billy, only I was positive that he was the man listed in the paragraph, too. And I had absolutely no reason to believe that the baby was me, but I saw the date and knew for certain that when Burt had said, "Evelyn and the child," he'd meant me, that he wasn't as delusional as I'd thought.

I read the paragraph over and over again, hunting for details that weren't there, something I'd read wrong, some indication that the wife wasn't Evelyn. That the husband was significantly older or that he was an engineer, anything other than a seismologist. That the newborn was a boy. That he had died. All the details checked out. Evelyn would have been thirty-four, the same age Mom was when I was born. Billy was an earthquake scientist. The baby was a girl, born on my birthday.

A numbing concoction of fear and intuition seized me as I scanned my memory for a sign that I should have known all along. Had I ever seen my birth certificate? Wasn't I born at UCLA? Didn't Mom tell me she was in labor for thirty-three hours? Didn't she say that the first time she took me in her arms she felt a sense of completeness that she'd never known before? I wanted to call Mom, to ask her about my birth certificate, about the hospital where I was born, about my first breaths, then another truth came crashing down on me. Mom wasn't my mom. My life as I'd known it had been a lie.

I walked out of the library in a strange haze, an impossible calm that couldn't last. I didn't feel anger toward Mom and Dad. Only sadness. A profound loss. It felt like the ground beneath me was slowly collapsing. I didn't try to fight it. I just let myself fall.

"Dear!" the librarian called as she ran outside with a book. "Is your name Miranda?"

Was my name Miranda? Was I named after *The Tempest*, Evelyn's—my mother's—favorite play? And if I weren't Miranda, who else could I possibly be?

The librarian handed me *Bridge to Terabithia*.

"Our library read," she explained. "Katherine Paterson wrote it to help her son cope with his best friend's senseless death. Poor girl was struck by lightning."

"I don't want it." I tried to give the novel back to her.

The librarian shook her head, refusing to accept the copy. "I've been holding this for you for over a year. Stipulation in

funding the library read was that I get you this copy." She
tapped the cover of Paterson's novel. "It's an important lesson
on grief for us all."

After she disappeared inside, I threw the novel into the trash
can. Whatever clue it held, wherever Billy wanted to lead me,
I didn't want to follow anymore.

By late afternoon, the heat was still strong. I waited for it all to
make sense, some peculiar look the Conrads, our neighbors and
my parents' oldest friends, had given me, some cryptic comment
Billy or Mom had made, some way I'd always felt out of place in
my own skin. But I felt the same. I still felt like me. The me I'd
always been.

I walked away from the water, toward Big Bear Boulevard.
The lake carried the sounds of Jet Skis zooming across its surface, the chatter of people having fun. I tried to imagine what
that would have been like, if there had been no carbon monoxide, if Evelyn and Billy had raised me and we'd summered
here as a family. Billy, teaching me how to fish. Evelyn, braid-
ing my hair so it wouldn't fall into my eyes as the wind carried
me across the lake. And what about Prospero Books? Would
I have spent my afternoons there doing homework? Would
Evelyn have helped me between customers? I grabbed my phone
from my back pocket and found the photo I'd taken of her and
Mom from their high school yearbook. Mom sticking out her
tongue and cross-eyed. Evelyn's eyes shut, trying to contain her
pleasure. They were young. They were silly. They were best
friends. I searched Evelyn's pinched nose, the perfect arch of
her eyebrows, the straight hair that fell into her face. I squinted,
then opened my eyes wide. Blurry or clear, she looked nothing
like me. I focused on Mom instead. Her eyes were the same
shape as mine, her lips as thin as mine had always been. Billy
had thin lips, too. He had our deep-set eyes. I always thought
I looked like Mom, but I looked a lot like Billy, too.

I turned right on Big Bear Boulevard, past ski shops and

sporting stores, the sheriff's department. I didn't want to be Billy's daughter. I didn't want two parents who were dead. I wanted the parents I'd always had. I entered a bar. It smelled like stale beer. The customers were talking too loudly. I continued walking. On the next block I found a quiet café with lace curtains on the windows. I went inside and picked a table in the back.

I wasn't hungry. Or maybe I was. I didn't know anything anymore, not even the desires of my own body. When the waitress called me "doll" and asked me what it would be, I heard the word *coffee* from my mouth and wondered if I liked coffee, or if I only thought I did. She returned with a ceramic mug and a bowl of creamers.

"Doll?" the waitress asked. I stared up at her. "You have to believe what's true."

"What?" I said.

"I said, 'Do you want something to eat?'" She exaggerated each word, like she wasn't sure we spoke the same language. "Are you hungry?"

"No, I'm fine."

She pointed to the counter. "I'll be over there if you need anything."

The coffee was lukewarm and watery. I drank it slowly, savoring the minutes where I was just a customer, where I wasn't a daughter or a niece, where I wasn't anyone. I peered over at the waitress. When we locked eyes, she looked away. I was glad she didn't want to get involved. If she asked me if I was okay, I knew I wouldn't be able to hold back the tears anymore.

You have to believe what's true. I swore she'd said that, and yet she merely asked me if I wanted something to eat. *You have to believe what's true.* Did I know what was true? I had evidence, external facts. I didn't have truth; I didn't have the life and soul of my history, the details that might explain how I'd been raised by my aunt and uncle, how they'd decided—not just Mom and

Dad, Billy as well—to let me think I was someone else. I threw some money onto the table and ran out of the café. I sprinted past the ski shops, the sheriff's department, the bars, through the library's parking lot, to the trash can by the door. I couldn't avoid this quest. I couldn't avoid who I was.

The novel fell open almost to the end where a bookmark was sandwiched between a highlighted passage on one page and a black-and-white illustration of a boy carrying a lifeless girl on the other. I read the passage.

> **He ran until he was stumbling but he kept on, afraid to stop. Knowing somehow that running was the only thing that could keep Leslie from being dead. It was up to him. He had to keep going.**

Senseless death, that was what the librarian had said. A parable on senseless death. I'd never read *Bridge to Terabithia*. Billy had never given it to me. Mom had never given it to me, either.

The bookmark was a simple one, cut from cardboard. Prospero Books in letters so winding they were almost illegible. It took me a moment to find the clue in that curly font. At the bottom of the bookmark, I spotted the artist's name, Lee Williams. While I didn't remember Lee's surname, I remembered Lee, the way he tried to comfort me when I'd gone searching for Billy and found only his absence. Lee, who had always been friendly but stilted, like he didn't know how to interact with kids. Maybe he just didn't know how to interact with me.

I DROVE STRAIGHT TO MY PARENTS' HOUSE. I DIDN'T TURN ON the radio or the air-conditioning, and the car was hot, filled with the rattle of the overworked engine. I focused on driving the speed limit, not sure if I wanted to get there faster or slower. I didn't know what I would say to Mom when I saw her, whether I would hug her or never speak to her again. I kept my attention fixed on driving steadily, on remaining calm, on keeping my speed consistent across the long and flat distance. My phone buzzed and Jay's name sent a chill through me like hearing from a ghost. I debated picking up until it went to voice mail. He didn't leave a message. I didn't call him back. I couldn't think about Jay. I couldn't think about Philadelphia. I couldn't even think about Prospero Books. All I could think of was Mom. Mom, who wasn't my mom but my aunt. I'd never had an aunt before. I didn't know what an aunt was supposed to be to you. Someone you saw twice a year on holidays? Someone who was like a second mom or more of a friend?

Mom was in the kitchen when I arrived, singing as she cut peaches. A Janis Joplin song, softer and sweeter in her voice than it was meant to be sung. And that was Mom. She turned everything beautiful and safe, even lyrics written in heartbreak and protest. I dropped my purse audibly on the counter.

Mom jumped. "Honey, I didn't hear you."

The knife hovered in her hand an inch above the peaches. Juice dripped from the cutting board onto the floor. Mom remained motionless, gripping the knife, watching me.

"Oh, Mom." My voice faltered. Mom dropped the knife and ran to me. I let her envelop me, burying my face in her curly hair that looked like my curly hair, clutching her narrow frame, the same size as mine, my entire being a facsimile, a lesser reproduction, of hers. I squeezed her, feeling small again, like a child. Like her child.

Mom kissed the top of my head. I waited for her to tell me it wasn't true, that it was all a big misunderstanding. I waited for her to rebuild my world, to make everything the same as it had always been.

"We wanted to tell you," she whispered.

Those were the exact words I didn't want to hear.

I pushed her away from me. "I shouldn't have come here."

I headed toward the door. Mom darted in front of me, blocking my path. "Miranda, don't leave. Let's talk about this." Her eyes implored me to stay.

"Please get out of my way." I wasn't asking. It was all I could do not to curse at her. Instead, I said truer words, more hurtful. "She's my mother, not you."

"We wanted to tell you." She grabbed both my shoulders. "I wanted so much to tell you, but Billy... He didn't want you to know."

"Don't you dare blame this on Billy," my voice roared.

She dropped her arms by her sides. "You're right. This was my mistake." She buried her face in her hands and started to cry.

"You're not allowed to cry right now." She cried harder. "Stop!" I screamed, startling her. For a moment, everything grew still. "Just stop." I slid past her and headed to the door.

"Where are you going?"

"I don't know, but I can't be here. Not with you. I'm sorry, I can't." I didn't storm off. I didn't slam the door. I didn't say anything cruel even though I wanted to. I simply walked out. And what was worse, she let me go.

CHAPTER SEVENTEEN

I GOT AS FAR AS THE CORNER. ONCE MY PARENTS' HOUSE WAS OUT of sight, I couldn't drive any farther. Not my parents' house. My aunt and uncle's. I didn't know where to go. To the airport to get the first flight back to Philadelphia? Across that familiar path to the east side? Or should I drive, no destination, just pick a highway, any highway, until I arrived somewhere that felt right? Could you disappear if you'd never really existed?

It took me a moment to register the buzzing as my phone. I was relieved when it wasn't Mom, when it wasn't Jay, either.

"If you don't get here soon," Sheila said, "I'll have to order a third martini, and it will be all your fault."

"Get where?" It seemed impossible that life had continued, that martinis existed, that plans were made.

"To Westwood. Please tell me you're close. You know I hate drinking alone."

Westwood. I checked the calendar on my phone.

"Joanie's play." I couldn't believe I'd forgotten. Even with everything going on, this was Joanie's big break, when she'd be praised or panned, or worse, ignored.

"It starts in twenty minutes," Sheila said.

Sheila was expecting me. Joanie was, too. Joanie, who had

slept at my house most weekends in high school. Joanie, who went to restaurants with my family and helped Mom whip egg whites until they peaked. Joanie, who laid across my bed with me as we talked about boys and avoided our homework. Joanie, my oldest friend. Joanie, who knew me better than I knew myself.

"I'm on my way," I said, turning over the engine and pulling away from the curb.

SHEILA WAS WAITING FOR ME OUTSIDE THE GEFFEN PLAYHOUSE, fidgeting like a nervous mother.

"Come on, come on." She rushed me into the theater. We found our seats moments before the lights went down.

The curtain opened to the Prosorovs' living room. Joanie played Irina, the youngest sister in *The Three Sisters*. As Olga and Masha busied themselves with reading and work, Irina was lost in thought. Joanie wore a simple white dress and stared vacantly at the audience. The first line of the play was Olga's: *Father died just a year ago, on this very day.* The anniversary of his death was also Irina's name-day. Olga continued to explain how in a year they'd healed from a death that had felt impossible to overcome. Already, they were dreaming of the future, dreaming of returning to Moscow. I tried to focus on Joanie— beautiful, young Irina, the only sister who was happy—as she rambled about the value of work. My mind drifted to my own dead father, trying to locate moments when I should have discovered the truth.

When Mom and Billy had fought on my twelfth birthday, my first instinct was that they were arguing over my party, and they were. Billy had promised he'd be there. As my father, he should have shown up. All those times Billy didn't turn up, Mom never grew exasperated. Or perhaps she did. Perhaps she'd hid it from me, so I didn't have to be disappointed, so I didn't have to realize the truth. I thought about the afternoons when

Billy took me to Prospero Books, how I always imagined the store was waiting for me, and it was. It was waiting for me so much more than I'd understood.

In the final scene of the play, the three sisters embraced, sharing their unfulfilled desires and misguided dreams of Moscow. Joanie hugged those two actresses. They seemed like real sisters. While I'd always considered Joanie a sister, she had blood sisters, a connection we'd never know no matter how close we were. She had a mother, too. A neglectful mother but one who was hers.

"I would have interpreted the ending differently," Sheila said as the actresses took their final bow. "I've always found the end sad. Determined, not hopeful. Maybe we need the end to be hopeful. Maybe we need to believe that life will decide and life will choose right." I laughed bitterly at this, and Sheila eyed me, suspiciously.

We walked outside where several people milled around a fountain, sipping wine as they waited to meet the cast.

"How was your trip?" Sheila grabbed a glass of white wine from a tray. She asked me if I wanted one. I shook my head.

"Did you know?" I searched Sheila's calm demeanor for the sign of a lie.

"Did I know what?" Sheila exclaimed, eager for a bit of gossip.

"You told me you came to our house when I was a baby. Do you remember?" I stood at full attention, ready to pounce the moment she twitched or stammered or did anything that seemed off.

Sheila rested her hand on my shoulder. "Miranda, I know I'm old to you, but I'm not senile. Of course I remember."

"You said my mom was breast-feeding me," I said.

"And?"

"Are you sure?"

"I think so," she said, not understanding.

"My mother couldn't have breast-fed me."

Sheila crossed her arms, considering this fact. I waited for her to ask why it mattered, not certain I was ready to tell her my family's sordid tale, to put it out in the open, particularly to a writer who might see it as a story rather than a life.

She snapped her fingers. "You know what, I dated a man after Billy whose sister had also had a baby. She might have been the one who breast-fed. I can't remember."

I wanted to push Sheila on her memories of that evening at my parents' house, to help her find something amiss, a look Billy gave me, something my mother said that had struck her as off. Before I could say anything, the patio erupted in applause. Joanie and the two television actresses walked through the crowd, arm in arm. Joanie beamed. She was radiant. I wanted to be excited for her, but it was difficult to fight through my emotions, especially since I knew I couldn't pull her aside to talk about me. I couldn't steal this moment from her.

Sheila rushed to get in line to greet Joanie. Joanie was gracious with her fans, shaking hands and posing for photographs. When Sheila reached the front of the line, she handed Joanie a program and asked Joanie to make it out to her favorite middle-aged woman.

Joanie hugged us both before she was pulled away by an older man in a suit who introduced her to a circle of older men in suits. Some guy recognized Sheila and begged her to join him for a drink. She asked if I minded before dashing off. Joanie reappeared at my side, and we watched Sheila and her new friend vanish onto Le Conte Avenue.

"I want to be like that when I'm her age," Joanie said wistfully. I didn't mention that Sheila's husband had killed himself, that Sheila's confidence was an act, a way to fight the grief.

"You were amazing," I told Joanie.

"Thank you," she said in the rehearsed way she'd been thanking everyone on the patio, then she laughed at herself for pretending with me. "I was so nervous I don't remember a second of it. I don't think I missed any of my lines."

"If you did, no one noticed." I grabbed her hand and she squealed. We scanned the patio. "So tell me who's important."

As Joanie started to explain that the man in the suit was a producer, someone stopped behind Joanie and put her hands over Joanie's eyes. She had dyed blond hair and wore layers of makeup. Joanie grabbed her wrist and turned to hug her.

"Jacks." It was Jackie, Joanie's eldest sister. Her mother and her other sister, Jenny, were standing behind Jackie. They formed a huddle, a secret meeting between family that I watched from the outside.

Joanie's mother pet her hair. I tried to remember the last time Joanie's mom had shown up to support her daughter. She'd missed every school play, leading roles at the tiny theaters on Santa Monica Boulevard. She continued to stroke Joanie, saying, "talented" and "star" and "famous" and "amazing" and "my daughter." My daughter. I wanted to tear her hand away and scream that you can't just turn up when someone succeeds, you have to be there along the way, but Joanie was glowing under her mother's praise. Those comments meant more to her than the accolades of the executives and directors who had been at the show, the ones who might make her career.

Joanie and her family were going to have a drink somewhere on Westwood. "You'll come?" Joanie asked me, her arms linked with her sisters.

I told her I was tired.

"Let's get lunch tomorrow before my curtain call? No, wait, Chris's parents are coming. Then his brother's going to be here with his family. What about next week? Shoot, Lonnie and Sarah are flying in for the show." I didn't know who Lonnie and Sarah were. "The play will be over after Labor Day. We can do a weekend getaway to Ojai or something?" Joanie frowned. "You'll be gone by then."

"Joanie, it's fine." It was fine. It had to be. I was going through something, but Joanie was, too. I couldn't take this away from her, but I couldn't be part of it, either.

"Joanie, we should really get going," her mother said.

"You were wonderful tonight," I told her.

"You really think so?" she said, the perfect ingenue.

"Just don't forget about me when you're rich and famous." I did my best to sound chipper.

"I'll take you anywhere in the world you want to go." She blew me a kiss as her sisters guided her through the gate. I watched the four of them disappear across the street, arms linked, a force against the chilly night.

WHEN I GOT BACK TO PROSPERO BOOKS, I LOOKED UP LEE WIL-liams, ruling out several Lee Annes and Mary Lees, a college football star and a glassblower from Detroit. There were still thousands of Lee Williamses in America. The Lee Williams I was searching for didn't have a Facebook page. He didn't use Twitter or Instagram. His picture didn't even come up in images. I Googled Mom instead. Her likeness filled the screen. Dad's arm around Mom at a formal event, Mom's pretty face flush with wine and the energy of the room. Mom's professional photo from her website, hand on hip, hair straightened, no-nonsense gaze. Mom and one of her clients, whom I could tell was an actress from her extravagant clothing, from her comfort at being photographed. I scanned the pages of photographs of Mom. I didn't find any pictures of her with me. I couldn't remember the last time we'd been photographed together. My parents weren't big picture takers. They weren't the type to commemorate every moment, to share the details of their lives with everyone they knew. I'd assumed it was because they were private, but they must have not wanted something to become obvious in photographs that I hadn't seen in life. Maybe everything they did was decided around keeping their secret.

IN THE MORNING, THE STORE SMELLED OF BURNED TOAST FROM a bagel Lucia had forgotten in the toaster. She stomped around the tables, slamming plates of food before customers. Dr. Howard clapped to the beat of her stampede until she scowled at him.

When I asked her what was wrong, she said, "You're joking, right?" I followed her into the kitchen, watching as she smashed a slab of cream cheese between halves of a bagel. "Where the hell have you been?" Lucia glared impatiently at me, ready to attack.

"I can't deal with this right now." I started to walk out of the kitchen. Lucia blocked me, the plate with the bagel poking me in my rib cage. "Aren't you supposed to toast that?"

"You're suddenly the expert?" Lucia dropped the plate on the counter and started pacing. "You waltz in here and ask us to turn everything upside down, then you can't even bother to show up." She was like a peacock, sticking out her head, releasing exotic colors of emotion all around her. "Malcolm had to deal with the pipe by himself. Do you know what a pain in the ass that was? Then you miss my crochet circle not once but twice. You completely bailed on your turn to run the classics book club. Now, Alec's canceled and, like, half the people who bought tickets for the gala want their money back." When I gave her a look—*Who's Alec?*—she widened her eyes disdainfully. "The DJ?"

"So we'll get someone else to DJ." I really didn't care about DJs or books clubs or pipes.

"You know another world-class DJ who's going to do our gala for free?"

"What does that even mean, a world-class DJ?"

She grabbed the plate with the untoasted bagel, the slab of cream cheese like a block of ice in the middle. "I know you're only here temporarily, but we were counting on you." She stormed out of the kitchen. Only temporary. That was me. Here and everywhere.

Amy Meyerson

Malcolm was reviewing the literature section, clipboard in hand, jotting notes as he surveyed a shelf. It was nearing mid-August, and the store was empty. Other than Dr. Howard, Ray the screenwriter and some guy I didn't recognize, unfortunate enough to have ordered a bagel, none of the regulars were camped out in the café, not even Sheila. Two girls with backpacks and long brown hair browsed the literary section, competing to see who had read more. I recognized in the way they pointed to books without pulling them from the shelves that they weren't going to buy anything.

"Someone had sticky fingers with the Didion," Malcolm said. He flipped the page and scanned the next list of books, scribbling checkmarks beside the titles. Lucia threw a chair into the table. Mugs clanked as she grabbed the bus tub. "Don't pay attention to her," Malcolm said. "It was, like, twenty tickets. She's in the midst of her monthly fight with her boyfriend. She wants to feel like everyone's let her down because he's acting like an asshole. If she doesn't cool down in a few minutes, I'll tell her to take the day off." Malcolm continued checking the books. "I've put in a few calls to musicians I know. I'll find someone to play. Besides, we don't really want to be saved by a bunch of EDM-loving millennials, anyway." He flipped the page on his clipboard and began examining the next shelf.

"I'm sorry." All the emotion I should have felt since Big Bear poured into me at once. My legs buckled and I leaned against the shelves so I wouldn't fall. My headed pounded. I couldn't see straight. My ears rang painfully. Malcolm peered over at me, the two of him that I saw, suddenly worried. He put the clipboard on the shelf and stepped closer to me, resting his hand on my shoulder.

"You okay?" he asked. I gasped for air but my lungs blocked it. "Hey now, you're okay. Come on, let's sit down." He threw my arm across his shoulders and walked me to the desk.

I sat in the desk chair as Malcolm went to get me a glass of water. I leaned down, placing my head between my knees and breathed. Was I dying? Was this a panic attack? Malcolm returned and handed me the water. He rubbed my back as I took a few small sips. The water seemed to expand my throat; my breath returned. My head still pounded, only I could no longer hear it in my ears, and my vision focused until there was only one Malcolm standing beside me, still concerned. Suddenly, I wanted to say everything to him that I'd hoped to hear from Mom. "I'm so sorry for before. I know Billy was your friend. I haven't really thought about what this must have been like for you. I'm sorry I haven't been more understanding. I'm sorry—"

"Shh," Malcolm said. His hand was still on my back. "It's okay. You're okay." I continued to breathe as Malcolm studied me. He was so calm I started to feel embarrassed. But he looked at me like he'd seen it all before, like it was no big deal.

"I really am sorry," I said.

Malcolm nodded. "It's cool. I know it's been hard for you, too, Billy's death. I'm sorry, too." He leaned against the desk, and I could tell he wanted to say something more to me. "Billy and I have season tickets to the Dodgers. There's a game tomorrow. You'll come?" His tone was so flat I wasn't sure if he was asking or telling me to come.

"I'd like that," I said, and he nodded like the matter was settled. I watched as he returned to the shelves, found his clipboard and continued to do the inventory check. I felt my heartbeat not quite race but pulse, and it gave me hope that if I could feel excited about something again, I'd be able to feel other normal emotions at some point, too.

I finished the water and walked to the café to put the glass in the bus tub. Malcolm smiled when I passed him, his gaze soothing, and I doubted I could ever get used to those eyes, that they could ever lose their hold on me.

The café was so silent I could hear Dr. Howard scribbling on his legal pad. I found my bag, which I'd abandoned at the back table when Lucia had started yelling at me. *Bridge to Terabithia* rested on top of my wallet. I put it on the table, twisting the bookmark in my hand. I stared at Lee Williams's name. Lee was always in the store on the afternoons when Billy brought me to Prospero Books. I never remembered a closeness between him and Billy. Still, Lee must have known how I ended up being raised by my aunt and uncle. Billy must have told him something that would help me understand what I was supposed to do now that I had no mother or father, now that Billy had imploded my reality without creating a new one in its wake.

Lucia left without saying goodbye. She didn't even say hi to Charlie when he traded places with her, just brushed past him. He rolled his eyes at me as she slammed the door on her way out. Her anger was misplaced. She was really angry at Prospero Books, that everything wasn't working out so easily. That was a good anger. It was one that would drive our fight to save the store.

Charlie sat at my table, flipped through *Bridge to Terabithia*. "Poor Jess Aarons."

"Poor Leslie," I said.

Charlie carefully put the book on the table as though it were an antique, capable of breaking. "I don't think we're supposed to pity Leslie. She died, but it was a brave death. She taught Jess to be brave, too."

"So then why do you pity Jess?"

Charlie considered my question. "Maybe not at the end, but watching him deny her death, the guilt he felt because he abandoned her that day. It's so real."

Charlie pet the book before hopping up to check the coffee thermoses. *He ran until he was stumbling but he kept on, afraid to stop.* Jess had tried to outrun Leslie's death. He wasn't faster than Leslie when they'd raced at school. He wasn't faster than her death, either. And when he stopped running, he discovered how to memorialize his friend, how to keep the magic of Leslie alive, the magic of Terabithia, too.

DODGER STADIUM WAS TWO AND A HALF MILES FROM THE STORE, through Elysian Park, mostly uphill. Along the walk, I replayed Malcolm's words in several tones. *There's a game tomorrow. You'll come?* he said hopefully. *You'll come?* he ordered. *You'll come*, he begged. *You'll come*, he condescended. None of those tones felt right. I kept repeating his sentence with other inflections, distracting myself from the fact that I hadn't found Lee Williams, that I hadn't heard from Mom again, either.

Despite the brisk weather, I was perspiring by the time I reached the parking lot. My seat was on the reserve level, above home plate. I walked between rows of blue chairs toward a familiar mop of hair. I didn't realize I was holding my breath until I exhaled. Even though I saw Malcolm nearly every day, we'd never been together outside the store before.

Malcolm jumped up when he saw me, spilling half his bag of peanuts. I sidled through the row of people, stopping when I arrived beside him. He hesitated, then hugged me, the embrace over as quickly as it had been initiated.

"You made it," he said.

"Did you think I wouldn't?"

"Never know with you," he said as if I were an enigma, some inscrutable puzzle he couldn't solve. I sat in the seat beside him. Our knees touched as we watched the game.

Malcolm tossed peanuts into his mouth, cracking the shells with his teeth. The Dodgers' pitcher threw the first strike. Malcolm clapped after the batter struck out. The second batter hit a single to center field. With the bases loaded, the batter hit a fly ball, and the Dodgers filed into the dugout.

Malcolm stood up. "Do you want a beer? I'll get you a beer."

I sat alone, watching the away team warm up for the second

inning. I hadn't been to a game since middle school, when Dad used to get us tickets to the studio's box. Throughout the game, I'd sit in the front row, eyes peeled on the field, glove on my left hand, ready for a fly ball even though it would have been near-impossible for a foul ball to have reached the box. Dad would sit on the couches inside, chatting with his colleagues. Often, I was the only kid. Rather than feeling lonely, it made me proud. This was a business event, and still, Dad wanted to bring me. Every inning or so, he would sit beside me for a batter, pointing out the batter's perfect form, the telltale signs that the pitcher was about to throw a fastball down the middle. *When you step up to the plate,* he said, *make sure to look the pitcher in the eye. You see how the batter just did that? That lets the pitcher know you're not afraid. Baseball is like the rest of life,* he told me. *You have to decide how you want to be.*

Malcolm reappeared with two beers. We sipped from our plastic cups as we watched a Dodger stake out his position in the batter's box. I kept thinking about Dad. Mom must have told him I'd stopped by the house. He hadn't called me. He hadn't sent me a commanding text to come home. I snuck furtive glances at Malcolm as he focused on the game. I still wasn't sure why he'd asked me to come. Perhaps he'd put together an offer to buy me out or wanted to talk about the transition after I left. Malcolm didn't mention Prospero Books, and the longer we watched the game, the more it felt like an outing between friends.

"You come to a lot of games?" I asked.

"Billy and I usually made it to a game a week when the Dodgers were home. Billy hated to go a series without a game. He said it gave him cold sweats."

"I didn't realize he was a sports fan."

"Only baseball." Malcolm stood as a ball soared into the outfield. "Go, go, go." He twisted his body like a novice bowler hoping to steer the bowling ball from its natural trajectory toward the gutter. The baseball fell foul. "Damn." Malcolm sat down and popped another peanut into his mouth. "This is the last home game we have tickets for. I don't know if I can get season tickets next year without him."

I began to put my hand on his back, then felt awkward about it. I took one of Malcolm's peanuts and cracked it open with my fingers, digging the nut from the shell.

"That's cheating. You have to crack it with your teeth and spit the shell." He made a clicking sound as a tiny piece of shell arced out of his mouth.

The Dodgers were down 3-2. Malcolm chewed his nail. I sensed that this game mattered more to him than to the Dodgers' record. The batter walked toward home plate like he'd already struck out.

I stood up and started clapping. "All right, batter, batter, batter."

I motioned to Malcolm to join me and we screamed like it was the bottom of the ninth. Our energy was contagious. A man with a mullet stomped his feet. A blonde my mother's age danced. The batter watched two strikes go by.

"Swing, dammit!" Malcolm shouted. The bat cracked and the batter hesitated before running to first.

"Thank you!" Malcolm slapped me a high five.

Everyone stood for the leadoff hitter. This was the Dodgers' chance to break ahead. Cheers cocooned us, enclosing Malcolm and me into a small world of our own. He put his arm around me and swayed my body with his as we cheered. I felt the warmth of his chest, certain this was something more than a game with a friend or at least that I wanted it to be. Memories of Phillies games with Jay flashed through my mind. I quickly shook them off. It didn't feel quite right, being here with Malcolm when things were still so uncertain with Jay, but it didn't feel quite wrong, either. The leadoff hitter struck out. Malcolm muttered a string of nasty words as he sat back down.

The music got louder as the Dodgers tumbled out of the dugout. The screen above the scoreboard went black and the words Kiss Cam appeared inside a pink heart. An old couple's faces materialized in the heart. When they caught their profiles on the jumbo screen, they leaned into each other. Malcolm and I watched the pitcher warm up on the mound, both pretending we weren't monitoring the screen.

"When are you headed back to Philly?"

"In two weeks or so. School starts the first week of September."

"You excited to head back to work?"

The old couple's image disappeared, replaced by a mother and son. He squirmed as she tried to kiss him.

"I don't know if anyone is ever excited to go to work." My sarcasm surprised me. I'd never been flip about the start of the school year. By the time the summer was over, long days filled with reading and sleeping and a newfound, quickly abandoned exercise regiment, I'd itched to feel useful. Sure, the first morning my alarm went off at 5:15, I'd always asked myself, *Can I really do this again?* but I was never glib.

"I always am." He smiled. The Kiss Cam continued to capture couples, startled, then passionate, and I felt a subtle disappointment each time Malcolm's face and mine weren't broadcast across the screen. Malcolm had plump lips. They looked like good kissing lips. A tinge of guilt as I recalled Jay's lips, how a few months ago I'd hoped he'd be the last man I'd ever kiss.

"Once I'm back in the classroom, I'll realize how much I missed it. For now, it doesn't seem real that I'm leaving," I said.

In the bottom of the ninth, the Dodgers hit two doubles and a home run to win the game, and we were in the mood to celebrate. We stopped at a bar that was once an old cop haunt now overrun by recent college graduates. With the arrival of the new patronage, the owner had repurposed the neighborhood bar into a nightclub, fashioned with a dance floor and photo booth. Tonight, it didn't matter if you were old Echo Park or new, because everyone was a Dodgers fan. Even I had a Dodgers hat on. Malcolm bought it for me on one of his trips to the bathroom.

After a few beers Malcolm grabbed my hand and we danced to Michael Jackson beneath the glittering disco ball. The music's beat was a call to action. While I wasn't exactly comfortable, I was fluid, organic. Malcolm was a terrible dancer. That didn't stop him from breaking out every move from his junior high days.

When the Dodgers bar got too crowded, we stumbled down Sunset toward Prospero Books. It was over two miles and our drunken banter fizzled out as the cold night sobered us up. We stopped at a red light.

"Should we get a car?" he asked.

"We're more than halfway there at this point."

"But you're shivering." He took off his coat. "At least take this."

The light changed and I pulled his jacket tightly around my shoulders. It smelled like Malcolm. Cinnamon salted with sweat. I didn't realize I knew his scent. I inhaled deeply, trying to lock it in as a sensory memory, something I could return to when I thought about Malcolm, something that from across the country would help me remember this night.

When we got back to Prospero Books, Malcolm guided me around the store like I'd never been there before, introducing me to the books he loved, others that were Billy's favorites. I showed Malcolm the books I loved, biographies on Washington, Jefferson, Lincoln. I told Malcolm that Thomas Jefferson loved books, that he spent weeks in seclusion, reading and rewriting sections he didn't like. He even edited Shakespeare. Shakespeare.

"I bet he didn't change Miranda," Malcolm said. "'But you, o you, so perfect and so peerless, are created of every creature's best.'" I was surprised he knew the line. "It's from *The Tempest*," he explained, grinning ear to ear.

"I know what it's from," I said warily. His sincerity caught me off guard.

Malcolm consolidated Billy's titles on the staff table to make room for mine. He wrote my name on a card and sketched a caricature of me. My eyes were bigger in the drawing than in life, my lips pouty. I took the most recent biography on Paul Revere—one that highlighted his role in the Revolution while debunking Longfellow's myth of the man—and put it on an empty stand. Malcolm watched me. Soon, his face approached mine. He kissed me tentatively at first, expecting me to stop him. When I didn't, his kiss deepened.

Malcolm's mouth traveled toward my shoulder, grazing my clavicle. Jay flashed into my brain, but there was the pressure of Malcolm's lips and it felt incredible. Besides, Jay and I hadn't spoken in a month. Could you really feel guilty about cheating on someone you hadn't spoken to in a month? Was it even cheating? Malcolm's hands pulled my hips toward him until our stomachs touched, our inner thighs, our shoulders, and I forgot about Jay. I forgot about anything outside Malcolm, unsure how this was happening now, why it hadn't happened before, in disbelief that it was happening at all. I remembered how calm he'd been that afternoon as he'd watched me unravel, how nonjudgmental. As he continued to kiss my neck, I thought of how beautifully he'd recited the line from *The Tempest*. *But you, o you, so perfect and so peerless, are created of every creature's best,* his voice steady, like he'd been waiting to recite it to me from the moment he met me, and I realized, suddenly, that he had.

I pushed him away. "Billy told you I was named after *The Tempest.*"

"What?" He reached for me again. I pushed him away harder.

"You sent me the copy of *The Tempest*, in Philadelphia." I'd thought Elijah had sent me the book, but he'd said *letter* not *package.* A letter after Billy died, which would have arrived after the news of Billy's death, after I'd left Philadelphia. "You lied to me."

Malcolm leaned against the cooking section and ran his hand through his hair. "I wanted to tell you."

Those words were no better coming from Malcolm than they were coming from Mom.

"You said you were mourning," I screamed.

"I was mourning!" he screamed back.

"You made me feel like an insensitive asshole even though you really were lying. Do you realize how fucked up that is?" I became a beast turning at full moon, a wild animal let loose. I had no idea what I was saying to him. It involved a lot of *fucks*, a lot of *assholes*, a lot of *liars* and *manipulative pricks* and every other word I could lash at him. That anger was the first thing that had felt good in a long time, the first thing besides Malcolm's kiss, which paled in relation to the uncontrollable fury radiating out of me. "You think I'm an idiot? Dangling me along on your little leash. What the hell is wrong with you?"

"Miranda, stop." Malcolm grabbed me by the shoulders. "Just stop yelling."

I caught my breath. "You told me you were mourning. You used my uncle's death against me."

"I know," he said, "I know I did. And I was. I am. I am mourning."

"But you were lying to me, too."

"I was trying to help Billy."

"By *lying* to me!" And then I said the words that really hit him, the words that drained all the color from his face and caused him to stop trying to get me to calm down. "You knew Billy was my dad."

"He told me you were his niece," Malcolm insisted.

"But you knew."

Malcolm turned away. "You look just like him."

"And you didn't think to tell me? You didn't think I had a right to know?"

There was a beast in Malcolm, too, one I'd poked and prodded until he'd had enough. "Tell you what?" he yelled. "What exactly could I have told you? *Hello, I know we don't really know each other, but you know that uncle of yours, the one who used to own this store? Surprise! He's actually your dad.* Explain to me how I could have told you that?"

"You could have told me about the scavenger hunt." I ran my hand through my hair. "You could have admitted that you knew who I was at the funeral. You could have told me anything instead of making me feel like a complete shithead for asking you what you were hiding."

"I didn't like lying to you." Malcolm reached for one of my curls.

"Well, I guess that makes you citizen of the year."

His fingers felt like water as they tickled my scalp, and it would have been so easy to reach for his hand, to pull him to me and return to the part of the evening where we were learning how to please each other.

"You're right to be angry with me. I get it." His voice returned me to the room, out of the trance of his touch, back to his words, back to his lies.

"How noble of you. Jesus, you're arrogant." I yanked my hair away from his touch.

Malcolm folded his hands, not quite sure what to do with his restless energy. "I was trying to be a good friend to Billy."

"By pretending not to know who I was?"

"What difference would it have made? If I'd told you about Evelyn—"

"You knew about Evelyn, too!" I felt like I might vomit.

"Billy wanted to tell you this way." Malcolm watched me, his eyes doleful and even bluer. "I was trying to be a good friend. I don't know what else you want me to say."

I wanted him to say he was sorry. To say that he'd wanted to kiss me from the moment he first saw me. To say I had no idea how hard this has been on him. I wanted him to say anything that might let me be comforted by him. Instead, he repeated the words I didn't want to hear. "This was the way Billy wanted it."

I slid to the floor and leaned against the cooking section. "You were the only person who could have encouraged Billy to know his daughter." I was dizzy from the alcohol and the truth and the desire I still felt for Malcolm. He reached down to comfort me. I kept my face hidden from him, kept myself locked away where I hoped he couldn't find me.

"I know it doesn't mean much, but I really am sorry." I could feel him towering over me, so I burrowed my face farther into my palms.

"I'll go," he said. When I didn't fight him, I heard his feet shuffle toward the café. A chair scraped against the floor as he lifted his jacket off the back. "Sorry," he whispered again. He quietly slipped out the back.

I stayed on the floor after Malcolm left, in no rush to get up. How many times had I asked Malcolm to tell me the truth? How many times had he lied to me, manipulated me? I felt foolish. Absurd. Naive. I believed Malcolm was sorry, that it was hard for him to keep a secret, that he thought he was helping Billy. He wasn't helping, though. Malcolm should have pressed Billy to contact me sooner. And Billy should have reached out to me on his own. He should have wanted to have a relationship with me when I could have known him, when he still could have been my father.

CHAPTER EIGHTEEN

EVENTUALLY, I GOT UP OFF THE FLOOR. I WENT UPSTAIRS AND washed the shame from my face. When I climbed into Billy's bed, my father's bed, I couldn't sleep. My brain returned to *Bridge to Terabithia*, to Lee, to the rest of Billy's quest I still hadn't completed. The last time I saw Lee he'd called Mom and she'd whisked me away from Prospero Books. Did he know that was the end of my relationship with Billy? Did he feel guilty? I'd told Malcolm he was the only one who could have encouraged Billy to reconnect with me, but he wasn't. Lee could have, too. He could have prevented Billy from disappearing in the first place.

I searched the internet again for Lee, using every word I associated with him: bookstore, manager, books, reading, Silver Lake, Nancy Drew, coffee, literature, recommendations. I'd never asked him enough about himself to know anything about his personal life. I didn't know if he was married. I didn't even realize he was gay until I located a two-hundred-word piece in *LA Weekly*. *Neighborhood says goodbye to beloved bookstore manager.* The article was from 2001. It explained that Lee and his partner, Paul, were relocating to Santa Barbara.

IT WAS A PERFECT SOUTHERN CALIFORNIA MORNING AS I DROVE to Santa Barbara. Clear blue skies, air salty from the ocean. In Malibu, surfers rode the modest waves that bordered Highway 1. I had telephone numbers and addresses for nine Lee Williamses listed in Santa Barbara County. One was Thomas Lee. Another Joseph Lee. I didn't know if Lee was his first name, and besides, nine wasn't that many. My plan was simple: I'd visit each one until I found the Lee I was looking for. I could have called before I left, but I just needed to go. I needed the fresh air, the drive, the distance from Malcolm and our fight. The distance from Mom and our fight, too.

The traffic lights grew sparser along the highway until they disappeared. Mansions clung to the bluffs, threatening to collapse onto the open road below. By seven-thirty, Malcolm would have arrived at the store. When I didn't surface downstairs, would he brave the steps to the second floor? Would he knock on my door? And when he realized I wasn't there, would he think I'd left for good? I checked my phone. No texts. No missed calls. Then I remembered. Malcolm didn't have my telephone number. I knew the way his breath tasted and the feel of his chest against mine but I didn't even know his area code.

I started to call the store, then dialed Joanie instead. When her voice mail picked up, all the stories I hadn't told her collected in my throat. It was too much for a voice mail, too much for the few hours she had before her next performance. After I hung up, I still needed to talk, to not be alone. I scrolled down to Jay's number, and almost hit Send. We hadn't spoken in a month. He would have been patient if I told him what was going on—but as soon as I thought it, I wasn't so sure. Besides, the person I really wanted to talk to was Mom. I put my phone away, and kept driving, toward Santa Barbara and the nine Lees that lived there.

The first Lee Williams was a Realtor, holding an open house near the old mission. A Spanish Revival with a layout like a

maze, making you lose all sense of direction until you magi-
cally returned to the front door. Lee was in the back. She was
statuesque with long red hair.

I called Lee Williams the attorney next. He was the right
gender at least. His tone was hostile when I explained that I
was trying to locate Lee Williams, the bookseller. "I don't have
time for whatever shenanigan this is," he said as he hung up.

That left seven Lee Williamses. Lee Williams the dentist had
immigrated to the US in the '80s. He had a subtle yet distinct
accent. The Lee I knew had a banal accent, one I'd assumed
was Midwestern even if, at twelve, I hadn't known what a Midwestern accent sounded like.

The next five Lees were equally dead ends. Lee Williams the
plumber was African American. His son, Lee Williams, Jr., was
the high school's star quarterback. Joseph Lee Williams the car
mechanic was too young. Thomas Lee Williams the retired police officer too old. Lee Williams the sommelier was the right
age, gender and race, but when I stopped into his restaurant,
he was too tall and skinny.

The last Lee Williams on my list remained a ghost. When I
tried the number I'd found in the white pages, it had been dis-
connected. I looked up his partner, Paul, instead and eventually discovered a picture of them dancing at a charity ball for
an LGBTQ organization, headquartered in downtown Santa
Barbara.

The organization's offices were on the other side of the 101
from the main strip of downtown. I passed Micheltorena Street,
turning on Figueroa, street names I recognized from Los Angeles. Of course they were historical figures, not simply street
names. General Figueroa. General Micheltorena. As I walked
toward the organization, I thought about how, if I'd taught in
Los Angeles or Santa Barbara, I could have printed maps of
the city, allowing my students to discover the historic names
of streets, using the city itself as a gateway into Alta Califor-

nia and eventually the Mexican American War. Remnants of California's Mexican legacy were scattered across the region like clues in a scavenger hunt. Remnants of the Revolution and the Early Republic were scattered across Philadelphia like clues in a scavenger hunt, too, only I'd never thought to teach the city's history that way.

The organization's offices were housed in a beige one-story building between a tattoo parlor and a dollar store. The man behind the front desk smirked when I asked if he knew Lee. "We don't normally give out our members' information," he said with feigned sweetness.

"Can you call him? He was friends with my uncle. My uncle died recently."

The receptionist cast me the expression of someone who had known many people who died but not so many that he'd grown immune to it. He told me he'd check with his supervisor.

While I waited for him to return, I looked at the picture of Lee and Paul on my phone. Their eyes locked as they danced, like they only needed each other. Mom and Dad danced like that. Billy and Evelyn had probably danced that way, too.

I couldn't look at that photograph anymore, so I browsed Prospero Books' website instead. Malcolm had uploaded the special offers of the day, signed first editions of *Jesus' Son* and *The Virgin Suicides*. His noir blog featured several neo-noir titles that in his estimation weren't entirely worthy of loathing. Photographs rotated at the bottom of the homepage. One of Charlie's most recent book club, a mommy-and-me reading of *Oliver Twist*. Charlie was dressed the same as the boys sitting on their mothers' laps, news cap and vest, a large print edition of the book opened between them. In another photograph, Lucia and four pale girls held crochet hooks toward the camera, balls of colorful yarn cradled in their laps. At the top of the homepage, I tapped the Gala tab. There was a link to purchase tickets, a description of the event, a list of items for sale at the silent auction and of the entertainment. Malcolm had added a new name for musical entertainment, a band called Raw Cow Hide, whose sound he described as a modern-day Velvet Underground. I didn't know he'd found a replacement for Lucia's DJ friend. He was making decisions without me, as if I was already gone.

I hit the About Us tab, expecting to find details on Malcolm, Lucia and Charlie, possibly Billy, not me. Beneath a lengthy description of Prospero Books, complete with Malcolm's explanations of the balance between new and used copies, titles you couldn't find in any big-box store, there was a photo of the four of us from the Fourth of July, empty beer bottles and tequila safely out of view. Malcolm's arms were around Lucia and me. Charlie sat on the opposite side of Lucia, petting her hand. Beneath the photograph Malcolm had written, *The Prospero Family.*

"You're in luck," the receptionist said when he returned. He handed me an address. "He's home now. He said he'd be delighted to see you."

LEE LIVED IN AN APARTMENT COMPLEX NEAR CITY COLLEGE where Paul taught statistics.

"Don't let him fool you," Lee said as he let me into their apartment. "Statistics is completely dull."

"Hush," Paul said from the kitchen. "It's a language like any other. You just don't know how to speak it."

Lee winked at me. His belly had ballooned since I'd last seen him, and his legs had slimmed to skin and bones. Traces of the man I remembered lingered on his face. He still had bushy eyebrows, now completely white. Full cheeks, now spotted with rosacea.

"Look at you," he marveled. "I can't believe you're here. How long has it been?" He knew how long it had been. We both did. "You're all grown up. You look—" I waited for him to tell me I looked so much like my mother. "I see so much of Billy in you," he said, reaching for my hand.

Paul brought in a tray with a pitcher of lemonade and a plate of cookies.

"I don't drink anymore," Lee told me. He took a sip of lemonade and sighed. "It's not a cold beer, but it's satisfying in its own way." Paul teasingly slapped his leg, making light of what must have been a longer, more painful story.

Paul said he had exams to grade and left us alone in the living room.

"Are you working?" I asked Lee.

"Volunteering," he said. "When we moved up here, I thought about working at another bookstore, maybe even opening my own shop. It would never have been Prospero Books. I knew I wouldn't be happy here if I tried to recreate the life I'd left."

"Why'd you move?"

"Paul's mom was sick. He wanted to be close to her. I didn't want to leave, but let me give you some advice. There are three things in life that matter—your partner, your job, your place. One of those three has to be number one. The other two have to come second. For me it was Paul. I loved LA. I loved Prospero Books. But Paul was numero uno."

"What about family? Where does family fit in?" I asked.

Lee's eyes shifted upward as he contemplated the role of family. "I don't know. I was never close with my family. Maybe it should be a list of four—love, job, place, family?"

"Or maybe family is part of place?"

"That sounds right. And for Paul, family and place were numero uno because he was coming back to care for his mom. I never begrudged him that. It didn't mean he loved me any less. In love, job and place, one partner picks love and the other picks something else that shapes their life together."

I tried to decide which would matter the most to me. I had a boyfriend who might be an ex, another man whom I'd kissed and then called a fucking liar. I had two jobs. They mattered to me in different ways. I had two places; I didn't know which one I preferred. The same went for family.

"You were working at Prospero Books until you left LA?" I reached for a cookie, then remembered the cookie I'd had the last time I saw Lee, how I'd broken it into smaller and smaller pieces, unable to take a bite. I put the cookie back on the tray.

"I told Paul we couldn't leave until I figured out a plan. Billy was always in and out, and he didn't know the first thing about running the store. It was a tough time. Paul was here. I was there. I owed it to Evelyn not to abandon Prospero Books. Plus, it was my home. Just because I picked love didn't mean I stopped caring about place."

"You owed it to Evelyn? You were friends with her?" No wonder I'd never noticed a closeness between Lee and Billy.

Lee returned his empty glass to the table and settled into his chair. "Evelyn and I both worked at a bookstore in Pasadena. It was a small store, sold mostly political books. I was there for five years or so before she started. She was kind and beautiful and that fooled everyone."

The store was home to communists, anarchists, to anyone with a taste for rebellion. Evelyn wasn't a rebel. She was a reader. Lee was a reader, too. They first bonded over their love of *The Tempest*. Evelyn loved Miranda, her purity, her willingness to trust and to love. Lee loved Ariel and Caliban, their desire to be free. When Evelyn started working at the bookstore in Pasadena in the late '70s, it didn't carry *The Tempest*. It didn't carry any Shakespeare. No copies of *Jane Eyre*. Nothing by Jane Austen, Henry James, Virginia Woolf, Nathaniel Hawthorne. None of Updike's Rabbit novels. There was a small political fiction section that carried *Catch-22, 1984, Fahrenheit 451* and *Dr. Zhivago*. Not *All Quiet on the Western Front* or *A Farewell to Arms*. *The Feminine Mystique*, not *The Bell Jar*. Those distinctions bothered Evelyn. What was war without love? What were cautionary tales without stories that celebrated life? What was a movement without the struggles of the individual? Evelyn saw more truth in Emma Bovary, Anna Karenina, Edna Pontellier and her awakening than in any of the pamphlets and manifestos the store stocked regularly. Lee agreed that the store needed books not overtly political. He thought the activists could learn a thing or two from the rhythms of Flaubert, Tolstoy, Chopin. What mattered to Lee was language. All those beautiful sentences he could never write. There was an art to appreciation. Lee excelled in the art of appreciation.

Evelyn always feigned ignorance to her effect on people. When she met your eye, you felt as though she really saw you. And she remembered everyone. Greeted them by name and asked them questions about their families, their pets, their jobs, questions that may have seemed generic or insincere coming from someone else. In return, they wanted nothing more than to please her. Lee wasn't immune to it, either. Every time she walked into the bookstore, a softness spread through his chest. A flurry like a crush.

Evelyn started with *The Master and Margarita*. She handed her dog-eared copy to the owner of the leftist bookshop as though she was handing him part of herself.

I think you'll like this. She smiled, turning Bulgakov into a secret between them. And what self-proclaimed communist wouldn't benefit from reading Bulgakov's critique of Stalinist Russia, its allegory of good and evil? Then she gave the owner her copy of Graham Greene's *The Quiet American*, then *Atlas Shrugged*, *The Grapes of Wrath*, *Orlando*, *The Bluest Eye*, until he gave her a corner of the store and told her to stock it as she saw fit.

Readings are a good idea. She twisted her emerald earring, batting her eyes at him as though the idea had been his, and it wasn't long before she had a reading series, wasn't long before the activists were also readers of literature.

"And that was Evelyn. She was a healer. She was generous. And she was unfathomably generous with me."

Lee didn't remember how it started. They spent hours in the store arguing about books they'd recently read, *Midnight's Children* and *The World According to Garp*. They always loved the same books for different reasons. Lee praised Jenny Fields and her individualism while Evelyn condemned Irving's patriarchal, so-called feminism. They had heated arguments about whether Mr. Rochester was a sociopath, Lee insisting that he'd been forced into an impossible marriage and Evelyn outraged that Lee would defend a man who locked his wife in the attic. Lee didn't believe half of what he said, but he liked how Evelyn's face grew red when she was exasperated. On one work, however, they always agreed. *The Tempest* was the perfect play. Prospero the perfect protagonist.

"I said something like, if we owned a bookstore we should name it after Prospero, and then that became a joke. If we owned a bookstore, we'd have an entire section devoted to literary criticism, with not one book of politics. If we owned a bookstore we'd have *Romeo and Juliet* appreciation day. We'd have a party in honor of literature's great lovers, and finally Evelyn said, 'Well, why don't we? Why don't we have our own bookstore?'"

For most people the answer would have been obvious—capital. Evelyn had a trust, modest by trust standards, but a trust nonetheless.

Well, why don't we? Evelyn said with that glint in her eye, and how could Lee possibly refuse her?

She deferred to him on almost everything. He'd been in books longer than she had. He understood which storefronts were too big, which were too small, how far down Sunset Boulevard the growing gentry of Silver Lake would be willing to venture. On one thing she was adamant. The walls had to be bright, almost blindingly green. She also insisted on the divisions between literary, historical and artist biographies, essays from memoirs. A table for first-time authors by the register.

"I wish she'd had more time there," he said. "We weren't open a year when it happened." Lee disappeared inside himself, appearing tortured by something he found there, something he could never forget. I'd thought Billy was using Jess to describe his own loss, but it was Lee's suffering, his connection to Terabithia, that Billy wanted me to understand.

"You found her?" I guessed.

"I've never told anyone what happened that day." Lee crossed and uncrossed his legs. "Paul was with me, and Billy never wanted to talk about it. It wasn't something I could ever tell anyone else. When Vince called this morning and said you were looking for me, I knew I was going to tell you. I knew I wanted to."

"It means a lot to me. I know it must be difficult. It means a lot that you'd return to all of that."

"I never left it," he said. "Looking back, it was reckless. Evelyn was over eight months pregnant. They never should have been there." Evelyn had insisted. They'd been up to the cabin the last three New Year's Eves, since they'd bought the place, and Evelyn wanted it to be their tradition. She'd never had traditions growing up.

I waited for him to tell me it wasn't true. I wasn't the baby. Some small part of me still hoped I could restore my family unit as it had always been.

"It was the last trip they'd be able to make before the baby—before you—arrived," Lee said. He didn't try to deny my origins. I didn't try to make him. "And once you were here, they needed to do a lot to the house before it was safe."

Lee studied me, trying to gauge my reaction. I remained perfectly still, seemingly calm, even though my body thudded with every heartbeat and I was worried I might start seeing double again. But I could breathe, so I breathed, in and out, steady, serene. I nodded to him to continue, that I could handle the details that would come next. And I could handle them. I needed to. This was the moment Billy had guided me to. The truth of my birth. The night of my mother's death.

"For starters," Lee continued, "the house needed a new roof." The roof leaked and was caving in. The vents were corroded and needed replacing. *It's like the opening credits for a horror film,* Paul had said the first time they saw the cabin, a comment he would regret for years to come. But the house's shabbiness was its charm. Pale blue paint chipping off the wood, a post missing from the porch railing. No television. No stereo system. Only a telephone, installed at Lee's insistence when he'd been unable to reach Evelyn after there had been a mix-up at the bank, and he couldn't proceed without her signature.

"Evelyn had been after Billy for months to fix the roof. Billy was pretty handy and he saw that house as his Sistine Chapel."

Billy had promised to repair the roof in the summer. Then he'd been busy at the lab. By the time things slowed down, the snow had arrived, and they would have to wait until the following summer to replace the roof.

Look at it, Evelyn said, pointing to the part where it curved downward. *A pile of snow and it could snap.*

If anything it will slowly leak. It's not going to buckle all at once, Billy reasoned.

And what about that? she said, pointing to a vent on the roof. *What if there's lead? Or if a squirrel crawls into the house?*

Then it will bite us and we'll go rabid. Billy nibbled her neck. She giggled, allowing herself to embody the moment, the happy couple about to be parents, her fears merely a new mother's nerves, evidence that she was ready for the baby and all that came with it.

Think about it in terms of probability, Billy told her. *Statistically, the likelihood of a roof caving in is less probable than getting in a car crash or getting mauled by a bear. Heck, it's less probable than get-*

ting mauled by a bear in a place called Big Bear. And Evelyn loved how he reasoned, how he removed the emotion and relied on logic. But that's the thing about probability, however unlikely. There's always a chance.

Lee and Paul were planning on coming up the afternoon of the twenty-ninth, after Lee closed Prospero Books for the holiday. A few customers had lingered and one of the employees had had trouble with the credit card processing machine. By the time Lee got through to the credit card company, the snow falling on Big Bear had thickened.

You'd better wait until morning, Evelyn said when Lee called to tell her they were finally getting on the road. *It's a whiteout here.*

Paul wanted to be on the first ski lift up the mountain, so the next morning he dragged a bleary-eyed Lee out of their apartment and into the car. They were already on the 210 when the sun's rays pierced the San Gabriel Mountains.

"For weeks after, I tried to imagine what we could have done differently," Lee said, "If we'd gotten there earlier that morning. If I'd insisted we have a party at Prospero Books instead of the cabin. But if we'd gotten there the night before—then we'd all be dead."

Lee stared at the ski mountain as Paul steered the car along the road that hugged the lake. At seven, the mountain was still closed. The ski trails were blank canvases, the trees separating them covered in milky white. Small dots of dark green foliage pierced through the snow, like specks of paint splattered across the hillside.

They turned off North Shore Road, into Fawnskin where the houses were small and old. Lee couldn't remember the address, so they tried the first street, looking for the wind chimes that hung on the porch. Lee had bought them for Evelyn as a housewarming gift.

You didn't think it might help to bring the address, Paul said. He was already wearing his snow pants. They made a swishing sound as his foot pressed and released the clutch.

It's part of the adventure.

Ski mountain sounds more adventurous to me.

They turned onto the next block. Lee knew it wasn't particularly efficient to drive around until they stumbled upon the house. Still, he liked searching for Evelyn's house and eventually finding it. It felt charmingly small town.

No chimes on the second street, so Paul turned at the end onto the next block.

This is completely ridiculous, Paul said.

Lee rested his hand on the back of Paul's neck. *The mountain isn't even open yet. Just humor me.*

Paul continued to weave in and out of the neighborhood, not finding humor in any of it.

Wait. Here. Lee pointed to a house three doors down from where Paul slid to a stop. The snow buried the broken banister and hid the old shingled roof, but Lee spotted them just as they passed. Patinaed copper and mahogany. The wind chimes.

Paul parked, and they followed the path toward the house. It hadn't been shoveled, and their calves disappeared into the snow. Lee laughed as he almost fell, kicking a bit of snow at Paul, who pretended to be annoyed. They knocked on the door. When no one answered, they knocked again. The house didn't have a doorbell. Lee figured Billy and Evelyn were probably in the kitchen preparing breakfast and couldn't hear the door. He carefully cracked the door open.

Evelyn? When no one answered, he stepped in. Paul followed. Garlic and burned toast lingered in the air. The floorboards creaked under their weight. Lee found the light switch next to the door.

"First thing I saw were Billy's socked feet dangling off the couch."

Billy's legs were crossed at the ankles, and when Lee saw them hanging like that, he knew something was wrong.

Bill? Lee shook Billy. He was lying facedown on the couch, seemingly asleep. *Billy.* He continued to shake him. *Evelyn? Ev?*

Paul rushed over and pushed Lee aside.

Billy, he said, grabbing Billy's shoulders. *Is he drunk?* Paul leaned in to smell his breath and shook his head. *He's breathing.*

What's wrong with him?

I don't know. Paul shook Billy, breathed into his mouth, shook him some more. Lee ran upstairs.

Evelyn, he called.

Evelyn, he screamed.

The bedroom door was shut. He hesitated for a moment, then pushed it open.

Evelyn was in bed, sleeping. Two pillows rested behind her head. Her long blond hair fell around her shoulders. She looked peaceful, beautiful. Too peaceful. Too beautiful. Lee shook her shoulders, softly at first, then violently. Evelyn's eyes remained closed. Lee felt woozy like his head had been hit with a hammer.

Paul, he shouted. *Come quick.*

Paul ran into the room.

She won't wake up, either.

Paul checked her pulse.

Let's get her out of here. Paul lifted Evelyn off the bed. Her head and feet dangled in his arms, her stomach an enormous beach ball between his hands. *Go call 9-1-1. Now.*

Lee sprinted into the kitchen, found the rotary phone on the wall.

This is taking too long, Lee called to Paul as he waited for the operator. He could hear Paul careening down the stairs, one foot at a time, his steps heavy with the weight of Evelyn's pregnant body. *Hello?...There's something wrong. They won't wake up... What?...I don't know...Yes, they're breathing...No, I don't know what's happened...The address? I don't know. We just got here...I don't know the address.* Paul rushed into the kitchen and searched a drawer. He handed Lee a piece of mail and Lee read the address to the operator. He hung up. *They're on their way.*

In the living room, Paul had seated Evelyn next to Billy on the couch. Billy was contorted at an awkward angle. It seemed painful. If it was, Billy couldn't feel it. Evelyn was seated upright. Her head had fallen back like she was drugged. Lee's head was pounding now. He massaged his temples. The throbbing didn't go away.

We should get them out of the house, Paul said.

Lee found their jackets in the closet. He leaned against the doorframe, dizzier, out of breath. He willed himself to focus. He threw their coats to Paul. Focus.

Lee sprinted outside. The air stung his lungs and cheeks. He thought he might fall he was so dizzy. He fumbled with the keys as he tried to unlock the door. Focus. Why had Paul even locked the car, anyway? Lee got into the car and turned over the ignition. He cranked the heat on full blast and rushed back to the house to help Paul.

Move, Paul shouted as he wobbled with Evelyn in his arms. *Jesus, Lee, get out of the way. The door. Get the car door.*

Lee rushed back to the car and opened the door, helping Paul put Evelyn inside.

I'm sorry, Paul said once Evelyn was safely in the car. He stroked the side of Lee's face.

Never mind. Let's go get Bill.

Lee followed Paul to the front steps. *Wait here,* Paul instructed. *I don't want you going back inside the house.*

What's wrong with the house?

I don't know. Paul covered his mouth with his sleeve as he swooped back in, but there was nothing to protect himself from. Burned toast and garlic. That was it. No odorous gas. Nothing obviously poisonous.

When the ambulance arrived, the EMTs asked a few questions that Lee didn't remember answering. They strapped Evelyn and Billy to gurneys and intubated them.

Do you know what's wrong with them? Lee asked the EMT who was checking his vitals.

They'll do tests at the hospital. The doctors will be able to tell you what's happened.

Lee felt nauseous and didn't refuse when an EMT placed a mask over his face. He remembered the EMT's hands were cold and surprisingly brittle. Paul insisted he was fine, then threw up all over the white snow.

At the hospital, Lee and Paul were rushed in one direction, Billy and Evelyn in the other. Lee and Paul sat in a sterile room, confined to plastic chairs by oxygen tanks. The mask was claustrophobic. All Lee could hear was the inhalation and exhalation of his steadying breath. He looked over at Paul, who blinked at him with watery eyes. He reached over to take Paul's hand, and they sat like that, hand in hand, staring at each other until the doctors returned.

Lee learned the term *carboxyhaemoglobin* from the doctors. Their faces were grave when they said that Evelyn's and Billy's carboxyhaemoglobin levels were astronomical. Lee didn't know what that meant but he understood that it was bad. And then they used a term he did understand.

Carbon monoxide.

"They didn't have a detector?" I asked Lee.

"I don't think they were even on the market yet."

"So how did it happen, the carbon monoxide?"

"I never got an exact story. It had something to do with a clogged vent on the roof from all the snow."

"You never got an exact story?"

"At the hospital, the doctors told us that Evelyn was in surgery. Billy was stabilizing. We weren't family, so they didn't tell us anything else. The police asked us some questions, then the doctors told us to go home and get some sleep. We checked into a motel nearby. In the morning your parents were there."

Lee spotted Suzy and her husband—"David," I told him. Lee had only met him that one time in the hospital and couldn't remember his name—in the waiting room. Suzy was leaning against David's shoulder, crying.

Is that Bill's sister? Paul asked Lee. *Don't you want to sit with her?* When Lee hesitated, Paul said, *Go sit with her.*

Lee wasn't sure Suzy would recognize him. Whenever she came into the bookstore, she said hello as though she was trying to remember who he was, even though he was one of three employees at Prospero Books and had been friends with Evelyn for years. When he sat beside her, Suzy immediately said, *Lee,* and hugged him.

"That's how I knew. If it had been Billy, she wouldn't have hugged me. That's how I knew it was Evelyn."

The baby's in NICU, but Evelyn— Suzy was unable to finish her sentence and Lee clasped her hand, indicating that he understood.

Lee sat beside Suzy, holding her right hand. David held her left hand. When the doctors told Suzy she could see the child, she thanked Lee for coming.

Miranda, Lee told Suzy. *Evelyn was going to name her Miranda.*

Suzy nodded. Lee couldn't tell if she knew the reference. He watched as she followed the doctors farther into the hospital. As she disappeared, a quote from *The Tempest* appeared to him. *Thy mother was a piece of virtue.* It was the single reference to Miranda's mother, a figure otherwise absent from the play, absent from Miranda's life, absent from her memory.

CHAPTER NINETEEN

I SHIFTED ON THE COUCH, TRYING TO GET COMFORTABLE AS LEE continued to talk about Evelyn's death. While the cushions were firm, it was the story itself that cramped my arms and back. I couldn't have remembered that time. Still, it seemed like it should have felt familiar, like it was part of me.

"After Ev died, I didn't see Billy for six months or so," Lee said. "They had a funeral, but there was some big fight between Evelyn's father and Billy, so they kept it to family."

Lee was mourning. The devotees of Prospero Books were mourning, too. So they decided to throw a memorial of their own. At the store, the employees and the regulars each read a passage that reminded them of Evelyn. Lee didn't tell anyone what had happened to Evelyn, but tragedy had a way of revealing itself, of spreading like streams between people.

The store still overflowed with Evelyn. Boxes of books she'd ordered continued to come in daily. Lee cried when he saw the cover of *The Handmaid's Tale*. Gray stone walls. Crimson garments. Evelyn had been so excited to read it. Her handwriting remained across the classics and literary correspondences sections. Lee knew he'd eventually have to take down the shelf-talkers she'd written. The store would have to recommend other, newer books. He held off on removing her notes until they were yellow and disintegrating.

"So Billy didn't contact you for six months?" I asked Lee. "Did that seem strange?"

"It's hard to know how to behave when someone you love passes. Lots of things feel wrong. Nothing feels right. I think for Billy, coming to the store must have felt wrong until one day not coming felt worse."

Lee froze when he noticed Billy lingering by the door. He'd lost weight since Lee had last seen him.

"Billy and I weren't that close when Evelyn was alive. We spent a lot of time together, couples' time. Evelyn and I gravitated to one conversation, Billy and Paul to another. They had mathematics in common. It was clear to anyone who saw Billy and Evelyn together how much he loved her, so I respected him for that, but we never really had a connection."

Once Billy returned to Prospero Books, he started visiting the store regularly. He and Lee never spoke about what had happened. He would ask Lee about the sales, if Lee needed anything from him. Lee assured him everything was fine.

"Those were the days when the store thrived. We were the only bookstore around. This was before huge commercial retailers and the internet, before DVR and on-demand. Back then a bookstore was a viable business."

There was nothing Billy needed to do, which seemed to comfort him.

"What about me?" I asked. "Did Billy tell you how I ended up living with my parents?"

"Not directly." Lee paused, studying me. I remained calm, externally, anyway. "Are you sure you want to hear this? I can't explain why Billy did what he did. I won't justify it."

"I'm not looking for you to justify it. I want to know the truth. I think that's why Billy wanted me to talk to you. He knew you would tell me the truth."

"I'm not sure I know the truth. I know what I saw."

"I want your truth, then," I insisted.

"Well," Lee began, debating how honest he should be. "Truth is, first time he came in, he didn't mention you. I thought you'd passed, too." Billy told Lee that he was staying with his sister. He'd said, *I'm staying with my sister*, not *we, we're staying*. "Then one day he said something about his niece, Miranda, and of course I knew."

Billy had been coming to the store for several months. After close, they would sit at one of the tables in the café, drinking whiskey as Billy amused Lee with stories from his latest adventure abroad. Billy treated his body like armor meant to be abused. He'd returned from Taiwan with his arm in a sling after tripping on debris from the Tsaoling landslide. In Tehuacán, he'd been stung by a swarm of bees. Welts rose on his legs and neck. Lee let Billy talk. All his stories were about his travels. Never about Evelyn. Never about me.

He said it so casually Lee didn't immediately register what he'd heard.

What book should I get for a one-year-old? It's my niece Miranda's first birthday. My first birthday, also the one-year anniversary of Evelyn's death.

Lee wanted to ask him, *Miranda? You mean your daughter? She's still alive?* He wanted to ask Billy how he'd never mentioned his daughter. He wanted to ask how his daughter had become his niece. Billy fumbled with his whiskey glass, not meeting Lee's eye, and Lee understood that this was Billy's way of confessing he'd been unable to care for me. Lee was speechless. He wanted to shake Billy, screaming, *This is Evelyn's daughter, you can't abandon her*, but Lee saw in Billy's distant and nervous face that anything he wanted to say to punish Billy, Billy had already inflicted upon himself.

I'm sure we can find something for your niece, Lee said. Billy looked visibly relieved when Lee handed him a copy of *Goodnight Moon.*

"From that point on, you were Billy's niece. I wonder what would have happened if I'd said something to him."

"He probably would have stopped coming to see you," I said because it was true.

"That's probably right," he agreed. From that point forward I was Billy's niece, which worked because I looked like Mom. I became her daughter.

"It's not that you don't have Evelyn in you. You have her energy. Her calm. That's what people loved about Evelyn. It was her demeanor, her poise, that made her not just another pretty girl. I see that in you."

"You don't have to say that."

"I saw it the first time I met you."

When Billy first brought me to Prospero Books, he'd held my hand as he guided me inside. Lee watched my eyes wander around the store taking everything in at once, giggling like I had an inside joke with the space, the books. He saw instantly that I was Evelyn's daughter.

Can we find something special for my favorite niece? Billy said when he introduced me to Lee.

For years, Lee had known that I was being raised as Billy's niece, but seeing me in Prospero Books, saying to Billy, *I'm your only niece,* Lee understood in a way he hadn't before that Evelyn was gone.

I held on to the ends of my pigtails, swaying foot to foot in anticipation of the perfect gift. Lee had no idea what book to give Evelyn's daughter, what might be special enough. Nothing seemed right, not E. B. White, not Roald Dahl, not Frances Hodgson Burnett. Lee peered down at my freckled, eager face, searching for sadness that wasn't there, for that eerie foresight children sometimes have. Between the pigtails and the freckles, and my striped T-shirt, Lee thought I looked like Pippi Long-stocking. Unable to come up with a better choice, he guided me to the children's section and handed me all the Pippi Long-stocking books that were in stock.

Right away, Lee realized it was a mistake. He watched as Billy began to read to me about Pippi's mother who had died when she was very young, about her father who had been swept to sea. Lee waited for Billy to glare at him, castigating Lee with his eyes. But Billy kept reading, his voice even and his attention remaining on me.

Do you like this story? he asked me.

I had pointed to the page. *Read*, and Billy continued to read how Pippi never believed her father was dead, how she waited for him to return to her. Lee debated whether he'd subconsciously chosen this book to urge Billy to be honest with me. Truth was, Lee didn't remember the story of Pippi Long-stocking. He remembered she had pigtails and freckles. He saw mine. It was just a terrible mistake.

As we were leaving, Lee grabbed Billy's arm. *I'm so sorry, Bill. I forgot what the story was about.*

Don't give it another thought. She loved it. Lee searched Billy's face. He sincerely looked content. Happy to be with his niece. Happy to have given her a book she loved. Lee watched Billy and me leave, hand in hand, missing Evelyn terribly.

"So after that, Billy brought you into the store every few months, and as the years passed, fewer people in Prospero remembered Evelyn." Lee chuckled suddenly. "You used to prance in like you owned the place." Lee said I would strut up to any kids in the store and tell them that it was my store, that it was up to me whether they were allowed to have any books. Billy should have scolded me or lectured me on the virtues of sharing. Instead, he would muss my hair and lure me away from the shelves with hot chocolate.

"The perils of being an only child," I told Lee. "You never have to learn to share."

"They were all your books, though. The store was always yours."

"Do you remember the last time I came? When I was looking for Billy?" My voice was weak. I wanted him to remember. I didn't want him to remember. I still didn't know what I wanted.

Lee nodded. "I didn't realize it was a mistake to call your mom until I saw the look on your face."

You called my mom? I'd said so desperately, so terrified Lee realized that Susan didn't know I was at the store.

When Susan arrived, she threw the door open, her eyes racing across the room until they found Lee's. *Where is she?* she asked frantically, and Lee saw that even if she hadn't birthed me, she was my mother. He pointed to the back. *Thank you, Lee. Thank you for everything.*

"You should know," Lee said, massaging his hands. His fingers were thick, swollen. "Billy talked about you for years. It took me a while to realize that he didn't see you anymore. I noticed he didn't bring you to the store. I figured since you went there when you weren't supposed to, it became some symbol of disobedience."

Billy still came to visit Lee at the store whenever he was home between devastating earthquakes. He'd detail an earthquake that struck Turkey, the thousands of people who had died, tens of thousands who were severely injured, hundreds of thousands left without homes, focusing on one person: me. *Miranda would say hummus sounds gross, but it's actually pretty good.* He said I would like the Blue Mosque. The baseball stadiums in Tokyo. The puppets in China. *Would like.* The conditional tense. Never, *Will like.* Never the future.

"How'd you respond when he said things like this?" I asked.

"I just let him talk," he said.

"So Billy took over the store once you decided to move?"

"Paul's mom started to get worse around 2000."

So you want to move back to Santa Barbara? Lee had asked after Paul broached the topic one night over dinner.

I've always wanted to move back to Santa Barbara, Paul reminded him.

Who will manage the store? Lee asked, and Paul understood what he was really asking.

It's been fifteen years. You need to let her go.

Love. Work. Place. There was only one person Lee couldn't live without, no matter how much he loved Prospero Books, no matter how much he missed Evelyn.

They reached an agreement. Lee wouldn't leave until he knew Prospero Books was in good hands. He wasn't certain how long it would take him to find someone who understood the changing neighborhood, its reading preferences, someone who would get along with Billy, who knew how to turn a profit, not that the store had turned a profit in years.

"That was the era of *You've Got Mail,* stand up to the big, bad chain store." If Billy ever noticed how few people bought books, how the taxes had increased, how more cafés had opened around Sunset Junction, luring coffee addicts away from Prospero Books, he didn't let on. Billy checked the finances each month, or his lawyer did, Lee wasn't sure. All he knew was that every time finances were dangerously low, money would appear in the account. Lee didn't see how Billy could afford it, but like most topics with Billy, they never spoke about money.

Lee was waiting for the right time to tell Billy that he was quitting, even if Paul said there'd never be a right time. The earth had been particularly mobile those months while Lee tried to find a good time to quit, or possibly Billy was particularly restless, or maybe Paul was right, maybe Lee was simply stalling.

Then one day, after Billy had returned from Taiwan, for some reason Lee couldn't listen to another one of Billy's stories. His stories were all the same. They had different epicenters, dif-

ferent magnitudes, different death tolls, but they were all trag-
edies that never belonged to Billy. Lee was tired suddenly of
all the things they didn't say to each other. Or maybe he was
cranky. The drives back and forth to Santa Barbara were taking a toll on him.

We're moving to Santa Barbara, Lee told Billy. Lee explained
that Paul's mother was sick and he needed to be with her.

Lee expected Billy to fight him, to be his usual self, not
understanding others' needs, particularly when they were in-
convenient or undesirable to Billy.

Instead, Billy said, *Of course you should go. You have to take
care of family.*

I'll wait until we find the right replacement, Lee said.

Who can we trust? Lee frowned sympathetically at Billy. He
had invested in a dying industry. Not dying. Fatigued. Billy
had invested in a fatigued industry, and Lee didn't know who
they would find that could put up the necessary fight. It was a
romantic job, but like most romantic jobs it paid little. Billy's
face beamed. *Me. We can trust me.*

Come on, Billy. You're always away.

That can change. Billy sounded more eager than Lee had heard
him in a long time.

You love your job, Lee told him.

Not as much as I love it here. I'm serious. At that moment, with
the store closed, glass of Scotch in hand, Lee had no doubt that
Billy was serious. What about a week later, when an earthquake
crippled some village in Italy or Indonesia? Would he be serious then? Or when he was invited to lecture at a conference in
Osaka or Buenos Aires—would he decline the invitation? *You
don't think I can handle it.*

It's a quiet life, Bill. There aren't adventures.

There are thousands of adventures here. There were adventures.
Overflowing toilets, difficult customers, delayed deliveries—
not the type of adventure Billy chased.

Day in, day out. It's the same thing, Lee said.

Maybe I want that, Billy said.

It's not as a romantic as it looks, Lee replied. He wasn't sure if he was talking about the job or about being in Evelyn's space, all day, every day, without her.

"Maybe for Billy it was the greatest adventure of all, staying still, confronting his past, finally learning how to live without Evelyn. I didn't agree to it right away, not that it was my choice. It wasn't until the earthquake in India that I was comfortable letting go."

January 26, 2001. The Gujarat earthquake. Republic Day. At 7.7 on the moment magnitude scale, the quake was felt from Bangladesh to Pakistan. Over twenty thousand dead. Other seismologists, engineers and sociologists rushed to investigate the damage before cleanup missions began. At ten that morning, Billy was waiting outside Prospero Books like it was any other day. He ordered his coffee, occupied what had become his regular table and read about the destructive quake in the newspaper. It was then that Lee believed Billy was serious about staying put.

January 26, 2001. I was a freshman, recently fifteen, trailing Joanie through the halls of our high school, trying to mimic her ease as we passed groups of older boys, her indifference. I didn't hit puberty for another year, and I had nothing to fear from those older boys beyond their total disregard for me. By high school, I'd lost interest in getting a dog. Instead, I was obsessed with the breasts I didn't have, the curves that never appeared, how when I stood beside Joanie I looked like her younger cousin rather than her best friend. I wasn't thinking about Billy. It didn't occur to me that he'd still be traveling across the world, that he might have returned to LA. I was a teenager, coming of age. I had an excuse for not thinking about him, or at least a reason. Billy didn't. He'd decided to stay put. He'd decided to face his fears. Still, he didn't try to find me.

Lee stood abruptly and walked to a cabinet in the corner of the room. He opened the top drawer, and handed me a padded envelope. "Bill left that for you about a year ago. He didn't tell me he was sick, but I knew."

While Billy had looked tired and thin, it wasn't the physical symptoms that made Lee realize Billy was dying. It was the nature of their last exchange.

Billy and Lee sat on the balcony of Lee's apartment, watching the ocean below as each wave broke and rolled onto the sand.

You're happy here? Billy had asked. *This is what you want?*

Lee wasn't sure how to answer. He missed walking the stairs of Silver Lake, evenings at the observatory, dinners in Thai Town. He missed his friends, the regulars at Prospero Books, but this was where Paul was. So, Lee told Billy that he golfed whenever he wanted, that he sat on his balcony every afternoon, watching the ocean. He told Billy that he was happy.

That's important, Billy said.

Eventually, it grew too brisk to sit outside, and Billy said he should probably get going. Before he left, Billy handed Lee the padded envelope. *If she comes, please give this to her.*

Lee didn't ask whom he meant. He shook Lee's hand, and the handshake seemed oddly formal. Lee knew he would never see Billy again.

I held the package. Hard and square. Another book. Part of me didn't want to open it because I knew it had to be the last.

"How'd you find out he passed?" I asked.

"Malcolm."

Of course Malcolm knew where Lee was along with all the other things he knew about me. I fidgeted in my chair, uncomfortable in my body again.

"Don't hold it against the boy." Lee frowned. "Billy put him in a tough spot."

I was about to fight him, then I pictured Malcolm and Billy

behind the desk at Prospero Books, Malcolm picking at his thumb as Billy tried to tell him about his death plans. Malcolm had hidden that story from me, too. Even when we were fighting, he didn't force me into that moment, when he had learned that his best friend was dying.

"The bookstore will never make you rich," Lee said as he saw me out. "But if you watch your budget and find ways to bring in more folks, you'll get so much more than fortunes out of it. I guarantee you that."

I hugged Lee and he hesitated before putting his arms around me. It was the closest I'd get to hugging Billy. The closest I'd get to hugging Evelyn, too.

I WALKED DOWN TO THE BEACH WITH THE PADDED ENVELOPE in my right hand, imagining what it must have been like for Lee, not talking about that morning in Big Bear, if every time he thought of Evelyn he saw her lifeless body, that image erasing those of her smiling or laughing. I hoped telling me about it had made him feel better. I wondered what it must have been like for Billy, too, returning from trips abroad, that moment before he stepped into Prospero Books, a glimmer of hope that he might find Evelyn inside. Someone else would have sold the store. Instead, Billy gave up his career, denied himself any chance at a life outside Prospero Books to remain where job, place, love were all one. Where they were all Evelyn.

On my phone, I found the photograph I'd saved from Mom and Evelyn's yearbook. Their faces pressed together. Mom's tongue out, her eyes wide. Evelyn laughing at her best friend, demure, poised. Joanie and I had similar photos. She was always doing something theatrical and uninhibited while I smiled beside her, the straight man to her one-woman performance. Lee was right. I shared qualities with Evelyn, attributes that were as much a part of me as my curly hair, my brown eyes, my features that made me look like Billy, like Mom.

From the beach, I could see Lee's dirty apartment building. The chairs on the balconies were all empty. I kept watching them as if Billy and Lee might slide open the door and sit down to talk about happiness as the waves unfurled onto the beach.

I walked along the shoreline where the sand was sturdy and cold under my feet. The coast in Santa Barbara looked different than in Los Angeles, more sailboats undulating with the waves, paler sand, bluer water. I pictured Mom in her hooded sweatshirt from the Quaker school where I taught, her regular walks on the beach in Santa Monica. What was it like, living with that big of a secret? Did she think about it every day, during those hours alone as she strolled toward Malibu, staring into the vast Pacific? Had she buried it so deep that she'd learned to forget I wasn't hers? Or was it more like a scar, something permanent, no longer feeling, something neglected yet always there? I'd discovered the secret she kept, but I still didn't know about the fight that had driven my biological father out of my life. I opened the padded envelope Billy had left for me.

The journey came full circle. Same cover. Same rogue wave. Same doomed vessel. Same betrayal. This time, a different speech from *The Tempest*. In the fifth act, an envelope marked the last scene where Prospero told Ariel he would swear off his magic books, he would relinquish his thirst for revenge, he would forgive his brother even if Antonio didn't regret what he'd done to Prospero. Prospero's famous words were highlighted.

The rarer action is

In virtue than in vengeance.

I ran my nail beneath the envelope's seal and unfolded the letter.

August 1, 2012
Miranda—

"Now my charms are all o'erthrown,
And what strength I have's mine own,
Which is most faint."

Like Prospero, I have reached the end of my story and I am alone onstage, asking you to forgive me. You have every right to be furious. You might even be so angry you abandoned this journey as soon as you discovered I'd lied to you. But I hold out hope that despite the years, I still know you. You will see this quest to the end, even if it only brings betrayal.

A year ago, when I discovered I was sick... It's true what they say about your life flashing before your eyes. Only the life that flashed before mine wasn't the one I'd chosen, but the one I'd ruined. I could see it clearly, wheeling Evelyn out of the hospital, holding her newborn daughter in her arms, our newborn daughter, Miranda, you. I could see us tucking you in each night, first in your crib, then your bed. I could hear you sprinting down the stairs of our cabin in Big Bear, off to swim at the lake, Evelyn reminding you to be careful and worrying until you were home safe. Evelyn was always a worrier. Even as I imagined the life we could have had together, I couldn't escape that. She worried. I made light of it. Sometimes I was right to calm her restless nerves. One time I wasn't. The time I can never take back.

I haven't told anyone I'm sick. Even as I write this, no one knows what little time I have left. I don't want their pity. Mostly, I'm not ready to admit that I am going to die, that my life has amounted to this, a man who allowed his anger to grow stronger than his love, so much so that at the end of his life he has no family, not even his daughter.

And I was angry. I was angry at your mother. I thought I was like Prospero, a victim of my sibling, who had betrayed me. Overtaken my kingdom and cast me away. It was an easy anger, and I held on to it for years because it allowed me to ignore what I had done. It was my choice to let you go. Not your mother's.

I will always feel responsible for Evelyn's death. No matter how many people tell me it was an accident, I know it was my fault. I deprived my love of the thing she wanted most. Growing up, Evelyn never had family dinners, holidays, movie nights. I took the possibility of that from her when I failed to make the house safe. When I failed to keep her safe. I told myself that I didn't know how to keep you safe, either, that I didn't deserve to create a family without Evelyn. Really, I was afraid of all the ways you reminded me of Evelyn, all the ways you didn't. I was afraid that you would never know her. I was afraid that we would never be complete, and so I told myself that I would give you a complete life, one where your birth wasn't paired with tragedy, one with two parents and a stability I could never provide. I thought I was being noble. I thought I was being brave.

When I realized that giving you up was cowardly, not courageous, I tried to fix my mistake. It was too late. I blamed your mother for that, but it was my fault. I had waited too long. I didn't know how to be your uncle anymore, so I left. There was no courage in that, and for that, I can simply say I'm sorry.

It wasn't your mother's fault. I put her in an impossible position. She'd learned to treat you as her own. She loved you like a mother. She is your mother. It wasn't fair of me to give her that, then to try to take it away from her. Maybe she shouldn't have accepted it, but I didn't give her much of a choice. Once I let go of my anger, I saw my mistakes clearly. Despite forgiving her, I didn't want to apologize to her. I didn't know how to apologize to her. But I do want to apologize to you. I know how to apologize to you.

And so, in the words of Prospero...
"As you from your crimes would pardon'd be,
Let your indulgence set me free,"

Billy

I sat on the beach, rereading his letter as the waves stretched toward me, grazing my toes with their cold fingers. The summer after first grade, we spent nearly every afternoon at the beach, me, Mom, Billy. Mom would pack a cooler with peanut butter sandwiches and juice boxes. A beach bag with shovels and a bucket. To anyone who saw us, we must have looked like a family, Billy and Mom holding my hands and swinging me into the air on the count of three. Were they both thinking that Evelyn should have been holding my hand in place of Mom? When Mom let us bury her in sand, turning her into a mermaid, when she broke through the bust and engulfed me in her dirty arms, carrying me into the ocean, was she acting the way she thought Evelyn would? And when Billy came barreling into the water, when he held me high above the waves and Mom spotted me so I didn't fall, was he thinking that Evelyn would have spotted me, too, that she had been right to worry? I could still see the way he gaped at me as he held me high above the waves, like everything was perfect, only it wasn't. It couldn't have been. It wasn't surprising Mom and Billy had a falling-out. It was unbelievable that they'd pretended for so long.

I put the letter in my back pocket, and watched the middle-aged men who fished off the pier. Some of the men cast lines into the calm waters. Others used both hands to haul buckets filled with seaweed and fish. They sorted through the buckets, throwing back the fish that were too small, fish that got caught in the hooks at the end of nearby lines, an endless cycle of catch and release where the fish were never big enough to keep. Still, the men measured them, hoping they'd somehow grown. I didn't want to be in an endless cycle, reading that letter over and over, hoping for something more from Billy. I wanted to understand why he and Mom had stopped pretending. I wanted to understand the catalyst for their life-changing fight. I still didn't.

I rolled up my jeans and stepped farther into the ocean. The swell engulfed my ankles and retreated. *Let your indulgence set me free.* Billy had asked me to release him, but I was still trying to capture him. I took the letter out of my pocket, the wind threatening to tear it from my hand but I held tight. I wasn't ready to let him go.

Besides, what did it mean to set Billy free when he was already gone? Was he asking me to forgive him? Was he asking me to let Prospero Books go? Lee had said that he and Evelyn had named the store Prospero Books because they both loved Prospero. Maybe the past would have been different if they'd given the store another name, even Tempest Books or the Bard's Store. Maybe Billy wouldn't have become Prospero. Maybe he wouldn't have needed forgiveness. Maybe I wouldn't have become Miranda. Maybe I would have known my mother, *a piece of virtue.*

Prospero Books. I missed it more than I'd realized. I missed the after hours when the store was mine. I missed the daytime when it belonged to the neighborhood, those rare hours when it was busy, the mornings when the regulars populated its mosaic tables. I missed Dr. Howard teaching me about Annabel Lee and the zipless fuck. I missed how Ray the screenwriter would nervously peer at other writers, as if they might steal his material. I missed Sheila, how she always seemed to be waiting for someone to recognize her. I missed Lucia, and her tattoos, Charlie and his tattoos. I missed Malcolm. Most of all, I missed Prospero Books, how it was love, job, place and—my addition to Lee's list—family.

What was I saying? Could I stay? Did I want to? School started in three weeks. I couldn't quit three weeks before the trimester started. After five years, I couldn't do that to my principal, my colleagues, my students. Plus, I loved history. I loved sharing competing versions of the past, even though few of my students understood what I was trying to teach them.

But that was just it. It wasn't the teaching I loved but the history. The past.

CHAPTER TWENTY

I HELD MY PHONE IN MY HAND, STARING AT MY PRINCIPAL'S number as I willed myself to hit the call button. She would have every reason to be furious with me, and she was good at anger. She'd had enough practice with students. While she would make me feel horribly guilty, guilt was better than regret.

"Miranda, I'm just sitting down to dinner. Is everything okay?" she asked when she picked up.

"Everything's fine." I dug the big toe of my right foot into the cold, wet sand. It was soft like clay.

"So what's up?"

My heart raced. "My uncle died."

"I'm sorry to hear that."

"I had to come home to manage his estate." Stop stalling, I chided myself. You're making this worse. "It's been a pretty unexpected summer. There's no easy way to tell you this. I'm afraid I can't come back to school in the fall."

"What do you mean you're afraid you can't come back? School starts in three weeks."

"I know the timing is terrible."

"Your timing couldn't be worse."

"You know how much I love our school. It's such an important part of who I am." The waves buried my feet in their white foam. The bubbles tickled my calves.

"It can't be that important if you're calling me three weeks before the trimester starts."

"I have a responsibility to my family," I said.

"You have a responsibility to us." She waited for me to apologize. "What am I supposed to say here, Miranda? You want me to tell you it's okay? It's not okay. This is completely irresponsible and inconsiderate. I'm so, so disappointed in you."

"I know you are." When the water withdrew, I followed its path farther into the ocean.

"This is final. No calling back tomorrow and telling me you made a mistake."

"I'm not making a mistake," I said as I hung up.

The water cut my legs with its cold, and each time my legs acclimated I stepped a little farther, daring the water to punish me again. I still had one call to make. One I should have made weeks before.

"Hey," Jay said cautiously when he answered. "I was wondering if I'd ever hear from you again."

"I should have called." The water splashed my jeans, threatening to soak my pants, but I kept my footing. I stayed grounded. I didn't run back to dry land.

"You okay?" Jay asked.

"I just quit," I said in a trance.

"You quit school? Fuck. That's big." He paused. "It's not because of me?"

His words snapped me out of my daze. Of course that's what Jay would think. "It was because of me. I'm staying here."

Jay didn't say anything for so long I thought maybe he'd hung up or fallen asleep.

"What should I do with your stuff?" Jay said indifferently. His apathy made this easy for me, but I didn't want it easy. I didn't want him to fight for me, either. I wanted some emotion, though, something that confirmed that we had happened, that it had mattered. There was a reason Jay and I weren't destined to be together. It wasn't Prospero Books. It wasn't my uncle. It wasn't even Malcolm.

"I don't know. I'll get someone to pick it up," I said.

"So that's it?" he said with the efficiency of a waiter who had taken my order and was ready to rush off to the next table.

"Yeah," I said. "That's it."

After we hung up, I stood in the ocean watching the waves crash against my calves. I waited for the panic to hit me. I'd just quit my job. Just broken up with my boyfriend. Just forfeited my life, a life that was by all accounts pleasant and easy. And for what? Prospero Books was still losing money. Even if we raised enough at our gala to keep the doors open for another month, we couldn't throw a party every time we were short on the mortgage. If we closed, where would I be then? But I didn't feel panicked. Only tremendously relieved. I took another step into the water. The waves flung icy water farther up my kneecaps, then receded, carrying my old life out to sea. It was going to be a struggle but I was up for the battle. And it wasn't just Prospero Books I needed to fight for.

As you from your crimes would pardon'd be, let your indulgence set me free. Billy had ended his letter with Prospero's final appeal to the audience members to remember their wrongdoings and forgive him as easily as they would have wanted to be forgiven. *As you from your crimes.* My crimes. Billy wasn't the only one who cast Mom as the villain. She'd been put in an impossible situation. She loved me like a mother. I could let her love me like a mother.

A shriek jolted me out of my head. A girl screamed in feigned disgust as her boyfriend tackled her into the water. The splash off their bodies rained down my arm. My feet had grown numb. Movement sent sharp pains up my calves. I trudged out of the shallow waves. I realized how I must have looked, a woman in drenched jeans and a T-shirt, walking out of the ocean. While Billy might not have known how to apologize to Mom, I did. I decided it was time to go home.

THE FOYER SMELLED OF ROSEMARY AND GARLIC AND WAS WARM from the oven. Mom leaned against the front doorjamb, blocking my path inside, and watched me. I waited for her to say something. She must have been waiting for me to say something, too. I was overwhelmed by the things I wanted to say to her. But the bravery I'd summoned to face my principal and Jay had vanished. I wanted her to make this easy on me. I wanted her to tell me what to do.

She stared at my pants. The bottoms of my jeans were caked. "You're covered in sand."

"I was at the beach," I said, as if that explained anything.

"Hold on." She left the door open while she rushed upstairs. Music was playing in the kitchen. I couldn't make out the song. I waited outside until she returned, laid a towel on the ground and waved me inside. She held out another towel, turning away as I took off my jeans. I wrapped it around my waist and Mom bent down. She cleaned my legs with a towel, gently rubbing off the sand, patiently caring for me, and I let her.

"There," she said. She squeezed my arm, using it as a crutch to stand. "All clean."

"This doesn't mean I forgive you," I said.

Mom sat on the bottom step, wringing her hands. "I should have told you years ago."

"What am I supposed to do here?"

"I don't know," she said. "I know what I want you to do. I don't know what you should do." The foyer was so quiet I could hear Mom's hands rubbing violently against each other over the distant music. "I always knew the truth would come out."

I sat on the towel Mom had placed on the floor. I was ready

to stay, ready to listen. I wasn't quite ready to sit on the stair beside her.

"I should have told you everything when you were twelve. You would have understood." She braved a look at me. I wasn't sure what she saw, what expression I gave her in return, but her hands slowly unwound and she rested them in her lap. "When you went to Billy's funeral. When you said you saw Evelyn's grave. I thought you figured it out. And then when you didn't, I chickened out again." Mom stretched out her legs, shaking them like she was trying to release the past from her tense muscles. "It was my fault. I knew what I was doing. Billy loved you, but he couldn't be a father. Not without Evelyn. Everything got so complicated. I should have told you when Billy and I got into that terrible fight. How do you tell a twelve-year-old that her entire life has been a lie? Maybe it wasn't about Billy. Maybe I just didn't want you to hate me."

"I don't hate you," I said.

"Billy hated me. He still does." And with that, the tears erupted. Mom hid her face in her hands. Her shoulders shook violently. I'd never seen Mom like that before. It was beautiful and confusing and violent, like Mom was rupturing, a fissure opening to expose her insides.

"This is so selfish of me. You're the one whose life has been turned upside down and here I am crying."

"So stop crying," I said coldly, and she did, startled by my callousness. It wasn't her turn to cry just because I wasn't. My eyes didn't sting. I didn't feel that tingling sensation like before you sneeze. I was emotionally exhausted, and I wanted the truth. I didn't want comfort. I certainly didn't want to comfort her. I wanted her, finally, to talk to me.

I walked over to the bookshelves in the living room and found a copy of *The Tempest*. I brought it into the foyer and sat beside Mom on the steps. I flipped to the second scene, Prospero's speech to Miranda, where Billy had left me the first clue.

"Billy sent me a copy of *The Tempest* before he died. It was the first clue." I waited for her to gasp and say, *Why didn't you tell me?* Instead, she took the book from my hands and read the dialogue on the page. "At the beginning, it seems like a play about vengeance but it's really about forgiveness. See here?" I pointed to Prospero's words. "Even as he explains how he was betrayed by his brother, he admits, 'I thus neglecting worldly ends, all dedicated to closeness and the bettering of my mind.' Prospero left the daily responsibilities of his estate to his brother while he was distracted by his studies. Billy didn't hate you. He knew that he was as much to blame as you were."

From there, I walked Mom through each of the clues after *The Tempest*, reframing them into the version of the past and Billy's quest as an apology to Mom: *Jane Eyre*, where Billy acknowledged his regret over their estrangement. "It wasn't meant as a dig. Jane's uncle always felt guilty about the fight he had with Jane's father, who died before they could make amends. That's how Billy felt about his fight with you." *Alice's Adventures in Wonderland*, where Billy initiated my journey into the fantastic world of his past. *Frankenstein*, where John Cook had exposed Billy's misguided attempts at grieving, where Billy was forced to accept that he could never bring Evelyn back. He couldn't figure out how to keep living, so he began running, chasing his own monsters. *Fear of Flying*, where Billy and Sheila had tried to allay their grief with their bodies, their desire. *Persuasion*, where Burt wasn't vain or superficial, but senile with regret. *The Grapes of Wrath*, where I went to Big Bear and saw the house.

"You were there?" Mom asked. Her face looked younger suddenly, like she was a teenager again, roaming the hallways of her high school, arm in arm with her best friend.

I found my phone and showed Mom the photograph of the banister. "Their initials are still on the railing." She ran her fingers over the screen as though she could feel the carving. "Do you remember Lee?"

"Who worked at the bookstore?" she asked.

I explained to her that *Bridge to Terabithia* had led me to Lee and he'd told me wonderful stories about Evelyn, and also stories about Billy's guilt. I flipped to the epilogue of *The Tempest* and showed Mom where Billy had left a letter, an apology asking us to forgive him, to set him free. "He wants you to tell me everything. He wants me to forgive you, too." And I realized as I said it that he did. Billy wanted me to free him. He also wanted me to free these secrets, to end the destruction they had caused.

"I still don't know what you fought about on my birthday," I said. "I know it had to do with Billy being my father, but he didn't tell me what happened. He wants you to show me. He wants me to understand from your perspective."

None of the people I met—not Sheila, not Lee, not Burt—knew what had happened between Billy and Mom. He hadn't told them about their fight. In his letter of apology, he hadn't told me, either. He said he didn't know how to apologize to Mom, but he did. He was allowing her experience of their argument to be the only account that existed.

Mom closed *The Tempest* and placed it in her lap. "Where should I begin?"

I DON'T UNDERSTAND, MOM SAID WHEN THE DOCTORS FOUND her in the waiting room. *Carbon monoxide?*

The police will complete an investigation to determine how carbon monoxide got trapped in the house, the doctors reported in practiced voices. *It likely had to do with the storm.*

Are they okay? Oh, Mom, any time you had to ask that, you already knew the answer.

The doctor started with the good news. Billy was still on an oxygen tank, but he was stable. They were monitoring his levels closely. Too much oxygen could lead to its own problems. He was partially conscious and they'd begun to administer decongestants to help with the barotrauma and sinus problems.

The bends, the doctors explained. *Like scuba divers sometimes get.*

The doctors said they would have to monitor him for a few days, but the chances of any lasting effects were unlikely.

And Evelyn? Mom asked.

You never know how you will react. Mom would have imagined she'd be frantic, on all fours, pounding her hands on the cold linoleum floor. She didn't even cry. Not until the funeral when Evelyn's body was slowly lowered into the ground. Evelyn's father had wanted a Catholic ceremony. Evelyn was atheist, and Mom was glad she hadn't been so paralyzed by grief that she hadn't known to fight Burt. Billy was useless at that point. He could barely put together a sentence much less a cohesive argument.

In the ER, the doctors continued their story. They'd had to do an emergency C-section. The baby's pulse was faint. They'd incubated her and she was stable. She'd have to stay in the hospital for another week or so.

"You were a fighter from the beginning," Mom said. "It's a miracle, really. You shouldn't have survived."

And Evelyn was a fierce protector to the end, her body holding on until the baby was cut out of her.

How's Evelyn? Mom asked again. She needed to hear them explain it. She had to remember. She knew she had to be the one to tell Billy.

There were complications during the C-section. The doctors said they had been monitoring her oxygen levels and pulse closely, but once she began to seize, they were unable to save her.

I don't understand, Mom said.

She'd had an amniotic fluid embolism, which had caused the seizure.

We're very sorry, the doctors said in the same practiced voices.

Mom kept saying it: *I don't understand. An embolism? A seizure?* Until Dad pulled her into his chest.

Can we see the baby? Dad asked the doctor.

"Evelyn was desperate to be a mother," Mom told me. From the moment she and Billy got married, she'd started planning the family they were going to have—three kids, and a dog. A golden retriever because it was the type of dog the perfect family would have in a movie and that's what they were going to be, perfect, nauseatingly so. For four years, Evelyn monitored her menstrual cycle, her ovulation. When, month after month, her period arrived, she visited fertility specialists, three in total. She'd tried everything. Insemination, ovulation induction drugs, nothing worked. "She'd given up hope. And then one day... And then one day..."

Mom was waiting for Evelyn at a booth in the diner where they always met. As soon as Evelyn walked in, Mom sensed something about her was different. Nothing obvious. She was only about six weeks pregnant. Her cheeks were rosier than usual, and she seemed like she wanted to burst into song.

Look at you, you're glowing with life. Mom hugged her best friend and said all the things you're supposed to say. *Congratulations. I'm so happy for you. You're going to make a wonderful mother.* These things were true. She was happy for Evelyn. Evelyn was going to be an incredible mom. But everything was about to change. It was ugly, Mom knew. Still, she couldn't shake a prevailing disappointment that they couldn't continue to be women without children together.

"After, that was what I felt the worst about. The entire time, as she grew bigger and bigger, I kept wishing that she wasn't pregnant, that she wouldn't become a mother." Mom cried harder, and I had to fight the urge to console her. I wasn't ready to commiserate with her, to help her forgive herself.

"I never wanted kids," Mom said once she'd steadied her breath. Even in her thirties, she'd still clung to the open road, to the possibility that with one phone call, she could take off. Of course, she couldn't. She had Dad, and besides, that mystical phone call never did appear. "I didn't want kids. I only ever wanted you."

Mom said she'd never seen so many tubes on such a small baby. Mom was hit with a maternal desire like a hot flash.

"You were so blue," Mom said. The nurse let Mom touch my head, and she cupped my small skull, bluish skin peeking between black fuzz like bruises. Evelyn would never get to touch me like this, Mom thought. She would never get to touch me at all.

Mom didn't know how Burt had learned that Evelyn was in the hospital. Somehow, he was always abreast of Evelyn's life, as if he had private detectives monitoring his distant daughter's every move. He barreled into the hospital demanding to see Evelyn.

I want to see my daughter, Burt barked at the nurse unlucky enough to be sitting at the station when he arrived.

Mom rested her hand on Burt's shoulder. He regarded her without recognition.

Suzy, she explained. *Billy's sister. Why don't you come sit down.* She guided him toward the waiting room.

After Mom repeated what little information the doctors had given her, Burt asked if Mom knew who was in charge of the investigation. Had they been to the house yet? Had they interviewed the emergency responders? How long did Evelyn seize before she died? The ideas were building behind Burt eyes.

Billy, he said. *This is Billy's doing, isn't it?*

"Burt never approved of Billy. It didn't make sense," Mom said.

In high school, Burt didn't like Evelyn seeing a college boy, even though Evelyn and Billy had been dating since before he was in college. When they got back together, Evelyn would bring Billy to their monthly dinners, and Burt would ignore Billy's questions about advances in fertilizers or cross-breeding trees. Each month, as the women Burt brought to dinner changed, Billy remained, and each month while Evelyn was polite to the woman in rotation, asking her questions about her burgeoning acting career or her humanitarianism, Burt would act as though he didn't know what Billy did for a living or where he was from. Billy's Judaism, as nominal as it was, became the issue when they decided to get married. *Think what your mother would say*, Burt told Evelyn, making her so angry she stopped speaking to her father for three months until Billy insisted that she invite him to their reception.

"I guess I shouldn't have been surprised when Burt blamed Billy," Mom told me.

Billy was in the hospital for another week of unprecedentedly low temperatures. The snow didn't melt. It grew hard and turned to glass, cracking under your feet as you walked. "We were lucky for the cold weather. Otherwise, the police might not have figured out what happened." Or unlucky, perhaps. If they hadn't located the vent on the roof, clogged with snow, maybe Billy wouldn't have blamed himself. Maybe Burt wouldn't have blamed him, either.

Burt stuck around Big Bear long enough for the snow to begin to melt, long enough to cause trouble. He went to the house. He met the detectives. He forced the issue of foul play, which the detectives dismissed, making Burt more determined.

"We didn't learn about the independent investigation until Burt began fighting Billy for the inheritance, for custody."

"Custody? Of me?" I tried to imagine what that life would have been like, Burt's big house filled with employees in place of family, furniture in place of friends, wives in place of mothers.

"The whole thing was terrible. It lasted nearly two years. Burt refused to let it go. Billy would say, 'Let him have it all, I don't deserve it. I killed her.' So, we couldn't let Burt's lawyers near him. Dad had to take care of everything. It was horrible, what Burt put Billy through."

Ten days old, I was finally released from the hospital. Billy and I came to stay with Mom and Dad. They set up a bassinet in the room where Billy would sleep. Billy took one look at the bassinet and shook his head.

I can't. Put her in the other room.

Billy, a newborn shouldn't sleep alone, Mom explained.

Will you watch her? Billy asked, his attention shifting from Mom to Dad.

I don't think that's a good idea, Dad said.

You've got to get used to her, Mom added.

I don't trust myself. Please, Suze. Please don't make me do it. And Billy looked so desperate that Dad moved the bassinet into their bedroom, sure to tell Billy that this was only temporary.

For the first few weeks, Billy wouldn't even hold me. "All new fathers are afraid of babies, like they'll break them, but this was different." Billy would watch Mom rock me, singing sweet lullabies.

You're such a natural mother. Look how she responds to your voice.

She'll respond to you, too, Mom said, holding me out to Billy. He shook his head. *It's not your fault. It was a terrible accident. You can't keep blaming yourself.*

Billy would nod absentmindedly before leaving the room. Eventually, Mom stopped asking Billy if he wanted to hold me. She stopped telling him accidents happen. She stopped pleading with him that he shouldn't blame himself.

WHEN I WAS SIX WEEKS OLD, BILLY LEFT. *GOING TO SEE AN OLD friend*, the note on the dinner table said. *Be back in a few days. —B.* No, *thank you.* No *Please take care of my daughter.* Just *Be back in a few days. —B.*

Dad was the first to see it. Mom was still in bed after waking up with me three times in the night. Dad stormed into the bedroom, holding me against his chest as he waved the letter toward Mom. Mom was stunned by how natural Dad looked with me in his arms.

Did you know anything about this? Dad shouted. I started to cry and Dad rocked me, cooing to me and kissing my head.

Of course I didn't know, Mom said, reaching for the letter.

He just leaves?

Mom read the note. *It says he'll be back in a few days.*

So we're supposed to take care of Miranda? He was glowering, but his voice rose with my name, like the prospect excited him.

We take care of her, anyway. I'm happy to do it.

That's not the point, Dad said, storming out with me still in his arms.

Mom remained in the bedroom, half-asleep, trying to piece it together. Where did Billy go? Why hadn't he left a phone number? A name? Was he trying to disappear? He wouldn't do that, she decided. Billy would never abandon Evelyn's daughter.

Dad was sitting at the table, drinking a cup of coffee, and rocking me in the bassinet. He made funny faces at me, and Mom watched, realizing that Dad never made funny faces, that he was always serious. It was nice seeing him with his tongue curled, his eyes crossed. It was fun seeing him relax.

I'm sorry, he said as Mom sat down beside him. *It's not your fault. It's just…the longer we let this continue, the harder it will be for Billy.* Mom knew what he was really saying. The longer they cared for me, the harder it would be for them to let me go.

"I don't know where Billy was those few days. It did something, though, because he started going to group therapy after that. Pretty soon, he started holding you. He'd give you back as soon as you started to cry, but he was engaging with you. It was never meant to be permanent. We were doing everything we could to get him back to normal." The new normal, anyway, which would never be normal. Still, Billy had to try.

AFTER SIX MONTHS DAD HAD HAD IT.

This can't continue, Dad said to Mom. They were in the

kitchen, talking in whispers. Billy was upstairs, asleep in the guest room. I was asleep in their bedroom. *It's been six months.*

I know how long it's been.

And you're okay with this? He's never been alone with Miranda. He won't even change her diaper.

What will you have me do, David? He's mourning.

He can't live with us forever.

No one's talking about forever. He needs a little more time. You want me to let Miranda live alone with him when he's still like this?

They were staring intensely at each other, until Dad looked beyond Mom, and she followed his gaze toward Billy. He leaned against the island, his eyes wild with pharmaceutically induced sleep.

Just getting some water, Billy explained, walking past them toward the sink. They watched him fill a glass of water and walk out of the kitchen. They heard his rapid footsteps up the stairs, the door to the guest room whisper shut.

Do you think he heard us? Mom asked Dad.

Of course he heard us.

Maybe he needed to hear them because the next morning, when Mom wandered downstairs with me on her hip, she found Billy in the kitchen, dressed in a shirt and slacks, loading a bowl and mug into the dishwasher.

I've got an interview for a new job, Billy told Mom as he knotted his tie at the mirror.

Billy, about last night. Their eyes met in the mirror.

Don't give it another thought, Billy said.

We're happy to have you and Miranda here for as long as you want.

David's right. I can't stay here forever. He tugged on the knot of his tie, shoving it toward the collar.

"Even at the time, it struck me as odd how he said it. 'I can't stay here forever.' I guess I should have realized that he never had any intention of taking you with him. I'm not sure he even realized what he was saying."

By six that evening, Billy wasn't back. Mom called his house in Pasadena. He probably hadn't gone there, but she had no other way of reaching him. When he didn't answer, she left a message. *Billy, it's Susan. I don't know when you're planning to be back. If you get this, will you give me a call, let me know what's going on?*

By seven, she called Prospero Books. Lee picked up. She asked for Billy. *It's Susan*, she explained.

There was a pause.

We thought Billy was staying with you. We haven't seen him in months.

He is. I thought he may have stopped by. I'm sure he'll be back soon.

Will you have him call us? We've been worried about him.

Mom promised she would without confessing that she was worried about him, too.

By seven-thirty, Dad returned home from work to find the table set for two. I was in a playpen by the table.

I don't know where he is, Mom said, setting a plate of chicken and roasted potatoes at Dad's seat.

He'll be back, Dad assured her. He lifted me from the playpen and bounced me on his knee. He kept me in his lap as he began to eat. Mom waited for him to resume the conversation they'd been having in the kitchen the night before. She was prepared to agree with him. This couldn't continue. Not the disappearances. Not the spare bedroom. Not the bassinet in their bedroom. Not the parenting. *He'll be back*, Dad promised again.

"I wanted to call the police, but they were in the middle of the lawsuit, and your father said it would hurt Billy's case if Burt's lawyers knew he'd disappeared. Oddly enough, the longer he was gone, the less worried I was. If he was dead, I figured we would have heard something."

Each day that Billy didn't return, Mom's fear morphed further into rage. She tried to remind herself that he was grieving, but she was grieving, too. She was grieving, and still she got up in the middle of the night to feed me. Still she went grocery shopping, cooked dinner, scheduled doctors' appointments, changed diapers. Billy, he just disappeared.

What angered Mom most was that she loved motherhood. She had to turn down two gigs because Dad was working late, and she didn't want to leave me with someone who wasn't family. But she didn't mind. She loved how I recognized her voice, her smell, her face. She loved that each time she took me to the grocery store, other women would coo at me, telling her she had a beautiful daughter. She loved afternoons at the park, where she would hold me as we watched the older children run around the playground. She loved how the other mothers smiled at her. She would smile back, feeling as though she was part of their maternal society, until she remembered. I wasn't her child. Billy would come back. If he wanted me, she would have to let me go.

CHAPTER TWENTY-ONE

"IS THAT WHY YOU STOPPED SINGING?" I ASKED. WE WERE STILL sitting on the bottom step. I leaned back, allowing my knee to graze hers, allowing us to sit together. "Was it because of me?"

Mom shook her head. "It was time. It was more than time. You helped me feel okay with wanting to do something else with my life." I wasn't sure I believed her. I could see in the look she gave me that she wanted it to be true. She wanted me to have saved her.

"So when did Billy come back?" I asked.

"He was gone for more than a week." She laughed in disbelief. "Right when I thought we'd never see him again, he comes prancing in like nothing happened."

The guest room had been cleaned, the windows opened to let in fresh air. Mom had bought a crib and converted the office into a makeshift nursery. It was a Sunday. She was preparing chicken for the grill. The bell rang and Dad carried me to the door. From the kitchen, Mom heard Dad say, *Look who it is, Miranda. It's Billy.* Mom noticed that he said Billy, not "your father." She wondered if Billy had noticed, too.

Mom didn't hug Billy. She was unwilling to embrace him, to instantly forgive him. He handed her a rectangular box.

Inside were four cloisonné dishes, black with golden birds at their centers.

I got them in Beijing, he said.

Beijing? she asked.

There was a conference.

What the hell, Billy?

I know. I just needed to get away.

Mom wanted to scream. She hadn't slept all week she was so worried. He couldn't take off like that, not without telling anyone. It was selfish. It was more than selfish. He couldn't leave his daughter and jet off to Beijing. And how did he even happen to go to Beijing? He'd never been anywhere, always insisting that California was enough of a seismological minefield for any career. Was this really the right time to suddenly become a world traveler? She wanted to yell at him for all this and more. He seemed so young standing before her, waiting to be scolded.

Instead, she told him the plates were beautiful.

Over dinner Billy regaled them with stories from his tour of China. Dawu, Yecheng, Tangshan and other regions Billy had trouble pronouncing. Many areas were rural and the surface ruptures were still visible from earthquakes several years past. Mom and Dad listened patiently, waiting for Billy to turn the conversation to his daughter, to how she'd grown in the week he'd been gone. Billy didn't mention me. He didn't apologize or thank my parents for taking care of me.

After dinner, Billy helped Mom carry the dishes into the kitchen. When I started to cry, Mom lifted me out of the playpen.

Time for bed. She kissed me and started upstairs. She heard Billy behind her.

She's sleeping on her own now? Billy asked when they entered the makeshift nursery.

She's outgrown the bassinet, so we set up the crib in here. A crib and a changing station and a small bookshelf filled with children's books that she read to me each night.

Mom began to change me into my pajamas.

Do you mind? Billy asked, reaching for me.

Careful when you put the shirt over— Billy had buried me in the pajama top, and I began to wail. His face went slack and he darted away from me. Mom rushed over and pulled the shirt over my head.

She doesn't like her head covered. She always cries.

Billy stood against the far wall, watching from a distance as Mom put me down.

Mom and Billy joined Dad in the living room. She assumed they'd have the conversation they'd been avoiding all night. When Mom offered Billy a cup of tea, he told her he should get going.

Going where? Mom asked.

Home, Billy said.

What about Miranda?

Jesus, Billy, you can't just leave her here. There was that hopeful inflection in Dad's voice.

I'll be by tomorrow to spend some time with her, Billy said as he left.

Mom and Dad watched him reverse out of the driveway.

You know he won't be back tomorrow, Dad said. *This is totally inexcusable.* But his tone was eager again.

That night Mom couldn't sleep. What had happened? Was this Billy's way of asking them to keep me? And could they keep me? What about Burt? Wouldn't he get custody before they did? And what if he did return the next day? What if he decided he wanted to take me? Would Mom be able to let me go?

"After the earthquake tour of China, Billy started traveling nonstop." He joined a reconnaissance team that deployed regularly after calamitous earthquakes. And when there wasn't an earthquake, there were conferences, delegations, facility visits.

He came to our house between trips, staying until I was asleep. His visits home were infrequent enough that I didn't learn to recognize him. He would return from Mexico or New Zealand, making exaggerated faces to make me smile. Instead, I cried, the pleasure falling from Billy's face as he handed me back to Mom.

Give her a few minutes. She'll warm up to you, Mom said, but Billy wouldn't reach for me again until his next visit, when I would cry again and he would return me to Mom, again.

"And then you started to talk." Mom had always heard *Dada* was easier to say, yet it was her I called to. She was in the middle of a project for one of the executives at Dad's studio who was redecorating his living room. The executive and his wife were going for a hunting aesthetic, even though their house was made of glass and concrete, set in the Pacific Palisades. It wasn't her job to judge, only to curate. They were her first clients and she was doing the project practically for free. As she laid paint swatches and leather samples across the dining room table, she tried to tune out my unintelligible mumble. Suddenly, I slapped my hand on the bottom of the playpen.

Mama, I shouted. *Mama.*

She lifted me from the playpen and held me close to her face. *No, Miranda, I'm Auntie. Aunt Susan.*

Mama. Mom saw Evelyn's eyes looking out from my face, yet she couldn't fight the pleasure those two syllables gave her. Ma-ma.

THEY HAD TO TELL BILLY. THAT WAS THE FIRST THING DAD SAID when he returned home. *We have to tell Billy.*

Of course we have to tell Billy, Mom said defensively.

Dad lifted me from the playpen and spun me in the air. *We should never have let this go on for so long.*

In the year they'd been watching me, Mom had stopped auditioning. She'd enrolled in night classes for interior design because it sounded like something she might like, the type of job she could do part-time. Dad was right. They'd allowed this fantasy to continue for too long.

Billy was out of town, Mom wasn't entirely sure where. He always left abruptly, claiming he didn't have time to let them know, although how much time did it take to make a simple phone call? Mom checked the newspaper until she spotted an article on two earthquakes in Taiwan that had occurred within hours of each other. She tried to imagine him in Taipei. She always wondered who Billy was when he was with the other scientists, the engineers, the sociologists. Did they know he was a savior out of guilt? Perhaps they were all guilty, a society of the regretful. Why else would they constantly surround themselves with so much tragedy, so much death?

They heard from Billy a few days later. He had just returned from Taipei where he was investigating the remains of a two-story market that had collapsed. Could he come see Miranda? Mom cautiously told him that he could.

When Billy's headlights flooded the driveway, Dad carried me to my room. It was too late for a nap, too early for bed, but they didn't want Billy to hear me say *Mama* before they'd had a chance to tell him.

He was at the door with a box of loose tea for Mom, a smile across his face until he registered the concerned looks on my parents'.

Where's Miranda? Is she okay? Billy asked.

She's upstairs, Dad said.

Mom took the tea and gestured for Billy to sit in the living room. A bottle of wine rested on the coffee table even though Mom and Dad didn't like to encourage Billy's drinking, a practice that had become noticeable since Evelyn's death. But if ever a glass of wine was called for, this was it.

You're starting to scare me, Billy said, eyeing the wine.

Miranda spoke her first word, Mom said.

Well, that's right on schedule for her age, isn't it? That's great news.

Billy, she said "Mama."

Billy's face continued to glow for another few moments until he understood.

Susan and I think it's time to reconsider our arrangement. Dad was using his lawyerly voice. Mom hated when he spoke that way to her. In that moment, however, she was thankful that he could turn on his professional persona so easily. *We've grown very fond of Miranda, but we fear she's starting to get confused.*

It could be very damaging, psychologically, if she's unclear on who her parent is, Mom added. Parent. Singular. Why did Mom have to say that?

Won't it be traumatic for her if I take her away now? Billy asked.

I could come stay with you, until she's used to your home. She's still young, she'll adjust quickly, Mom said.

And when I have to leave for work, she can still stay with you?

Billy, you're going to have to stop traveling. I'm sure the lab would be happy to hire you back, Dad said.

Maybe you can travel again, once Miranda is older, Mom added.

I can't quit, Billy said.

Dad started to fidget and Mom could tell his patience was waning.

Billy, you're a father. You need to put that responsibility first, Mom said.

I don't know how to take care of her.

That's because you haven't tried, Dad said. *You've left all the responsibility to us. You've been completely delinquent.*

We know you miss her, Billy. We miss Evelyn, too, but your daughter needs you. Mom moved closer to Billy and took his hand in hers. She couldn't remember the last time she'd held his hand. It was possible she'd never held his hand before. *You have to forgive yourself.*

You don't understand. Every time I hold her, I'm afraid I'll drop her and she'll crack her head open. When I watch her try to walk, I think she's going to trip and fall just wrong.

That worry is normal. Kids fall. And when they do, you learn not to worry so much, Mom said.

All I do is worry. She needs a normal childhood. That's what Evelyn would have wanted.

Billy—

You have to keep her.

Billy— Mom said again.

It's the only way.

And what will she think? Dad asked. *Being raised by her aunt and uncle while her father flitters around the world, in and out of her life as though he can't be bothered to care for her. That's going to make her feel normal? You think that's what Evelyn would have wanted?* Mom tried to signal to Dad that he had gone too far, but his full attention was on Billy, staring him down.

Why does she need to know I'm her father?

Billy— Mom said again.

Will you stop saying my name like that.

We're not going to lie to Miranda, Dad said. *Do you even hear yourself?*

Billy began to talk all at once. About Evelyn. About how much she'd wanted to be a mother. She'd had everything figured out. Miranda, then two years later, Pip, followed as soon as possible by Sylvia. That was why they'd bought such a big house, to fill it with the laughter of children. He paced, pulling at his hair. How many times had she asked him to fix the roof? All she wanted was to make the house safe for their family. For Miranda. Then Pip. Then Sylvia. Why did he have to take all that from her? How could he be Miranda's father when he'd killed her mother?

Billy, you didn't kill Evelyn, Mom tried to tell him.

But he did. Accident or not, he hadn't fixed the roof when she'd asked him to; he had convinced her that mathematical probability made them safe. He'd been negligent. He didn't know how to not be negligent. He'd never forgive himself if something happened to me.

Mom didn't remember agreeing to it. At some point she must have. Dad must have, too. Billy kept talking, and it was all so crazy that it started to make sense. Of course they should take me. Of course they should raise me as their own. Of course I shouldn't know that Billy was my father when he was so naturally my adventurous uncle.

"We waited until after Burt's lawsuit to file the adoption papers." Mom couldn't believe it was finally over. Two years back and forth with mediators until finally an arbitrator decided that Burt had no grounds for contesting the communal ownership of their properties, no basis for evoking The Slayer's Act, since the death had been a no-fault accident. Two years, and then in one afternoon it was done.

When Mom and Dad signed the adoption papers, Dad asked Mom, *You really think this is a good idea, hiding the truth from her?*

What else can we do? Mom asked.

If we tell her when she's young, it will be something she's always known. It will feel normal.

Knowing her father would rather be halfway around the world than with her will never feel normal. I don't want her to hate Billy.

She might end up hating us, Dad reminded her.

"I knew he was right. I knew you would find out one day. You would blame me. I told myself it was better than having you blame Billy. I really believed it was the only way he wouldn't disappoint you. The only way we could all be family. I thought I was doing the right thing." Mom reached out to put her hand on my knee. I shifted away so she couldn't use me as a crutch.

"You couldn't have really thought that. I don't understand why you didn't try harder. He was my father." My mind raced through every Sunday I ran to the door, screaming, *Uncle Billy!* Every time he asked Mom what time he should have me back, every riddle he'd written, crafting a private language that we alone understood. Through all of it. He'd known he was my father. Mom had known, too. "You should have tried harder."

"I should have," she agreed. She was no longer crying. Her voice was steady. "The longer we waited, the more impossible it became to tell you. The more unfathomable it was that I could lose you."

With the adoption papers signed, the inheritance lawsuit decided, I became Mom's. I learned other words—*Dada, home, family, uncle.* We saw Billy whenever he was in LA. Almost immediately it began to fester. Billy would arrive on Sunday nights with a present for me, and when I would say, *Mommy,* and run to her with the beaded necklace, the wooden toy, Billy would look jilted. Mom would look guilty. She would remind herself that this was Billy's idea. Still, each time I said *Mommy* in front of him, she wished I would call her something different.

They never spoke about it, and the tension grew. Dad felt it. During Sunday dinners, he asked Billy so many questions—about the food, landslides, ground motion—his tactic to defuse tense situations. And Billy talked at length. He said sushi wasn't as fishy as he'd expected. He said, in Quebec, they ate French fries with gravy and cheese curds. In Peru, the specialty was guinea pigs. *Guinea pigs,* I'd said horrified. I was in second grade, and we had two guinea pigs in my classroom. Billy promised no one would eat them.

Billy was always deferential. When he asked if he could take me up to San Francisco after the Battle of the Bay earthquake, Mom suggested we all go together, and we loaded into her station wagon for the six-hour drive. When he wanted to take me to San Diego for a Padres game, she suggested the Dodgers. Bumper cars in place of go-karting, wake boarding in place of surfing, snorkeling not scuba diving. Billy never fought back, never insinuated that it should be his decision. He just said, *You're right. That's smarter,* and adopted Mom's suggestions as if they'd been his own.

"So that's how it was for years. We didn't talk about our arrangement. We didn't even talk about Evelyn. Sometimes I'd almost forget he wasn't your uncle." She never forgot that I was Evelyn's daughter. Billy didn't, either.

THERE WAS ALSO THE ISSUE OF THE VODKA. MOM DIDN'T KNOW when that had become Billy's liquor of choice. She didn't remember him drinking it when Evelyn was alive. She didn't remember him drinking anything beyond the occasional beer. Mom kept a bottle of expensive Russian vodka for Billy's visits. The more expensive the bottle, the quicker Billy drank it. So she stopped stocking vodka, bracing herself for his response when she told him they were out, but Billy shrugged and reached into the pocket of his sport coat for two airplane bottles.

I don't like this, Dad said as he threw the tiny empty bottles into the trash.

He's an adult, David. He's allowed to drink. Dad never drank. He thought any regular consumption constituted a dependency and any dependency constituted an illness. Just because his father's consumption had been a disease didn't mean Billy's was.

"Dad's father was an alcoholic?"

Mom nodded sadly at me.

"So the car accident?"

"I thought you knew."

"I had no idea." I'd always been told that Dad's family was driving late at night and his father had swerved to avoid a deer, hitting a tree instead. I'd never asked Dad enough about his family to realize he hid the truth of their deaths.

"Billy usually kept his drinking under control. There were a few episodes." Mom said the night of my twelfth birthday party wasn't the first time Billy had shown up overly energized, his breath smelling of vodka. It was, however, the first time he'd knocked on our door in the middle of the night.

"Your birthday was always hard for Billy." Mom never knew

where he went on those days. She knew better than to ask. "For some reason, Billy was intent on coming to your party that year." He claimed a weakness for skee-ball, a desire to see me hit a round of baseballs, and Mom thought he might be entering a new phase. Billy had even offered to bring the cake. Fortunately, she hadn't taken him up on it.

"I wasn't even upset that he missed the party. You were running around with your friends. You didn't notice he wasn't there. It was really no big deal, not until he showed up in the middle of the night."

Mom was always a light sleeper. She heard the car pull into the driveway and rushed downstairs before Billy rang the bell.

Is she still awake? Billy tried to squeeze past Mom. She blocked the doorway. Alcohol emanated from him like he'd bathed in vodka. He stood on his tiptoes trying to peer into the house behind her. *Miranda?*

Shh. She's asleep.

Oh, Suze. I don't know how. I didn't mean to. It was noon, and I was about to leave my house, then—he looked at his wrist even though he'd never worn a watch—*oh, Suze, I didn't mean to miss her birthday.*

Suze. She tried to recall the last time Billy had called her that.

Mom opened the door. *Come on, I'll make up the guest room for you. You can take Miranda out for breakfast in the morning.*

Billy reached into his pocket and held a pair of emerald earrings toward Mom. Mom's chest seized when she recognized them. They were teardrop. Encased in fourteen-karat gold. Entirely inappropriate for a twelve-year-old.

Do you think she'll like them?

You're not serious, Mom said.

I want her to have them.

Bill, they're not really something you give a kid. Her heart started racing. Her eyes watered. She wiped away the first tear as it trickled from her eye.

They're Evelyn's.

I know whose earrings they are. Mom had been with Evelyn when she found them at an antique store in Beverly Hills. They were walking down Robertson. Evelyn stopped when she saw them in the window, turning white as she stared at the earrings through the glass, and told Mom they had belonged to her mother.

Come inside, Billy. Mom motioned him in. *We'll figure this out in the morning.*

Don't do that. You always do that, Billy said.

Do what?

Treat me like a child.

I'm not treating you like a child. I'm treating you like a drunk middle-aged man who wants sympathy for forgetting his niece's birthday.

They fell silent. Billy's glassy eyes looked past Mom. She followed his gaze to me at the top of the stairs.

Miranda, go back to bed. When I stalled, she added, *Now.* I sprinted back to my room.

Nice, Billy said.

Excuse me?

You shouldn't yell at her like that. He was still holding the earrings in his palm. They were a dark, opaque green. Evelyn had worn those earrings nearly every day. Mom assumed she'd been buried in them.

Please don't tell me how to raise my daughter, Mom said.

My daughter, he said indignantly.

"I should've gone back to bed, but we needed to fight. It'd been sitting under the surface for so long. I wanted the fight as much as he did."

Billy started yelling and cursing. His words came out fast and jumbled. *Liar. Evelyn. Miranda. Secrets. You wanted this. You stole her.*

You've got some nerve, showing up in the middle of the night and blaming me, Mom said when she could get a word in. *Some fucking nerve.*

He jabbed his middle finger at Mom. *You preyed on me when I was weak.*

Is that how you remember it? Mom was trying to control the volume of her voice. She could feel the rage like bile in her throat, and she stepped onto the porch, closing the door behind her. *Because in reality, you abandoned her. In reality, we did everything we could to get you to take her.*

You knew I was mourning, and you took advantage of me.

I was mourning, too, she screamed. The anger wrapped itself around her. It made her feel alive. It made her feel strong. *But I kept my shit together, Billy. I lost my best friend, but I changed her daughter's diapers. I woke up in the middle of the night to feed Miranda. She is not your daughter. She was never your daughter.*

She will always be my daughter. Billy scowled at her. She never forgot that look. Although his eyes were dazed from the vodka, they held hers. He snorted indignantly. His jawbone protruded from the intensity of his clenched teeth. He appeared almost rabid. *You took her from me.*

You made things this way. Mom lowered her voice again, hoping I wouldn't wander downstairs, open the front door and ask why they were standing on the porch. *You hear me? This was your choice. Don't you dare blame me.*

Her knees started to shake. It wasn't in her head. They were actually quaking.

Billy clasped his hands around the earrings and put them in his pocket. *You should be ashamed of yourself. You were always jealous of her. You were never happy for us.* Billy stormed off. Mom knew she should stop him before he got into his car and had a chance to hurt someone else. She was too stunned to react, too stunned to go back inside. She watched the driveway after Billy was gone, realizing it was true; she'd never been happy for them. Her brother had always known this. Evelyn had probably known this, too.

"I remember the next morning I sat by the phone waiting for Billy to call. I should have realized it would come to this point. I knew how much it hurt Billy to see you with us, and I chose to ignore it. At first, I thought it could be a good thing. We needed to talk. I really thought Billy would call and we'd finally have an honest conversation." Or he would feign ignorance, inebriated amnesia. But Billy didn't call.

Mom went to him instead. His BMW was in the driveway, as rusted and chipping as ever but otherwise unscathed. She sat in her car and watched the dark living room through the windows. The roses that lined the house had been deadheaded and stood barren beneath the windows. She wondered whether Billy had noticed that the roses had been cut to stubs, if he realized that the front lawn was always freshly shorn, because Mom had employed a gardener for regular upkeep. If he realized that his floors were always mopped, his dishes always put away, because in addition to the gardener, Mom had hired a housekeeper. She'd done so many things to make his life easier, so many things he never noticed, let alone thanked her for. A figure moved from the kitchen and switched on the light in the living room. Mom got out of the car. She reminded herself to remain calm.

The color waned from Billy's face when he found her on his porch. His lips fell open. Mom thought if she stepped closer, she would smell alcohol on his breath. She kept her distance.

They watched each other, waiting for the other to initiate the conversation. Of course it would be Mom. It was always Mom.

Are you going to let me in? Mom asked.

He opened the door and followed her into the living room. Mom sat on the leather couch. Billy stood at the far end of the room. He held a tumbler, rolling clear liquid against the glass. He didn't offer her a drink.

Things got out of hand last night, she began.

I meant everything I said.

I know you did. I just wish it hadn't take you twelve years and a liter of vodka to tell me how you felt. Mom reminded herself to remain calm.

It had nothing to do with the vodka.

So what do you want to do?

There's nothing we can do.

If you want to tell Miranda, if you want to rearrange our situation, we'll make it work. We can talk to someone, get some advice on how to do this.

It's too late. Billy turned away from her, staring out onto the perfectly kempt backyard.

Mom walked over and lifted her hand to comfort him. *We can figure this out, Billy.*

Please don't touch me.

Mom's hand lingered behind his head. Billy still had a thick head of reddish brown hair. Every morning she found another white hair lining her auburn curls. Whether it was from age or the sun she wasn't sure. Billy's hair looked as youthful as it did when they were teenagers, when Evelyn had first noticed that his hair shined copper in the sun, when this had all begun with a simple and unlikely crush.

I was jealous, but I always wanted the best, for all of you. When Billy didn't respond, she said, *I'll let myself out.*

IN THE WEEKS OF SILENCE THAT FOLLOWED, BILLY'S WORDS RE-turned to Mom as she washed the dishes, drove me to school, forced herself to smile at the young actress who was decorating her first house. *There's nothing we can do.* Did Billy actually believe that? Mom should have pushed him to stay in therapy. He'd quit the group after a few weeks. One-on-one would have been better. Or they could have done couples counseling, and they were a couple, inextricably linked. Mom believed in that inextricability. They were family. You don't have to like your family, you only have to love them. And she loved Billy. She chose to see him as sensitive instead of selfish, as adventurous instead of unreliable. Billy chose to see himself as the aggrieved widower swindled by his resentful sister. And that's what hurt Mom most, that Billy chose to see her this way.

There's nothing we can do. Billy's words were true. Only, it wasn't *we*, it was *I. There's nothing I can do.* There was nothing Mom could do in high school when she knew Evelyn would crush Billy. Not in their twenties when she knew their getting back together was a mistake, even if she couldn't have guessed that the mistake would prove fatal. And there was nothing she could do now to convince Billy that I could handle the truth, that whatever he wanted to do, they would figure it out together.

She knew he wouldn't call. Still, she grew nervous each time the phone rang. Then when Billy finally called, it was to talk to me.

"Billy always came inside when he picked you up," Mom continued. "That day, he waited in the driveway. I was certain he was going to tell you, that you would hear his version and hate me."

Still, Mom let me go. *There's nothing I can do,* she told herself. If he wanted to tell me, she wouldn't stop him. Instead, she chose to trust me, our bond. From her bedroom window, she watched Billy's car idle. She watched me jump in, the car speed away, and in that moment she felt resigned but free. At least now it would be over.

"I never imagined that he'd... I knew he'd be unfair. I didn't think he'd be cruel."

A few hours later, I ran into the house, holding a box. Mom was in the kitchen, still in her robe. If Dad had been home, he would have made her change.

Mom, I shouted even though she was sitting not twenty feet from me. I was still calling her Mom. That was a good sign. Perhaps things could return to normal, after all. Then I pulled a golden retriever puppy from the box. A golden retriever. Mom remembered Evelyn's plans for her nauseatingly perfect family. She knew Billy did, too. *Can you believe Billy bought me a puppy?*

You can't keep that. She headed toward the stairs to change. *We're taking it back right now.*

I followed Mom upstairs. The puppy squirmed in my hands, nibbling at my index finger.

You haven't even met him yet.

We've been over this. How could you bring a dog home? She felt her voice rise, but she reminded herself that I wasn't the one who had angered her.

I sat on the bed and continued to pet the puppy's head. *I thought once you saw him, you'd change your mind.*

Mom sat next to me and let the puppy gnaw at the side of her hand. *You know it isn't about that.*

Before Mom left the house, she called Billy. *What the hell is wrong with you?* she screamed into his machine. *Is this supposed to be some sort of fuck-you? Well, I hear you loud and clear. How dare you use her against me.* She wasn't sure if she meant Evelyn or me, which one of us he was using against her.

Mom didn't make me go to the store with her. When she returned, I was in my room with the door closed. She decided to let me sulk until dinner. She tried Billy again. Surely he was home by now. *Don't ignore me, Billy,* she shouted into his machine. *How dare you manipulate her.* Mom slammed the phone down. She didn't feel better, so she walked to the beach.

The cool ocean breeze didn't help. Neither did her ire, so she tried a different tactic. *Billy,* she said calmly into his machine. *I'm sorry I got so angry before. It was a nice gesture, but you can't buy Miranda a dog without consulting me first. We should talk about what happened. Obviously, this isn't working anymore. We need to find a way to fix this.*

He didn't return her call, so she tried again, pleading, *Please, Bill, don't shut me out. Let's talk about this.* And when he didn't call back, she left another message. *Bill, we've got to work this out. We're each other's only family. This isn't want Evelyn would have wanted. Bill, are you listening? Call me back.*

After two weeks of calling to no avail, she was livid. *This is it, Billy. I mean it. If you don't call me back, we're done. And you can say goodbye to your relationship with Miranda, too. You hear me? This is your last chance to have us as your family.*

"I didn't really mean it," Mom said. "I just needed to shake him." Mom stood and motioned me to get up, too. She held her hand out to me. "Come on. I want to show you something." I followed her upstairs to her bedroom. She found a shoebox in the back of her closet and handed me an envelope she'd addressed to Billy. It was stamped, but wasn't postmarked.

The old adhesive had lost its grip and gave way easily.

Bill,

If you're reading this, I'll take it as a sign you want to work things out. I'm sorry about the messages. If I could erase them I would. Maybe it's good, though, that you know how much this is hurting me. I'm only sorry that that hurt was expressed as anger.

Do you really feel like we stole her from you? I hope that's your hurt talking as anger, too. You're right to be upset. I can't imagine how impossible it's been to watch your daughter being raised by someone else, even if that someone else is family. I know you must look at Miranda and think that she will never know Evelyn. We should have talked about her more. We should have enabled Evelyn to live in Miranda.

I'm sorry for everything I said, and I know you are, too. But it's not about us. Do you know how much Miranda misses you?

Please don't shut us out, Billy. Tell me how we can fix this.

Susan

Mom rummaged through the box, locating an earthquake report authored by Billy and two other scientists. *The January 30, 1998, Antofagasta Earthquake.* The introduction detailed the seismology of the 7.1 earthquake off the coast of Chile, the one life that was lost, the damage to old buildings.

"I wrote that letter after I picked you up at Prospero Books." In the morning, before she went to the post office, Mom saw a human-interest story on the news about a family that had been separated during the earthquake and were recently reunited. "I don't know how I missed the earthquake in the paper. It was big enough—there must have been some mention of it. I'd assumed Billy was home, listening to each of my messages and deleting them. All that time he'd been away."

I'd assumed Billy was home, too, listening to my messages and deleting them. I'd thought he'd betrayed me when I'd gone to Prospero Books. I thought he'd told Lee to call Mom. Instead, he returned from Chile to an answering machine full of messages, Mom's interwoven with mine: *Mom made me return the dog. She's such a bitch; How dare you use her against me; Me and Mom are done. I'm going to stay mad at her forever; We should talk about what happened—we need to find a way to fix this; I tried, Uncle Billy. Really, I did; Don't you dare shut me out; You know Mom. You know how she is; We're done. This is your last chance to have us as your family.*

"After I saw the story on the news," Mom said, "you remember, on the car ride home from the bookstore, how I told you I thought we could work it out?" I'd heard something different.

In my memory, she had said she didn't know if they could. We had competing recollections of the past, but one wasn't more right than the other. "When I saw the story about the family on the news, I realized the letter wouldn't have helped. We were never going to work it out."

For the next several months, Mom mourned Billy. She started seeing a psychologist, who assumed her brother was dead. Mom didn't disabuse him. After a few sessions, he inferred that Billy was still alive. He'd pressed her on why she'd misled him. Mom didn't go back to therapy. At that point, she hadn't spoken to Billy in six months. Sometimes, they'd gone two even three months without talking, never half a year. When six months turned into seven, eight, a year, she stopped skimming the newspaper for shock waves across the world.

I heard car wheels crunch against the gravel as Dad pulled into the driveway. Mom closed the box and returned it to her closet. From the window, I saw Dad push open the car door with his leg, and slowly heave his body out of the car. He walked around to the trunk where he steadied his weight to lug a pile of wood out of the car. I didn't hear Mom walking up behind me until her hand rested on my shoulder.

"And Dad?" I couldn't imagine what this had been like for him.

"You know your father. Talk to him about someone from history who was adopted and he'll understand."

Eleanor Roosevelt was adopted. Nelson Mandela, too. Gerald Ford, Bill Clinton, John Lennon. Dad and I often spoke through history. Before I started college, he reminded me of Lincoln's work ethic. The first time I was dumped, he told me about Thomas Jefferson's young heartbreak. But rock stars and first ladies, political prisoners—no one's adoption could stand in for mine.

"Maybe I should have a direct conversation with him?"

"Yeah," Mom agreed. "That's a good idea." We watched Dad rest the wood against the house as he struggled to get the key into the lock. He pushed open the door and disappeared inside. The weight of Mom's hand was growing heavier on my shoulder. I didn't shrug it off. I let her continue to rest it there, feeling connected to her, grounded.

CHAPTER TWENTY-TWO

IT WAS DARK BY THE TIME I GOT BACK TO SILVER LAKE. THE store's gate had been pulled down, most likely by Malcolm. I found the lights and walked around the bright, quiet bookstore. *My* bright, quiet bookstore. The sketch Malcolm had drawn of me was on the recommendations table beside the books I'd selected. In the black ink, I looked confident in ways I'd never been. I didn't remember picking all of the titles on my side of the table. I was drunk and nervous and delighted by Malcolm, by what was building between us. I'd grabbed any book that might define me as a student of history. I'd always seen American history as the origins of my life, but it was a passion I hid behind. One that masked my relative disinterest in a more personal history, a past I should have known. The books on that table didn't represent me. Now, I had other books that did.

I took the books off the table and restocked them in the American history and biography sections. I browsed literature, feminist fiction, young adult, pulling down *Jane Eyre, Alice's Adventures in Wonderland, Frankenstein, Fear of Flying, Persuasion, The Grapes of Wrath, Bridge to Terabithia*. Those books might seem an arbitrary collection to a customer, even the regulars. I would know they weren't random. Malcolm would, too.

Behind the front desk, I found the binder with the financial records for the first half of August. The numbers were worse than I'd expected. We were selling in a day what we should have sold in an hour. I imagined Malcolm printing out those numbers, watching them get smaller and smaller. He must have panicked, even if he hid that panic from everyone. He must have doubted we could save the store. He must have feared that, soon, everything would change. It would change, but not everything had to change for the worse. I left a notecard on the desk for him to find in the morning. It read simply, *I'm sorry*.

IN THE MORNING, MALCOLM KNOCKED ON THE APARTMENT door, holding two cups of coffee. He handed one to me and I invited him inside. We sat on the couch, steadily drinking our coffee, waiting for the other to set the tenor of our conversation, whether it would be reconciliatory or a continuation of our argument.

Malcolm put his mug on the chest in front of the couch. "You know, this is the first time we've been up here together. It's the first time I've been up here since…" He braided his hands, resting them in his lap.

"You found him?"

I followed Malcolm's eyes to the floor by the door. "I heard a thud, so I came up."

"I had no idea." I wanted to hug him, to squeeze his hand, to comfort him in some way, but I didn't know if he would let me. Our eyes wandered around the living room. "I haven't changed much. I think I've been afraid to change anything. I have to now, now that I'm staying."

Malcolm choked on his coffee. "You're staying?"

"Don't worry, I'm not trying to take your job."

"No, I wasn't." He inched closer to me, as if I wouldn't notice.

"I just couldn't leave." I inched closer to him until our legs touched. Malcolm didn't reach out for me, and that made me more certain that he would, eventually.

"You'll make the apartment yours, with time." His fingers ran down the side of my face, and it was exhilarating in its innocence, maddening in its tenderness.

"I'm sorry." His face was so close to mine that my exhales became his inhales.

"I'm sorry, too." I waited for him to ask me how I was feeling about Billy, if things were okay with my family. Instead, he pressed his lips into mine. He kissed me urgently, like he wanted to make up for the time we'd lost in our anger.

"I'm glad you're staying," Malcolm said.

"I'm glad I'm staying, too," I told him. "What are we going to do about the store?"

"We'll figure it out," he said, and I trusted the *we*, that we would do it together, that we'd try.

AUGUST INTO SEPTEMBER WAS A WHIRLWIND. MALCOLM AND I bought tickets to more Dodgers games, walking together from the store through Echo Park where he showed me every Mexican bakery that had disappeared, the murals that had been painted over, the new graffiti that he consecrated as art. Every Sunday, the Brooks Family Cookout seemed to outdo the ones of my youth. Mom made homemade pickles and jam for a cheese course, hand-churned ice cream for dessert. Over grilled lobster and whole fish, Mom talked about the books Evelyn got her to read, not only *Fear of Flying* and *Jane Eyre*, others by Umberto Eco, Milan Kundera. Dad remembered the time Evelyn brought an author to their house, a writer as famous for his drinking as he was for his prose. He'd broken a mirror by careening into it, shards cutting into his shoulder, staining his white shirt red. They had to take him to the emergency room where the nurses posed for pictures with him. When he sobered up, he announced to Dad that he had an idea for his next novel. It went on to win the Pulitzer.

September days stayed long and hot. The neighborhood returned from family vacations and camping trips, from summer music festivals. After too much day drinking, too many screaming children, they were eager to resuscitate their minds with the help of our website, our frequent buyer programs, our book clubs. Malcolm's *Literary LA* was written up by *LA Weekly* as a Top Things to Do This Fall after it had turned into a pub crawl. Malcolm guided packs of pale, malnourished-looking men to the bars where Charles Bukowski picked fights, to Raymond Chandler's regular haunts in Koreatown. Lucia seized control of our Instagram account with an enthusiasm that was extreme even for her. She spent hours organizing piles of books into sculptures and crafting the perfect foam arrow through a heart of what she was calling her signature cappuccino. Charlie organized several book fairs for the fall, at elementary and middle schools across the city. I started an American history book club, which turns out was as much teaching as I needed, sitting around one of the mosaic tables with adults who were old enough to appreciate history, old enough to understand how the choices of the past shaped the present.

I didn't even realize that Labor Day had passed and schools across the country were back in session until Malcolm and I helped Charlie load up his dented sedan with boxes of picture and chapter books for a book fair we were hosting at an elementary school. We waved goodbye like proud parents, and I realized that school in Philadelphia must have started, too. I imagined my principal giving my replacement a tour of our campus, telling her about the nightmare of a former teacher who had bailed on them at the last minute. I saw my replacement as me, only younger, more eager, with straighter hair. I imagined Jay, now the veteran teacher, training her, telling her which students to watch out for, which parents to cajole, which ones would never show up for parent-teacher night. She would laugh as he listed the nose pickers, the overachievers, the slackers and the kiss-asses, an energy building between them that would soon lead to more.

Malcolm relinquished some of the control of the store over to me, and I became the official buyer for our history, politics and social science books, the head organizer of the gala. Nearly every day we were fielding calls from people who wanted to buy tickets, even after they had sold out, from vendors who wanted to donate three-course dinners, wine tastings, massages and facials, a bread-making class. Together, those donations didn't add up to the money we still owed, even after the ticket sales, but silent auctions were designed for people to overpay. We had to hope they would. Our patrons were our last chance.

Despite the stories Mom and Dad told about Evelyn, they still hadn't been to Prospero Books. I'd invited them to readings, to book club gatherings, even to Lucia's crochet circle. I asked Dad if he would serve as an adviser to my newly formed history book club. Although he emailed me reviews of books he thought the club might like, he never met with us. And Mom was constantly in motion. Running from houses to antique shops to lighting stores. *Once this project is over, I'll stop by,* she'd promised, then she'd sign on a new project before the last one finished, fearful that any downtime might turn into an involuntary retirement. While she insisted she was merely busy, I could tell she avoided Prospero Books, fearful that it held too many memories of Evelyn or possibly too few. But our gala didn't belong to Evelyn; it didn't belong to Billy; it didn't even belong to me. It belonged to everyone who didn't want to see the store disappear.

AT LAST, THE DAY OF THE GALA HAD FINALLY ARRIVED. THE scent of cinnamon and chocolate wafted through the café as Charlie and Lucia covered the tables with linen and set out plates of truffles and mini apple tarts a bakery had donated for the event. We were still a few thousand short on October's payments, but the Mexican restaurant down the block had donated platters of flautas, the flower shop had compiled arrangements for each table. A local artist had painted a temporary mural on our picture window, a literary map of LA with Prospero at its epicenter. It seemed like anyone who could offer something did. The entire neighborhood had gone above and beyond anything we could have expected, and that was the surest guarantee of any that the night would be a success.

When Charlie saw me arrive downstairs, he took off a top hat and bowed. I lifted the thin fabric of the white dress I'd found at a thrift shop to resemble the white nightgown Miranda wore in every staging of *The Tempest*, and lowered my head, a wreath of flowers fastened to my hair. Lucia's simple white dress was similar to mine but her hair was unadorned and she carried a cookbook. Tattoos peeked out of her sleeves like undergarments. She said she was Tita from *Like Water for Chocolate*. Tita could make people feel through her food.

Malcolm walked out of the kitchen holding a tray of pies. His hair was hidden beneath a cowboy hat. Yellow aviators tinted his eyes turquoise. An unlit cigarette dangled from his mouth.

"What?" Malcolm said when he caught me staring. "You said I couldn't be Philip Marlowe." Malcolm sauntered away in his best approximation of Hunter S. Thompson's strut, muttering lines Thompson may have said.

For the first hour, people milled around in their costumes, imbibing and nibbling sweets, scribbling bids for the silent auction.

Joanie and Chris were dressed as Harry Potter and Hermione Granger, whom Joanie often insisted should have ended up together.

"Hopefully everyone gets so drunk tonight that when Halloween comes around, they won't remember we've already worn our costumes," Chris said.

Joanie jokingly shoved him. "You're not supposed to go around telling everyone."

Chris shrugged and wandered off to talk with Malcolm and Ray the screenwriter, dressed as Sherlock Holmes.

Joanie and I stood by the door, taking in the growing crowd. We hadn't seen each other in a few weeks. Since her play had ended, she'd been on countless auditions, landing a small role in a studio film. I wasn't even sure she was going to make it to the gala, but this was my big night. She would support me as I'd supported her, constantly from a distance. We watched a woman dressed as Edgar Allan Poe snuggle up to a woman dressed as Jack Kerouac. A lorax ate tart after tart, cleaning off an entire plate. Dorothy from Oz chatted with Dorothy Parker.

Joanie scanned the room. "You got a good turnout."

"Let's hope it's enough," I said.

"Did you finish Billy's quest?"

"I did."

"And?"

"It led me here." I waited for Joanie to press me for more information. Instead, she squeezed my hand.

Sheila took the stage wearing a voluminous dress with a white hat and parasol. She was Caroline de Winter from the portrait in the minstrel's gallery at Manderley. "Or maybe I'm the second Mrs. de Winter or *Rebecca*. Or maybe I'm them all," Sheila said. "Thank God no one recognizes me. Otherwise, they'd see my arrogance in pretending to be so young."

Everyone stopped talking as Sheila approached the podium. There weren't enough seats, so people squeezed onto the floor, covering every inch of Prospero Books.

"This is something new. I'm not sure where it's going. It's inspired by this place." Sheila cleared her throat and shuffled the papers in front of her. "People sell aging as graceful. Because the process happens slowly, we're encouraged to embrace it as we would an aria. You can accept aging with dignity and civility, but the daily injustices of growing old have very little music to them." Sheila continued to detail the realities of aging—panting while climbing a set of steps, a hangover from a modest glass of wine. The crowd laughed at her self-deprecating confessions as she replaced grace with something more human. Soon, her reading turned and I found myself listening to an essay about me. She changed my name, left Billy and the store out of it. The essay detailed what it was like to befriend someone thirty years younger than she. I glanced over at Joanie, and she winked. I searched the room, realizing most people didn't understand how her piece connected to Prospero Books. Malcolm stood behind me and rested his hand on my shoulder.

"You're a muse," he whispered.

As Sheila continued, the bell on the door interrupted her reflections on *The Three Sisters*. My parents stood tentatively in the entryway, surveying the crowded room. Mom in a pink blouse tucked into khaki pants, Dad in a blue-and-white-striped golf shirt. They could have been parents in an Updike or Cheever story. Mom's eyes lit up when she spotted me, and that familiar sensation flooded me. I wanted to run into her arms, to be young again, but too many bodies blocked my way. Dad indicated that they would find me when Sheila was finished reading.

Sheila ended her essay full circle, with the stupidity of those who argued that age was merely a state of mind. "You're only as old as you feel, they say between shots of cortisone and fists full of aspirin. I feel old, and I am indeed old. You are young, and I will not hate you for it. I will not pretend that I wish I were you." Sheila took off her glasses and accepted the crowd's applause. "I'm still working out that last part."

Malcolm hopped onto the stage and became the auctioneer, jiggering as he goaded the crowd. Bidding for a dinner with Sheila started at fifty dollars.

"I didn't realize I was such a cheap date," Sheila said. Several people bid, but Dr. Howard outbid them all. He trotted onto the stage, twisting the mustache he'd grown for his Shakespeare costume. He raised his arms in victory as he grabbed Sheila's hand, twirling her before holding her in a dip. The crowd went wild.

People wove in and out of conversation. I found my parents, still by the door, taking in the coordinated dance of the crowd. Mom sipped her red wine, her eyes darting around the room. She motioned with her chin toward the green brick. "That was Evelyn's favorite color. The brighter the green, the better." I hugged her the way she always held me, never wanting to let go.

We had three additional readings scheduled for later in the evening. At eleven, Malcolm's friends were set to play. By the time Raw Cow Hide took the stage, napkins littered the wood floors. Empty glasses cluttered the tables. Malcolm and I stood against the wall, watching the crowd dance. My parents were at the center, Mom's blouse untucked, Dad's golf shirt darkened with sweat. Joanie shimmied up to Mom, and they held hands and stomped their feet like they were dancing the hora. Malcolm asked me if I wanted to dance, and we joined Mom, Dad, Joanie and Chris in a circle. The song ended and we danced to the rhythm of the drunken conversations as we waited for the next song to begin. Raw Cow Hide slowed it down with a Fleetwood Mac cover.

"I love this song." Mom shut her eyes and swayed. Her face was rosy from the warmth of the room and the two glasses of wine she'd drunk. The heavy guitar buried her voice, but I saw her lips move, I saw her face soften, I saw that she could still disappear into the song, not yet hardened by life.

I whispered to Malcolm and he ran up to the stage to talk to the guitarist. His friend nodded and resumed his musical interlude.

"Mom? Would you want to sing with the band?"

Mom opened her eyes. She stopped dancing. Dread paralyzed

her face as the lead singer waved to her. Mom and I studied each other. I'd thought she would want this, to reclaim the spotlight, to defy age in a way Sheila had protested the old couldn't. She looked scared. The band dragged out the instrumental interlude, but they wouldn't wait forever.

We continued to stare at each other as the room faded away. It was Mom and me, and the guitar's chords. Suddenly, a smile surfaced on Mom's face, no hand covering her mouth, just the parted lips of unadulterated happiness.

At first, she sang timidly, barely audible above the drums. As the song continued, her voice grew louder, and at one point she tilted her head back and began belting the lyrics to "Landslide."

The song ended, and Mom whispered something into the lead singer's ear. He signaled to his band, and they started in on a Rolling Stones cover. Mom marched up and down the stage. She allowed her short curly hair to mask her face, not quite as emblematic as the ironed hair of her former self, but I could see Suzy with her long, straight hair and bright miniskirts. She was still there.

Dad and I watched Mom walk toward us, exhilarated and a little bit sweaty. "Isn't she glorious," Dad said, never taking his eyes off her.

"She is," I agreed.

Raw Cow Hide was halfway through its set when the cops arrived. Although bars up and down Sunset had lines snaking their exteriors, one of our neighbors had called in a noise complaint. Malcolm briefly argued with the cops until they noticed the wineglasses and asked if he wanted them to check everyone's identification. The party thinned quickly.

Mom was sitting at a table in the corner, mopping sweat from her neck. Dad whispered into her ear, and she laughed from her beautiful, wide-open mouth. They collected their things and found me to say goodbye.

"It's about three hours past our bedtime," Dad said.

"Speak for yourself," Mom said. Mom and I waited while Dad got the car. "I can't remember the last time I had this much fun," she said as he pulled up. She took my hand in hers. "Evelyn would have loved it." She gave my hands a squeeze and ran outside. Dad waved goodbye as they sped off toward their lives on the Westside. As I watched them go, I saw that Mom was finally free. But Billy was still trapped in Prospero Books. Evelyn was, too.

Malcolm found me by the window after my parents left, staring onto Sunset. "It seems like they had fun."

"I think so," I said distractedly.

"What's wrong?" he asked.

"It's really over," I said. "Billy's quest is really over."

"Now your journey begins." Malcolm put his arm around me. "Too cheesy?"

"A bit." I elbowed him. "I like it."

After the last guests left, Lucia sat behind the desk, counting our profits. Joanie and I broke down the tables while Charlie swept the floor. Sheila and Dr. Howard sat in the corner smoking a cigar as they watched us work.

"You missed a spot," Sheila said, using the cigar to point out a plastic cup Charlie had overlooked in his haste.

We could hear Chris and Malcolm laughing outside as they smoked pot. In a state where anxiety or back pains offered you access to a smorgasbord of cookies, lollipops and popcorn laced with THC, I didn't know why I was surprised. I'd never seen Malcolm smoke before.

"It's going to stink in here tomorrow," Malcolm shouted as he came in from the back.

"On the contrary," Dr. Howard argued. "We're cleansing the space. What would you prefer, Cuba's finest or stale beer?"

"Neither!"

Sheila exhaled and handed the cigar to Dr. Howard. She

walked over to Malcolm and put her hands on his cheeks. He tried to shake his head free of her hands.

"Tonight was a good night." Sheila kissed him on the cheek. "Enjoy the success."

Malcolm found the remains of Billy's Scotch bottle in the kitchen and poured each of us a glass—Sheila, Dr. Howard, Joanie and Chris, Lucia, Charlie, me. We crowded around one of the mosaic tables.

"This is the end of Billy's bottle," Malcolm said, and we all raised our glasses.

"'I would give all my fame for a pot of ale, and safety,'" Dr. Howard recited as he downed the Scotch.

"'I say the gentleman had drunk himself out of his five senses,'" Sheila said, shaking her head.

"The Merry Wives of Windsor," Dr. Howard said. "Impressive, my fair lady."

"'As you from your crimes would pardon'd be, Let your indulgence set me free.'" Everyone stopped talking and turned toward me. Some of them surely recognized Prospero's famous line. Others didn't. They all stared at me, waiting for me to explain. "At the end of the play, Prospero asks the audience to release him."

"Well, really, it's Shakespeare talking through Prospero. It was his last play," Dr. Howard explained, and Sheila swatted him to shut up.

"Not every table is your podium," she said.

"We need to change the name," I said. At the end of The Tempest, Prospero left his enchanted island. It was time for Billy to leave his, too. His charms were overthrown and we needed to set him free.

"Of Prospero Books?" Charlie couldn't decide whether to be hurt or offended.

I glanced over at Malcolm for support. He looked deep in thought. Or maybe he was just stoned. I felt the first tinge of frustration with him, a comforting irritation, the way you can let someone annoy you disproportionately because you know you'll eventually get over it.

"Miranda's right," Malcolm finally said. "The store's changed. If we want it to survive, it can't keep living in the past."

Lucia choked. "Says the man who's decried every lost Laundromat in the neighborhood."

"I'm not saying get rid of the Prospero Books," he said, his voice ripe with condescension, "but it's changed. It has to keep changing in order to stay the same."

"That's stoned logic if I've ever heard it," Lucia said.

Dr. Howard tugged his goatee. Sheila tapped her nose with her index finger. Lucia nudged Malcolm with her toe, goading him for her own entertainment. Joanie swayed with her eyes shut to a melody she alone could hear, and Chris had almost certainly fallen asleep. Only Charlie searched for communion, for someone else who seemed as alarmed as he was.

"Yesterday's Bookshop," I said. "It commemorates the past but acknowledges that we aren't still living in it."

"Every day has a yesterday." Dr. Howard continued to stroke his goatee. "They are inextricably linked."

"And every day has a tomorrow," Sheila agreed.

"Yesterday's Bookshop," Malcolm said. "I can get behind that."

Dr. Howard and Sheila continued their garden variety musings on the past and present. Malcolm started listing changes he could make to the store, hanging pictures of old Silver Lake on the walls of the café, making the front window look like an apothecary. I stopped him when he mentioned the walls.

"They stay green," I said, and he agreed, knowing why they were green, whose favorite color it had been. Malcolm put his hand on my shoulder and leaned over to kiss my forehead. It was the first time he'd kissed me in public, and I didn't need

⏘ scan the room to gauge everyone's reaction. I didn't need to get used to it. It simply felt right.

Lucia and Charlie began to argue about who was going to be more hungover in the morning. Joanie chatted with Malcolm, who kept his hand on my shoulder, rubbing it absentmindedly. I watched my oldest friend, the friends I'd recently made, the people who knew me before I knew myself. Yesterday's Bookshop belonged to them as much as it did to me, but Prospero Books was Billy's. Evelyn's. We were giving the store a chance to survive. I needed to give myself a chance, too. It's what Prospero had wanted for his Miranda, not to be burdened by the past but to know it farther, to prepare for the future.

★ ★ ★ ★ ★

ACKNOWLEDGMENTS

FOR YEARS, WHEN I FANTASIZED ABOUT PUBLISHING A NOVEL, one of the things I was most excited about was writing the acknowledgments. Whenever I sit down to read a new book, the first thing I do is turn to the acknowledgments page. I love hearing about a writer's community because it reminds me that, although only the author's name appears on the front cover, so many other people have contributed to the process through their encouragement, wisdom, hard work and faith. For me, this novel has been a labor of love, and I simply could not have done it without the insight and enthusiasm of my teachers, friends and family, as well as all of the wonderful people I've met along the way.

Thank you to my incredible agent, Stephanie Cabot, her equally incredible assistant, Ellen Goodson Coughtrey, and everyone at the Gernert Company. To the magnificent trio at Park Row Books: Erika Imranyi, who took a chance on me, and my tireless editors, Liz Stein and Natalie Hallak. And to Shara Alexander, publicist extraordinaire. Words cannot express how fortunate I feel to have had such smart and kind women working with me on this project.

Thank you to my thoughtful readers and talented fellow writers who helped me through the messy first drafts: Lynn Elias, Alexandra D'Italia, April Dávila, Corey Madden, Erin La Rosa,

Jackie Stowers, Kelly Morr, Will Frank, Yance Wyatt, Tatiana Uschakow, Mary Menzel, Lauren Herstik, Taiwo Whetstone and Jessica Cantiello. To the talented Amanda Treyz for her beautiful photographs and for many talks over many meals. To Katie Frichtel and Troy Farmer at raven + crow studio for the awesome website and their awesomeness generally. To Kevin Doughten for his editorial insights and support from day one, probably even before day one.

To all of my wonderful instructors and mentors at USC, especially to Judith Freeman, who was the first person to see promise in this idea, and to Aimee Bender, who has encouraged me in more ways than she knows. To my colleagues in the Writing Program—through you, I've found a nurturing and supportive home at USC.

Thank you to Steve Salardino at Skylight Books for giving me an insider's glimpse into independent bookstores and to Eoghan O'Donnell for sharing stories of his dad's used bookstore. Independent bookstores have been a vital part of my reading and writing life. Whenever I travel, I make sure to save a good chunk of time—and luggage space—for browsing local bookstores. I'm constantly inspired by the celebration of books, ideas and reading that persists in our communities through these bookshops. Prospero Books is my ode to you and your shelves.

To my family: the Meyersons, the Perrottas and the Chans. A special thanks to my parents, who encouraged me without ever seeing a page (now's your chance!). To my brother, Jeff, for his advice and support through the process. To Lindsay and Jan Perrotta for their enduring enthusiasm. To Jessica Chan for her sage medical advice and to Jen Chan for her social media savvy. And to my exceptional friends; I am indeed very lucky to have such a vibrant and inspiring community.

Finally to Adam, who always believes in me, even when I don't believe in myself.